Regency England comes seductively to life in Julia London's THE ROGUES OF REGENT STREET—acclaimed novels that feature a trio of dashing aristocrats as infamous as they are irresistible. Whether risking their lives on the dueling field or seducing the ladies of London's haute ton, they are men of unswerving honor and breathtaking sensuality.

And Arthur Christian, the untitled son of the duke of Sutherland, is no exception. . . .

THE BEAUTIFUL STRANGER

Arthur would never forget that tragic day: Lord Phillip Rothembow, his cherished comrade, killed senselessly in a duel. In an attempt to clear his late friend's name, Arthur leaves behind England—and the woman who broke his heart—to journey to Scotland. How could he know that his travels would lead him to the most enchanting woman he has ever seen? Desperately fighting to hold on to the land her husband lost in a foolish business venture, widowed Kerry McKinnon cannot believe that this beautiful stranger has come to seize her home and leave her to a terrible fate. Yet from the moment they meet, something powerful ignites between them. Theirs is a passion that is reckless, scandalous . . . and impossible to resist. But a shocking crime will force Kerry to flee with Arthur to England, where propriety rules, and where desire can lead to certain ruin. Unless a determined woman can ~~~~~~ ~~~~~~~-weary rake that a life ~~~~~~ ~~~~~ ~~~~~dal of all. . . .

THE ROGUES OF REGENT STREET

The Beautiful Stranger

JULIA LONDON

A Dell Book

THE BEAUTIFUL STRANGER
A Dell Book

PUBLISHING HISTORY
Dell mass market edition published July 2001
Dell reissue / June 2008

Published by Bantam Dell
A Division of Random House, Inc.
New York, New York

This is a work of fiction. Names, characters, places, and incidents either are the product of the author's imagination or are used fictitiously. Any resemblance to actual persons, living or dead, events, or locales is entirely coincidental.

Dell is a registered trademark of Random House, Inc., and the colophon is a trademark of Random House, Inc.

ISBN 978-0-440-23690-0

Printed in the United States of America
Published simultaneously in Canada

www.bantamdell.com

OPM 14 13 12 11 10 9 8 7 6 5

For
Brocodile, January Jones, Don Vito, the Virgin
Henley, Filbert, Princess Shoes, Scoop, Happy
Jack, Slick and Kaffiene

Thanks for keeping the Dimwonkie sane. . . .

I met a lady in the meads,
*   Full beautiful—a faery's child,*
Her hair was long, her foot was light,
*   And her eyes were wild. . . .*
She look'd at me as she did love,
*   And made sweet moan.*
I set her on my pacing steed,
*   And nothing else saw all day long,*
For sidelong would she bend, and sing
*   A faery's song.*

—LA BELLE DAME SANS MERCI
John Keats

Prologue

THE CHURCHYARD WAS so choked with weeds that one could scarcely read the markings on the headstones. This was worrisome to Arthur—who would tend to this grave? Who would lay flowers at his headstone as Phillip lay rotting beneath the earth? As the vicar glanced up at the leaden sky and cleared his throat, Arthur glanced surreptitiously at the two dozen or more mourners huddled around, mentally assessing who among them could be depended upon to tend this grave.

Not one of them.

In a low bass voice, the vicar began the funeral hymn, and the mourners, in their black crepe armbands and funeral bonnets, joined him in the lugubrious melody. Nothing more than morbid curiosity had brought this throng here—they had come only to gawk, to see if the fantastic rumor was true, to look upon the grave and witness with their own eyes that one of the infamous Rogues of Regent Street was dead.

Arthur lowered his gaze to the plain pine box in the hole yawning before him and imagined Phillip inside, his arms folded serenely across what was left of his chest, his gray face free of pain, and the death shroud wrapped loosely about him. He regretted he hadn't found something better in which to clothe him, but unfortunately, there was nothing better to be had at Dunwoody—it was little more than a hunting lodge and used infrequently. There had been just an old nondescript suit of clothes to give the undertaker, but Phillip had not been quite as large as the previous owner and with a good portion of his torso gone, the fit was atrocious. Not that Arthur believed that what he wore to the afterlife was important. It was just that Phillip had always been so foppishly meticulous about his dress; he would despise spending all of eternity in an old, ill-fitted suit of clothing.

And besides, if Arthur didn't think about what Phillip wore now, he would think about how goddamned furious he was.

Why did he do this? What divine providence gave Lord Phillip Rothembow the bloody right *to do this?*

The sudden surge of anger was as razor-sharp and white-hot as it had been the moment Julian had lifted his head from Phillip's bloodied chest and uttered the words that still seemed to reverberate throughout the forest: *"He is dead."*

The mourners' voices suddenly swelled to a crescendo, then fell again as they began a second verse. Arthur cringed, forced himself to look up, blinking into the cold mist that enveloped them.

What in God's name were they doing here?

This could not be real. It had all started so innocently, just another respite at Dunwoody, the four Rogues gaming and whoring with their friends, lazily planning a bit of a hunt the next morning. Adrian Spence, the earl of Albright, aloof and distant, his mind undoubtedly on the latest row with his father. Julian Dane, the earl of Kettering, charming the skirts off the two demimondes who had accompanied the luckless Lord Harper. Cards, copious amounts of bourbon, and Phillip, naturally, drunk as usual.

If only Adrian hadn't asked Phillip to stop cheating.

If only he had laid down his hand, called it off. But he had asked for Phillip to stop—very politely, really—

and that had been the beginning of the end. Phillip had taken offense and had stunned them all by demanding satisfaction. Adrian had accepted Phillip's drunken challenge, thinking, as they all did, that he would sober and retract it the next morning. But Phillip had come staggering onto the dueling field with a bottle in his hand and no intention of backing down.

A wagon rumbled past the little churchyard at that moment, and in its reverberation, Arthur could almost hear the distant report of the first pistol fired that awful morning—Adrian, deloping. And just as he had then, he could feel the weight of impending doom laying hard on his chest, the shock of disbelief when Phillip, Adrian's own cousin, had responded to Adrian's generous act by firing on him. He misfired terribly, of course, because he could hardly stand erect. But it had seemed to fill him with a gruesome determination—he twisted about, grabbed Fitzhugh's double-barreled German pistol and knocked that fool to his arse, then whirled as gracefully as a dancer and fired at Adrian's back.

Why? Phillip, why?

The question beat like a drum in his head, a relentless pounding to which there was no end. They would never know *why* Phillip had forced Adrian's hand because the bloody coward had denied them any plausible explanation for his actions by succeeding in getting himself killed. Just moments after firing on Adrian's back, Phillip lay in the yellow grass, his azure-blue eyes staring calmly at the sky, his life having quietly seeped from the gaping hole in his chest.

Dead. One of them dead, one of the immortal Rogues of Regent Street, killed by one of their own.

God have mercy on us all.

Arthur glanced to where Adrian stood as rigid and unmoving as Julian beside him. The four of them— Adrian, Phillip, Julian, and himself—were the idols of the younger members of the British aristocracy. They were the Rogues, renowned for living by their own code, for risking their wealth to make more wealth, for their fearless irreverence of law and society. They were the Rogues who toyed with the tender hearts of young ladies among the exclusive shops of Regent Street by day then extracted intended dowries from their papas in the clubs at night, saving the best of themselves for the notorious Regent Street boudoirs.

Or so the legend went.

It was all fantasy, of course. They were only four men who had grown up together, who rather enjoyed the recklessness of one another's company and the pretty women of Madame Farantino's. There was nothing more to the Rogues than that—not one of them had ever done anything too terribly unlawful, had never sullied a lady's reputation or driven a man to debtor's prison in a single card game. There was nothing particularly remarkable about them at all . . . except that one of them had found life so bloody unbearable that he had, in essence, killed himself by forcing the hand of his cousin.

Thereby proving that neither were the Rogues immortal.

Arthur closed his eyes as the mourners began the last chorus of the hymn, the bitter rage burning as it rose like bile in his throat. He hated Phillip, *hated* him for ruining everything, for ending it all on that yellow field!

He hated Phillip almost as much as he hated himself.

Ah God, the guilt was bloody unbearable. He had watched it happen, had stood aside and watched Phillip drown in despair when he might have led him to a different course. Lord Arthur Christian, the third son of the Duke of Sutherland and once destined for the clergy, stood aside and had watched it happen. *He* might have pulled Phillip from the edge of the abyss, not Adrian, not Julian. *He* might have.

The voices rose one last time, putting an end to the wretchedly morose hymn. Silence fell; the crowd shifted about uneasily. Some of them peered up at the increasingly gray sky as the vicar puffed out his cheeks and fumbled through the little prayer book. With a pointed look at Adrian, he at last spoke. "All those who mourn him, may ye know in his death the light of our Lord and the quality of love . . ."

Damn him for what he had done to them!

". . . Ah, the, ah, quality of life, and know ye the quality of mercy. Amen."

"Amen," the mourners echoed.

The quality of life? Of mercy? God yes, Arthur would know the quality of life from this day forward, would know it every time he looked at a sunrise or held a woman in his arms or inhaled one of Julian's fine cheroots! And the *quality* of his life would be measured by the weight of his guilt and his anger and his bloody remorse! *Phillip!*

Arthur staggered backward a step, sucking in his breath through clenched teeth as the gravediggers began to shovel the dirt into the hole. Yes, yes, he would know from this day forward the quality of life all right, for each and every day he would carry with him the burden of having let Phillip down in the worst imaginable way. He would bear the gnawing wrath he held for one of his best friends, the humiliation of having been denied the opportunity to stop him, to set everything to rights again, to at least *try* and slay the demons that could devour a man's soul and leave him so desperate for death.

Damn him.

Chapter One

If Arthur Christian should ever be captured and subjected to the worst of all torture, his tormentors could do no better than to arrange an evening such as this.

It was his own fault. It was his ball after all, his mansion on Mount Street, his indifference that enabled the lowest quarter of the *ton* to come walking through his door. Yet in spite of hosting this elaborate affair—and many just like it during the Season—Arthur would rather be drawn and quartered than suffer one more come-hither look from Portia Bellows, much less her pawing of his leg.

The pawing was, of course, also his own fault. He'd been too inattentive of his guests and therefore hadn't seen her coming until it was too bloody late. Portia had very neatly cornered him in the little alcove off the main corridor, which was where they were at that precise moment, her hand brazenly roaming his thigh. "I've never forgotten you, Arthur, not for a single moment," she murmured in her best bedroom voice.

"Of course not," Arthur drawled, and reached down into the swirl of Portia's heavy satin skirts around him to peel her hand away, finger by finger.

"It is you I imagine when he is on top of me," she

whispered huskily, and lifted her hand to the large black pearl nestled at the swell of her bountiful bosom, carefully tracing a line around it that dipped lower and lower into the décolletage of her gold satin gown. "It is you who makes love to me in my dreams."

Actually, he'd wager the bitch was thinking of Roth's rather sizable fortune when he was on top of her . . . yes, drawn and quartered, thank you, with his limbs scattered to the far corners of the earth just so he should never hear this tripe again.

Her fingers stubbornly sought the inside of his thigh again. "I didn't mean to hurt you, darling." She said it in exactly the same voice she had used when they were eighteen, the same soft purr that made Arthur profess his undying love to her a dozen times over. That voice, along with her smoldering look, had sent him off to breathlessly ask his father for permission to offer for her, to which his grace had quietly informed him that Miss Bellows was already betrothed to Robert Lampley. Two years older than Arthur, Robert Lampley was destined to inherit a fortune *and* a title—exactly one more attribute than Arthur possessed. It was the first time in his life that he had understood just how insignificant the untitled third son of a powerful duke could be.

Now, at six and thirty, he understood how tiresome women could be, and calmly removed Portia's hand again. "My Lady Roth, you know that I don't believe a word that passes between your lips," he said, and smiled as if she amused him, though nothing could be further from the truth. Everything she did humiliated him and when she was really in top form, she made a colossal fool of him. Ah, yes—Portia Bellows had duped Lord Arthur Christian of the Duchy of Sutherland not once, but *twice,* thank you, and evidently, judging by the way her fingers were boldly flitting across his groin now, she had in mind to attempt an astounding third supreme humiliation.

Standing in the alcove, hidden from any guest who might be wandering off to the privy by one of the large potted plants Arthur's sister-in-law Lauren was inordinately fond of forcing on him, Portia boldly moved to cup the protuberance between his legs in her palm. She smiled wickedly; Arthur matched her smile with an insouciant one of his own, knowing that there was nothing the woman could do that would ever get *that* reaction from him again. He circled her wrist and squeezed hard. "Your husband is not fifty feet away," he softly rebuked her.

Her cheeks flushed, she carelessly shrugged her lovely shoulders. "He cannot see us, and even if he did, he would not care."

"Ah, but I do," he said, and squeezed so tightly that he feared he might actually snap her bones before she finally let go of him.

Pouting like a child, she jerked her wrist from his grip and stepped back, rubbing the offended appendage. "You are horribly mean-spirited! You would fault me after all these years for merely seeking a way to survive this cruel world!"

With a low, irreverent chuckle, Arthur casually folded his arms across his chest. "I fault you for many things, love, but surviving is not one of them."

Her dark brown eyes flashed with ire. "You've no idea whom you insult, my lord!"

"On the contrary," he said, giving her a mocking bow. "You have the distinction of being the one woman I wouldn't bed if even to save my very life."

Portia's eyes widened; she caught a small cry of indignation in her throat. "There is no need to be hateful!" Arthur grinned indolently. Portia pressed her lips together in a thin line, turned abruptly, and marched toward the double mahogany doors leading into the ballroom, cutting him in a way only a thoroughbred aristocratic woman could do. A footman just barely reached the door and opened it before she sailed through, her gold skirts swinging against the man's legs with her strut.

Smiling lazily, Arthur adjusted his neckcloth and smoothed back a thick, unruly wave of golden-brown hair. Portia was still a beauty, he would give her that. Red hair, alabaster skin . . . but a viper all the same, and no one knew it better than he. After she had crushed his foolish young heart when they were eighteen, she had married Lampley, given him a daughter a few years later, then had watched him die from some fever. She was still in her widow weeds when she had sent for Arthur, artfully dredging up sentiments he had thought long buried. She had been persistent—when at last he relented, she had tearfully confessed it was him she had loved all those years. Although she was a fool to think it would affect him now, those words had moved him then, and well she knew it. Nonetheless, he was resistant, eager to avoid having his heart dashed to little pieces a second time.

And he might have actually spared himself the humiliating sting of her claws had Phillip not died when he did.

It was immediately following the events of Dunwoody that he had found himself drifting, quite unable to find his stride. It was when the dreams had begun, dreams of Phillip walking about with the gaping black hole in his chest, mocking Arthur with his death. It was during those long, black hours that he had turned to Portia, seeking a comfort he recalled from summers long since faded. Portia had eagerly given herself to him, had whispered sweet promises in his ear, made him believe that she truly *had* pined for him all those years. Sorry fool, he was—it was a great shock to read in the *Times* one morning that Lord Roth was to marry Portia that spring.

Oh, Portia had wailed prettily when Arthur confronted her—what, she had cried, was a poor widow to do? Worse yet, he discovered that she was toying with not one, but *two* other suitors, each titled in their own right. But not him, not Arthur Christian, not the son who probably should have bowed to the family's wishes years ago and joined the clergy in some quiet little parish.

With a sigh, he shoved his hands into his pockets and strolled to the ballroom entrance, pausing there to look around the room crowded with the elite of the British aristocracy.

The room fairly sparkled—the light of dozens of candles suspended on crystal chandeliers glittered against the ornate jewels on the hands and necks of the silk-clad ladies. Everywhere he looked there was opulence—heavy crystal flutes of champagne engraved with the Sutherland seal, gold-filled fixtures, fine bone china, hand-carved furnishings, great works of art.

In addition to the two hundred or more guests whom Arthur knew would give their firstborn to be in attendance tonight, there were also those dearest to him—his mother and lady Aunt Paddington, or Paddy as they affectionately called her. His brother Alex and his wife Lauren. Kettering and his wife Claudia. Only Adrian and Lilliana were missing, kept in the country with the birth of their son. This was, he thought indifferently, a Sutherland home, there was no doubt of it. This was a scene that was played out many times throughout the year. This was the *haute ton* at its highest caliber.

Arthur wished he were anywhere but here.

There was nothing for him here, nothing that held his interest or inspired him to greater things. He felt as if life was slowly marching past him while he hosted one grand fête after another, taking his youth with it and any sense of purpose he might have had as a young man. He had no idea where he belonged anymore.

His gaze inadvertently fell on Portia, who was now smiling prettily at Lord Whitehurst. The look on her face made him want to turn and walk out the door of his home and keep walking until he escaped the reverie and reached the Tam O'Shanter, the Rogues old haunt, but his brother Alex caught his eye and started toward him. Arthur dutifully waited, trying very hard to maintain an expressionless façade.

Alex paused to take a flute of champagne from a heavy silver tray a footman extended to him as he reached the door. "Need to warn you, old chap," he said, glancing behind him, "my darling wife has a maggot in her head to introduce you to Warrenton's daughter"—he gave Arthur a look—"she's a bit on the plain side."

"Marvelous," Arthur drawled.

"Ah, and here she comes now," Alex muttered before beaming a smile over Arthur's shoulder. Arthur turned, smiling, too, as Lauren neared them, extending her hand.

"Arthur! You are a dreadful host! I've been looking all over for you," she playfully scolded him as he took her hand in his.

"I humbly beg your forgiveness," he said gallantly, bowing low over her hand. "I was unavoidably detained with a small housekeeping matter."

"Oh," Lauren said uncertainly, then suddenly grinned again. "Well now that I've found you, I am so very eager to make an introduction—"

"Ah, Kettering!" Arthur quickly interrupted, nodding in the general direction of the hearth. "You will excuse me, but I've an important matter that really can't wait," he said, and inclining his head politely, stepped aside before Lauren could object.

"Liar!" he heard her mutter cheerfully under her breath, followed by Alex's throaty chuckle.

Arthur flashed a grin at her before disappearing into the crowd. He made his way deeper into the room, pausing only to greet his mother and aunt. The dowager duchess smiled warmly. "You look devilishly handsome," she whispered to him. Arthur idly glanced down at the black superfine coat, the heavily embroidered silk waistcoat. He thought he rather looked as he did every day—trussed up like a Christmas goose.

"Never mind *that*," Paddy said excitedly, and clapped her hands like a girl, making the fat white sausage curls dance around her cherubic face. "Miss Amelia, the daughter of the *very* important Lord Warrenton, is in attendance tonight!"

Aha. So Lauren had already gathered her troops for the attack. Arthur loved his sister-in-law dearly, but she seemed absolutely determined to see him shackled to a debutante from here to eternity. "I am certain Miss Amelia will have a grand time of it." He patted his mother's hand then carefully extracted his arm. "Ladies, you will excuse me?" Ignoring Paddy's blustering protest, he continued on until he reached the sideboard where his butler, Barnaby, had laid out an impressive array of liqueurs and brandies. Shooing a footman away, Arthur poured champagne into a heavy engraved crystal flute.

"Rather thought you were going to abandon me to the conspirators in Miss Amelia's new courtship."

Arthur chuckled and turned toward the familiar voice of Julian Dane, the earl of Kettering. "What then, are they all quite afraid I shall be put on the shelf before the year's end?"

Julian laughed. "You and Miss Amelia both, apparently," he said, and signaled the hovering footman to pour him a brandy.

"It appears I shall be forced to have another frank discussion with my sister-in-law. Speaking of impossible women, what have you done with your wife?"

Julian chuckled as he accepted the imported French brandy from the footman, then nodded lazily to where a small string orchestra was resting for a brief interval. Claudia was perched on the edge of a French settee, her elbows on her knees as she pressed home what was an undoubtedly very important point to the rather vapid

Lord Perry. "I predict Perry will hand over everything he's got in the three-percents before he even realizes what has happened," Julian said, hiding a proud smile behind his snifter. Arthur had no doubt that was true. If there was a force in London who could raise funds for worthy causes, it was Lady Kettering. She had the ability to charm a man right out of his stockings—literally, in Julian's case. He was about to comment as much when Barnaby suddenly appeared at his elbow. "Beggin' your pardon, my lord, but Lord Rothembow insists upon a word."

Rothembow. The name evoked a flash of his dream last night—a ballroom just like this, glimpses of Phillip, trying to catch him to demand an explanation, a *reason.*

Bloody hell.

Arthur exchanged a look with Julian as he set aside his champagne flute. "Show him to the morning room," he instructed Barnaby, and turned only to see Rothembow pushing through the crowd, bearing down on them. The crowd seemed to turn as one toward the three men as Rothembow came to an exaggerated stop in front of them. It was exceedingly awkward; Rothembow had not been invited; his dress clearly indicated as much. But regardless of what anyone thought, Arthur would not deny the man entrance, he would not deny him anything, really, and simply nodded his head in greeting, "My lord."

Rothembow's thick gray eyebrows shot together in one long frown. A full head shorter than Arthur, the rotund man snapped his head back to better glare at them. "Christian, I would have a word if you please," he said gruffly, and reached into his coat pocket, withdrawing a folded paper. "I have in my hand a matter of some consequence. It would seem that the Christian solicitation offices have failed me once again."

Arthur exchanged a quick, wary look with Julian. "I beg your pardon, sir, but if this is a matter of business perhaps it best would be discussed—"

"I will not be put off, my lord!" he angrily interjected. "I received this letter just today, and while the contents of it were quite disturbing, let me assure you it came as no surprise to me to learn that at least one of you was involved—"

"Shall we adjourn to the morning room?" Julian asked sharply. Rothembow paused, mouth open, then thought better of what he would say and quickly shut it. With a curt nod of his head, he stepped aside so Arthur could lead the way.

Arthur could hardly fault the man for despising the Rogues as he did; he supposed it was quite natural for a man to assign blame when he lost a son, particularly in the manner Rothembow lost his. But the same Lord Rothembow who had once taught four young boys to play cricket now made his disdain for them known at every opportunity, and even publicly refused to be in the same room with Adrian. As Arthur stepped into the crowd, his thoughts and old despair carefully masked, he felt the old but familiar sense of anger with Phillip he had harbored these three long years now.

They moved silently down the thickly carpeted corridor with Barnaby hurrying ahead, and paused as one just across the threshold of the morning room, waiting patiently for Barnaby to light several candelabrum. As the door shut silently behind Barnaby, Arthur turned and looked at Rothembow. "My lord?" he asked coolly.

Rothembow's small blue eyes turned to ice. "You wouldn't stop him, would you? Not as long as you stood to gain a pound or two," he spat and tossed the folded paper onto the desk. It slid across the highly polished oak until Arthur caught it. "I am quite certain you were aware of this . . . of this *lunacy!*"

Julian cast a questioning glance at Arthur as he quickly unfolded the paper. It was a letter addressed to the Christian Brothers' offices, signed by a Mr. Jamie Regis, Esquire, of Stirling, Scotland, dated July 1, 1835— almost two years past. Scanning the words neatly penned on the thick vellum, words like *debt* and *arrears* and *taxes* leapt out at Arthur, and slowly, he began to understand what he was reading.

Phillip's cattle.

This had to do with the land and cattle in the central highlands of Scotland in which Phillip had invested only weeks before his death. Arthur had forgotten about it, but he saw now that his instincts at the time had been correct—it was, apparently, a very foolish investment. He shoved the letter toward Julian, turned away from Rothembow, and walked to the hearth, his mind whirling with sober memories. Oh he had known of it, all right, and had thought it a terribly ill-advised thing to do, sight unseen, particularly when, over the last several years, many cattle enterprises in Scotland had been lost to sheep farming.

But Phillip had been ecstatic, his boyish enthusiasm for the venture making him almost giddy. Apparently, a Scot farmer, up to his neck in debt, had offered part of his holdings in exchange for a cash infusion. Phillip had been so enamored of the deal that he had offered to subsidize the purchase of cattle, believing that the cattle market would be revived and make him a rich man, provide him a means for getting out from under his own mountain of debt. Arthur had warned him that it would take years of profits to reduce his debt, during which time the interest would continue to mount. But Phillip had cavalierly waved him off as if that was no concern and proceeded to arrange the purchase through the Christian Brothers' offices. And Arthur, as he was so damn good at doing, had kept his mouth shut and thereby allowed Phillip to dig his hole a little deeper. That ridiculous purchase had been some sort of desperate grope for sanity on Phillip's part, an attempt to turn his life around and make a fresh start . . . an attempt at equilibrium.

"I don't understand," Julian said behind him. "This letter is two years old."

"Apparently it has been misdirected for some time," Rothembow muttered.

"I wasn't aware that Phillip had invested in land in Scotland," Julian said, more to himself.

"*Yes,* my lord, he purchased a *worthless* herd of cattle and an even less desirable parcel of land only weeks before he was killed!" Rothembow fairly shouted. "And now *I* am to pay in excess of twenty thousand pounds for it, but God save me if that will be all!"

Arthur glanced over his shoulder; Rothembow fixed an angry glare on him and continued. "You knew about this, Christian! He entered that ridiculous venture through *your* offices!"

"Yes, I knew it."

"Then you *knew* he was throwing good money down a rat hole! My God, how in good conscience could you have allowed it? Surely you could have at *least* stopped him from making such a foolish purchase!"

Surely he could have at least stopped Phillip from killing himself. That's what Rothembow wanted to say, and they both knew it.

"Here now, my lord," Julian quickly interjected. "Phillip was a grown man, responsible for his own actions!"

Rothembow turned on him. "He was a *drunkard!* A worthless, penniless drunk! He was doomed from the moment he met the likes of you," he said, gesturing wildly at both of them. "My Phillip was a good boy until then, a very good boy, but you *ruined* him! The Rogues ruined him, and now . . . *now* . . ." Rothembow's voice suddenly trailed off; his blue eyes skirted the walls and ceiling before his shoulders slumped. He glanced blindly down at his feet like a defeated man and exhaled a long, weary sigh.

The three men stood in silence for a long moment until Arthur asked quietly, "What would you have us do?"

The small sound of grief from Rothembow scored Arthur's heart. "I would that you give me back my son,

Christian," he said hoarsely, and lifted a watery gaze. "Short of that, I would very much appreciate it if you would instruct your offices to handle this unseemly matter at once and clear my son's name. Do whatever it takes, but dear God, at least allow my son's name to be respected in one corner of the kingdom! Let him have his peace somewhere!"

Arthur glanced at the letter lying on the library table. "I don't know what can be done, but I give you my word, I shall endeavor to repair it, my lord."

With another subdued sigh, Rothembow looked at Julian, then turned and walked slowly to the door. "I fear this will never end," he said raggedly as he reached for the handle. "My son will never rest in peace." He closed the door loudly behind him.

"If his son never rests in peace, it is his own damn doing, not ours!" Arthur muttered resentfully at the closed door.

With a halfhearted shrug, Julian moved to a drink cart and poured two whiskeys, holding one out to Arthur. "Rothembow will always believe we killed him. Nothing will ever change that."

"Phillip killed himself! And he made his own foolish decisions," Arthur responded, gesturing angrily toward the letter. "Why in God's name would he buy a herd of Highland cattle?" *To have something to hold, something to make him normal.* Arthur strode angrily to the table and picked up the paper. The lawyer's neat script detailing the troubled property made the indignation mount, but for who or what, Arthur suddenly wasn't sure. It seemed that everything Phillip tried ended in one disaster or another, as if the heavens were dead set against him. He folded the paper and put it in his coat pocket, then tossed the whiskey down his throat.

"Come on, then. Your guests will wonder where you've gone off to," Julian said.

Arthur glared at the door. "Heaven knows I have tried to understand why he did it, but I can find no reason for it. Nonetheless, I didn't force him onto that field any more than you or Adrian, and I am sick unto death of taking the blame for it, I swear to God that I am!"

"Then don't, Arthur," Julian said quietly. "We can never understand why he did what he did." He opened the door, waiting for Arthur. "And a man could make himself insane trying."

For the rest of the evening, Arthur ignored the letter burning in the inside pocket of his coat. Almost mindlessly, he did what was expected of him—he spoke at length to the dimwitted Perry, despite feeling as if he was talking to the wall. He bantered a bit with Sir Fox about the horse races, charmed a group of young ladies who giggled like children, and suffered through two quadrilles. In the dining room, where tables and chairs had been set up for the dancers, he talked amicably with Miss Amelia, Warrenton's homely, but well-endowed daughter—both physically and financially, as Julian discreetly pointed out—over a plate of goose and asparagus awash in French crème sauce.

He played his part well, but he scarcely recalled a thing he heard or said—he could not stop thinking about Phillip. He hadn't thought about him like this in months, had managed to push his anger and resentment down until he could pass several days without thinking of him. *Until another dream would come, unwanted.*

But now this—honestly, had Phillip really believed that an ill-advised venture in Scotland would make a difference to his situation? Why hadn't he asked for advice, sought counsel on his growing debt from the finest solicitation offices in the kingdom? Offices that just happened to belong to one of his closest friends? *Why did he kill himself?*

When several of the guests returned to the dancing, and a few select men gathered in the library, Arthur watched Julian turn a beaming smile to Claudia as she glided past. He could see the adoration shining in Julian's eyes and felt a faintly familiar tug in his chest that felt, oddly, a bit like envy. It could not be envy, however—Arthur Christian did not envy men their wives. All he had to do was look at Portia to remember why that was.

After the men had exhausted their talk of politics in the library and had vowed to support Alex in his reform efforts in the Lords, they rejoined the ball. Arthur followed, filled to the brim now with a growing anger at Phillip, and worse, the old anguish buried deep inside him that Rothembow had stirred. He stood alone like some abandoned soul, staring morosely at the dancers, anxious for the evening to end.

When he had at last made himself quite miserable with the incessant rumination of Phillip and life and what might have been, he slipped out of the ballroom and onto the terrace behind the mansion's breakfast room, away from the guests who had filtered into the gardens.

The flare of a match caught him by surprise; he glanced over his shoulder as Julian extended a cheroot toward him. "Made with the finest blend of American tobacco. Delivered just this morning."

Arthur took the cheroot and inhaled, then watched the smoke slowly rise up to the ink-black sky.

"I take it then you are finished with the dancing," Julian remarked.

Arthur shrugged. "I needed some air."

"You've allowed Rothembow to unsettle you."

Arthur shot a curious look at Julian; he shrugged, exhaled the smoke of his cheroot. "Face it, Christian, you've always been a bit too sentimental for your own good."

"Dear God, here we go again," Arthur snorted. "From one sentimental fool to another."

Julian ignored that. "I wasn't aware that he had invested cattle or land in Scotland."

Frowning lightly, Arthur shoved his hands in his pockets. "I knew," he admitted quietly. "It just seemed . . . at the time he seemed quite desperate for it, as if that bloody land would solve some monumental problem. The worst of it is that I didn't advise him against it in spite of seeing that it was a rather foolish thing to do."

"Phillip Rothembow was responsible for his own affairs, Arthur, not you. You can't punish yourself forever."

Apparently they were destined to have this conversation again, the one in which Julian would insist Arthur didn't deserve to shoulder the blame for what had happened to Phillip, that he was sliding too far into isolation where guilt would consume him. And then Julian would insist that what happened to Phillip was *his* fault, that he had known Phillip better than most, had been close enough to see his demise.

"I don't disagree, really. But you can't deny I might have advised him—"

"And you might have let him make his own decisions, like any man. You wouldn't presume to advise Albright against a purchase like that unless he sought your counsel. You certainly wouldn't think to tell *me* to invest in the percents instead of those dusty old manuscripts. Why should Rothembow have been any different?"

Julian's interminable logic never worked in this conversation. Phillip was different because he was *Phillip.* Unwilling to argue, Arthur looked away, into the dark beyond them. "Nevertheless, I promised Rothembow I would look into it and do what I could. I suppose I shall have to send someone up there—Redmond, perhaps. He's done quite well for us. He might enjoy—"

"*No.* You believe it all your fault? Then *you* go," Julian said sharply, and Arthur looked up, surprised. "*You* go, Arthur, and clear Phillip's name, do whatever it takes to release this enormous guilt you carry if you think you can."

"Go to Scotland? Don't be ridiculous."

"What's so ridiculous about it? You rarely leave London. You've mentioned a desire to see one of the Scottish clippers that are beating the Christian fleet to every port. And since you insist on bearing Phillip's death like your own personal cross, what better way to help him now? Really, Arthur, what have you to lose? It's not as if there is anything to hold you here!"

To his credit, Arthur managed to hide his considerable irritation at that remark with an indulgent smile. "Thank you for your advice, Kettering. I shall consider it."

With a look of pure disdain, Julian tossed down his cheroot and ground it out with his heel. "Very well, then, wallow in your guilt," he said irritably, and walked away.

Arthur watched him, almost laughing aloud at the absurdity of his suggestion. But by the time he returned to the ballroom, the smile had faded, replaced by a feeling of distraction.

He couldn't just up and go. Edinburgh was not an easy journey; it would take some time. And there was far too much to be done here. *Or was there?* A dozen or more highly trained solicitors handled the Christian family wealth; they hardly needed him for anything other than to lend his signature to papers and bank drafts. And he really was rather keen on examining the Scottish clippers that were outpacing every other ship on the seas.

Still . . . Arthur shook his head. A journey deep into Scotland was hardly the same thing as popping over to Paris. And it wasn't as if he knew anyone there at all— he'd be virtually alone. Yet it wasn't as if he was engaged in any meaningful activity here. His life consisted merely of another Season's events, which included, he thought with a grimace, the constant parade of unmarried debutantes under his nose, the occasional outing with Julian and Adrian when they weren't engaged with their families, and the periodic call to Madame Farantino's to tend to his physical needs. There was nothing: no purpose, no reason for him to be here. He did not really *belong* here.

A movement to his right caught Arthur's eye and he glanced across the room, his gaze landing on Portia. She was smiling seductively at him while her husband chatted with another gentleman, fingering the pearl at her bosom again, openly stroking herself.

No, it wasn't as if there was anything or anyone to hold him in London.

He owed this to Phillip, didn't he? He had failed him miserably; the least he could do was try and clean up the mess he had left in Scotland and establish his good name again.

Arthur pondered it until the early morning hours when the ball finally began to draw to a close. Julian and Claudia were among the first to escape. As they stood beneath the great stone portico and waited for a runner to fetch their driver, Claudia slipped her hand into Arthur's and smiled up at him, winking mischievously. "I've convinced my stubborn husband that we ought to have a supper party, Wednesday next. Wouldn't you please come, Arthur? I'm rather keen to invite Miss Wilhelmina Bentson-Fitzmayor. She is a dear friend of mine and her father a rather generous benefactor to the Whitney–Dane School for Girls, but she hasn't been introduced as of yet. You'd be doing me a great honor."

Arthur returned Claudia's bright smile and squeezed her hand affectionately. "I am terribly sorry, but I'm afraid I must decline," he said smoothly.

Julian chuckled as their coach pulled to the curb. "I assure you, Miss Wilhelmina Bentson-Fitzmayor is a far sight lovelier than her name."

Arthur bent to kiss Claudia's cheek, then returned Julian's smirk as he helped her into the coach. "I don't doubt for a moment that she is, but I shan't be in London Wednesday next," he said as Claudia settled herself on the squabs.

"Indeed?" Julian drawled as he stepped inside the cab. "And where exactly might you be, old chum?"

Arthur smiled. "Scotland."

Chapter Two

Mr. Jamie Regis, Esquire, stared at the man sitting across from him in the leather winged-back chair, quietly reading a letter. He didn't like the looks of Lord Arthur Christian very much; he had that air of suffocating wealth about him. Not that Jamie Regis had anything against wealth . . . he just didn't like being *summoned* by it.

And summoned was exactly what Christian had done, sending him a letter one month ago dictating exactly where and when he would be expected to show himself, without any thought as to how difficult it might be for Jamie to come all the way to Edinburgh. The English Ass had business in Edinburgh, and therefore expected the world to come to him, just like the rich sheep farmers Jamie often represented.

Look at him. He was awfully pleased with himself, wasn't he? Sitting there like the king himself, right in the middle of the drawing room of the fancy Kenilworth Hotel, one leg draped casually over the other as he read the bank's letter. Jamie considered himself rather dapper in his grooming, but the Ass was wearing a dark brown coat made of a material so fine it had to have come all the way from Paris. And his waistcoat—Lord, the pale green waistcoat was silk, Jamie was quite certain of it, and embroidered with rose and dark brown thread that exactly matched his coat. His pale green and brown neckcloth was impeccably tied, and the cut of his hair— a bit longer than the current style, Jamie thought smugly—was trimmed in such a way as to tame the waves in it. Even the man's side whiskers were, impossibly, perfectly matched. It just wasn't possible for a man to be that exacting on himself!

He shifted his gaze to Christian's hands and smirked. They were big, large hands—perfectly manicured, a heavy gold seal of some sort on the left ring finger— hands that had never worked a day.

Jamie's smirk faded as his gaze dropped to the man's feet—and he quietly sucked in his breath. It was Christian's boots that held him in awe. Rich, supple leather, tanned to shining perfection, rising up to a flaw- less fit just below his knee. Jamie Regis would have laid down his life for a pair of boots like that.

"Mr. Regis?"

Caught salivating over the man's boots, Jamie col- ored. He looked up, felt instantly overpowered—the other thing the Ass possessed was a very sharp hazel gaze. "Aye?" he responded tightly.

"I'm still a bit unclear. You handled Lord Rothembow's investment in property in . . . where was it again . . . ah yes, Glenbaden, in Perthshire, is that cor- rect?"

Jamie nodded.

"I imagine it is rather picturesque there."

When Jamie refused comment again, Christian smiled knowingly. "And you negotiated a settlement on the land and cattle with the Bank of Scotland for one- half the purchase price of eight thousand pounds to be paid at signing, and a loan against the other half for which the tenant had a responsibility to pay with pro- ceeds from the sale of six beeves per annum over three subsequent years?"

He had to think hard about that succinct summary; slowly, he nodded.

Christian cocked his head to one side. "Please help me to understand, Mr. Regis. This letter from the bank clearly states that the debt owed on one-half the purchase price is in arrears and the taxes have not been paid since the loan was granted. I understood that a rather sizable herd of cattle was purchased with the land—was it not considered collateral against that loan?" he asked smoothly.

Lord, the man's gaze did not waver at all; Jamie felt as if it was actually piercing him all the way through his skull and to the chair behind his head as he waited for an answer. Unnerved, he hastily dropped his gaze and fumbled through a stack of papers he held on his lap. "Milord, it appears that ah . . ." *Christ, what was the tenant's name again?* He hadn't been to that glen in three years now, but God Almighty, whoever would have thought his practice would explode as it had . . . "Ah, Fraser," he quickly continued, latching onto the man's Christian name from some dust-covered memory. "*Ahem.* Aye, milord, Fraser did not make the payments to the bank as was agreed. Now, in thirty-four, there was quite a drought, quite a drought indeed, and I rather imagine there was no grazing land to speak of. And then in thirty-five there was a great influx of sheep to the region. That would be—"

"Mr. Regis," Christian smoothly interrupted in a way that made Jamie grit his teeth, "shouldn't this . . . *Fraser* . . . have contacted you and asked for arrangements to be made with Lord Rothembow's handlers in London when he missed the first payment? Or the second? Certainly the third?"

There was no arguing that point; Jamie stopped fumbling through his papers and met the man's gaze head on. "Aye, milord, he certainly should have. But I *did* send a letter to Lord Rothembow at once upon receiving the correspondence from the bank."

A slight frown crossed the Ass's features and Jamie imagined that were *he* a solicitor here, he would personally call on his clients to see after things instead of relying on them to tell him when something was amiss. Well bloody hell, he could hardly be blamed for the fact that his practice had tripled in the last five years. Surely even the perfect Lord Arthur Christian wouldn't have turned down the sheep herders that came to him, even if they were spread between Inverness and Fort William and Skye and—

"Please take note, Mr. Regis," the insufferable man said, and templing his fingers, narrowed his eyes and stared into space for a moment before continuing. "You will call on Fraser directly and inform him that, due to the deplorable state of his covenant with Lord Rothembow, the covenant is hereby and immediately suspended." He paused, sipped delicately at a whiskey, then glanced curiously at Jamie. "You are making note, I trust?"

Miraculously, Jamie refrained from saying what was on the tip of his tongue, bent his head, and gripping his pencil so tightly that his fingers hurt, scratched out the instruction he had just been given. "I am taking note, milord," he said tightly.

"Furthermore, you may tell him that he is to be evicted forthwith from the property and the land and remaining cattle to be put to sale as soon as possible, the proceeds of which will go to retire the outstanding debt, the taxes owed, and the interest accumulated these four years." He paused again, quietly waiting for Jamie to finish writing his exact instructions. When Jamie at last lifted his head again, Christian leaned forward, commanding Jamie's undivided attention. "When you make this call, sir," he said low, "you should be quite clear with Mr. Fraser that I fully intend to pursue all remedies afforded to me by Scottish law in an effort to recoup the losses he has caused the late Phillip Rothembow, and that I will do so as the lawful agent of the Rothembow estate and with the full authority of the British Crown. Is that understood?"

He spoke like a mercenary, as if he handed down such cold edicts all the time. Jamie nodded dumbly.

Christian responded with a curt nod of his own. "Very good. In the meantime, I shall travel to Dundee upon concluding my business in Glasgow and pay the interest due as well as the taxes owed so that we may dispose of the property without hindrance."

He paused again, caught the eye of the servant across the room and nodded faintly at the whiskey glass next to his elbow before turning to Jamie again. "I shall expect to hear from you as to a date we might meet again and conclude this ugly business. But please understand that I fully expect to be on a ship to London by the end of the month and will brook no delays. I believe that is all, sir. Thank you for coming."

Jamie blinked. He couldn't be entirely certain—the Ass spoke awfully fast in the clipped tone of the aristocracy—but he thought he had just been dismissed. His eyes narrowed slightly; he puffed his cheeks and loudly gathered his belongings, fuming over the notion that he had come all the way from Inverness like a dog at this man's summons, only to be ordered about and dismissed like a servant. The thought so angered him that he stood abruptly and immediately dropped several of his papers.

The King leaned over the arm of his chair and retrieved them. "Your papers, sir."

Jamie quickly snatched them from his hand. "Why, *thank* you, milord," he snarled, and turned on his heel, fully intending to march away.

"Mr. Regis!"

Jamie stopped, debating whether or not to turn for fear that he might actually explode. Slowly, he glanced over his shoulder.

"You forgot to inquire as to where you may reach me. When you have completed your task, you may send word to the Sherbrooke in Dundee to the attention of Lord Arthur Christian."

"The Sherbrooke," Jamie managed to echo, and turned sharply, marching quickly from the posh drawing room of the Kenilworth before he did something foolish, like snap the man's neck. As he paused just outside the door to straighten his things and himself, he glanced back—Lord Arthur Christian was sipping a fresh whiskey that had materialized, casually reading a newspaper.

No, he did not like that haughty English Ass one bit. *Not one bit.*

Later, at a tavern near the highway where Jamie waited to board an overnight coach to Stirling, he looked at the notes he had made while suffering through that interview. He knew that Christian fully expected him to call on . . . Fraser? *What in the devil was his name, anyway?* But a trip to the central Highlands really wasn't practical just now. Jamie retrieved a leather-bound book from his satchel and opened it. There, in his neat script, was a list of appointments and legal matters he had pending. It was obvious from the extensive list that there was no time to go tramping about the Trossachs. Actually, he was desperately needed in Fort Williams where one of his clients was in a terribly heated dispute about a shipment of tobacco that sank off the French coast.

Lifting a tankard of ale to his lips, Jamie Regis pondered his dilemma.

In all honesty, a letter would have as much impact as his calling. He could simply write Fraser Whateverhis-name, explain the details of the eviction, and fix a date for his final call. The arrogant Ass would never know the difference—he'd get what he wanted, which was the settlement of the estate. Aye, this course was justified—he had far too much real work to take the additional time. He would simply pen a letter, inform Fraser that he would call four weeks hence to "conclude this ugly business," as Christian put it, and tend to his business in Fort William.

Right.

A letter.

That's what he'd do. Just as soon as he found the man's blasted name.

Chapter Three

WHEN THE HAPLESS young Willie Keith delivered the weekly post to the scattering of modest homes in Glenbaden each week, the residents—what few of them were left, anyway—gathered in their yards and waited. Not for Willie, of course, but the widow Kerry McKinnon. Mrs. McKinnon had the task of actually delivering the post because young Willie was so desperately in love with her, he couldn't rightly read the names on the vellums, much less find his way down the rutted lane snaking through the glen.

So every Wednesday, Willie Keith rode through the barley field of their peaceful little glen on the back of his mule. He looked neither left nor right, but simply disappeared over the knoll that led to the big white house of the late Fraser McKinnon. And every Wednesday, shortly after Willie's arrival, Mrs. McKinnon would appear on the knoll with a basket in her hand, leaving the poor young Willie to stare after her with such longing on his freckled face that the residents couldn't help but worry that this would be the week he would actually expire with it.

Yet there wasn't one of them who didn't feel his obvious longing stir something deep inside their own venerable souls. Not that a casual observer could tell from looking at any of them, but once they had all been just as young as Wee Willie.

On a particularly clear and cloudless summer morning, however, no one was chuckling at poor Willie Keith—they were far too concerned with the urgency they sensed in Kerry McKinnon's step as she marched down the rutted lane with the basket of letters clutched in her hand. The dozen inhabitants stood in their little yards with their chickens, dogs, and children at their feet, warily exchanging looks as she handed out the neat bundles of letters. It was unusual to see her so distracted—she had forgotten her always-cheerful greeting, her inquiry into their respective well-being.

She hardly spoke at all.

More than one wondered if the pretty, dark-haired lass wasn't feeling a wee bit ill. Little wonder if she was—the lass worked like a dog to keep them all going, rising with the first gasp of the day and toiling well after its last sputter into the night. In spite of the work it took just to keep the crops growing, the livestock fed, the house and barn in repair, Kerry McKinnon also found time in every day to see after them, each and every one. She called on Red Donner to see after his gout, made sure the old hag Winifred had awakened to another sunrise (and blast it if she hadn't), helped the young mother of three, Loribeth, with her chores. She was the glen's lifeblood, and to see even the slightest crease of a frown on her fair brow made them all feel a little out of sorts.

But unbeknownst to the residents, Kerry McKinnon had started the day in perfectly fine health. In fact, she had been feeling so robust that she had tackled the very daunting task of cleaning the old barn, attacking it with gusto—until Willie brought her the weekly post. She smiled at the carrot-topped lad, asked after his sister who had been ailing. Even though she saw her mother's handwriting on one folded vellum—which caused her to shudder involuntarily as it always did—it was the neat little signature of Mr. Jamie Regis, Esquire, on the back of a very heavy vellum that caused her stomach to churn.

Kerry remembered the name of Regis all right, but worse, she remembered Fraser had done something through him that she had never fully understood and had suspected was quite ill-advised. A sense of impending doom had immediately tightened her throat. She snatched the letter from the little basket, hastily broke the seal, and unconsciously lifted a hand to her neck as she began to read, choking on the contents.

After the necessary and extremely wordy felicitations, the letter very simply said that the land she was standing on was forfeit and marked to be sold, that she was to be sued for Fraser's debts, and *oh God* . . . immediately evicted.

Evicted!

Her hand suddenly shaking, Kerry had quickly grabbed the left side of the letter to steady it and read it once more, certain she had misunderstood, positive there was a clause that she had missed.

Unfortunately, she had understood it all too well.

Somehow, she had managed to smile at Willie, to send him to the kitchen and the freshly baked biscuits there. Somehow, she had managed to put the post in her basket and start down the lane toward the cottages that dotted the glen. She had forced herself to smile and greet her neighbors as she handed out the mail, and now, she was miraculously managing to walk out of their midst, away from their curious gazes, turning at the end of the lane toward the loch, her head high.

Blind to the path in front of her, she walked, seeing nothing but Mr. Regis's neat script citing irreparable debt and mismanagement, and the ridiculously short time of four weeks allotted her to pay her debt and avoid any legal consequence.

This was unbelievable! Fraser had sold a large portion of the family land, had owed money she had no inkling of before his death, and now she stood to lose everything because of it, be tossed away like so much garbage, along with his cousins, Angus and May, and Thomas, too. Not to mention the others in Glenbaden, the last of Clan McKinnon, his own family! Dear God, where would they go? What would they *do?*

An invisible vise suddenly clutched her stomach; Kerry abruptly stopped and bent over, her pain real in the wake of understanding what the letter meant.

But after a moment, she forced herself up. She couldn't let the others know of this disaster, not yet, not until she had thought of something. Anything! They would panic; Thomas would do something rash. No, she couldn't let them know, not until she had tried everything to save them.

But Mr. Regis had given her only four weeks!

Despairing, Kerry continued walking, moving woodenly toward the loch as her mind raced, desperately seeking solutions to this catastrophe. But there was nothing—she had no money, nothing of any value. There were no options, nothing save her mother . . .

Not that. Never that! She stumbled to a stop again, brought a hand to her eyes as she squeezed them shut. Tears burned her eyes, but she pushed herself forward, told herself to keep moving, keep thinking, which she did almost unconsciously until she found herself on her knees beside her husband's grave, staring at the little cross, the awful letters clutched in one hand.

"You lied to me, Fraser."

She had *believed* him when he told her everything would be all right. Yes, well, it *was* all right for Fraser now, God rest his soul, as he had died last fall. But he had left her in a morass from which she had no idea how to extract herself.

Kerry glanced around at the little cemetery on the banks of a stream where the McKinnon ancestors were buried alongside her husband, trying to force down the anger she seemed to battle every day. She shouldn't *feel* such anger—poor Fraser, he hadn't been very old at all, just four and thirty when he had finally gone to meet his maker. She winced and wiped her palm down the side of her neck.

There it was again, that little feeling of relief that he was gone.

Certainly she was glad he was no longer suffering, but that small, yet distinct feeling made her question if she hadn't been more relieved for herself than for Fraser. All right then, truthfully—Fraser had been so sick for so long, that in Kerry's heart, he had died years ago. He had taken ill only two years after they had married and had lingered in worsening degrees of ill health another seven years. They had ceased to live as husband and wife at the onset of his illness, and in the last two years of his life the pain had been so debilitating that he had required her constant care.

And so had the glen.

The McKinnon family had lived in this glen for more generations than Kerry knew. They had fished the little loch fed by the larger Loch Eigg, had cultivated a strip of land that would support a bit of barley in the good years. Fraser's grandfather, an officer in the old clan system, was fortunate enough to have owned some acreage in his own right, which had eventually passed to Fraser. Along with the land they had leased from Baron Moncrieffe, they had lived quite comfortably. Until Fraser fell ill, that was, and then there seemed nothing that she or Fraser's cousin, Thomas, or anyone else in Glenbaden could do to keep the cattle from dying or the barley from withering.

She had known things were bad, of course she did, but she had not known *how* bad.

Abruptly, she lifted her head and looked up at the white house with the green shutters she loved, sitting majestically on a small foothill, mountains dotted with cattle rising behind it, a stream below it running serenely into the loch. She loved this glen.

Oh God, she was in deep trouble—so deep, she was barely treading water.

Fraser, damn him! It wasn't until her husband had died that she began to discover the depth of her trouble. No sooner had she buried him when the first piece of correspondence came, a letter from the Bank of Scotland curtly informing her that taxes on the property were in arrears and that interest on the loan—a loan she was shocked to discover even existed—was past due, and the creditors quite anxious to be paid.

As if that astounding news wasn't enough, a second piece of correspondence had arrived from her mother, insisting that she come to her in Glasgow at once.

Kerry could not say which letter had frightened her worse.

The letter from the Bank of Scotland had, in hindsight, been easy to ignore. None of it made any sense to her then, and besides, she had been too panicked by her mother's letter.

After years of trying hard to love her mother, Kerry had finally reached a point where she acknowledged to herself that she could not. Her childhood memories were awful—Alva MacGregor had been a religious zealot who believed that every malady befalling a body was God's punishment for disobeying His word—as *she* interpreted it, naturally. As far back as Kerry could recall, Alva had never said a kind word about anyone, and for some reason, saved her most vehement condemnations for her husband and daughter.

One of Kerry's earliest memories was being locked in a closet as punishment for having accidentally broken a vase in her play. She was only five years old when her mother had pushed her into the dark closet, deaf to her fearful screams, shouting that Kerry should beg God to forgive her. But all Kerry could think of was the Devil— she was certain he was in the closet with her, because her mother had told her so, and that he ate naughty children.

In spite of the bright sunlight, Kerry shivered unexpectedly at the memory.

Fortunately, her father, Devin MacGregor, was not as devout as her mother and did not tolerate that sort of punishment. The result of his extreme displeasure upon finding Kerry huddled in the corner of that closet was to send her off to Edinburgh to a passable girl's boarding school he could ill afford. There Kerry remained until she was a young woman, returning home only in the summers when she was forced to endure her mother's harsh condemnations of anything and everything.

It was little wonder that she had begun to dream of escape, and when Fraser McKinnon had paid particular attention to her one summer evening at a harvest season gathering, she had shamelessly encouraged him. It hadn't been hard to do—he was rather pleasant looking and was fortunate enough to own land nearby. When Fraser began to court her, Kerry could taste her freedom. She turned all the feminine charm she could muster on him, and they were married after a few short weeks. Not a moment too soon, either, as her father was found dead in his bed one morning just a month after they were wed.

That was when Alva seemed to lose what was left of her mind. She began attending the gatherings of an evangelical minister who was gaining quite a reputation around Perthshire. Alva grew very enamored of the Reverend Tavish, and much to Kerry's horror, within a month she had sold the family's land to a sheep farmer and turned the profits over to Tavish. That was astounding in and of itself, but Kerry was bowled over when Alva up and followed Reverend Tavish to Glasgow, where he had, apparently, established some sort of enclave. He and his followers lived and spent their days among the Glasgow poor, condemning them for their heathen ways and coaxing them into his fold. It wasn't too long afterward that Kerry received word her mother had married Reverend Tavish and was expecting his child.

Her contact with her mother was sporadic after that, amounting to no more than a dozen letters exchanged in eight years.

But when news of Fraser's death reached Alva, she suddenly began writing with a vengeance. Fraser had been gone only a month when Kerry received the first letter demanding she come to Glasgow. That letter was followed with alarming frequency by others, boldly ordering her to give up her morally decrepit ways and come make a good, obedient wife to a Believer.

Kerry would just as soon die.

She glanced down at the latest missive from her mother. Morbid curiosity filled her; she unfolded it, shaking her head wearily when the letter began immediately with a tirade about the Glory of God, the Sins of His Children, the failings of the Church of Scotland, and of course, the litany of Kerry's particular faults. It ended with the usual demand that she come to Glasgow, but interestingly, Reverend Tavish himself had deigned to add a line, instructing her to honor her mother's wishes, deny the temptations of the flesh, and come to Glasgow at once, her only hope for chastity. With a roll of her eyes, Kerry stuffed the letter into the pocket of her gray skirt.

She was chaste, all right, and God help her, she'd remain that way for the rest of her life before she would go to Glasgow.

Aye, Thomas's plan was beginning to look better and better all the time.

Thomas McKinnon, bless him, was Fraser's cantankerous cousin who had never stepped foot out of Glenbaden in all his life—although he threatened on a daily basis to do so. But Thomas loved this land. He *knew* the glen, knew what it would yield. It was his opinion that the land could not support cattle long term, as the grass was neither rich nor vast enough—but it was perfect for sheep. Sheep and barley, he told her, were the future; sheep and barley would turn the profit she needed to pay Fraser's debts.

But . . . in order to make the transition from cattle to sheep, Thomas had urged her to borrow the money necessary to buy the sheep. If they could just turn a profit in this year's cattle, he said, they could repay half of what they borrowed for the sheep, and hence, were halfway there. Thomas had thought of borrowing from the bank to purchase the first dozen sheep. But then the letter from the bank had come, and once he had recovered from his shock, he had quickly devised another plan— borrow from Baron Cameron Moncrieffe.

Borrowing from her neighbor was loathsome to Kerry, but Thomas's suggestion had played in the back of her mind, in part because she had nowhere else to turn, and in part because Cameron Moncrieffe had been such a frequent visitor to her house in the last two years of Fraser's life.

Moncrieffe, a wealthy man, lived in Glenbhainn just beyond Loch Eigg. Kerry had once heard he farmed a thousand head of sheep. She didn't know if that was true or not, but the man lived in high enough style. She knew this because when Fraser could get around, he often called at Moncrieffe's renovated castle and had once taken her to a summer ball there. And when Fraser's health deteriorated, Moncrieffe called at Glenbaden. It had been a terribly thoughtful thing for him to do, and truly, Kerry had appreciated his concern for her husband.

Yet there was something about the man that made her uneasy, matched only by her extreme discomfort with his son, Charles.

All right, then. She could not admit it to another living soul, but she could at least admit it to herself. Charles Moncrieffe was a ten-year-old lad arrested in the body of a thirty-year-old man. It was indeed a man's body and the way Charles looked at her, the way he smiled . . . may she rot in hell for her thoughts, but poor Charles Moncrieffe made her skin crawl.

Kerry looked again at the two letters, trying to ignore the queasy churn of her stomach. As she could see it, the letter from Mr. Regis left her with two options. She could watch what was left of the McKinnon land be seized, the rents increase, and tenants lose their homes like hundreds of Scots before them pushed out by the sheepherders. They would be displaced to America or to the rocky shorelines to farm seaweed while she went to Glasgow, to her mother.

Or she could go to Moncrieffe.

The grandeur of Glenbhainn and Moncrieffe House always took Kerry's breath away, but today, standing in the middle of such a beautiful place in her old black bombazine, she felt like a ragged beggar. Alone in what was once the great hall, she marveled at the oak paneling, the brass light fixtures, the polished pewter framing the oval mirror just above a library table. Even the new marble floor had been swept and rubbed to a sheen, which seemed especially remarkable to her—she was fortunate if she could just keep the mud from the floors of her modest home.

Kerry nervously wiped a damp palm on her skirts, then shifted the bonnet she held from one hand to the other.

"Mrs. McKinnon. What a pleasant surprise!"

The deep voice of Cameron Moncrieffe startled her; she jumped a bit as he sailed into the hall through a heavy oak door, followed by a small butler who carefully avoided her gaze. Moncrieffe was, as usual, impeccably dressed. She had always thought him fairly handsome, but he looked quite genteel with his gray hair fashionably crimped and combed and his thick side whiskers neatly trimmed. "Thank you for seeing me, my lord," she said, dipping into a curtsey.

"It is my great pleasure, madam. My day is considerably brightened by such a . . ."—he lifted her hand to his mouth, his lips lingering on the back of her hand for a long moment before slowly rising—"such a lovely caller."

Her skin prickled unpleasantly; Kerry gently withdrew her hand from his and clutched her bonnet tightly, forcing a smile to her lips. "You are too kind, sir."

"Nonsense," he said, taking her elbow. "Shall we be seated?" Without waiting for her response, he looked over his shoulder at the butler. "Tea," he said curtly, then propelled Kerry forward to a grouping of furniture covered in blue china silk. She briefly wondered what it cost to cover a chair the exact color of the summer sky and sat gingerly, vaguely fearing she might somehow ruin the silk coverings. Her host selected a chair across from her and, casually crossing one leg over the other, folded his hands on his thigh and regarded her kindly. "Now, then. To what do I owe the extraordinary pleasure of your call, Mrs. McKinnon?"

Right. That. She glanced uneasily at the hearth, feeling a bit ridiculous—how exactly did one go about begging for money? "I, ah, I must admit I come on a matter of some delicacy, my lord." Her voice sounded weak; she stole a look at him from the corner of her eye. His expression blank, he patiently waited for her to continue. "I suppose I should just come to the point, no?" she asked quietly.

Moncrieffe nodded.

Just speak. "I've not come on a social call, really—although I am pleased to see you well," she hastily added. He inclined his head in acknowledgment of that. "But . . . but there is a matter of business behind my call." Oh aye, *business.* She liked the sound of that and forced herself to relax her grip on her skirts.

"Is there indeed?" he asked with an indulgent smile.

"Aye . . ." *I should like a large sum of money, please.* "I, ah, have found myself in a wee bit of a predicament." A wee bit of a predicament? It was a full-fledged catastrophe!

Moncrieffe nodded encouragingly. "Please continue, Mrs. McKinnon. If you are in a . . . ah, *predicament* . . . I should like to help you if I can."

That was encouraging, but they were interrupted at that moment by the appearance of the butler carrying a silver tea service. She chewed on her lower lip, stared at her hands as she waited, feeling the pressure of her heart against her breast and fearing that he could hear its thunderous beating.

"You were saying?" Moncrieffe asked politely as the door shut behind the butler, and moved to pour her a cup of tea.

"My lord, I . . . I have nowhere else to turn," she blurted, wincing at the bluntness of her admission. "Unfortunately, and m-much to my surprise, I have learned that my husband . . . Fraser . . . owed—that is to say, *owes*—quite a lot of money to the Bank of Scotland. And . . . and taxes."

Moncrieffe lifted a delicate cup of bone china to his lips and sipped his tea as if he heard such devastating news all the time.

"And, ah, some creditors of some sort," she shakily continued, "although I confess I am unclear as to the details." She paused again, certain that was enough to shock and disgust him.

"Is that all?" he asked pleasantly, then waved airily at the tea service. "Please, drink your tea before it grows cold."

Is that all? Drink your tea? Good Lord, had the man heard a word she had said? Incredulous, Kerry stared at him. "You . . . surely you understand—I wouldna come to you, I wouldna *burden* you had I any other option, but really, I've come upon my wit's end. Yet I want you to know that I am not without a plan. My . . . my cousin, Thomas, he believes that if we can sell a few healthy beeves this year, we might transition from cattle to sheep, because the sheep are much better suited to the grass—but even with a decent showing at the cattle market, I fear it is not nearly enough! I'm in desperate need of cash to hold the bank for a time, but I am certain—"

With a chuckle, Moncrieffe abruptly silenced her

rambling plea as he set his teacup aside. "I beg your pardon, Mrs. McKinnon, but sheep?" He chuckled again, shaking his head, as if that was a perfectly ludicrous notion. "You have been sadly misguided, my dear. You've not enough acreage for sheep. Your little scheme would never work."

That declaration threw her—she trusted Thomas's opinion so implicitly she was hardly prepared to argue his plans. "But Thomas said—"

"You would be advised to forget what your cousin told you, madam," Moncrieffe interrupted, his voice noticeably cooler. "He does you an injustice by filling your pretty head with such fantasy. And frankly, I doona think it particularly important if it be cattle or sheep— you've simply not enough land to support the livestock you will need to buy back your debt. Aye, you are quite right, Mrs. McKinnon—you are in somewhat of a predicament."

Stunned, Kerry could only stammer. "Aye, I-I realize—"

He held up his hand. "I doona think you do," he said, and slowly leaned forward, his blue-eyed gaze piercing her fragile composure. "Your husband's trouble began when the plague killed his herd three years past. How do you think he paid his debts that year? He sought my considerable help, that is how. And again the following year. When *last* year's bull was ill-disposed to father a single calf, he rather gave up trying to appease the bank *or* me. Quite frankly, Mrs. McKinnon, your debt is greater than you realize. I am personally owed more than five thousand pounds."

Five thousand pounds? The air seemed to leave her lungs; she suddenly could not catch her breath. The sum was overwhelmingly large, staggering, almost as grand as the sense of betrayal she felt. She slumped against the chair back, too stunned to move or speak or even *think*. Fraser's lies seemed to pile on top of one another, pushing her down into a morass so deep that she almost felt as if she was drowning, right there, in a sky-blue chair. A flurry of memories whirled in her mind, of the dozens of times Fraser had assured her everything would be all right, that she had nothing to fear—

"Here, now, drink this."

Moncrieffe was thrusting a dram of Scottish whiskey into her hand. Kerry sluggishly remembered where she was and pushed it away, shaking her head. "I . . . I didna *know*," she whispered hoarsely as she forced herself to sit up straight.

"I am certain he didna want to burden you."

That caused her to snort indelicately. "He hasna exactly left me without a burden."

"There now, Mrs. McKinnon. You'll only make yourself ill," he said with a twinge of condescension, and strolled to one of six windows to gaze out at a green lawn below. "He knew he was dying, and there was little he might have done to reverse the course of things. He knew you would be adequately provided for, so he chose not to cloud the last few months of his life on this earth."

That brought Kerry's gaze up and around to where Moncrieffe stood. "He knew that I would be adequately provided for?" she asked, aware that her voice sounded shrill. "Surely you understand my situation now, my lord, and I therefore canna imagine what you might possibly mean!"

"Indeed I do understand," he said, turning toward her. "Better than you know." The strange smile that spread his lips made her blood suddenly run cold. "Your husband and I came to some agreement about the debt, you see, and he was rather insistent that your future be part of any agreement between the two of us. I was very happy to oblige him."

Fingers of dread scraped at Kerry's belly. "*What* agreement?" she forced herself to ask.

Moncrieffe extended his hand in a gesture for her to join him at the window. "Come here, will you? I would show you something."

Her legs and arms did not want to move. Kerry rose slowly, moved stiffly across the large expanse of room, the dread thickening. As she neared the window, he put his arm around her shoulders and smiled warmly. "See there?" he asked, pointing to the green. His son Charles was on the lawn, holding a stick and playing a game of keep away with two dogs, exactly as a young boy might play. To one side, under the canopy of a tree, Thomas leaned against the wagon, watching him from beneath the brim of his hat. "Charles has now reached his thirtieth year. I think it rather obvious he will never possess the mind of a grown man, but I've seen to it that it will never matter. Charles will inherit considerable wealth. In addition to the property I own now, and will soon repossess from you, I rather suspect that the Bank of Scotland will be quite pleased to sell me your land, Mrs. McKinnon."

Now he was confusing her. "But . . . but the land in question apparently belongs to someone else. The Bank of Scotland has written me so."

"An absentee owner who has never so much as set foot on the property. I rather imagine he, too, will be quite happy to be relieved of the debt."

This wasn't making any sense. Kerry shook her head. "I doona understand," she said, moving away from his arm draped heavily around her shoulder.

"Then let me explain it simply," he said, as if speaking to a child. "The bank will want what is owed them. The owner will want to be relieved of what has become an extraordinary debt. I can purchase your paltry acreage for perhaps a fraction of its market value and make both owner and bank happy."

Her mind was swimming; her gaze shifted to the figure of Charles on the lawn, and she vaguely noted that his shirt had come loose from his trousers and his hair was flying in all directions—a perfect contrast to his neatly attired father. "I doona believe you," she muttered. "Fraser intended for me to remain in Glenbaden.

He wouldna have agreed to give what was left to you or anyone else."

Moncrieffe laughed, put his hand on her shoulder, and leaned down so that his mouth was just a breath from her ear. "You are quite mistaken. He didna want Thomas McKinnon to have you, so in exchange for forgiving his debt, Fraser agreed that you would make a lovely wife for my Charles."

Something in her breast exploded; Kerry leapt from his reach and whirled, her hand pressed against her racing heart. "How *dare* you!" she cried as the thick dread quickly turned to bile in her throat. *How dare Fraser? How dare he betray her so?*

"Come now, it's not as if you have any other options!" he reminded her. "When you rid yourself of those widow's weeds, do you think any decent gentleman will come running to your door? Even McKinnon willna have you then! You have *nothing!* Your only alternative to my rather generous offer is to seek shelter with your mother, whom I daresay *will* find a man to provide for you!"

No words would come; her tongue was frozen. The shock was too great; she felt herself crumbling under the weight of it.

A heavy sigh escaped Moncrieffe. "You couldna hope for a better solution, Mrs. McKinnon. I'll grant you my Charles is rather slow, but you will have all that you want—"

"I will *never* marry Charles," she said, surprised at how calm she sounded. "And I willna be coerced, by you or anyone else."

Moncrieffe pressed his lips tightly together as he considered her for a moment. "Think before you speak, Mrs. McKinnon. You might regret such rash words."

"I will regret nothing," she said, her voice growing stronger. "I willna marry your son, not under any circumstance." Moncrieffe's face turned red in response to that, and Kerry was suddenly anxious to be gone from there. "You will have your five thousand pounds," she said haughtily, and turned on her heel, marching for the door, unable and unwilling to think just how she might accomplish that extraordinary feat.

"Mrs. McKinnon!"

Her hand stilled on the door handle; her instinct was to flee while she could, but she lifted her chin, forced herself to turn and meet his gaze. His eyes were blazing with anger, his fists clenched tightly at his sides. When he spoke, it was through gritted teeth. "You canna possibly manufacture five thousand pounds! But I will allow you to try—as it is, you are no use to us in your mourning habits. You have *one* month, and then you will honor your husband's debt to me, do you quite understand?"

Oh, she understood all right. Understood so clearly that she almost laughed out loud at the absurd impossibility of it. "As I said. You will have your five thousand pounds," she said with false confidence, and jerked the door open, walking through with her head held high as if she had some notion of how she might produce the bloody miracle of five thousand pounds.

Chapter Four

THOMAS WAS FIT to be tied when Kerry announced her decision to go to Dundee and meet with an agent from the Bank of Scotland. "Waste of bloody time, that is. No point in it," he had said again and again, arguing that the bank wouldn't loan her any money for any purpose. But as he didn't have a better idea, Kerry was determined. She was *not* going to let Moncrieffe win, not until she had drawn her last breath. So she had donned her black bombazine, packed a small, worn red satchel—complete with the gun Thomas made her take—and slipped a beautiful, triple strand of pearls into a small pocket sewn on her petticoat.

When May protested her intention to use the pearls as collateral against the debts, Kerry had lost her patience with the lot of them. Could they offer a better solution? No. She had no idea what she was doing, was frightened unto death with what she was about to do, and did not need their doubts at this moment.

What would the bank say to it? The pearls had belonged to her great-grandmother, then her grandmother. Her father had given them to her as a wedding present. The memory of her wedding did not improve her black mood, nor the memory of the summer ball at Moncrieffe House, the only other time in her twenty-seven years she had worn the pearls. The good Lord above knew it pained her to risk losing them—the pearls were the only things from her childhood that held any meaning for her—but unfortunately, they also were the only things she had worth more than a few farthings. And she was not going to lose her land, not to Moncrieffe she wasn't, and on that point, she was absolutely, unequivocally determined.

Her shock, indignation, and choking despair upon leaving Moncrieffe House had slowly turned into a ravenous anger. There had been moments in the last twenty-four hours that she was actually *glad* Fraser was dead, because if he were living, she might very well have strangled the last breath from him. It was impossible to fathom that he could have defamed his own cousin then bartered her away like that—and to Charles Moncrieffe of all people! Mother of God!

Fraser had done worse than betray her horribly; he had destroyed every feeling she had ever had for him, and the worst of it was that she couldn't demand an explanation from him, couldn't ask him *why* he had done this to her. She had nursed Fraser until he had finally succumbed to his illness, had kept their land with what little she had—she had been a *good* wife to him! The depth of betrayal scored her, and she believed, as the coach thundered through the serene countryside, that she had lost everything because of him.

The anger had, however, compelled her into action. It seemed as if all doors of escape were slamming shut, but she was not ready to give up. There simply *had* to be a way, and at the moment, that "way" seemed to be in Dundee.

So to Dundee she had come, using a portion of their dwindling funds to buy passage on a public coach departing from Loch Eigg before the sun was even up. Kerry traveled a full day and a half sandwiched between a woman with arms that looked like roasting turkeys and a man who smelled to high heaven. In Dundee, she had waited patiently for four hours before the bank's agent, Mr. Abernathy, could see her. He had apparently just returned to Dundee that very day from a lengthy absence. Although he was quite flustered, Mr. Abernathy was a kind old man, a grandfatherly sort, who patted her hand frequently as he explained that the value of the pearls was simply not enough to cover even the interest on the loan. Apparently, Kerry possessed a very pretty triple strand of mediocre pearls. Mr. Abernathy did, however, *keep* the pearls. Not that he hadn't been terribly sympathetic about her plight—he had generously offered her until the end of the month to come up with something else of value she might use to make a payment of some sort. *Any* sort.

It seemed as if the whole world was waiting to collapse at the end of the month.

Even after that disheartening interview with Mr. Abernathy, Kerry still would not admit defeat. She spent two of her last twenty-five pounds on a small room in a boarding house, where she paced until the early hours of the morning and it was time to board a public coach bound for Loch Eigg by way of Perth.

The public coach almost emptied in Perth when the road turned north, save Kerry and two men. She hardly saw the heath-covered hills roll by between towering hedgerows and pines and maples that cast long shadows on the road. She responded coolly to the efforts of the two male passengers to engage her in conversation. How could she converse with them? If she opened her mouth, she was certain the fear and frustration would produce enough tears to drown them all. She could not recall ever feeling so abandoned and alone.

Or so angry!

It was over. She would lose all she ever had, all she ever wanted. Fraser had once promised her a rich life filled with children, family, and a comfortable hearth. That faded memory seemed almost a figment of her imagination now.

With a soft groan, she closed her eyes, wishing for mind-numbing sleep, just a few moments away from the hell that was suddenly her life. And she might have found it, too, had the coach not suddenly swerved sharply to the right in a screech of metal, tossing her onto the floor. The two men cursed as the coach righted and came to a very bumpy halt.

Fabulous. Just when she thought there was nothing left to possibly go wrong.

"Here now, lassie, are you quite all right?" one of the men asked her.

"I am fine." She was lodged awkwardly between the seats, halfway on the bench and on the floorboards, and clumsily managed to fumble her way back up on the bench.

"What in thunder?" the other one demanded, and swung the door open, almost hitting the driver.

"Very sorry, lads. Seems the axle threw a bolt," the driver said apologetically. Kerry had no idea what that meant, but the two men immediately groaned and rolled their eyes at one another. The news obviously wasn't good. Kerry looked to the driver, who lifted his shoulders in a sort of half-shrug. "Sorry, lass. We'll have to turn back to Perth, we will."

"Perth!" Oh *no!* This was disastrous! She could not afford to spend another two pounds on a boarding room and she had to get home—her time was running short. "Can't you drive on?" she asked, aware of the desperation in her voice. "Surely there is a village close by—"

The driver shook his head. "Too far. Perth's closer. Ah, lassie, doona look at me like that!" he exclaimed, wincing. "If we drive on, we could ruin the whole axle! The parts, aye, they rub together without that bolt—"

"But I'm expected home, sir! I canna go back to Perth! Is there no village nearby where I might hire another coach?" she insisted.

The driver absently pushed his hat forward so that he could better scratch the back of his head as he pondered that. "Well . . . I suppose you could wait at the crossroads here. There's a coach from Crieff that comes through regular, headed north for Dunkeld and Pitlochry." He paused, consulting his pocket watch. "Aye, an hour, no more than two, I'd wager. You could wait."

"I beg your pardon," one of the gentlemen quickly interrupted. "I wouldna advise it, lass. We are far from civilization and the public coaches are wholly unreliable—"

"Beggin' your pardon, sir, but *this* service arrives in Perth every evening at eight o'clock on the button and leaves promptly at six o'clock every morning, arriving at Blairgowrie precisely at—"

"Beggin' *your* pardon," the second man snapped, "but are we or are we not about to turn *back* to Perth?"

"Well now, you expect a bit of mechanical trouble now and again, you do!"

"Are you certain about the Crieff coach?" Kerry interrupted.

The driver glowered at the men before answering. "I am indeed, lass. You'll do right well to wait here for it."

She extended her hand, ready to climb down. The smaller of the two men tried to stop her with a hand on her arm. "Madam! There's naught but wilderness about you now! If you wait for that coach, you do so at your own peril!" he pleaded.

As if anything else could happen to her—Lord, even *Job* had not suffered so many trials! Kerry smiled at the two gentlemen as she shook off the one man's hand, then fairly leapt from the coach. "Gentlemen, I thank you for your kind concern, but I am rather determined to reach Pitlochry by nightfall." And she continued smiling as the driver fetched her satchel from the back running boards.

The larger of the two men threw up his hands in a gesture of defeat. The driver, however, seemed rather pleased with her decision. "Our service willna fail you, lass," he said cheerfully, and grinning broadly, tipped his hat to the men before slamming the coach door shut. He showed Kerry to a spot where the road from the east curved into another road running north. "Wait here, and he'll be along in an hour or so, mark me. You'll be right safe, doona you worry," he added, placing her satchel at her feet.

"Thank you." She inclined her head to his jaunty wave good-bye, then watched him and another driver turn the coach around and roll slowly in the direction from which they had come.

As the coach disappeared from sight, Kerry glanced around at the unfamiliar and very deserted surroundings. The shadows were already lengthening; it wouldn't be long before the mist would roll in, shrouding everything. She peered into the dark forest behind her, unable to see past the dark greenery of the first line of trees. The foliage was thick and deep, seeming almost impassable from where she stood. And as she peered into the dark shadows, she was struck with the memory of Mary Blain, a schoolmate of hers years ago who had a penchant for telling the most ghoulish stories.

Kerry scoffed, turned away, and looked up the road. She was not going to stand here like a child and think of beasties and fairies and trolls living under bridges. How absurd! Nor would she allow Thomas's dire warnings of robbers and generally unsavory characters bother her. This was a minor inconvenience, nothing more. That sound that kept coming from the woods behind her was just a squirrel. The Crieff coach would be along in no time at all.

She had nothing to worry about.

Just like the driver said.

But the coach was not there in an hour. Or two. Or even four.

Arthur was rapidly coming to the conclusion that he was not overly fond of Scotland—or perhaps it was just

Scots he took issue with. The country was beautiful, he could not deny that. Deep, swift running rivers cutting through dark green rolling hills, tall stately trees. But the *people,* well . . . he had learned that they were a stubborn lot and not exactly enamored of the English. One of them even had the audacity to call him a Sassenach.

No, he was not overly fond of the Scots, a conclusion he firmly reached standing in the paddock of a stable just outside Perth. Absently slapping his gloves against the palm of his hand, he waited for the impudent stable master to bring him the mount he had purchased at a swindler's rate. Not that he'd had any choice. It had taken him a full day just to *find* a stable where he might purchase a mount, as the Scots apparently didn't have the same need of horses as the English. He routinely received a blank stare when he inquired as to where he might locate a stable for the purpose of purchasing a mount.

"How'd you get here, then?" one man had asked, apparently puzzled that a man might have need to actually *purchase* a horse.

"I hired a private coach."

"Won't that do for ye now, milord?" the man replied, scratching the top of his balding head.

Good God.

In all honesty, Arthur had rather enjoyed Edinburgh and certainly the journey to Glasgow and up the River Clyde. One particular ship builder was ecstatic when, after showing Arthur about his shipyard and onto a new clipper, Arthur had arranged to purchase one for the Christian Brothers' fleet. So ecstatic that he threw a fete in Arthur's honor that entailed excellent lobster, Spanish wine, and a pretty wench who was happy to warm Arthur's bed that night. Ah yes, he had rather enjoyed the River Clyde.

But not Perth.

He slapped his gloves against his palm again and

glowered at the stable entrance. What could possibly be
taking the man so long? This entire ordeal just confirmed that he was quite mad for continuing on to
Dundee on horseback. But when he had returned from
his review of the new Scottish clippers, a letter from that
funny little Regis had been waiting for him at the
Sherbrooke, requesting a meeting in Dundee to discuss
the final disposition of Phillip's land—in *three* weeks—
precisely four longer than previously set. That did not
set well with Arthur. He was quite certain he had told
the hapless solicitor that he fully intended to be on board
a ship bound for England by then.

Frustrated and restless, Arthur had gone on to Perth,
where he had arranged to meet Mr. Abernathy of the
Bank of Scotland, and thereby save him the unnecessary journey to Dundee. It did not help his disposition to
learn that Mr. Abernathy had been called away to
Inverness and was not expected in the area for some
time. When he had asked exactly how long that might
be, the banker's assistant had responded with the very
definitive and very helpful, "Couldna rightly say,
milord."

Faced with a wait of an indeterminate amount of
time, Arthur had then made the uncomfortable discovery that there was absolutely nothing for him to do in
Perth and found himself hopelessly bored. A few jaunts
beyond the town proper had revealed a glimpse of a
beautiful wet and green wilderness, steeped in history,
replete with an occasional castle ruin and Celtic cross.
Arthur was curious enough to want to see more of it. So
curious that he came up with the notion of having a look
at Phillip's land for himself while he waited.

He inquired with a clerk at the less than serviceable
Kinrossie Inn where he had taken up residence. The lad
had told him that the glens were just beyond Pitlochry,
which was actually rather close by, and had sketched a
map of the general area, suggesting that the distance was
nothing more than a leisurely ride of a day or two. In

Dunkeld, he could inquire as to the exact location of the land . . . if he ever reached Dunkeld, that was.

"Confound it all, you stupid nag!"

The shout came from just inside the stables. Arthur lifted his gaze and watched the stable master emerge, fighting a mare into the paddock. Ah, just bloody grand—he had paid a premium for a *green* horse. With a weary sigh, he donned his leather gloves and strolled into the paddock. As he neared the man and horse, he could see that the bit was fastened too tightly, and immediately reached to loosen it. The mare jerked her head at his touch, but Arthur stroked her nose and cooed softly as he loosened the leather straps. The horse calmed considerably; the stable master's eyes widened with surprise.

Idiot.

"Oh, she's broke," he hastily assured Arthur when he saw his dubious expression. "A wee bit ornery she is, that's all."

Yes, he could see she had been broken—not five minutes ago, he'd wager. "My bags," he said, and nodded imperiously toward the edge of the paddock where he had left two large, soft leather bags. The swindler flushed; he awkwardly thrust the reins at Arthur and retrieved the bags, dropping one into the dirt rather carelessly when he returned so that he could jerk the leather straps tight around the other. When he picked up the bag at his feet and moved to the other side, the mare moved uneasily, snorting loudly as the man once again jerked the straps too tight. He stepped back, rubbed his palms together; Arthur politely handed him the reins, loosened the straps so the horse could breathe, and pausing to adjust his hat, gestured for the reins again.

The horse, however, was not of a mind to be mounted and began to dance impatiently, nickering at Arthur when he put his foot in the stirrup. A smug smile lifted the corner of the man's mouth, but Arthur had faced tougher mounts than this and swung up, immediately reining the horse hard right when she began to buck beneath him, squeezing her with his knees at the same time and signaling that he was in command. After several minutes of snorting and jerking her head about, dipping her shoulders to dislodge him, and kicking her back legs out as if she intended to buck him, the mare finally calmed. Relatively speaking. Arthur glanced down at the stable master. He no longer looked smug, but mildly awed.

"I rather think you misrepresented your stock, sir. You gave me a price I would expect for an experienced filly."

"W-what's that? She's broke, I swear it!" the man blustered.

Arthur rolled his eyes and nodded toward the paddock gate. He had the mare under control for the moment, and the difference was not enough to haggle over. "If you would be so kind," he drawled, and spurred the nervous mare forward, fighting for control with every step.

Once the gate opened, the mare bolted from the paddock, galloping down the rural lane. By the time they had reached the main road going north, Hellion, as Arthur quickly named her, was handling somewhat better but remained skittish. Traffic scared her; if another horse approached, it was all he could do to keep her in check. They struggled for what seemed hours to him, until she was finally trotting smoothly beneath him, resigned to her fate.

The road wound through an increasingly rural countryside, past deep vales and crystal clear streams. As the road grew narrower, the pines grew taller. The region seemed completely deserted, and had it not been for the old woman draped in plaid walking along the road with the aid of a dog just as old as she, Arthur would have believed it so.

By late afternoon, he was beginning to wonder if he hadn't missed a turn. He reined the mare to a stop at a small stream beside an old stone cross marking the location of God knew what, and let Hellion drink her fill as he studied the crude map the hotel clerk had drawn. An *X* supposedly marked Dunkeld, the village where the clerk had suggested he seek further direction. By Arthur's calculations, the village should have been just about where he was standing. He glanced at the sun, gauging his direction. Head north, the clerk had said, to Kinelaven. Kinelaven was, judging by the map, immediately adjacent to Dunkeld, which looked to be no more than ten miles from Perth.

With a soft groan, Arthur rubbed the nape of his neck. He was fairly certain he was that distance and more from Perth. Then again, perhaps it only *felt* that far because of all the trouble with Hellion. He led the mare back onto the road to continue north, deciding that if he hadn't reached a landmark in another hour, he would turn back.

After another hour, having passed nothing more than the stone foundation of what once had been a keep, he was irritably despising of the whole of Scotland, and in particular, Perthshire, when he reached a large *Y* in the road. There was no *Y* on his map, nothing but an *X* for Dunkeld and another for Kinelaven. Oh yes, and a very helpful arrow pointing north, as if he hadn't already ridden across the bloody continent because of that goddamned arrow. He jerked his head to the right, glaring at the road leading north.

All right. There was no point denying it. He was plainly lost.

Hopelessly so it seemed, as there had been absolutely no evidence of civilization with the exception of the woman in plaid, and that had been two hours past. What, had he ridden into the wilds? Uncharted territory? Encroached upon the bloody moon, perhaps?

Hellion began to graze on a patch of long blade grass as Arthur pondered his predicament. He turned to view the route curving to the north, and—

What? Something lying on the edge of the road. A satchel?

Arthur leaned to one side and cocked his head to assess it. It was indeed a satchel, red and leather-trimmed, and seemingly stuffed full. The discovery elated him—where there was a satchel, there was surely a body, one that could speak and tell him where in God's name he had gone wrong. Arthur quickly dismounted and began to tug Hellion forward, but the horse resisted, far more interested in the grass than the satchel. Sighing loudly for the horse's benefit, Arthur carelessly tossed her reins over a low-hanging limb of the hedgerow, then stepped away to have a look around.

The road was bordered by a thick copse of trees on one side and on the other, sloped down into a grassy clearing on the edge of a forest. Slowly, he turned full circle, searching the landscape for any evidence of life, realizing as he did that the satchel likely had fallen from a passing coach.

"Bloody *marvelous*," he muttered, and walked back to the satchel, nudging it with his boot. Perhaps there was something inside that could help him—although he had no earthly idea what. A map! A *real* map. He sank down on his haunches and opened the satchel.

A frilly white cotton garment sprang free. *Ah, bloody hell, then.* The satchel belonged to a woman, which meant he'd find nothing of use to him. But he removed his glove nonetheless and with a snort of displeasure, plunged his hand deep inside, past more frilly garments and other things he paid no attention to until his fingers scraped the bottom of the bag.

Nothing.

He was about to toss the damn thing aside in frustration when he heard the unmistakable sound of a gun being cocked.

Wasn't that just *lovely*—now he could add being robbed to the wonderful events of his day! He heard the rustle of clothing as the bounder moved toward him—

apparently on tiptoe—he was certainly light on his feet. That struck Arthur as odd; he rather supposed any self-respecting highwayman would keep a fair distance from his prey in the event such prey was determined to surprise him, as he was about to do. What alternative did he have? He couldn't reach his gun before the highwayman could shoot him. No, unfortunately, what he had here was one of those unenviable situations where he would just have to spring on the rotter and hope for the best, for he was *not* in a mood to be robbed of all his possessions.

He waited, listening closely to the soft rustle until he could practically feel the bandit at his back. With a grunt, he suddenly whirled, springing to his feet and swinging his arm out at the very same moment the gun discharged, scorching through his flesh like fire and knocking him flat on his back.

Chapter Five

It was several moments before Arthur could pick himself up and grope about his person to assess the damage. Fortunately, it seemed that the bullet had only grazed his arm, doing nothing more than ruining his very expensive riding coat and giving him a nasty flesh wound that stung like hell.

Nonetheless, it was about all Arthur Christian could endure of Scotland for one day.

He jerked around to where his assailant would be standing—*should* be standing—and his mouth dropped open in astonishment. A *woman* of all things, flat on her bum and furiously rubbing her elbow with a grimace that suggested she had struck the ground hard. The kick of the pistol obviously had knocked her down. Lying in the road as it was, Arthur could see why—the thing was positively ancient and loud enough to scare an advancing—

Hellion.

Arthur whirled around to where he had tethered the horse and released a very colorful oath. The sorry horse had bolted, taking all his belongings with her. He was running before he realized it, racing down the road in the vain hope that she was only hiding in the woods, but it was obvious that the damn nag had fled for the comfort of her stable in Perth. He stopped, gasping for breath, and pressed a hand to the stitch in his side. "Damn it. *Damn it!*" he bellowed, and pivoting sharply, stalked back to the scene of the crime, growing angrier with each step. He stopped just short of marching over the wench with the ancient gun and stood, legs apart, hands on hips, glaring at her sprawled on the road with her boots sticking out from beneath her skirts. She stared back at him with a deceptively wide-eyed look of innocence that made his pulse pound with fury. He took several deep breaths in a struggle to calm his rage, but it was impossible. "What in the *hell* did you think you were *doing?*" he shouted.

Something sparked in the woman's eyes—they narrowed menacingly. "Protecting my belongings, that's what!" she responded hotly. "And what did you think *you* were doing, then?"

"Did it occur to you that you might simply *announce* that the bag was yours before firing on an unarmed man?" he countered angrily, and leaned over, growling at her startled gasp when he caught her elbow and jerked her to her feet. She immediately wrenched her arm free of his hold and stumbled backward, glaring daggers at him as she carelessly adjusted her bonnet.

That was precisely the moment Arthur noticed she was wearing black. *Black.* Marvelous. He had been brought down by a widow! He groaned loudly and looked away.

"You really shouldna paw through things that doona belong to you!"

That unexpected admonishment was delivered with a bit too much superiority to suit Arthur, in spite of his assailant's pleasingly soft burr. He turned slowly and raked a smoldering gaze across her as she shook the dirt from her skirts with such force that he half-expected them to tear clean of the gown's bodice. "I was not *robbing* you, madam! Trust me, if I was of a mind to *rob*, it should be something a bit more enticing than a filthy, old red satchel!"

She paused in the dusting of her skirt, met his angry glare, and raised it with a look of such fury that he felt a bit of a chill flit down his spine. "If you didna intend to rob me, just what *did* you intend to do, then?"

"Pardon me, but it isn't often one encounters a satchel in the middle of a deserted road! I thought it might contain some sort of clue as to its owner or destination!"

Her glower receded into a look of confusion; he could almost see the light of understanding dawn like a halo above her head. "Oh," she muttered.

Oh, indeed. Releasing a sigh of great exasperation, Arthur watched her dust the dirt from her derriere and asked reluctantly, "You've not harmed yourself, have you? Nothing broken?"

"Not anything that shows," she said, eyeing him suspiciously with orbs that Arthur suddenly realized were the palest, crystalline blue he had ever seen. They were beautiful, the irises rimmed with a dark circle of gray and long, dark lashes—

"You are from Edinburra, then?" she asked.

He blinked. "I beg your pardon?"

"Edinburra. You must be from Edinburra," she said, nodding.

As if it wasn't perfectly obvious from whence he hailed. "I am from *England*," he corrected her, and the little gasp and sudden flash of her brilliant smile caught him completely off guard.

"I was once acquainted with a lass from England!" she exclaimed as if they were being introduced over tea, and then just as suddenly—before he could even respond—her smile faded. "Holy Mother, I *shot* you!"

And the light above her bonnet grew even brighter. "Why yes, I believe I mentioned that earlier," he drawled, following her gaze to his arm. Not a pretty

sight, that—frankly, he had forgotten it in his anger—
but seeing the blood that covered what was left of his
coat sleeve, the pain of the torn flesh was suddenly quite
vivid.

"It must be bandaged." She moved so suddenly that
Arthur took an involuntary step backward. Fetching her
satchel in one fell swoop, she instantly rooted around inside and extracted a white cottony thing that Arthur
could not quite identify. "You'll remove your coat, will
you?" she said, and dropped the satchel to tear the white
thing apart.

Oh no. He might have been shot by a widowed lunatic, but he really did not care to be doctored by her,
too. Shaking his head, he stepped back, just beyond her
reach as she advanced on him, her pale blue eyes now
brimming with determination as she eyed his arm.
"Thank you, madam, but you have done quite enough as
it is."

"You are *bleeding*," she needlessly reminded him.

"It is merely a flesh wound—"

"*Och,* what foolishness. Kindly remove your coat."

"I will be quite all right until we reach a village.
You'd be a much greater help to me if you fetched your
carriage. Where is it?" he asked, glancing down the road.

"My carriage?" She laughed. "I doona have a carriage, sir!"

"Then your *mount,* or whatever the conveyance by
which you are traveling today," he insisted testily.

"My *conveyance* would be my *feet*."

Now she was being coy, that was all, and Arthur was
in no mood for it. He leaned forward, scorching her with
the fiercest scowl he could muster. "Madam, I have had a
rather long day of it. As you have managed to shoot me
and chase my horse away, I should very much appreciate
it if you would produce your mode of travel and let us
be on with it!"

"You should have tethered your horse."

Arthur's head snapped back with surprise; he

clenched his jaw and stared at her, wholly unaccustomed to being spoken to in such a careless manner. Oh yes, he would hand the wench over to the authorities in Perth with absolute glee. "Perhaps I should have," he said smoothly. "And perhaps *you* should have *announced* yourself instead of firing that rusty old pistol! Now *where is your horse!*"

With the long strip of white cotton dangling from her fingers, the other arm akimbo, the woman's pale blue eyes sparkled with feminine ire. "Perhaps the shot ruined your hearing, eh? I doona *have* a horse! *Or* a carriage! I was waiting for the coach from Crieff when you paused in your little jaunt to rob me!"

"I did *not* . . ." Whatever he might have said died on his tongue, because he suddenly realized she was telling the truth. And if she was telling the truth, that meant they were stranded. *Stranded!* In the middle of a bloody wilderness with dusk falling and a mist rolling in. *Please God, what had he done to deserve this?*

She realized it at exactly the same moment, he knew, because her eyes grew impossibly round and she murmured, *"Oh no,"* before clamping a hand over her mouth in dismay.

"Oh *yes*," he said, and the absurdity of their predicament all at once struck him as ridiculously funny. If he hadn't known better, he would swear he was an actor in one of the halfpenny plays on Drury Lane. The laughter bubbled up in his chest, spilled out, and he was suddenly laughing so hard that tears blinded him as he struggled out of his coat. Still laughing, he thrust his arm out so that she could bandage it. "Have done with it then!"

Bloody wonderful this was. The stranger was insane as well as angry, Kerry thought. Aye, well, he had every right to be angry—she winced as she looked at the wound and motioned to it again. "It should be cleaned first," she said, and inclined her head toward a small clearing.

Still chuckling, the stranger nodded. Kerry moved

immediately, picking up her satchel and marching briskly. And she kept moving, past an old stone fence, practically sprinting to a stream she had discovered earlier in her haste to get away from the robber.

On the stream's banks, she fell to her knees and took several deep breaths, completely unnerved by the experience of having just shot someone, particularly when said someone might very well be the world's most beautiful stranger. Lord God, as if her life could possibly get any worse, this man had to ride into her life like a thief and scare her half out of her wits! How was she to know he was a gentleman? What could she possibly have thought when she saw him stride to her satchel and begin to rummage through it? In her haste to hide when she heard him approaching, she had forgotten it. And then she had shot him—*shot* him!

She plunged the strip of her cotton drawers into the cool water, then wrung the excess moisture from it.

All right, well, she had shot him because she feared for her life, thank you very much. Thomas had warned her about the highland thieves—but good *God*, he was hardly a thief! He was a gentleman from *England,* of all places, who had thought to find the owner of the satchel she had left lying in the middle of the road! Aye, but there was something odd about him, something a wee bit insane. . . . Kerry forced herself to her feet and turned. The beautiful stranger was sitting on what was left of the old fence, his hands braced against his knees, staring . . . rather, his gaze was boring a hole right through her.

Making her knees tremble.

Trembling knees or no, she would bandage that wound before they parted company. It was the least she could do, having inflicted it. She willed her legs to move and walked toward him, feeling the intensity of his gaze trickle down her neck and spine. When she reached him, she avoided that pointed gaze altogether by dropping to her knees, setting her satchel aside, and peering closely at the wound. When she carefully probed it with her fingers, he flinched, sucked in his breath, gritted his teeth . . . but kept staring at her with those hazel eyes.

Kerry abruptly sat back on her heels. "It's naught more than a flesh wound."

His eyes narrowed. "I gathered as much."

Kerry dabbed lightly at the wound with the wet cloth. "It was an accident," she heard herself say. "I didna intend to harm you, I promise you that. I . . . I jumped when you jumped, you see, and for some reason it just, ah . . . *ahem*. Went off." She shot him a quick glance. "I'm really very sorry for it, truly. Mortified, if you must know. I've never shot another being in all my life."

"That's somewhat reassuring," he remarked dryly.

"You've naught more to fear," she babbled on. "I doona know how to load it." Oh honestly, what was she *saying?*

Her remark certainly gave him pause—he cocked his head to one side and looked at her as if *she* were the deranged one. "I beg your pardon, madam, but do you often go traipsing about the wilderness with nothing more than an old gun you don't know how to fire, much less load?" he asked incredulously, frowning slightly when she shook her head. "Might I inquire then as to the *reason* you are here with that ridiculously old pistol?"

"I *told* you," she responded impatiently, "I am waiting for the coach from Crieff. The Perth driver said it would be along directly."

His handsome face lit up at that. "Aha! A rescue! How directly?"

"Well . . . perhaps not *directly*," she quickly corrected him.

He frowned. "Then *when*, exactly?"

Kerry suddenly dipped her head, hiding beneath the rim of her bonnet as she fussed with the dry half of the white cotton. "Noon," she muttered, and could almost sense the rise of his chest as it filled with steam.

"Do you mean to tell me that you have been waiting alone here for a coach for more than six hours? That driver ought to be hanged for abandoning a defenseless woman!"

"I am *not* a defenseless woman! I have a gun!"

"Oh, righto, that you do—a gun you don't know how to use or reload!"

As there wasn't any good response to that, Kerry concentrated on wrapping the dry cloth around his arm, tying the loose ends into a neat little bow with the lacy ends of the fabric. The beautiful stranger looked down and groaned. She sat back, slapped her hands together, and pretended to ignore him as he examined her work. "All in all I suppose it isn't too badly done," he drawled, then flicked a hazel gaze to her. "For a pair of ladies' drawers."

"A half pair," she indolently corrected him, and gained her feet, busying herself with the straightening of her skirts—anything but looking in those eyes.

The stranger sighed loudly and came to his feet. "Well then, I suppose we ought to find something that will pass as shelter before night falls."

Shelter? "I beg your pardon?"

"Shelter," he said, his hands sketching an imaginary house between them. "From the elements. Wind, cold, that sort of thing."

"N-no, sir," she stammered, taking several steps backward. "I will wait here for the coach!"

"What in God's name is the matter . . ." his voice trailed off. He shook his head, glanced up the road for a long moment before fixing his gaze on her again. "Mrs.— Pardon, but now that we are on the most familiar of terms," he said, gesturing to his arm, "might I at least have your name?"

"McKinnon," she mumbled.

"Mrs. McKinnon, I am pleased to make your acquaintance. Arthur Christian at your service."

"How do you do?"

"Why just *splendidly,* thank you. Mrs. McKinnon, the Crieff coach is not coming. Now, as I see it, we have two choices. We can begin the walk back to Perth now—"

Kerry snorted. "I've no intention of returning to Perth now!"

"All right, then, on the morrow," he said blithely. "In the meantime, we can endeavor to find a place where we might wait out the night and hope to high heaven that the coach actually comes on the morrow."

She gaped at him. "Mr. Christian! I doona know who you are or what your custom is in England, but . . . but surely you know that to *seek shelter* with . . ." she stopped, looked down the road that curved to the north as she released her fluster in one long breath, nervously adjusted her bonnet, and whispered loudly, "It would be the height of impropriety to seek shelter with a man I doona know. Any man, for that matter." She paused, glanced at him from the corner of her eye, and felt the prickly heat under her collar. "I'm right sorry about the shot, I am, but I canna do more. I must bid you a good day."

Mr. Christian's eyes rounded with the apparent disbelief that she would not seek some sort of shelter with him. "Mrs. McKinnon, I could not, in good conscience, allow you to stand here all night and wait for a coach that is not going to come. Given the circumstance, I think you may trust that your reputation will be spared."

She could feel the flames in her cheeks with the implication behind that statement and quickly stooped to retrieve her satchel, which she held tightly to her chest. "You willna dissuade me, Mr. Christian. I'm to wait here for the coach. Good day." As if that wasn't definitive enough for the man, she waved him along.

But he didn't move. "Mrs. McKinnon, you are being rather foolhardy—"

"Excuse me, sir, but is it considered acceptable behavior in England for ladies to go wandering off with perfect strangers?" she interjected quickly and, tightening her grip on the satchel, leaned to peer around him and up the road. Where in heaven's name was that blasted coach?

"I honestly don't know why I should bother," he said to the sky. "Very well, Mrs. McKinnon. You win. *I* shall seek shelter and *you* may wait all night for your imaginary coach." He shrugged back into what was left of his coat and began marching across the tall grass of the clearing toward the hedgerow.

But halfway across the clearing, he stopped, pivoted about, and marched back, past Kerry, who was still rooted to her spot, and to the road. There, he retrieved her useless pistol and returned it to her. "If you are set upon by strangers, at the very least you could strike them with the butt of this gun. That should put a body down for a good twelve hours," he said, and with a mock tip of his hat, began walking in the direction of the trees again.

Set upon? *Set upon?* Her pulse quickened. "Mr. Christian!" Kerry fairly shouted after him.

He stopped, turned slowly. A faint smile turned the corners of his mouth. "Yes, Mrs. McKinnon?"

"W-what do you mean . . . if I am set upon?"

"Set upon," he said with a slight shrug. "Attacked. Robbed. Highwaymen, Mrs. McKinnon. You will do well to strike them with the butt of your pistol as a means of self-defense."

Highwaymen.

"Good day and good night!" he called, and continued walking toward the trees as Kerry's mind filled with the ominous possibilities of attack, the faces of horrid thieves and murderers who would find her here, alone, unprotected—save for the butt of an old pistol.

She squeezed her satchel even more tightly to her chest.

When Arthur reached the forest, he skirted to the right and found a place where tall grass afforded a barrier of sorts from the road and extended beneath the trees. It seemed as good a place as any to bed down for the night. He couldn't help himself; he glanced over his shoulder. Mrs. McKinnon was standing in the exact same place, staring up the north road, her satchel still clutched to her chest.

Obstinate wench.

He half-hoped a highwayman would come along and frighten her almost to death for being so stubborn. What, was the entire Scottish nation born with some sort of malady that made them all so bloody hardheaded?

He tore his gaze away from her and looked around him. A few handfuls of the tall grass would make a bed of sorts, and where the grass gave way to dirt and ivy beneath the trees, there was enough kindling to start a small fire. Fortunately, in taking stock of his pockets, he discovered he had a cheroot or two and some matches, along with his gun, a small purse—thank God he had put the bulk of his funds in an account with the Bank of Scotland—and a kerchief. If he was to build a fire, he best be about it—the mist was beginning to settle over the treetops.

Arthur momentarily forgot Mrs. McKinnon and set about gathering wood.

A half hour later, he stood looking down at the fire he had built—in spite of his aching arm, thank you—feeling rather pleased with himself. It had been quite a long time since he had started a fire from scratch. Barnaby, his head butler, saw to such things as the hearth at his various estates. The only time he had made a fire was when he was a boy; he and the Rogues had begun several small ones in places they weren't allowed such as the kitchen, the laboratory, and on one particularly cold night, beneath the headmaster's bedroom window.

He turned and looked up toward the road. Dusk had

fallen with the mist and he could no longer see Mrs. McKinnon. But he could well imagine her standing there, her spine ramrod stiff, that awful satchel clutched tightly to her. He heard the sound of an owl in the distance, answered by the howl of a wolf even farther away. She knew where he was. If she wanted the warmth of a fire, she could come down here and risk her blasted virtue.

Arthur made himself comfortable near the fire, his back propped against a tree and one leg stretched in front of him, the other bent at the knee. How long he sat, he had no idea, really, but it rather surprised him to realize that he actually enjoyed the peace and tranquility of this particular wilderness, this bit of solitude. There was nothing but the sounds of the woods—the scratching of tiny paws as squirrels chased one another around the trunk of a pine tree, or the limbs of the trees creaking as they settled under the weight of the changing night air. If he were a betting man, which he was, he'd wager Phillip's debt that before the mist grew so thick he could no longer see a sliver of moon, Mrs. McKinnon would come walking into this little nook of the clearing, having given up on her ridiculous notion of a coach.

He heard the owl again, only closer now, and got up to gather a little more wood for the fire.

The sound of her shriek ripped through the peaceful evening like a knife. Arthur reacted without thinking, yanking his gun from the holster at his side as he raced into the clearing, trying desperately to see beyond the little ring of light his fire cast. He almost missed her hurtling toward him in that black bombazine, spotting the flash of her red satchel just as she plowed into him. She threw herself at him, threw her arms tightly around his neck and buried her face in his shoulder as he fought for balance.

"Robbers!" she shrieked into his coat.

He held her trembling frame tightly to him as he

peered into the black. "Be still, be still now. Take a breath and tell me what you saw."

She shook her head, knocking strands of lavender-scented hair into his mouth. "Not saw. *Heard*. I *heard* them!" she gasped, and leaned back from her death grip of him just enough to peer up at him with eyes as round as blue china saucers. "A-a crackling sound . . . a-and a whistle of a sort! I am certain they are just on the other side of the road!"

Crackling sounds. Arthur fought a smile. "Wait," he whispered, pressing a finger to his lips to quiet her. She literally held her breath; her mouth was not two inches from his chin. After a moment, he heard the scratch of squirrels followed by the distant hoot of an owl. Mrs. McKinnon released her breath in one long sigh, right into his shoulder.

"Was that what you heard? A pair of squirrels, Mrs. McKinnon. The woods are teeming with them." She said nothing; her arms slid from his neck. He stooped a little, tried to see her face. In the weak light of the fire, he could see that her eyes were closed, her lips slightly parted, and her face deathly pale. He took pity on her, ran his hand soothingly down her back. "Would you like to sit with me for a time?"

She nodded, stepped away, and swept the back of her hand across her cheek in a self-conscious gesture. Arthur motioned toward the fire as he returned his pistol to its holster. "I was rather confused by the sound myself until I actually saw the little beasts," he lied.

With a meek smile, Mrs. McKinnon stooped to retrieve her satchel, then moved wearily to the small fire, sinking in a cloud of black, her satchel on her lap. For the first time since their unfortunate meeting, he noticed how tired she looked. It must have been a harrowing day for her, alone out here in the middle of nowhere as she was.

He left her for just a moment to gather some wood,

then built the blaze up before propping himself against the tree again. Mrs. McKinnon dug through her satchel, her forehead furrowed in concentration. She had lost her bonnet somewhere, and her hair, the color of midnight, gleamed in the firelight, particularly the thick strands that had come loose from the prim bun at her nape.

She actually had a very pretty face, he thought as she put the satchel aside and placed a small red bundle on her lap. Not a great beauty, but nonetheless very pleasing to the eye. Her eyes were her most stunning feature, her nose cute and pert, her full lips the color of young plums . . . yes, very pretty, actually. He might even go so far as to say exceptionally pretty—

"Biscuits," she said, working the knot of the bundle free. "May—my cousin—she packed them for me." She laughed nervously, smoothed the side of her hair with her palm. "I suppose she thought I might go starving in Dundee."

"So you've come from Dundee?" he asked, mildly curious as to what sort of business would have brought Mrs. McKinnon to be stranded here.

She nodded as she untied the knot, but offered no explanation. Reaching inside the bundle, she retrieved what she called a biscuit and held it out to him.

It was what he would call a scone. With a smile, Arthur gratefully accepted her offering. "Quite nice when served with a little Devonshire cream and a bit of jam. Thank you." He sank his teeth into the bread—and moaned with delight. In spite of being in the bundle for Lord knew how long, the scone was flaky and moist, practically melting in his mouth. "My God," he mumbled through another bite. "Food of the gods—my compliments to your May, Mrs. McKinnon."

She smiled then, that same brilliant flash of warmth that had captured him momentarily on the road. That smile . . . yes, *that* was the thing that made her exceptionally pretty.

"They are good, are they not? May makes them for Big Angus each Sunday." Mrs. McKinnon took a small bite of her biscuit and chewed slowly.

"Angus? Is that your son, then?" Arthur asked.

She blushed, shook her head. "May's husband, he is. I've no children."

Her voice carried a hint of wistfulness. "You've been widowed for a long time, then," he remarked unthinkingly.

"Eight months."

Eight months. Hardly any time at all. Poor girl—she undoubtedly still felt the brutal sting of it. God, he *still* felt Phillip's death, even though almost three years had passed. He glanced at the pretty widow, felt a twinge of sorrow for her. She was too young to have experienced the death of a loved one. Too pretty to have suffered the sting of it. "I'm terribly sorry for your loss."

She jerked her gaze to him, surprised. "Oh! Thank you—but my husband was ill for a very long time. He is at peace now, thankfully."

So the poor man had suffered. Arthur wondered how she had endured it as he munched his biscuit. Lady Whitehurst had endured her husband's long and painful death by carrying on with his groom. He mentally shook his head at that notion—for some peculiar reason, he could not believe that the woman who had shot him was as merciless as that.

They didn't speak for a long while; he ate two biscuits to her one. When he waved off her offering of a third, she neatly bundled the remaining two and stowed them in her satchel, then readjusted herself beneath her voluminous skirts, drawing her knees up to her chest and wrapping her arms around them. From his vantage point he could see her slender waist and square shoulders. She seemed a strong, healthy woman; Arthur had to pity the man who would catch the nefarious disease that would take him from the arms of a woman like Mrs. McKinnon.

After a moment of silence, she asked, "Do you live in Scotland, then?"

Arthur snorted. "Indeed not. I've come to settle some business matters for a friend."

"All this way?"

"Yes. In vicinity of Pitlochry."

"Aye." She nodded. "A wee bit north of here yet, but the coach passes through there, I think."

At the very least, it brought him a small amount of satisfaction to know that at least he had been on the right road. That idiot hotel clerk. If he should ever return to Perth, he would—

"I am really very sorry that I shot you."

Arthur started. He hadn't realized he was rubbing his wound and shook his head. "It's quite all right, Mrs. McKinnon. I'm quite certain the gangrene won't set in for a day or two."

That earned him a roll of her pretty blue eyes, which made him smile. "I am mortified, you know. I should have known just by looking at you that you were no robber!"

"And just how would you know by looking that I was not a robber?"

"*Och*, it's obvious," she said, flicking her wrist impertinently. "A robber would not wear clothing as fine as that, and he would surely be even filthier."

That made Arthur look down—he *was* filthy. Yet another new experience.

"And I think they doona shave."

He was with her—right up to the shaving part. "Not shave? Why shouldn't a robber shave?" he asked, confused by her logic.

"Why, he needs his whiskers to mask his identity! Once he has committed his robbery, he shaves his whiskers, so that not a single person can say with certainty that it was him."

"Aha. I had not realized that was how one went about a robbery."

"I read it in a novel," she blithely explained, and looked uneasily over her shoulder, peering into the mist, missing his broad smile. "I've heard there are highwaymen along these very roads," she muttered. "They camp in these woods, doona you think they do?"

Arthur rather doubted a highwayman worth his pearl-handled pistols would be so foolish as to camp *this* close to a road, even if it was practically deserted. "I rather think not."

Her hands fisted tightly in her lap. "What do you suppose happened to the Crieff coach?" she almost whispered.

"Mrs. McKinnon, you are unduly frightening yourself. The Crieff coach had probably already passed when the driver put you out. There are no highwaymen here. No one has been along this road in hours and I am quite certain a good highwayman would study the public schedules before embarking on his rounds."

She smiled with such relief that a curious shiver coursed right down Arthur's spine, landing in the pit of his belly. "Of course, you are right." She smiled again, but he noticed her hands were still fisted tightly in her lap. "I've read about England," she said, clearly changing the subject. "In school, I knew a lass who hailed from Carlisle."

"Carlisle. Near the lakes," he remarked, and taking her cue, launched into a rambling description of England beginning with the peaceful Lake District where the Sutherlands had their ancestral seat, to the rolling landscape of the moors where he had a small country house. Somehow, his remark upon that led to a mention of the stark beauty of the white cliffs at Dover, and then the magic of the forests in the Cotswalds.

Somewhere in the middle of his rambling, she shifted so that she was facing him, her funny little boots peeking out from beneath her gown. Arthur realized he actually had quite a lot to say—no one had ever really inquired about him or his home.

Mrs. McKinnon was either very good at listening or was as truly fascinated as she seemed. With the exception of the occasional nervous glance over her shoulder, she seemed to hang on his every word. He watched the light dance in her clear blue eyes as he spoke and realized, at some point in the conversation, that it was refreshing to sit with a woman who did not ask him about women's fashions, or what the latest rumor was among the *ton,* or what a pair of perfectly matched geldings might bring. Any one of a dozen questions Portia or any lady among the *ton* might have asked. Mrs. McKinnon asked about the English people, what they did to provide their living, where they were schooled, their hopes, their loves, their passions and fears.

"I beg your forgiveness, Mrs. McKinnon. I have put you quite to sleep," he said after a while and withdrew his pocket watch. The late hour astounded him—he had not felt the time pass.

"Oh no!" she exclaimed, adamantly shaking her head. "It's fascinating! I've not had the good fortune to travel beyond my home. I like hearing about England. It sounds so heavenly a place." She covered her yawn with her hand.

"Thank you, but I think we have quite exhausted the subject for one evening." He pushed himself to his feet. "I'll build the fire," he said, and walked into the forest to gather more wood.

When he returned a quarter of an hour later, Mrs. McKinnon was lying on her side, her hands pillowed beneath her cheek, fast asleep. She looked much younger in her sleep, he noticed, in spite of the dark smudges beneath her eyes. Arthur shrugged out of his coat and carefully draped it over her.

He turned his attention to the fire, and when he had kindled the flames, he glanced again at Mrs. McKinnon. What was the woman doing out here, alone? What had happened in her life? He moved to sit at the base of the tree next to her as he pondered that. He drifted to sleep, slipping easily into a dream in which Phillip appeared behind a tree, just beyond Arthur's grasp. But when he moved to catch him, he vanished, and Arthur struggled to remember if he had gone left or right, never really certain of where Phillip had come from or gone to.

The next thing he knew, he was waking in a dreamy state of arousal that strained against his buckskins. He forced his eyes open, noticed he was lying down, on his back, next to the dead fire. But he was not cold, because, as his mind slowly began to comprehend, Mrs. McKinnon—wrapped in his coat—was practically sprawled across him, her steady breath on his ear, her arm slung across his chest, and—merciful God—one leg hiked up and pressed against his groin.

Chapter Six

It was bad enough to have shot him. Worse to have gone running into his arms at the sound of a few forest creatures, but to awake practically on top of him—*oh!*

Kerry had almost killed herself getting off him, her arms and legs flailing as if she was being attacked by a horde of angry bees. She stumbled clumsily to her feet, at which point she had been completely unhinged by that wicked grin of his and had promptly tripped, just narrowly missing a headlong pitch into the grass. Her embarrassment only worsened as she tried to shove her skirts down—which wasn't exactly easy, seeing as she had managed to twist her crinolines into something of a mishmash. Then she realized her hair was falling all around her shoulders in one glorified tangled mess of curls. *Christ God!*

It did not help, not at all, that he just pushed himself up to his elbow and said in his wonderfully rich, silky smooth voice, "And top of the morning to you, too, Sunshine." Like a cat, he came gracefully to his feet, shook his fingers through golden brown hair that seemed one thick wave, then stretched his arms out wide and yawned. "Rather anxious to begin the walk to Perth, are we?" he asked over his shoulder as he strolled casually into the woods.

Kerry stared at his retreating figure, not sure if she should shout after him that she had no intention of going to Perth, or flee with all her humiliation in the opposite direction while she could. God, oh *God,* how was it that she had picked the most beautiful stranger in all the world to shoot? He was breathtakingly handsome—she had noticed that even when his face was contorted in that awful way when he was cursing the loss of his horse. His face, bless it, was shaped by angels, square and strong, with high cheekbones and a noble chin. And his *eyes.* His eyes were the most beautiful hazel eyes she had ever seen, tobacco-brown flecked with shimmering green and gold. And he was tall, over six feet, broad shouldered—when he walked into the woods, she swore she could see every muscle in his hips and thighs move in all their splendor.

She had felt his arousal under her knee—

Kerry suddenly whirled around. This was ridiculous! She had found herself practically panting last evening, watching his long, tapered fingers move as he spoke of England, the gentle curve of a smile on his lips, the sparkle of pride in his eye. How on earth she had ended up *sleeping* with him was beyond her—but it had given her a burning rash deep inside she could not scratch.

What madness! She had *shot* him! And in a few moments, they would go their separate ways, her apologizing one last time and he graciously making some little jest of it. She would not see this beautiful stranger again. So why was she almost breathless in her anxiousness around him? Had she forgotten she was a *widow* and barely eight months at that? For heaven's sake, he was the son of an English nobleman! This . . . this *preposterous* infatuation was just one more thing the good Lord had thought to throw at her, one more thing with which she had to contend.

All right, there it was then, a silly infatuation with an exceptionally handsome man. Fine. She would take her leave of him as she ought—but *not* looking a fright. Her hair felt a complete mess; the Lord only knew what had happened to her hairpins—no doubt half of them were up on the road along with her bonnet.

Kerry abruptly dropped to her knees next to her satchel, yanked it open with a jerk that almost tore the handles from it, and dug until she found her hairbrush. She frantically pulled it through her unruly hair, but froze at the sound of his cheerful whistle.

"Glorious morning, Mrs. McKinnon!" he opined. Kerry slowly lowered her arm and looked at him from the corner of her eye. He was blindly and artfully tying his neckcloth. "We should quite enjoy our walk." He retrieved his rumpled riding coat, gingerly putting his injured arm into one sleeve, seemingly oblivious to the fact that there was a gaping and ragged hole in it.

Oddly embarrassed, Kerry shoved her brush into her satchel. "Aye, it is indeed a bonny day. But I'll be walking to Dunkeld. Not Perth."

He paused in the dusting of his trousers to frown at her. "What, do you think to wait for that coach yet? I'd wager it is hours before one comes through, if at all. I should think our chances of finding suitable transportation are much better if we start toward Perth."

"I must be home, sir," she said politely, and came to her feet, self-consciously wrapping her hair into one big knot at her nape that she was fairly certain resembled a small animal attached to her head.

His frown deepened. "Mrs. McKinnon, Dunkeld could be miles from here. Please be sensible and return to Perth where you can take another coach."

"I doona intend to lose another day. My family will be frantic. And besides, I will find passage on a flatboat going upstream, not a coach." That, she thought, as the idea spilled out of her mouth, was a brilliant solution. If she headed due north, she would reach the River Tay, and from there, could follow the tributaries to Loch Eigg.

"I can't let you do that," he said solemnly.

Surprised by the arrogance, Kerry laughed. "It is not your decision!"

"I would be remiss as a gentleman if I let you foolishly wander off."

"*Foolishly* wander off? Surely I needna remind you who is Scot and who is not?" His shout of laughter was answer enough, but he replied with a resounding *"No."* *Arrogant cretin.* "Well then, I'll thank you for your help and I'll be off now."

"Mrs. McKinnon—"

"I'll walk to Dunkeld before I take even one step toward Perth!" she fairly shouted. Lord, *now* what was she saying?

His beautiful hazel eyes narrowed; his cheeks puffed out as he considered her, until he finally let the air go in one loud *swoosh.* "All in all, I'd say you are about the most obstinate woman I have ever encountered. Go on, then, carry your fool self off to some danger," he said, and stuffed his hat down on his head. "I don't intend to watch after you like a child."

"No one asked you to do so," she shot back. "Perhaps I should be watching *you* like a child—at least I would know to tether my horse."

His face darkened. "Is that so?" he drawled, lowering his head like a charging bull.

Something inside her twitched—Kerry quickly snatched up her satchel and took several steps backward. "Aye then. I am grateful for your . . . your, ah, companionship last evening, and I do so regret having shot you at all, but, well, accidents will happen, will they not, and I hope you have a lovely time of it in Scotland all the same, and a safe journey to England when the time comes, but if you will excuse me now, I really *must* get home."

Now he was advancing. She turned and walked quickly—sprinted, rather—across the clearing, to a point where the forest thinned and one could see through to another small clearing. She glanced over her shoulder—he had stopped, was watching her walk away, the scowl still on his face. She couldn't help herself; she lifted her hand. "Farewell!"

He didn't answer right away; a moment or two passed before he responded gently, "Farewell, and Godspeed, Mrs. McKinnon."

A vague but deep sense of regret invaded her. It had been a very long time that she had been near a man so virile, so handsome—*Enough!* There was no time to mope about a beautiful stranger; she had enough on her mind. With a jaunty wave, she marched into the woods, swinging her satchel at her side.

Arthur watched her walk into the copse, saw the tendrils of morning mist begin to close around her. The woman wouldn't listen to reason if her very life depended upon it. Moreover, she was too headstrong for her own good, she went about shooting unarmed men, she slept like the dead, and she was so damned alluring there ought to be a law against it.

So when his feet began to move independently of his head, Arthur decided he had lost his bloody mind. His feet put up the argument that, lest he forget, he was terribly lost, and for all he knew, he ought to be walking in the same direction as she anyway. If that wasn't enough, his heart further argued that he was a gentleman, and a gentleman did not allow a lady to walk off into potential danger—not a woman with a derriere like that, at any rate—no matter *how* infuriatingly stubborn she was, the silly little Scot! Ah, but what could he do? It was plainly obvious she was desperately in need of his help.

Before he even recognized what was happening, Arthur was suddenly only a horse length behind her, following the gentle bounce of that round bum to hell for all he knew.

What did he think he was *doing?* Kerry glanced over her shoulder a third time, moaned at his charming smile, and jerked her gaze straight ahead. Following her, that was what, and had been for a good hour or more. But to *where* for God's sake? He was so determined to go to Perth! This was impossible—she could not have a fancy Englishman follow her home!

Exasperated, Kerry paused by a fallen log at the edge of the heath where the forest rose up again and turned around. Her satchel by her side, her arms folded tightly across her middle, she glared at Arthur Christian as he strolled to where she stood as if he was out for his Sunday constitutional. "Do you *follow* me now?" she demanded.

"Absolutely not," he said, as if insulted by the notion. "I am going with."

Her mouth dropped open—indignation, confusion, and a strange, pleasurable heat swirled through her all at once. "Going *with?* You . . . you canna just follow me home!"

"Why not?"

"B-because!" she stammered, confused by the change in him. "Because it's not right! I doona even know you! *You* are to Perth, not the Highlands!"

"Actually, I am to Pitlochry. But it would seem to suit us both if I were to see you home and then continue on."

"But you *canna!* I can hardly go running about the countryside with a perfect stranger!"

"Why thank you kindly, madam, but I am hardly perfect," he said, smiling impudently.

Kerry gaped at him. How had she done it? How had she managed to get herself into such a predicament? Was the weight of the world not enough for her? Must she also bear this catastrophe? She sank down onto the fallen trunk and stared helplessly at him. "It's my punishment, no? I shot you and now you would ruin me."

He chuckled, sank down on his haunches next to her. "Actually, I'd prefer to strangle you," he cheerfully corrected her. "But the truth is that I am a gentleman, Mrs. McKinnon, and I cannot let you wander off alone. If you are too stubborn to return to Perth, then I shall just accompany you home. There is no point in arguing, my mind is very much set on it. Now. Since I've determined to be so very sporting about the whole thing, how about giving over one of those delectable scones?" he asked, motioning to her satchel.

She stared at him, tried to determine if those hazel eyes lied, but saw nothing other than an insufferably cheerful sparkle and the flecks of green. Apparently she had lost what was left of her senses, because after a moment, Kerry reached for her satchel. "They'd be called biscuits around here," she muttered.

They sat side by side on the fallen trunk, munching the last two biscuits. Part of her thought she ought to protest a little louder, but another part of her smothered what was undoubtedly a weak protest altogether. From all appearances, there was no life in this wilderness except sheep and, truly, she was grateful for the companionship. As for her reputation, well . . . she hardly cared anymore. Only one step away from being married to some religious zealot or a man with the mind of a child, she might as well throw caution to the wind. If she was to be ruined, it certainly did not hurt that it would be in the company of such a magnificent specimen of man.

When they finished their biscuits, she had made up her mind. He could accompany her to Dunkeld, and she said as much. The man smiled at her as if it had been a foregone conclusion all along, and offered his hand to help her to her feet. She ignored the tiny jolt of heat that went through her when she laid her hand in his; she dismissed the gratitude when he picked up her satchel and very jauntily perched it on his shoulder. And she refused to allow his gaze to melt her into a puddle by staring straight ahead at the ground in front of her as they set out.

"I would ask, however, if you are quite certain that the River Tay is due north?"

"I am quite certain," she responded airily. "We shall reach it by noon if not before."

But at the noon hour, they were still deep in the forest, guided only by an occasional glimpse of the sun above the treetops as they trekked across terrain that grew increasingly steep. Kerry's feet were killing her— the boots she wore were her good ones, handed down from Mrs. Wallace. They were too big for her feet, so she reserved them for church and important outings such as her disastrous call to Moncrieffe House and Mr. Abernathy in Dundee. They were not made, obviously, for long treks into the Highlands, and she could not help but envy Arthur Christian's fine leather boots. Her heels screamed with blisters, and now she was having difficulty keeping up with the beautiful stranger.

He had gone ahead; he was standing on top of a large rock, looking off into the distance when she finally climbed up a steep incline. "No sign of the river as yet, I'm afraid," he said apologetically, as if he were the one to have suggested this ridiculous trek.

The announcement brought her dangerously close to tears. She looked helplessly around them—nothing but trees and more trees, the only change being that the forest ground was growing rockier and they were moving higher. The air was cooler, too, and she could smell the faint but distinct scent of rain.

They were lost.

She had made them lost. For all she knew, she had led them in the opposite direction of where they needed to be. It was more than she could bear, and much to her mortification, her bottom lip began to tremble. She quickly bit down on it, convinced that the most humiliating thing she could do at this moment was cry.

"There's no cause for despair, Mrs. McKinnon," he said kindly, and leapt gracefully from the rock. "We've managed to keep on a northern course. We'll find your river yet."

One fat tear slipped from her eye and rolled down her cheek; she looked down. How could he be so kind? So . . . so *generous* after all she had done to him?

"Oh no, now that won't do," he said, and she heard the twigs snapping beneath his boots as he approached her. "No, no, we can't have this." He put a comforting hand on her shoulder; Kerry fought the urge to fling herself into his arms and sob. Instead, she hastily wiped the tear from her cheek and folded her arms tightly across her middle, ashamed unto death to be falling apart as she was. "I'm sorry, truly I am. It's just that . . ." *It's just that I canna take any more.* "It's my feet . . . they . . . they hurt a wee bit."

"A wee bit, eh?" His hand slid smoothly from her shoulder, down her back. "Well then, we'll just have to tend to them. We've too far to walk to be suffering, even a wee bit." He gestured toward the rock on which he had been standing. "Let's have a look then, Mrs. McKinnon."

"It's no bother, really. We should keep on—"

"A few minutes rest will do no harm," he said authoritatively, and gestured again toward the rock. The pain of her first step made her knees buckle; Arthur Christian made a sound of disapproval, and before Kerry could protest, he swept her up into his arms and carried her to the rock. "You should have told me sooner," he scolded her as he put her down. He went down on one knee before her and slid his hand to her calf. The quick, scorching heat of his touch through her thin stockings made her flinch; he looked up, brows raised. "You may put your modesty aside, Mrs. McKinnon. They are, after all, only feet."

Aye, they were only feet, but the feel of his fingers on her leg as he unlaced her boot was sending pulses of white-hot heat all through her. He leaned back on his heels, propped her foot on his thigh and gently massaged the bottom of her foot.

Oh Lord, she had died and gone to heaven. The sensation of his massage on her foot was *divine*—sweet and painful at once, soothing the muscles all the way up her leg. Kerry closed her eyes, let the gloriously wonderful sensation fill her. When his deep chuckle broke the spell, she reluctantly opened her eyes.

"You purr like a cat. Now then, we'll have to have those stockings off," he said, and nonchalantly reached to remove the boot from her other foot.

"We'll have what?"

"The stockings must come off. Your heels have been rubbed raw and must be bandaged."

Kerry blinked, amazed that first, he could tell her to take off her stockings without the slightest hesitation, and second, that she could take her stockings off in the presence of a man who was not her husband. But when he began to massage her other foot, all sense of propriety fled her head. She hardly cared if he was the Holy Pope in Rome—she would do just about anything for him to continue massaging her feet.

He laughed, patted her foot affectionately, and stood, smiling down at her. "I need to find something suitable for a poultice. Off with the stockings, my dear."

My dear. The small endearment drifted over her like silk, and Kerry smiled, a little deliriously, and continued smiling as he disappeared into the woods. Had she ever been so affected by a man? Certainly Fraser had never dissolved her with a mere touch. She dreamily did as she was told and removed her practical stockings, wincing at the sight of her blistered heels.

He returned a few moments later with a handful of ivy. He knelt before her again and, sliding his hand halfway up her calf, lifted her foot to examine it. "Dear God," he muttered, frowning, then carefully put her foot down. "You should have told me sooner," he said again, and popped several of the ivy leaves into his mouth, chewing them as he removed his neckcloth. He fished a knife from his boot and split the cloth, ripping it into two long strips. Then he removed the pulp he had made from his mouth and winked at her. "Forgive me, madam," he said, and pressed the chewed leaves to the blisters. The effect was instantly soothing—Kerry sighed as he wrapped one half of his silk neckcloth tightly around her heel and ankle.

When he was through wrapping the other foot, he instructed her to don her stockings so that he could help her into her boots, chuckling as he turned away to give her some privacy. Kerry smiled at his broad back. This man, this stranger, was titillating her with the heat of his touch and his apparent cheerful nature.

Perhaps she had done herself an enormous favor when she shot him.

"I'm done," she said.

He turned and fetched one boot. "All right, then, lets see if these boots won't last you a while longer." He carefully lifted her foot; between the two of them, they managed to slip the boot on her foot. He made her stand and walk before he would consent to moving on. The poultice buffered the blisters and the bandage kept the boot from slipping. While her heel hurt, it was certainly bearable.

"I canna thank you enough," she said, grinning her great approval as she sat to fit the other boot. "They are greatly improved."

Smiling, he took the second boot from her hand. "It occurs to me that with our new level of familiarity we might consent to using our Christian names, wouldn't you agree?" he asked, slipping the boot on her foot.

Oh aye, she would agree.

"Splendid. You may have your choice—my name is Arthur William Paddington Christian. Lord Christian to some. Merely Arthur to my mother. I suppose that should do just as well as any of them. And what is your name, Mrs. McKinnon?"

"Kerry. Just Kerry."

Arthur William Paddington Christian seemed taken aback by that; his hazel eyes locked with hers as he murmured, *"Just Kerry."*

The sound of her name on his lips was magical; he continued to hold her ankle and her gaze, his eyes seemingly probing her, down to where her heart was now pounding wildly beneath her breast. She hadn't experienced a man's touch in years, what seemed like a lifetime, really, and she hadn't known she was so hungry for it. Had Fraser ever looked at her so . . . *potently?* Kerry felt her face flood with heat, felt the tingle of his fingers on her skin, felt all of her senses suddenly sharpened by the mere presence of him.

And then suddenly he let go, dropping her foot to the ground and quickly lacing her boot before coming to his feet. "Well then, Just Kerry, shall we find the River Tay?" he said, and stepped away to remove his collar now that his neckcloth was wrapped around her feet.

Yes, she thought, they had best find the River Tay before she did something foolhardy—like throw herself on top of her beautiful stranger and kiss his breath away.

They walked for what seemed hours, but Arthur was damned glad of it, for every step he took moved him one step farther away from the insanity that had invaded him in the woods. For one long, incredibly intense moment, he had fought a raging desire to kiss the words *just Kerry* from her lips. It was the way she said it, the brilliant little smile behind it, the luster of her blue, blue eyes. Something in him had snapped and burst into a desire for a kiss that he had not felt in a very long time. And he had almost acted on it, too, imagining that he would start with her trim ankle, work his way up her shapely calf, then proceed to kiss every inch of Just Kerry.

It hadn't helped that he had awoken this morning

with that very shapely leg slung across his groin. He had thought about it all day as she had marched in front of him, that little bum swinging from one side to the other and back again . . .

Fortunately for them both, he still possessed some semblance of reason, but what in God's name was he thinking? That he would simply tumble a Scottish widow in the woods then deposit her on her doorstep before continuing on his merry way? All right, she was terribly alluring with that mess of black curls and pale blue eyes. And when she had unbuttoned the top of her traveling gown for a bit of relief from the heat, the hint of tender flesh exposed at her throat had almost undone him. He wanted to sink his teeth into that flesh, shove his hands through her hair, feel the soft curve of her bare breast against his skin.

With every bone-jarring step he prayed that the desire would disappear, and would have walked all day for it, but it did not feel enough. He had even tried to stop the absurd thoughts floating around his head by asking about her visit to Dundee. That tactic had actually boomeranged on him—listening to her halting description of a husband who had left her in what he gathered was a situation of some straits just made a strange, primordial anxiety surge to the forefront of his mind. Arthur had instantly disliked the deceased Mr. McKinnon.

His anxious state of mind grew even worse when she asked about his family. When he explained to her that Alex was the duke of Sutherland, she was as impressed as he knew she would be, exclaiming just like every other woman he had ever known. But then she asked what exactly it meant to be the brother of a duke, and he found himself explaining the structure of the aristocracy and the peerage, the hierarchy and use of titles, et cetera, the sound of his voice droning in his own ears.

"Do you have one of the titles, then?" she asked after his lengthy explanation.

Arthur's skin crawled with resentment. "No," he answered flatly.

To his amazement, she merely shrugged. "Seems like a bit of bother anyway, does it not?" She had sweetly remarked, then had launched into a discourse about a certain Mrs. Donnersen who apparently claimed to be a descendent of Swedish kings. Kerry blithely reported that it was the collective opinion of the entire glen that Mrs. Donnersen was actually the descendent of a pig farmer from the Lowlands. As she rambled on about the pig farmer's daughter, Arthur realized that not only had his lack of title not reduced him somewhat in her eyes—a reaction he was entirely accustomed to—but it hadn't even registered. The woman simply didn't care! It forced him to observe her in yet another new light—the light of a woman who was not impressed with titles or the delicate balance of power among the British elite. It made him feel . . . *free*.

As the day wore on, Arthur admitted to himself that he was quietly fascinated with Kerry McKinnon. It pleased him that she was well read. When he remarked on it, she dismissed it by saying that her husband had been ill a long time and that she had read to pass the time. He learned that she had boarded at a girl's school in Edinburgh, and that she lived in a valley called Glenbaden, where the McKinnon clan had lived for generations. She referred frequently to May and Big Angus, whom he now understood were relatives, and even more frequently to Thomas, another cousin, whom Arthur gathered she regarded more as a brother.

They reached a tributary of the River Tay in the late afternoon; when Kerry saw it, she jumped up with a squeal of delight. "Oh, thank God," she cried, and whirled toward him, her hands clasped anxiously at her breast. "Hurry with you now—there's bound to be river traffic!" With that, she picked up her skirts, running ahead of him, the black bombazine floating out behind her. Arthur shifted the satchel to his bad arm and calmly walked after her.

She was practically spinning in air when he finally reached the banks. "A flatboat will come any time now, you'll see!" she said breathlessly. "They travel up and down, between Pitlochry and Perth."

Perhaps, but as he didn't actually see one, or *any* sign of one for that matter, Arthur lowered himself to the ground under the shade of a tree to watch her pace, hoping for her sake that a boat did come along soon, because he did not like the looks of the dark clouds gathering in the east. Kerry's enthusiasm began to wane after a half hour of pacing—he supposed she imagined the river was virtually teeming with flatboats, all colliding with one another in their haste to take on passengers in the middle of nowhere. He, on the other hand, imagined it was much like her Crieff coach—there would be traffic on the main artery of the River Tay, but it likely would be nothing short of a bloody miracle to find a boat out on this little branch.

He was actually quite surprised when she came running toward him, pointing eagerly downstream.

Arthur tossed aside the long blade of grass he'd been absently chewing and came slowly to his feet as the edge of a flatboat slid slowly into view around the river's bend. It had a crude, box-like structure built at one end—the cabin, he presumed, only it looked more like a coffin. On the opposite end was a stack of crates, unmarked. He could just make out the heads of two men guiding the boat along with two long oars.

Kerry made a move; Arthur caught her wrist and pulled her into his side. "Stay here. I'll speak with them."

He walked down to the river's edge while the flatboat negotiated the narrow turn in the river. As the boat moved closer, Arthur saw that the two men manning the boat were twins. Built solid and square with perfectly round heads, they reminded Arthur of a team of matched bulls, practically indistinguishable from one another. "Good day, gentlemen!" he called as they straightened the boat.

The twins exchanged looks. "Aye, g'day," one of them responded, staring at Arthur curiously as he strolled alongside them.

"I wonder, sirs, if you would be disposed to helping a pair of stranded travelers?"

Neither man responded; they merely stared at him. Not exactly the talkative sorts, then. Arthur forced a smile. "We were put off a coach to wait for another, you see, but alas, it never came. We find ourselves without conveyance."

One twin cocked his head and raked a curious gaze over him. "You'd be English," he announced, as if that was news to Arthur.

"I am from England, that is true."

The twin immediately shook his head. "No. Canna take you."

What in the hell was this? Since when did a laborer refuse him? "I beg your pardon?" Arthur demanded with all the airs of aristocracy bred into him.

The twins looked at each other. "No Lobsterbacks or sheepherders."

Lobsterbacks? Sheepherders? "Now see here, sir! There haven't been any *Lobsterbacks* to speak of in more than twenty years! And furthermore, would you be-grudge a helpless *widow* passage?" he demanded hotly, gesturing wildly to where he had left Kerry standing.

"Aye, that'd be right," one said agreeably. "Ye can beg your passage from the next boat that comes."

"And when might that be?" Arthur snapped.

"Mayhap tonight," the man answered curtly, and turned away. "Or mayhap the morrow."

Their irreverent demeanor infuriated him. Arthur groped for the gun at his side, but Kerry's voice up-stream stopped him. He swiveled around, saw her stand-ing on the bank ahead of him, her satchel in one hand.

"Good day, laddies!" she called, smiling that brilliant smile of hers. She had one hand on her waist, innocently holding her skirt in such a way as to flash a hint of her calf at the two men.

One of the twins looked up; a smile instantly broke his stoic face. "*Och,* lassie! Got yourself in a wee bit of trouble, have ye?"

"On my honor, you wouldna believe me if I told you! A dreadful day!" she said, turning so she could stroll beside the boat slipping upstream. "I know you, surely! I've seen the pair of you in Dunkeld, no?"

The other twin smiled so broadly that Arthur feared his face would crack wide open. "Aye, we are through there often enough."

"Aha! I *knew* as much! I wouldna forget such handsome faces."

The two round-headed idiots chuckled in identical, sheepish tones, and Arthur realized they were bringing the flatboat to a halt alongside Kerry.

She glanced over her shoulder at him, flashed a brief but smug smile at his look of disbelief in their sudden transformation. "I'm desperate to reach Dunkeld now. My family will be awfully worried. You willna mind terribly if we come along?" She followed the gaze of one twin to Arthur and hastily added, "Ah, but he was particularly helpful when the coach didna come. I doona think he is a sheepherder."

What was the sudden fascination with sheepherding?

"He be a Lobsterback, lass," the more talkative of the two said, to which Arthur snorted.

"Aye, that he is," Kerry said, shooting him a quick, withering look. "But when the robbers came, he protected me with his very life. I would think that would mean he's done a bit of a turnabout, eh? He'll not be a bother, I promise."

"Robbers?" the other one asked.

Kerry nodded solemnly. "Highwaymen. *Four* of them," she said, holding up four fingers.

One twin looked suspiciously at Arthur, as if *he* had made that ridiculous claim. But the other twin, who had yet to peel his eyes from Kerry, piped up. "Aye, all right, then. We'll take him as far as Dunkeld," he said, ignoring the dark look of his brother.

"Ah laddies, thank you!" Kerry cried, and flashed a warm smile at them that even Arthur felt from several feet away. She turned her beaming grin to him and motioned him to hurry along.

With a low growl, Arthur stalked toward her, casting the twin bulls a look that clearly relayed his disdain as he helped Kerry onto the boat. He followed her, finding himself relegated to sit among the crates as the two bovine brothers pushed the boat into the river and continued their slow journey north. Much to Arthur's considerable annoyance, however, Kerry sat perched upon a crate, chatting with the two as if they were long lost friends. Exactly *why* it annoyed him, Arthur couldn't say. Other than he just didn't like the way Mr. Richey and Mr. Richey—as he finally learned their names to be—looked at her. Nor did he like the way she smiled at them. Or how her lilting laughter seemed to fill the air around them.

After an hour or more, he grew so disgusted with her cheerful chatter that could fill the sail of a ship, that he turned his attention to the increasingly black sky. He glanced at the crude box built on one end of the flatboat and suppressed another groan. When the first fat raindrops fell, Mr. Richey Number One suggested Kerry step inside the little hut. Kerry insisted Arthur be allowed to come, too. That suggestion was met by an argument before the brothers grudgingly agreed.

"How very kind," Arthur said snidely and stood, waiting for Kerry, who had moved to fetch her satchel.

That was the moment the downpour started, without warning. Instinctively, Arthur reached for her, but she mistook his meaning and thrust the satchel into his hand. "Come on!" he shouted, as rain came in sheets, and

Kerry nodded, grabbing onto a crate to inch her way around it.

The clap of thunder that boomed above them was matched by a fierce bolt of lightning that hit so close Arthur actually felt its jolt through his heart. He gasped, stunned by the sensation of it, and turned to look for Kerry.

She was nowhere.

He rushed to the edge of the flatboat, his fears confirmed when he glanced toward the Richey Brothers and one of them pointed downstream.

Bloody hell! With a heavy sigh, Arthur tossed her satchel to shore, cast a quick but fierce and final frown at the two Richey brothers, then plunged headlong into the dark waters of the River Tay tributary.

Chapter Seven

THE HARDER SHE fought, the deeper the current pulled her into the river's clutches. Kerry felt herself sinking with the weight of the voluminous bombazine skirts that marked her a widow. *Was this the answer, then? She was to die so soon?*

Her feet hit the sandy bottom—she had sunk so fast! *No!* her mind screamed, and she struggled again, kicking wildly but vainly against the weight of her clothing, dragging her arms against the water in a desperate bid to lift her head above the surface. Her lungs were burning, felt as if they would explode at any moment. *God grant her mercy, it was over!* She would die alone, drown in the river in her best black bombazine.

A strange sense of calm was beginning to wrap itself around her when she felt the hand of God clamp down on her shoulder. It *was* God—she felt herself being dragged upward, felt God's legs kicking for both of them, powerful strokes, propelling them upward, upward, until her face broke the surface. Kerry dragged air into her lungs with a ragged cry, gasping, unable to get enough into her lungs. Oblivious to the rain, to the pull of her body through the water, to the struggle to lift her onto the riverbank, she gasped for air, choked on it, sputtering bile and water, then gulped for air again.

It was several moments before the cloud began to lift from her brain and she realized she was on terra firma, rain pelting her upturned face.

"It's all right, Kerry, you are quite safe."

God had saved her—He had sent Arthur to save her life! The understanding of what had happened dawned harshly—tears erupted, blinding her, and she lunged into him, burying her face in his neck as she sobbed uncontrollably.

"There now, sweetheart. You are quite all right," he said soothingly, caressing the back of her head.

No, no, he didn't understand! "I almost *died*, Arthur. I almost died! You saved my life!" she wailed hoarsely, and choked on another sob.

Arthur forced her to lift her face to his, shook his head. "I would not let you perish, Kerry. And really, you weren't under terribly long. It's quite shallow."

He did not understand, could not fathom how close she had come to slipping the bonds of this earth but for him. "I thought you were God," she murmured.

That was met with a moment of silence as his gaze pierced hers hard, then slowly dropped to her mouth. "Not God. Just a man." And he bent his head to hers.

The unexpected, soft touch of his lips paralyzed her—until the sensation exploded within her core, jolting her back to life. It was so surprising, so tender, that her body reacted of its own accord, melting into him, clinging to the warmth of his lips.

A moan rumbled deep in Arthur's chest and suddenly his arms were around her, crushing her to him, nipping at her lips, sucking them, licking them. Kerry forgot the rain, forgot the river, forgot everything else as she opened her mouth and felt his tongue sweep boldly inside, tangling with hers, sweeping over her teeth, into her cheeks and producing a storm of emotion in her.

Her heart was pumping furiously now, stealing her breath again. She was aware that she answered the ardor of his kiss with an urgency of her own, one borne from years of unanswered desire, of living in a sick house with the wasting, rotting flesh of a man. She desperately explored his mouth, dug her fingers into the thick waves of his golden-brown hair, stroked his ears, his shoulders and arms, then gripped him with the same strength he had used to pull her from the waters so that he would not let her go. One large hand covered the whole of her ribcage; the other cupped her cheek and ear as he drew her bottom lip between his teeth, then dragged his mouth from her lips, to her chin, to the hollow of her throat.

The hunger burning in her was overwhelming; she feared she might shatter at any moment, that her limbs would fail her. She clung recklessly to him as she dropped her head to one shoulder and bared her neck to his mouth. Arthur's lips seared her skin, scorched the lobe of her ear. His breath in her ear sent a white-hot shiver of anticipation coursing through her veins. His hand swept the swell of her hips, pushed her body into his. Through the dripping fabric of their clothes, she could feel the ridge of his erection and inhaled a ragged, impassioned breath.

"Ah, God . . . Kerry," he murmured in her ear, then suddenly, as if she had been rudely startled from a dream, it was over. His hands slid up her arms until he found her wrists; he pulled her hands from his neck and clasped them tightly against his chest. "No more," he said, and closing his eyes, pressed his forehead to hers, seemingly as breathless as she was. After a moment, he lifted his head and tenderly laid his palm against her cheek. "We must find shelter or you'll catch your death."

Shocked by her brush with death, numbed by the raw life in his kiss, Kerry could not respond, afraid if she spoke she would ask for more. Arthur took her firmly by the hand; Kerry stumbled alongside him, heedless of the distant thunder or the river rushing nearby, blind to everything but the warmth of his hand wrapped around hers, the comfort and safety in it, and the desire to feel that hand everywhere on her body.

Arthur found an overhang of sorts, where the river had cut yards below the bank and the canopy of trees above blocked most of the rain. He led her to a ledge just barely large enough to hold them both. He helped her remove as much of her wet clothing as was decent, then his own.

Silent, Kerry sank down, exhausted and bewildered by a kiss that had awakened something long dormant in her. That awakening seemed the final straw—the weight of her life, the frustration and fears and hopes and needs came crashing down on her, and the tears erupted anew. She tried to stop them with every ounce of will she had left, but she was suddenly mired in an overwhelming sense of despair. "I'm sorry," she muttered miserably, appalled that she could not seem to make herself stop.

Arthur said nothing, but eased himself down beside her. Silently, he put his arm around her shoulders, pulled her head to his chest and held her, brushing the wet hair from her eyes and her face, caressing her back in long, comforting strokes while Kerry cried until there was nothing left in her. The last thing she knew before drifting into a dead slumber was the steady beat of his heart against her cheek.

What in God's name was he doing?

What insanity had befallen him, what monumental foolishness had seeped into his brain? Arthur stared at the woman sleeping beside him, her hair a wild mess of curls and dark corkscrew ribbons spilling all around her. Her lashes, thick and black, brushing skin with the luster of opals. A pretty widow . . .

But a Scottish crofter's widow! And one who was perched precariously on a ledge in the wilds of the Scottish Highlands at that!

Arthur looked away from her, stared at the black sky above, indistinguishable from the steep hills around them.

What, dear God in heaven, *what* was he doing? What divine forces had moved that he might find himself *here,* in the middle of absolutely nowhere, the sudden protector of a pretty young widow struggling to make her way home? Some protector—who was *he* to lead her out of this quagmire? And how could he possibly have allowed himself to *join* her in this quagmire? Bloody hell, he had no earthly idea what they might do now!

Except walk. Yes, keep walking, for surely they would eventually walk off the face of the earth or meet with some semblance of civilization.

He stole another look at her. *Jesus, he was a Rogue!* It was hardly as if he was so pure a gentleman that he never took advantage of women in vulnerable situations. Frankly there were times he had actually created vulnerable situations, but those situations had involved women of the *ton,* women who understood and knew how to play the game. This woman . . . this woman was as innocent about the world as she was stubborn. This was a poor crofter's wife who had, somehow, managed to find herself abandoned in the country and was trying her best to stand up to the mounting challenges of this extraordinary little journey.

All right, he had no right to have taken advantage of her. But devil take it, those crystal-blue eyes were drowning in tears, and her lips, *God,* her lips! He had meant only to comfort her, had only meant to kiss her once.

Righto. And he believed in fairies, too.

Worse yet, she had responded with such fierceness, such incredible longing, that just the memory of it made him hard all over again.

Kerry sighed in her sleep; Arthur silently extracted himself and gained his feet, jammed his fists into cold damp pockets and tried not to think how she had opened her mouth so eagerly beneath his, had thrust her hands in his hair and raked her fingers across his shoulders. *But he couldn't stop thinking about it.*

Damn it all to hell, but the woman had captivated him long before that kiss, had knocked him for a loop the moment she had marched off into the woods in search of the River Tay. She was impudent and vulnerable, courageous and timid all at once. Her financial woes, whatever they were, brought a glint of determination to her eye that was immediately softened by the glow of admiration when she spoke of Glenbaden, and her Big Angus, May, and Thomas. She had walked miles without complaint until her cheap boots had forced her to stop long after he would have begged for mercy. She had fallen in the river, kissed him with fierce passion obviously smoldering beneath that black bombazine, and then had cried herself to sleep like a child.

God, she was exhausting!

But she was unique, unlike any woman he had ever known. He was, as much as he was loath to admit it, completely enchanted by the widow who had shot him. There was something about her that made him feel strangely alive, as if she had awakened him from a deep slumber with that shot, shown him a sun and a moon and the millions of stars that seemed to hang above Scotland.

Oh yes, he was dangerously enchanted.

Bloody fabulous. Enchanted with a woman he could never have. He had come to Scotland for Phillip, not to fall victim to such treacherous emotions. *Christ God,* he would see her home, say his heartfelt farewells and put her out of his mind. He would settle Phillip's affairs and return to his life in England where women like Kerry McKinnon simply did exist. He had perhaps caught a Scottish star in his hand, but he could only hold it for a moment.

There was no other option. As much as she had captivated him, had sparked his dying imagination, deep down inside he knew that very well.

The feel of the sun on her skin forced Kerry to open her eyes. Her head ached something awful; her arms and legs felt leaden. The cloying scent of boxwood and moldy clothing made her queasy and she moaned, slung an arm across her eyes to shield the sun, felt the ache spread to every conceivable fiber of her body. She had never felt so battered in all her life.

"I daresay I've never known anyone to sleep quite like the dead as you do Mrs. McKinnon."

Oh no. Kerry peeked from beneath her arm at the scarred and muddied boots next to her face. Shifting her arm just a bit, she looked higher, past the sullied trousers, the stained silk waistcoat flapping open in the morning breeze, and what was once a very fine white lawn shirt opened at the neck. She blinked, tried to focus on the handsome face shadowed by a two-day growth of beard, but was suddenly besieged by the memory of her appalling behavior the night before and quickly covered her face again.

He sank down onto his haunches, pushed her arm a bit and bent to one side to peer into her face. "Do you intend to sleep all day, then?"

"No!" she croaked irritably and came to her elbows, ignoring his chuckle. "What time have you?"

He popped a dark purple berry into his mouth and shook his head. "I'm afraid I haven't any idea," he said, pulling his watch from his pocket. "That little swim of ours seems to have mucked up the workings of this thing." He frowned, shook the watch violently. "If I had to guess, I'd say the sun has been up an hour, no more."

An hour. She never slept so late. She suddenly bolted upright and attempted to stand. "We must be on our way!"

Arthur caught her arm and helped her to her feet. "Yes, well, we'll go soon enough. First, you will eat this." He held out a bunch of wild berries.

Amazed, Kerry stared at the berries. Berries that

looked like a feast for kings. Her belly rumbled loudly in response. "Where did you get them, then?"

"The market stalls," he said, and laughing, casually smoothed his hand over the top of her head. "It's the best I can do short of pine bark, but you must eat something before we continue."

She did not reply—her mouth was full of the wild berries. Arthur chuckled again and turned away from her, walked down to the river's edge, and went down on one knee to dip water to drink. *"Ach!"* he spat. "Foul stuff!" But he dipped his hands again.

Devouring the berries as if they were her last meal, Kerry watched the muscles of his back as he dipped his hands into the water and brought them to his mouth to drink, then thrust his wet hands through his hair in an attempt to bring some order. The effect was not what he undoubtedly intended, but made him look wild and masculine—

The memory of his kiss suddenly flared, inflaming the skin beneath her collar. She turned away from the sight of him, but the memory stubbornly lingered on her lips. That extraordinary kiss had awakened something dead inside her, something that was now ascending to her throat.

"I must say you look no worse for the wear, madam—as lovely as the moment you shot me." That backhanded compliment only made her flush deeper. She turned half-way toward the sound of his voice and self-consciously put a hand to her unruly curls. "You'll be pleased to know that I am healing nicely." He handed her the clothing she had discarded last night, and the smile he gave her made the blood in her veins feel as if it thickened.

She abruptly took the clothing and looked over her shoulder into the woods. "I, ah, I've got to . . ."

"Righto. I'll wait down by the river's edge."

Kerry scarcely heard him—she was already moving for the cover of the trees, afraid she was making a

complete fool of herself. She was acting as if she had
never been kissed before! *But she had never been kissed
like that.*

She did not know men like Arthur Christian.

And he undoubtedly did not know women like her.
She forced herself to regain her composure, managed to
don her damp clothing and stuff her hair into another
thick knot, then cautiously emerged from the woods.
Arthur had donned his coat again. It was remarkable
that despite the ragged appearance of his clothing, he
still managed to look terribly aristocratic. It was his
bearing; the grace came naturally, patently oblivious to
the ungodly circumstance in which she had put him.

He smiled in that devastatingly charming way of his
when he caught her staring. "I know you had your heart
set on a leisurely riverboat ride, but I've determined we
should follow the river's course on foot. If the foliage
doesn't kill us first, I believe we should stumble upon the
main artery of the River Tay 'ere too long."

Given her own keen navigational skills, Kerry could
hardly argue with him. He bent, then straightened, holding her satchel. The sight of the tattered red bag astounded her—he had even saved her sorry belongings.

"Shall we?" he asked pleasantly, and Kerry nodded.

So they walked—she, admiring his movement from
behind, he noting various genera of fauna to her, giving
her a bit of a botany lecture. When even he tired of that,
he asked about Glenbaden. Kerry told him what she
could, but it seemed impossible to impart the beauty of
her home, of the often-fierce winters that brought glorious springs. She tried to explain those of the McKinnon
clan who remained scattered across the glen, decades removed from the powerful clan they once were. She did
her best to avoid speaking of the hard times that had befallen them, but inadvertently, she mentioned a gaping
hole in the roof of her house.

"A hole? I should think the lot of McKinnons would

come to your aid," he said, pausing idly to examine the leaf of an ancient oak tree.

"That they would, had I the means to purchase the lumber," she said absently.

Arthur stopped his examination of the leaf. "What? You've still a hole in your roof?"

Kerry shrugged. "We'll patch it, we will."

Frowning, Arthur dropped the leaf, put his hands to his hips and looked down at his boots for a moment. He suddenly lifted a worried frown to her. "Pardon my asking, but is there no one who can help you?"

"Help me?"

He glanced at the river. "I mean to say, is there no one you can turn to for help with your ... financial situation?"

Ah God, how pitiful must she appear to a man like him. Her face flamed with shame at her circumstance. "I manage quite well on my own," she said stiffly.

"What of your father? Can't your father—"

"He is dead."

That garnered only a moment's hesitation from him. "Your mother, perhaps."

Kerry unconsciously raised her hand to her cheek; her fingers cool against her skin. "My mother," she forced herself to say, "has married a reverend who prides himself on austerity. I appreciate your concern, but I will manage."

He made no reply, just turned away to stare across the river to the other bank.

"It's not as bad as it must seem to you now—I'll not be destitute." She laughed, trying to cover that obvious lie, but her voice, her laughter, sounded hollow to her. It *was* as bad as he apparently thought, and in fact much worse. But she'd not disgrace herself further by letting him know just how bad it was. She had suffered enough humiliation for one outing and had no desire to suffer any more in the eyes of this beautiful stranger.

"We should walk on," she said, motioning ahead. He seemed to hesitate, if only for a moment, but he turned and walked on, leading the way through the undergrowth.

Suddenly anxious to turn her thoughts—and his—to anything else, she blurted, "What would be your friend's business?"

Arthur glanced over his shoulder. "Pardon?"

"You said you came to attend a business matter for a friend."

"Ah, yes," he said, still walking. "My friend met with an untimely death and left behind some property here. His father has no wish to keep it. I am merely acting as his agent."

"I am sorry," Kerry said, but her curiosity was piqued. "How did he die?"

Without missing a step he said simply, "He fell in a duel."

A duel! She almost gasped aloud—she had only heard of them, had never known anyone who had even seen one. The very thought of it made a shiver run up her spine; a million questions tumbled in her brain, but she kept silent, as his powerful legs were suddenly surging ahead.

By midmorning, the heavy underbrush had given away to sloping fields of heather dotted by the occasional black-faced sheep. The River Tay tributary snaked alongside the meadows, meandering north. By midday, they stumbled upon a series of small, cultivated terraces that caused Arthur to let out a *whoop* of laughter. "By God, it appears as if mankind actually *does* reside in these godforsaken hills!" he exclaimed happily, and grabbing Kerry's hand, forged ahead.

It was Kerry who saw the mule grazing across one field. When she stopped, Arthur, walking behind her, almost plowed over her. He caught himself on her shoulder. "What?" he demanded, his hand immediately going to his pistol.

She turned and looked up at him; a smile slowly spread her lips. "A *mule*."

Arthur jerked his head to the left, saw the mule, and shifted his gaze to her. "Splendid! That would suggest a settlement of some sort—"

He stopped, looked quizzically at Kerry as she shook her head. "They roam far from home. The grass, you know, it's not enough. He'll make his way home eventually, when he's had his fill."

"What, then there is no one about?" Arthur asked, momentarily confused, and looked at Kerry. An understanding passed between them instantaneously; a devilish smile lifted one corner of Arthur's mouth. "Madam, are you thinking what I am thinking?"

"A man will hang for stealing a horse," she warned him. "I doona think the penalty is much improved for a mule."

"Ah, but we should not consider this *stealing* exactly. Think of it as merely borrowing. Once we reach the River Tay, I shall hire a man to return him with a little gift for the owner. There, you see? Quite simple, really. So, madam, if you will kindly wait here while I fetch your mount." And with that, he dropped her satchel and went striding across the field, his arms swinging wide.

Kerry didn't object as she ought. In fact, she laughed as he strode purposefully toward the mule, walking right up to the beast as if he expected the thing to come docilely. And she couldn't stop laughing as she stooped to retrieve her satchel and followed him across the field. Apparently, mules were not to be found in England, or the poor man might have known a wee bit better than what he was doing.

Mules did so inhabit England. Arthur knew this because he had seen them at a distance. Not that he had actually ever been *near* one, but that hardly seemed important. He had a particular knack with horses, and quite naturally, he assumed that knack extended to the cousin mule. Which was why, therefore, he was so taken by surprise when the mule tried to butt him with its head.

Arthur jumped back, hands raised in a gesture of peace. "Come now, old boy, there is no call for that." He extended one hand, intent on stroking the mule's nose, but the beast jerked away. "Going to go like that, is it?" he asked, and began to slowly circle the mule, who glared at him over its shoulder.

"Now see here, Mr. Mule," Arthur continued in a very low, very soothing, sing-song voice, "I have walked for what seems days now, I am quite ravenous, absolutely exhausted, and hardly in the mood for disagreement. I'll just come around to your right flank and we'll have a bit of chat about that ride, shall we?"

The mule responded with a loud snort and a hard flick of its head. Arthur paused only momentarily before continuing his slow, steady movement, thinking to catch hold of the mane first, then the nose. After that, he wasn't quite certain what he'd do, but he thought he should at least be able to convince the beast that he was a gentle friend. On the mule's right, he very carefully reached forward, caught hold of the mane—

"What would you think to be doing?"

The sound of Kerry's voice startled the mule; it jerked around and snapped at Arthur, very nearly taking a bite out of his ribs. Arthur lurched to one side, just barely avoiding the enormous teeth, and seized the moment to clamp his hand down on the mule's snout. For that, he was suddenly catapulted over onto his side with a mighty shove from the mule. The beast's back hooves shot out, missing his head by a fraction of an inch. Arthur instinctively rolled into a tight ball and covered his head with his arms. The mule tried again, missed, and bucked away from Arthur before galloping to the far end of the field, braying as if he had been mortally wounded.

Slowly, Arthur unwound himself and pushed up on his arms, breathing heavily. Not only was he covered head to foot in dirt, he had eaten a mouthful of it. And judging from the particular odor he suddenly noticed, he had managed to stick his boot in a pile of manure. The muffled laughter he heard pierced his ego like a shot; he lifted his head and glared at Kerry. She was bent over, her shoulders trembling. When she at last raised her head, a hand clamped over her mouth, he could see the tears of her great amusement shining bright in her blue eyes.

That did it. He would kill her, strangle the little wench like he should have done the moment he was introduced to her pistol. He was up like a shot, barreling toward her. With a shriek, Kerry whirled, picked up her skirts, and ran.

And good Lord could the lass run! Her speed surprised Arthur, particularly given that she held her satchel in one hand. Nevertheless, she flew across the heather, her hair falling out of its little knot and streaming behind her like a standard. He almost caught her at the edge of the field, but she dodged artfully to the right and ran, incredibly, even faster. He pitched after her, skidding on more manure and catching himself with one hand to the ground before gaining his balance and barreling down a small hill after her.

He finally caught her on the banks of the tributary by the waist, jerking her back hard into his chest before forcing her around to tell her what he thought of her interference. But laughter was bubbling out of the imp like uncorked champagne. Her eyes sparkling, she pressed her hands against his chest and laughed so hard that her head fell back with absolute glee.

It all but undid him. Arthur couldn't help but do what he did, which was to catch her shoulders and yank her into his embrace, kissing the laughter from her mouth, her throat, and then her eyes. He kissed her so hard and completely that she shoved against him, gasping for air, then shoved again, backing out of his embrace, the glimmer of laughter still in her eyes.

"I shouldna think it necessary to inform a man of such considerable education, but mules really doona make very good pets."

An impudent little wench, he thought, watching her breast rise and fall as she gulped air into her lungs through bites of laughter. He wagged a finger at her. "Mrs. McKinnon, you almost had me trampled to death, do you know that?"

Kerry laughed again, her glorious smile stretching from ear to ear. "It wasna *I* who hit him on the nose!"

"No, but you shouted at the ornery ass," Arthur countered, taking two steps forward.

She instantly matched him by stepping backward an equal number of steps. "There is where you are wrong, now—the ornery ass I shouted at was *you!*"

Arthur laughed low, beckoned her toward him. "An ornery ass, am I? Then come here, Mrs. McKinnon, so that I might show you how ornery I can truly be," he said, and without warning, lunged for her. With a squeal of laughter, Kerry whirled around, but Arthur was too quick; he grabbed her and tumbled to the soft earth on the water's edge. She struggled beneath him, managing to roll over on her back, and looked up at him with the same, wide-eyed look of desire he had seen last night. With her bottom lip between her teeth, Arthur thought it was perhaps the most provocative expression he had ever seen on a woman in all his life.

"Are you hurt?" he asked gruffly.

She shook her head.

His hand went to her knee, bare beneath her bunched skirts. "Are you certain?"

She nodded very slowly. He moved his hands to her calf, gently kneading the pliant flesh, watching her blue eyes watch him, then up again, past her knee, to her inner thigh, and felt the vibration in her leg as she strained to hold still where he touched her. Her breath was coming unevenly now, but her eyes did not waver; she held his gaze with a power that almost seemed to bewitch him. Those pale blue eyes, the exact color of the cloudless sky, her body, as soft as the dark green earth. He could almost feel the silkiness of her skin beneath her drawers, the firm, supple flesh . . .

Kerry fell back on her elbows, and Arthur glided over her, never breaking the gaze between them until he lowered his head to kiss her. The succulent flesh of her lips torched his senses; his hand fell to the mound of her breast, skimming the cotton of her chemise before closing his fingers around her.

God, she was warm, the heat of her skin radiating through the cotton and inflaming every masculine nerve in him. Arthur breathed into her mouth as her fingers scorched him everywhere they touched. Her tongue was like a flame against his lips and teeth, setting him on fire, making him burn with an almost desperate need to have her.

"Arthur," she moaned, and the longing in her voice made his heart and groin pound relentlessly. He shifted; with his free hand, he unbuttoned her blouse and slipped his hand inside to the warm smooth flesh of her breast. His thumb grazed the rigid peak of her nipple; Kerry caught a breath in her throat and raised her knee between his legs, innocently pressing against his testicles. It very nearly sent him over the bloody edge—he dragged his head to her breast, freeing it from the chemise and laving it. She clasped his head in her hands, pressed him to her, lifted her breast to his mouth.

Arthur was drowning, completely submersed in her, nothing to stop him from taking her here, on the banks of the tributary, making love to her until her seemingly desperate passion was sated and his own fierce need appeased. He would have done it, too, had not the sound of voices interrupted the heat of the afternoon. The instinctive need to protect slowly gained ground over his desire; Arthur managed to lift his head and peer to the right, to the flatboat slowly approaching from a great distance.

Kerry was less sluggish than he, however—she suddenly shoved him off of her with a strength that surprised him and sat up, beating her skirts down to her ankles. The terror in her actions pierced through what was left of the lustful fog on his brain. Arthur came to his feet, yanking her up with him, and adjusted his clothing as best he could as she nimbly fastened her bodice. Wildly, he looked around, his heart drumming steadily with the realization of how close they had come to being discovered making love.

That thought instinctively compelled him to move away so quickly and thoughtlessly that he suddenly found himself down the banks of the tributary, waving to the approaching flatboat. "Ho there!" he called. "Ho!"

The flatboat, coming in from the north, slowed a bit. Arthur slowly lowered his hand. His eyes narrowed. His hands found his waist as he pressed his lips tightly together and reminded himself that their predicament meant that he could ill afford to antagonize Mr. Richey and Mr. Richey a second time.

Oh, it was the two oxen all right, the only change being that they were floating in the opposite direction of the last time they met, and their little flatboat was now covered with crates of squawking chickens.

All right. Was this some sort of heavenly jest at his considerable expense?

The flatboat drifted closer. Mr. Richey Number One eyed Arthur curiously from the stern of the boat as he stuck his oar into the earthen bank and brought the flatboat to a halt. "Aye?" he called.

As if he had no earthly idea what Arthur wanted! "Good afternoon to you, Mr. Richey. I should beg your pardon a second time, sir, as it would seem that Mrs. McKinnon and I are still quite lost and quite stranded. I hope that you could see your way into delivering us to the River Tay. We are in search of Dunkeld."

Mr. Richey Number Two emerged from behind a crate of especially disturbed fowl and looked at Kerry. "You be well past Dunkeld, lass," he said unemotionally, and leaned over the side of the boat to spit a wad of tobacco into the waters below. "And we just come from the River Tay."

"*Past* Dunkeld?" Kerry echoed, suddenly appearing at Arthur's side.

Mr. Richey Number One nodded.

Kerry cast a quick, confused glance at Arthur before turning to the Richey brothers again. "Then we'd be very near Pitlochry, aye? How far to Pitlochry, then?"

"Two leagues, not more," answered Mr. Richey Number Two.

Kerry's face lit up; she flashed a bright smile. "Oh, really? That's bonny, it is—Loch Eigg is just a bit past Pitlochry."

The Richey brothers exchanged looks. "Loch Eigg? We've been as far as that, lassie. Doona intend to go that way again," said one.

"But you must help us!" Kerry insisted. "We've come so far, and we've not eaten scarcely a bite, and I am certain my people are frantic by now! I'm naught called to leave the glen ever, you know, and oh Lord, they've surely called upon the laird for help and there will be no end to the trouble that will cause, and I shall not rest for all the grief I've brought them, especially now, because it's really *not* so very far, Mr. Richey, not so far at all . . ."

Fifteen minutes later, the Richey brothers had conceded that perhaps it was not so very far at all to Loch Eigg. Arthur didn't know if he should be impressed or appalled—Kerry had somehow talked them into reversing course and taking them to Loch Eigg for an exorbitant fee—which he had, of course, quickly offered to pay.

When they had at last agreed on a price, Mr. Richey

Number Two turned a rather dazed but smiling face from Kerry and frowned at Arthur. "Aye, well, on with you now. The day's awastin'," he said as Mr. Richey Number One helped Kerry step onto the boat.

"Righto," Arthur drawled, and waited until Kerry had settled onto the one crate that did not seem to contain livestock. When she turned an expectant look to him—along with Richeys One and Two—Arthur leaned to one side to pick up Kerry's satchel.

That was when he saw the sow.

An enormous one at that, munching happily in her pen.

Bloody fabulous. Just bloody rotten fabulous. Reciting a colorful little something in his mind, Arthur hoisted himself onto the flatboat and without being told, settled in, wedging himself between the crate of chickens and the sow, almost nose to nose. For some strange reason, an image of his father flashed in his mind's eye, and he rather imagined His Grace was spinning like a bloody top in his grave at that precise moment.

Chapter Eight

THOMAS MCKINNON WAS a man with precious few ties in his life—no unnecessary entanglements of the heart or mind, no one to disappoint when the time came to go. And eventually, he *would* go, would have gone long before now, had it not been for so many wee things in Glenbaden. He had never intended to stay so long. Aye, he would go, and soon, it seemed, for someone had to go have a look about for Kerry.

It was her fault he was still in Glenbaden. But the lass, she had a way about her that could seep into a man's skin. Thomas would never forget the first day he met her, scarcely a week after Fraser brought her home. With flour on her face and those loose, dark curls bouncing off her shoulders, she had smiled at him as if he was the Good Lord Himself and had offered him a plate of some of the best food he'd ever eaten.

But that was not what made him stay. It was the way she respected everyone in Glenbaden as if they were her closest kin, when in truth, one or two of them weren't any more industrious than the cattle. It was the way she had dealt with Fraser, treating him like a king when he wasn't any better than an ass. Thomas had never cared for Fraser, had not since they were lads—there was something ugly about him, something that gave a body a cold shudder from time to time.

But Fraser's worst crime was letting his wife work herself almost into the ground without a single encouraging word. Kerry McKinnon had done everything even a man could do to keep the land producing and rents paid at a time when it seemed everyone around the little glen was being forced from their homes in favor of Black-faced sheep.

And she had done it with a sunny disposition, too, even if she had become a wee bit desperate over the last two years. Any fool could see what was happening—the land was too rocky to support a cash crop. The beeves were too sickly with the fever in their bones. Fraser had not known what to do and had let some stranger buy in with a bit of cash. It had not been enough cash to save Glenbaden, though.

Well, no one knew the glen like Thomas, least of all Fraser, and he wasn't too proud to admit it. He'd meant to go a long time past, but he never seemed to find the right time. He could not leave them, not with things as bad as they were and getting worse. One thing led to another, and the next thing he knew, he was almost all Kerry had. Big Angus could not tend to the glen alone, not with a group of women and infirm old men.

So Thomas had stayed.

Which had brought him full circle back to his original conviction that a man should move on unless he wants his heart and his mind to get all wrapped around some unwanted entanglement. And dammit if he had not found himself with an entanglement. He was sick to death with worry about Kerry—the lass had been gone two days too long now—and he was just about as scared as he had ever been in his life.

He and Big Angus had discussed it over a plate of haggis last night, had decided if she didn't come home today, Thomas would go after her. Unfortunately, he had no idea where he was going—having never left

Glenbaden, he wasn't entirely certain how large a place like Dundee might be, or how difficult it might be to find his way there. He couldn't even assume she had actually *reached* Dundee, but he refused to let himself imagine the things that might have happened, and had snapped May's head nearly clean from her shoulders when she had begun to hypothesize on that point. He just preferred no one say a word, not a single word, because God knew his own conscience was talking enough for all of them.

Now that the day had come and almost gone with no sign of Kerry, Thomas donned the coat his father had left when he had died fifteen years ago and packed a sack of May's biscuits. Big Angus drew him a map—a bit sketchy, it seemed to Thomas, seeing as how Big Angus hadn't left the glen in a dozen years himself. But at least Big Angus knew where to find Pitlochry, and Thomas's plan was to reach it before nightfall, then start out from there the next morning.

He finished wrapping the biscuits and walked outside to say his fare-thee-wells, but was distracted by Big Angus's excited shout from somewhere near the barley fields. Thomas squinted across the field in the direction Big Angus pointed, and his heart actually skipped a beat or two. Thank the saints; he'd never in his life seen anything as wonderful as the sight of Kerry McKinnon walking across that field, even if she was trampling the new growth.

And he'd never in his life been as livid as he was with the man who was walking next to her.

Whoever the hell the stranger was, Thomas hoped for his sake that he had a damn good explanation for why Mrs. McKinnon was two days late and looked like *that*. Lord Almighty, her hair was loose and flying around her, her mourning clothes caked with dirt all the way up to her neck, and her pretty face was smudged with what looked to be mud. The lass looked as is she'd *rolled* all the way from Dundee!

He found it highly ironic, therefore, that Kerry was grinning.

Grinning.

Well, there it was, then. There was not a damn thing the stranger could say now that would save his bloody hide, and Thomas would take great delight in doing the killing, too. He dropped his bundle and walked out to greet them.

"Thomas!" Kerry cried, and ran the last few yards to him, laughing as she threw her arms around his neck and squeezed him tight. The sour smell of loch water assaulted his senses; Thomas wrinkled his nose as he pulled her arms from his neck.

"Been worried unto death about ye, lassie," he said gruffly, aware that he had yet to take his hands from her wrists.

"Oh, Thomas, you will never believe what has happened!" she exclaimed gleefully, but before she could tell him just what in the hell *had* happened, she caught sight of Big Angus lumbering toward them. "Big Angus!" She slipped from Thomas's grasp as May came running behind Big Angus, shrieking her thanks to the Lord above.

In the middle of their joyful reunion, Thomas turned and raked a very cold gaze over the stranger.

To his credit, the man calmly beheld him as Thomas took in the wavy hair, the beard that looked to be a few days old, the sorry state of his clothing . . . and the man's boots. The rest of him looked like hell, but those were some of the finest boots Thomas had ever seen in his life. He lifted a blistering stare to the man's face. "All right then, just who in God's name are ye?"

"Arthur Christian," he responded politely, and extended his hand.

Bloody hell, a Lobsterback on top of everything else! Thomas scowled at his proffered hand. "You see the lad standing just there," he drawled, jerking a thumb in the general direction of Big Angus. The stranger looked at

Big Angus, seemed to take in his enormous size and mess of bright red hair, then returned his gaze to Thomas.

Thomas gave him a wry smile. "Give me one reason why he shouldna wring your neck like an old hen."

Arthur Christian didn't so much as blink. But a corner of his mouth turned up ever so slightly, and he said in a voice as pure as Thomas had ever heard, "You must be Thomas McKinnon. A pleasure to meet you, sir."

That surprised him greatly; he folded his arms defensively across his chest and cocked his head to one side to better assess the scoundrel. "Aye, I'd be Thomas McKinnon. And if Thomas McKinnon finds that you've so much as touched a hair on her head, just a *single* hair, mind ye, so help me God I'll see ye dead, I will."

Incredibly, the stranger chuckled at that and looked to where Kerry was talking excitedly to May, her hands flying as she animated her story. He watched her for just a moment, but a moment in which Thomas had to suppress a groan—he saw something flicker deep in the man's eyes, from some place deep within him. From the place that caused entanglements a man did not need.

The stranger looked at him again, his smirk turning to a lopsided smile. "Frankly, sir, I find it nothing short of a divine miracle that I have somehow managed to survive this extraordinary little journey, and relatively unscathed at that. I assure you, you have nothing to fear—your Mrs. McKinnon is quite indestructible."

With a short of disgust, Thomas frowned at Kerry's back. He supposed he should not be too very surprised—after all, he knew better than anyone else that the lass had a way about her that could not help but seep into a man's skin.

An hour or more after May—who was as petite and dark as Big Angus was enormous and red—ushered Kerry to a waiting bath in the pleasant white house with green shutters, Arthur calmly considered the possibility that he might have to fight his way out of the tidy parlor, judging by the expressions on the faces of Thomas and Big Angus. Both of whom were staring at him from the door.

As no one had invited him to be seated, Arthur stood with one shoulder against the wall, his arms folded negligently across his chest, his legs crossed at the ankle, eyeing the two men with some amusement. He had seen similar looks on the faces of fathers and brothers in England, but never delivered with quite such . . . *intensity*. He rather thought he'd have a fair chance with Thomas, although his tall, slender frame belied sinewy muscles that Arthur could see outlined in his clothing. His dark hair, peppered with gray, was just as deceiving—he was a man in his prime.

While he might have had a decent enough chance with Thomas, Arthur was extremely doubtful he could succeed against Big Angus. He had driven smaller carriages than that man.

He sighed, glanced around the room again, taking in the furnishings. The house was certainly smaller than what he was accustomed to, but larger than it appeared on the outside, and much larger than the cottages that dotted the valley. Perhaps a little ragged around the edges, but all in all, like the glen, the house was very pleasing to the eye.

Actually, the view along the tree-lined path leading from the loch into the glen was spectacular. Fields of heather gave way to green slopes of new barley that swept down to the banks of a small stream. The main house, nestled in a clearing overlooking the stream was a white frame and rock structure, marked by green shutters on pane-glass windows. Below the house was a scattering of smaller quarters, mostly thatch and stone, with lazy streams of smoke rising to the clear blue sky. A large stable and barn dominated the foot of one hill, where one horse and two milk cows resided.

But while the exterior of the house was attractive in a rugged sort of way, the interior of the house startled a man's senses, and particularly that of an Englishman. It was quite obvious, even without the grand tour of the place Kerry insisted on giving him, that a woman ruled here. White chiffon curtains—from Edinburgh, May had proudly told him—lifted gracefully in the breeze, wafting across the muted floral prints that adorned every room. In the four main rooms that dominated the center of the house, there was evidence of many feminine hobbies.

Here, in the parlor, two worn but overstuffed chairs and a couch were covered with big pillows, each depicting a different rural scene in intricate needlework. Books ranging from breeding techniques, to a handful of popular novels, to history tomes and one very large atlas were carelessly scattered across various surfaces. In a small room at the end of the hall that served as an office, the account books lay open for anyone to inspect. Tiny little numbers were neatly recorded in the columns on a desk permanently stained with a large circle of ink.

It had taken Arthur a quarter of an hour to fathom that what was missing was any sign of a man. In the small cloakroom off the main entry, for example, there were no riding boots or crops, no hats. Instead, the pegs along the wall were draped with faded ribbons and tattered sun bonnets. Where sturdy boots should have stood was a pair of well-worn slippers. There was no tobacco box in the dining room; all port glasses were presumably tucked away in the scarred hutch. In the room with a basin, there were no strops or razors, no neckcloths or waistcoats or buckskins.

The only suggestion that men were even welcome was the presence of a small sideboard in the parlor on which sat one decanter of whiskey.

Only *one*.

Arthur had to admire Kerry's spunk—while he might

wonder who looked after her, he could not help but respect her bravery. Women were not supposed to milk cows, or balance books, or occupy their time with anything more taxing than an occasional ditty at the pianoforte. For her to struggle to keep this glen afloat was incomparably unique and wholeheartedly admirable. And to his own surprise, he found it quite refreshing—one woman, unfettered by the bounds of societal convention, living exactly as she pleased, and none of her family circle—including the crusty one—seemed to mind.

At the thought of her family circle, Arthur languidly shifted his gaze to Thomas again. As insufferable Scots went, Thomas McKinnon was in top form. "So," Arthur said amicably, hoping to lighten his stoic expression with a bit of civilized conversation, "I am given to understand that you raise cattle."

Thomas McKinnon did not even blink.

Arthur blithely continued, "Must be quite an endeavor, raising beeves. I would imagine it requires a good amount of acreage for grazing."

"What ye be doing here, then?" Thomas asked.

So much for civilized conversation. Apparently, the inquisition wasn't quite over. "I believe I have said. I've some business in Dundee on behalf of an old friend."

"Aye, and what business would that be?"

As if he owed the man any explanation at all. "*Private* business."

"Private," Thomas repeated, his blue eyes narrowing slightly. "Your *private* business would have naught to do with our Mrs. McKinnon, would it now?"

Good God. "I beg your pardon, sir, but I cannot speak any plainer than I already have. As Mrs. McKinnon herself told you, she shot me in the arm then insisted on running off into the wilderness as if she were Moses, without so much as a firearm to protect her. I was compelled as a gentleman to see that she did not come to any harm, and granted, although she returned to you quite mussed, I assure you the consequence might have been far, far worse indeed had I left her to her own devices. I am certain you have noted prior to this occasion that Mrs. McKinnon is perhaps rather headstrong, have you not? I should think it perfectly obvious that I have no designs on her, have never met her 'ere a day or two ago, and certainly do not intend to take advantage of her hospitality a moment longer than is absolutely necessary, given the unfortunate chain of events."

Thomas's scowl deepened. "Then ye willna mind sleeping in the barn, eh?"

"Oh, Thomas, don't be ridiculous! He'll sleep in the room at the far end of the hall!"

Kerry appeared behind Arthur's two guards, shoving her way in between their elbows with such force that she stumbled awkwardly but resplendently into the room. Her cheeks were rosy from the bath; her hair hung in one long braid down her back while little wisps of black curls framed her face. She had, thankfully, disposed of the black bombazine and wore a soft gray gown cinched tightly at the waist and buttoned up to a neckline that dipped well below her shoulders. Her smile was so deep that her fair cheeks dimpled.

Thomas grunted; Arthur could not help the grin that slowly spread across his lips.

"I found a few of the late McKinnon's things you might wear," she said, ignoring Thomas.

"I am much obliged."

"Big Angus will draw a hot bath for you"—she glanced over her shoulder—"will you not, Big Angus?" Satisfied with his nod, she looked at Arthur again. "We take our evening meal at nine o'clock if that suits you."

He rather imagined anything would suit him as long as she continued to smile at him like that. "I thank you for your generous hospitality. I look forward with great anticipation to an actual meal," he quipped, and pushing off the wall, strolled across the room. He paused in front of her and smiled warmly. "A rather dramatic improvement," he said, winking, and chuckled at Thomas's venomous look as he followed Big Angus out.

Kerry tried very hard to explain everything to Thomas, how he had saved her life despite her having shot him. Nonetheless, he remained stubbornly suspicious of Arthur. Big Angus didn't say much, but nodded in solemn agreement to everything Thomas said. Only May seemed unconcerned, muttering several times as she prepared the evening meal that Arthur Christian presented a fine figure of a man.

But there was nothing anyone could say or do to dampen Kerry's spirits. Freshly bathed and dressed in clean clothes, she felt like a new woman. Actually, she was ecstatic. First, because she had survived the adventure of her life and had proven to herself that she *could* persevere, in spite of almost having *died,* for heaven's sake. And second, well . . . second, because he was here.

He was *here.* In her house, just down the corridor, no doubt relaxing in a steaming tub of water . . . *naked.*

A delicious little flame shot up her spine so quickly that Kerry abruptly made a show of cutting the potatoes. Every time she thought of that charming smile and that wicked, *wicked* glimmer in his hazel eyes, her heart seemed to skip around her chest, she couldn't stop smiling, and she had to consciously remind herself not to hum. Not only was he so very handsome, he was courageous, entirely unflappable and, she was quite convinced, invincible. After weeks of despair, he had appeared from nowhere to make her feel lighthearted, as if she had been freed from some terrible burden.

Safe.

That silly sentiment almost caused her to laugh out loud, because nothing could be further from the truth. Her situation was far worse than she could have imagined—there was hardly any money left in the household fund and she had a mere three weeks remaining to come up with a bloody miracle.

Thomas was, as she knew he would be, furious with Mr. Abernathy and the Bank of Scotland. He expressed his frustration in some rather lengthy railings against banks and governments and sheepherders—the latter simply for good measure. He was so caught up in his speech that he had thankfully forgotten Arthur for the time being. Even when Kerry thrust a pile of plates in his hands with instructions to place them around the long wooden table that dominated the kitchen, Thomas would not stop. It wasn't until Arthur appeared in the kitchen doorway, bathed and dressed in a pair of heavy buckskin trousers and a crisp linen shirt that Thomas stopped.

They all stopped.

Kerry's heart stopped.

If she had thought him handsome before, he was positively virile now. His wavy hair was brushed back, still wet at the ends. The clothes were a tight fit—so tight that she could see the breadth of muscle in his shoulders and legs. The rough beard was gone, scraped clean by Fraser's old razor.

Arthur looked at them looking at him. "Is something amiss?" he asked after a moment and glanced down. "I suppose it's not the best fit."

"Mm-mmm," May muttered with a shake of her head, and turned back to the food preparations.

"Oh no! You look . . . You look . . ." . . . *majestic* . . . "refreshed," Kerry sputtered, and abruptly busied herself with the contents of a pot hanging above the hearth. Except that the pot was empty. "Would you like a pint of ale, then? Supper willna be long now," she said, motioning awkwardly to the kitchen table where Thomas and Big Angus sat.

"Ale," Arthur repeated, as if testing the word, then beamed a bright smile at her. "A pint of ale would be just the thing, thank you." He took a seat at the table next to

Thomas, gave Kerry a sly wink when she placed a pint of ale in front of him. "Something smells wonderful," he remarked, and turned his warm smile to May.

Thomas muttered something that sounded more like a growl and placed his pint down with a thud as May fairly burst with pride. "I hope you've a hearty appetite, laddie. Big Angus has brought us a fine piece of trout."

"I am ravenous, Mrs. Grant, and quite eager to try your trout. I had the pleasure of sampling your culinary skills when Mrs. McKinnon shared a biscuit. I think it was the most delicious bread I ever had the good fortune to taste."

May beamed with the pleasure of that compliment. Big Angus, however, exchanged a frown with Thomas, then turned that frown to Arthur, who blithely sipped his ale as if it had been served in a fancy crystal glass.

"What is it ye said brings ye to these parts?" Thomas asked.

"I said it was personal business," Arthur responded politely as Kerry slapped a plate of freshly baked bread in front of Thomas as a warning. "More than once."

Thomas ignored Kerry. "Strange, is it not, that an Englishman would have personal business all the way up here."

Arthur shrugged, calmly regarded Thomas. "I don't think it terribly strange a'tall."

"It's not as if he has business in Glenbaden, Thomas," Kerry interjected, piercing him with a sharp look. "Surely you havna forgotten the gentleman very kindly escorted me home."

Thomas scowled and looked intently at his ale.

"Actually, my business is in Dundee," Arthur informed them. "I am to meet a solicitor by the name of Regis."

Kerry's breath caught in her throat. *"Regis?"* she blurted, wincing when Thomas, Big Angus, and May simultaneously cast questioning looks in her direction.

"Oh, so you know him, do you?" Arthur asked pleasantly. "A rather industrious chap, I think."

Kerry carefully avoided the gazes of her family and smiled thinly at Arthur. "I doona know him. I overheard the name in Dundee," she lied.

"Yes, well, I was to have met him in Dundee this very week, but he has sent word he has been unavoidably detained in Fort Williams."

"For a fortnight," Kerry offered unthinkingly, and instantly bit her tongue for voicing her thoughts aloud.

Arthur glanced up at her. "Yes, for a fortnight," he said, his expression curious.

Kerry felt a rush of blood to her neck, tried to put down the ridiculous idea that popped into her head. She abruptly turned away, fetched a platter of steamed cabbage that she placed on the table. She was a fool—a *fool!*—to be thinking what she was thinking! But really, what was the harm? Inviting him to stay in Glenbaden until his appointment with Mr. Regis seemed the least she could do in return for her life. The *very* least.

With a surreptitious look at Thomas, who was regarding her closely, Kerry walked stiffly to where May was putting the finishing touches on the platter of trout.

It was her home, after all. And if there was one thing for which Scots were known, it was their hospitality, were they not? It would be the worst offense to send him off with nothing to occupy his time for an entire fortnight. "We would be honored to have you stay here until Mr. Regis returns," she said quickly.

The invitation was immediately met with a sputtering of ale from Thomas. Beside her, May smiled quietly as she arranged the trout on the platter.

"I shouldn't think of imposing, Mrs. McKinnon," Arthur responded.

Kerry turned, very nearly sighed aloud when she saw the smile glimmering in Arthur's hazel eyes. "It wouldna be an imposition, it would be our *pleasure*."

"*Och,*" Thomas muttered, but he thankfully said no more than that as he frowned deeply at the trout May set on the table.

"Well . . . I should make myself very useful, then. I would very much like to help if I can."

Thomas looked up, smiling thinly. "Would ye, now?" he asked, and chuckled.

The meal passed in light conversation, which suited Arthur perfectly, as he was far too intent on the excellent food to be bothered with talk of cattle and barley. The trout was prepared to perfection, the Yorkshire pudding delicately flavored, even the cabbage—a dish Arthur typically avoided as being far too pedestrian for his palate—was seasoned so deliciously that he could not resist a second helping.

When the plates had been cleared, and Thomas and Big Angus were deeply engrossed in a conversation having to do with sheep, Arthur leaned back in his chair and surreptitiously watched Kerry as she moved about the kitchen—rather, he watched her hips move beneath skirts free of petticoats, the long black braid swinging above them. He was filled with a lazy but potent desire to touch her, feel the softness of her skin beneath his fingers, his lips. Grateful when Thomas and Big Angus finally rose from the table, he flashed an indolent smile at Thomas when he told him that the day started early in Glenbaden.

"Indeed? And how early would that be, sir?"

"We rise with the sun here," Thomas stiffly informed him, then glanced at Kerry's back. "If ye think to be about, we could use the hand ye offered."

"I would be delighted," Arthur drawled, and dipped his head in mock salute to the crusty Scot. Thomas muttered something unintelligible beneath his breath as he followed Big Angus out of the kitchen. The lovely little May smiled dreamily as she floated past him after the two men.

With the Grants and Thomas McKinnon off to God knew where, Arthur watched Kerry in silence as she dried the last dish and placed it on a shelf. It occurred to him that he had never seen a woman in a kitchen other than Cook, and even that infrequently. Actually, he had rarely *been* in kitchens, was unaccustomed to the warmth. It was fascinating, really—Kerry moved fluidly among the pots and sacks and dried herbs. He felt an odd sense of calm watching her, as if in this one room, in this corner of the world, all was right.

When Kerry finished, she stood with her back to him, gazing out of the lone, unadorned window. Arthur stood and strolled around the table to stand beside her. "It was exceedingly kind of you to invite me to stay."

"We are honored."

"I think," he said, taking her hand in his, "not as honored as I." She glanced at her hand in his, and with a small sigh, surprised him by leaning against him. But she suddenly straightened and reached for the bucket of water she had used to clean the dishes. With a shy smile, she said, "I think there is naught lovelier than the moon over Glenbaden. Will you walk with me, then?"

Oh yes, he'd walk with her . . . right over the edge of a cliff if she asked.

Fortunately, he had to merely follow her outside, where she absently poured the water from the bucket onto what looked to be a garden patch, then set it aside and carefully wiped her palms on her apron. With a smile, Arthur held his hand out to her. Kerry looked at it so suspiciously that he could not help but chuckle. She smiled sheepishly at his laugh, slipped her hand into his, and the two of them strolled in comfortable silence into the heath beyond the house. The night air was thick with the scent of boxwood and heather; the small loch below them shimmered in the moonlight. Arthur glanced up at the sky, to the thin trails of mist streaking across the moon. Kerry was right; he had never seen anything quite as stunning as the light of a full moon spilling around them. "It is beautiful here," he murmured appreciatively.

"Aye," she softly agreed, and with a wistful sigh,

tilted her head back to gaze at the stars. "I've not been far beyond this glen, but I canna imagine a lovelier place in all the world."

Arthur was hard pressed to disagree with her and joined her in gazing up at the stars. There were millions of them, seemingly so close that it felt as if they almost touched his face.

He lowered his gaze and looked at Kerry. Her skin, bared to the moon above, had the rich luster of pearls. Her lips were starkly dark against her face, and Arthur was assaulted with the memory of those lips, the satin feel of her cheeks. He let go her hand and reached out to touch the column of her neck.

Kerry did not move; she held very still as he caressed the hollow of her throat, the long sleek line to her jaw. When he slipped his hand around to the side of her neck, she lowered her head and looked at him with luminous blue eyes that seemed to reflect his own growing desire.

Desire he had no right to feel.

He had no intention of staying in Glenbaden. He had had his little adventure; he would go in a matter of days. He had no right to kiss those lips, to perhaps relay a promise he would not keep. Yet he could not seem to tear his gaze away from those eyes, or the desire they reflected up to him. Wholly mesmerized, he gazed into the pale blue irises, his heart and mind seized by the moment, by the Scottish moon over Glenbaden.

Kerry leaned into him, rising slowly on her toes; he was confused in a vague way as to what she was about, until her lips brushed against his, settling lightly on his bottom lip, scarcely touching, but clinging to him all at once. Whether it was her boldness or the erotic simplicity of that kiss, it stunned him. He stood frozen in the moonlight, helpless against the heat that rapidly spread though his veins. But when he felt her falter, all his male instincts rapidly took hold—he quickly moved to anchor her, wrapping his arm around her waist, pulling her into his chest and returning the simple kiss with one that surprised him with its intensity.

He swept boldly into her mouth, drinking her in. Kerry responded with the fever she had shown him before—her hands swept up around his neck, her tongue darted out to tangle with his. When he dragged his mouth to her ear, she kissed his eye, his temple, her hands running down his arms, across his chest, bending her neck so that he might caress the slope of it into her shoulder with his mouth. Arthur heard her sigh, felt her mouth on his chest through the rough linen shirt, the grip of her fingers in his arm. He could feel her body against his, every quivering inch of it, but as his hand drifted up her ribcage, brushing against the side of her breast, she caught a ragged breath in her throat, shifted away from his caress.

It took Arthur a moment to gain his mind; scarcely able to think, he focused on the feel of her fingers as they drifted across his lips.

Kerry's fingers rested on his lips. "I . . . I fear I might abandon all morals to your touch, Arthur. I seem to be on dangerous ground here with you now."

As hard as he tried, Arthur could not think of a reassuring response to that; it seemed odd that she chose those words, words that struck so very close to what he was feeling.

And had he been able to think of a reassuring response, it would have drifted into the night on the tails of the mist, because Kerry slipped away, walking quickly to the house and leaving him to stand alone in the heath.

Leaving him to a hunger that he feared would not now or ever be completely sated.

Chapter Nine

THAT NIGHT ARTHUR dreamed of England.

He stood in the formal drawing room of his Mount Street home, Portia beside him as he greeted guests. Then Phillip appeared, his blond hair wildly mussed, his shirt stained red with blood, weaving in and out of the crowd, smiling at Arthur over the shoulders of his guests. He came so close, but when Arthur reached for him, he melted into the crowd. He turned to Portia, only it was Kerry now standing beside him, wearing a plain gray broadcloth amid the sea of pastel silks, her blue eyes glittering. He leaned forward to kiss her . . . but she stopped him cold with a punch in the ribs. He groped for the injured rib, but she hit him again, hard.

Ouch.

"*Och,* ye sleep like the dead."

The gritty sound of Thomas McKinnon's voice dragged Arthur from the depths of a very comfortable sleep. He felt the discomfort in his side again and opened his eyes. In the dim light of a single candle, he could see it was the toe of Thomas's boot that was striking him in the ribs, the bloody bastard.

He rolled away, presented Thomas with his back, and asked through a wide yawn, "Is there something I might do for you at this ungodly hour, Mr. McKinnon?"

"I told ye that we start early in Glenbaden. If ye'll be up, we could use yer back," he said, nudging Arthur again with his boot. "Up with ye now."

The next thing Arthur heard was the *clip clip clip* of Thomas's boots as he walked out of the room.

With a groan, he slowly raised himself and focused his blurry gaze on the window. He blinked, tried to clear the sleep from his eyes, because it looked pitch-black outside. He blinked again ... God's blood, what time *was* it?

He dressed, stumbled to the kitchen, and frowned. Thomas was there, sipping from a cup of steaming coffee, a bowl of oats next to a platter piled high with scones in front of him. Kerry was there, too, busy at the basin. She glanced over her shoulder and flashed a brilliant smile that only made Arthur's head hurt. "Good morning, Arthur Christian! You slept well, then, I trust?"

Arthur fell unceremoniously onto the wooden bench beside him. "Very well indeed, until a few moments ago."

Thomas lifted a wiry brow. "I suppose then that the English doona believe in a full day's work."

"The English, sir, are so very efficient at a full day's work that there is never a need to rise in the middle of the bloody night!" Arthur snapped irritably. "Now where did you find that brew?"

Thomas casually inclined his head toward a table and an iron vessel beneath the window. Arthur pushed up and dragged himself to fetch a cup.

"Big Angus, he'll be along in a moment. Have ye any experience with livestock?" Thomas asked.

Arthur poured steaming coffee down his throat before answering. "I am rather remarked upon for my skill with horses, so yes, I suppose I've a bit of experience," he said testily, and ignored Thomas's derisive chuckle.

"Thomas McKinnon, mind you now," Kerry said from the basin. "I'll keep him occupied, you needna worry over it."

"Aye," Thomas said, his blue eyes smirking, "I'd see that ye do."

The sun was only beginning to creep above the horizon when Arthur realized that a self-proclaimed skill with horses did not necessarily translate into any discernible skills with livestock, and in particular, hogs. He could scarcely believe it when Kerry handed him a large bucket filled with a most foul smelling, rancid-looking offal and pointed toward a pen of hogs in the middle of the cluster of thatched-roof cottages. Arthur looked at the hogs, then at the slop, then at Kerry.

"They are not particular," she said, her nose wrinkled in offense to the slop.

"I beg your pardon, I am to do *what?*" Arthur asked again, still incredulous.

"Toss it about. The hogs, they'll root about for it," she said patiently, then frowned lightly at his apparent distaste for the task. "If you prefer, I'll—"

"Oh no," he said quickly. He was not about to give Thomas McKinnon the pleasure of humiliating him. If the residents of Glenbaden slopped hogs, then by God, so would he. "I'll be quite all right." And very nobly putting down the urge to flee, he walked to the pen, swallowing the obscenity on his tongue when the hogs began moving toward him, their round snouts wiggling furiously as they tried to touch him. Aware that Kerry watched him—and for all he knew, *Thomas*—Arthur took a deep breath, held it, and began to pour the slop for the hogs.

After he had finished that chore—satisfactorily and in record time, he was quite certain—Kerry cheerfully led him to a barn that looked as if it would collapse at any moment. Inside, one sway-backed dairy cow munched contentedly on her hay. "She's to be milked," Kerry said, and shoved a bucket into Arthur's chest. "I'll gather the eggs, providing that old hen cared to grace us with any."

"Really, haven't you a milkmaid or someone of similar occupation to do this?" Arthur groaned as he took the bucket.

Kerry laughed. "Take care with the teats, now," she warned him in all seriousness. "Nell willna care for it if you squeeze too hard. There you are, then," she said, and with a jaunty little wave, turned and walked out of the ramshackle barn, assuming, apparently, that he was quite the expert in milking cows.

Lord God. With a heavy sigh, Arthur warily approached her, carefully positioning the milk stool and bucket before patting the old girl's rump. "I've not had a complaint yet, Nell. We wouldn't want to dampen a man's spirit with one today, now would we?" he said, and lowered himself to the stool, studied the mechanics of her udder, and grimacing, reached beneath to relieve her of her milk.

A half-hour later, he considered the milking, like the slopping, an astounding success—Nell complained three times, but she only managed to butt him off his stool once. Arthur was wise to her after that; with grave determination, he righted the stool, informed Nell that he would have her milk if it killed them both, and doggedly continued until every teat was dry.

By late morning, when most self-respecting English gentlemen would only just be rising, Kerry was dragging Arthur through a thick mist over a very rutted path. On his back, Arthur carried heavy stone-cutting tools, the purpose of which, Kerry explained, was to help Thomas shore a fence. Arthur could scarcely wait.

But first, Kerry would apparently make a few calls.

At the first cottage Kerry stopped, Arthur was introduced to Red Donner, a man almost as big as Angus, with gray streaking through his bright red hair. He had, evidently, sliced one of his sausage-like fingers, but was adamant that Kerry not apply the salve she withdrew from her basket. He was so fearful of it that he scarcely noticed Arthur at all, merely nodded his enormous head before objecting again to Kerry's plan, half in English, half in Gaelic.

"We'll not be without your fiddle, Red Donner," she insisted firmly, and in a matter of minutes, Red Donner's hand was in hers, and she was spreading a very offensive-smelling unguent into his wound while the man wailed like a child.

The second cottage was set back in a thick copse of trees, around a bend in one of the many hills that bordered Glenbaden. The location of the cottage was curious, Arthur thought, as if the owner had intended to be removed from all neighbors. Kerry did not bother to knock, but stooped and disappeared through the small door.

A few moments later, a hideous shriek rent the tranquility of the glen; Arthur started toward the cottage, but Kerry emerged, her face a wreath of smiles. "Winifred," she said with a roll of her eyes. "She's as old as this glen, curses every day she lives to see, and threatens to shoot me for bringing her bread. Yet she eats it, and she's no gun," she said, and walked on.

The last cottage, situated just where the rutted path ended, belonged to a young widow with three small children. Loribeth's husband, Kerry explained, had drowned trying to save their youngest child, who had wandered off and into the loch. They never found the baby's body, and Loribeth had never been the same. When the young woman appeared at her door, looking drawn and ragged, Arthur's heart went out to her. He wondered exactly how she might put food in the bellies of three children, but then he realized how—Kerry had brought biscuits and a rasher of ham.

Upon leaving Loribeth's cottage, Kerry turned into what seemed like an endless meadow of tall grass, moving on to where he was to meet Thomas. The thought of

Thomas suddenly reminded him of the heavy stone-cutting tools on his back. "And what exactly do you suppose Thomas means to do to me with these?" he drawled, adjusting them again on his back.

Kerry laughed gaily. "He's ornery I'll grant you, but he'll be grateful for the help, he will."

Arthur doubted that. Doubted it even more when they reached the piece of fence in question. As Thomas gruffly explained that his task was to shore an old rock fence to keep their few head of cattle from wandering too far, Arthur wondered just where in the hell Thomas was afraid the cattle would go, what with rocky hills sweeping up either side of the meadow. But he rather supposed that question would earn him nothing more than another look of complete disdain. The old fence was disintegrating, and for the life of him, Arthur could not imagine how shoring this one spot could possibly make any difference.

"Well then, I suppose I shall leave you to your work," Kerry chirped, and with a wave and a soft smile, turned to make her way across the meadow again.

As if on cue, Thomas dropped a large stone at his feet that landed with a deep *thud*. He very tersely instructed Arthur how he was to collect a few stones and split them, and then use the pieces to rebuild the fence, showed him how to wield the axe, watched him a time or two, then abruptly turned around and began to walk back across the meadow.

Arthur watched him for a moment before he realized Thomas intended to leave him there. "Ho, McKinnon! Just where in the bloody hell do you think *you* are off to?"

Thomas scarcely paused to glance at Arthur over his shoulder. "I've me own work to do!" he called, and kept walking, leaving an incredulous Arthur alone to the chore of repairing the fence. Well, that convinced him. Thomas fully intended to kill him.

Thomas almost succeeded.

Splitting the rock was backbreaking labor. Even though the day was cool and the breeze steady, Arthur dripped with perspiration. His hands ached from holding the cutting tool he used to spall the large stones and the muscles in his back burned with the effort of lifting the stones to the wall. He was beginning to feel parts of his body he had not even known existed. But as miserable as his body was, there was something very cathartic about the activity. The physical exertion made him feel alive; in a rather strange way it was far more rewarding than he ever might have imagined. He could feel and see the fruits of his labor, the progress toward an end, the concrete results of his exertion. In London, a full day's work meant various social calls where little was truly accomplished. But here in Glenbaden, it seemed that every activity had a purpose, and every purpose was the common good.

He had been raised from the cradle to avoid physical labor, so it was therefore nothing short of astounding that it was as exhilarating as it was this day.

But oh God, he hurt!

Shortly after midday, Arthur paused to stretch his back. He glanced across the meadow and a slow smile spread his lips. The sun had finally penetrated the blue mist; he could see Thomas and Kerry walking toward him. A pail swung carelessly at Kerry's side; she moved languidly through the tall grass, her thick black braid of hair draped carelessly over one shoulder, her free hand skating across the top of the grass. The simple gray gown she wore hugged her slender frame and Arthur could remember the feel of it in his arms, her hips pressed firmly against him. The memory of that kiss seeped into every bit of his consciousness; his pulse began to rise steadily as he turned fully toward her, enchanted by the sight of her gliding as if on air, as if she and this landscape had stepped out of a master's painting and into life.

"Mind ye doona let the spittle drip onto that borrowed shirt," Thomas said as he walked past him on his way, presumably, to inspect the fence. Arthur sliced a quick and impatient gaze across the man's back, dropped his cutting tool, and moved forward to greet Kerry.

She graced him with a beatific smile. "I should have known," she said as he reached to relieve her of the pail she carried. "Thomas would put the king himself to work." She stopped, lifting a hand to shield her eyes from the sun as she gazed up at him, eyes dancing with mirth.

"I am quite convinced he may succeed in seeing me dead by day's end."

Somewhere behind him, Thomas snorted at that. Kerry's rich laughter drifted across the tall grass. "Aye, he's a bit hard around the edges, but he's a good heart."

Frankly, Arthur would require more evidence of that before he'd be convinced, but he wisely chose not to argue the point and glanced at the pail. "What have you got here?"

"Cheese and eggs, some bread, and from May, a bit of shortbread." She smiled, winked coyly. "It seems our May has taken quite a fancy to you."

"Has she? I rather suspected the woman had uncommonly good taste."

Kerry laughed again, lips stretching across even teeth. Through no conscious thought of his own, Arthur impulsively reached for her, slipping his hand around her wrist and squeezing fondly. "I love to hear you laugh," he said softly. "It is music to me."

Her smile faded slightly; she opened her lips to speak, but whatever she might have said was forever lost to Thomas's intrusion. "Well then, ye'd best eat," he said sharply, and took the pail from Arthur. "We'll take a moment, no longer. More than a wee bit of work to be done here," he informed them both, and stalked away with the pail.

"He doesna like it when I interfere with the work," Kerry whispered with a wry smile, and then to Thomas, she called, "You'll bring the pail, will you not, Thomas?"

"*Och*, aye, aye," he said through a mouthful of biscuit.

She glanced at Arthur from the corner of her eye, still smiling. "I should go now."

Stay. Perhaps she read his mind; she didn't move immediately. Her gaze seemed to lock with his and for a moment, Arthur believed she could see deep inside him, to the rather warm, lustful thoughts that were racing through him. But before he could look away, Kerry's gaze dipped. Her cheeks pinkened; she giggled softly. Arthur followed her gaze, realized he still held her wrist and reluctantly let go, his fingers wistfully brushing her hand.

Still smiling, she stole one last look at Thomas and stepped away. "You'd best hurry before he eats your share." Arthur nodded; Kerry began to walk backward, her steps reluctant, her smile terribly alluring. He couldn't take his eyes from her, kept watching her, feeling his smile broaden when she at last turned and stole one last look at him before she moved into the meadow.

He stood there until she was halfway across, and only then did he turn around. Thomas had apparently finished his luncheon and was inspecting the work Arthur had done, slowly shaking his head. *Devil take him.* Famished, Arthur walked to where he had left the pail to have a look. One egg, a half-eaten biscuit, and a small block of goat cheese were all that remained. He jerked his gaze up to where Thomas was standing.

He could have sworn the old dog was laughing.

After a thorough critique of Arthur's technique—naturally—Thomas left him again, returning for him as the sun was beginning its descent into the west. Arthur painfully gathered up his tools, quite certain his legs would never carry him across the meadow, much less up the rutted path, but just as certain that Thomas McKinnon would never know how he ached. Somehow, he managed to get the tools on his back. Somehow, he managed to flash Thomas a grin that suggested he could continue his work for several more hours, and somehow, he was able to start out with what he hoped was a jaunty pace.

As they walked, Thomas eyed him suspiciously. Arthur supposed he was hoping he would collapse at any moment, and honestly, he was waiting for the very same event. In a very vain attempt to cover his discomfort, he sought to distract Thomas with conversation and cheerfully remarked, "Looks to be fertile land you've got here. You must support quite a lot of cattle on it."

Thomas astounded Arthur by actually laughing at that. "This land wouldna support a bean," he said, and chuckled again. "The beeves are sickly and the barley crop good only one in five years. Aye, Fraser McKinnon was a fool to have bought more beeves, he was—the land canna support more than sheep."

Fraser . . . the name caused Arthur to misstep. It was the same name of the man from whom Phillip had bought land, then joined in buying livestock. No, it could not be . . . Fraser was the man's surname—not McKinnon. Still . . . "Fraser McKinnon?" he asked.

"Aye. Kerry's late husband. Dead almost a year."

It was a ridiculous assumption, an inconceivable notion that it could be the same man. Besides, his Fraser was alive and well and owing quite a lot of money. "If the land doesn't support cattle, then why do you raise them?" he asked, forcing the ludicrous thought from his mind.

Thomas glanced impatiently at Arthur as if he was being purposefully obtuse. "The wee bit of Clan McKinnon land in this glen belonged to my cousin Fraser. It was he who bought the beeves—beeves so sickly we lost almost an entire herd to fever. What few were left have not produced 'til now. If the market holds, we'll sell the beeves if they birth and take as many Blackface in trade as we can. We'll have to make do 'til then."

The condition of the Scottish livestock market was not something Arthur knew a whit about, with the single exception of knowing that sheepherding had overtaken most other agricultural pursuits. This he knew because some of the Christian Brothers' clients had invested heavily in the future sheep markets.

They walked on in silence.

Yet something Thomas had said nagged at the back of Arthur's mind. If *his* Fraser McKinnon had lost a herd, it would explain why payments hadn't been made on the note. And if one assumed it took two or three years to rebuild the stock, then one might assume that payments were not made for several years. But still, the coincidence was too much—how was it possible that he should stumble upon Phillip's land in such a bizarre manner? No, it wasn't possible.

It simply *couldn't* be possible.

Thomas made sure Arthur put the stone-cutting instruments away in their proper place before showing him a pump where he could wash. Only then was he allowed into the white house, as he had begun to think of it, where the mouth-watering scent of freshly baked bread greeted him. His stomach was suddenly screaming with hunger; he wearily made his way to the kitchen, smiled when May beamed at him, and shrugged when a clearly irritated Big Angus growled.

May motioned him onto the wooden bench at the table. "Thought ye'd never come in," she said cheerfully. "Kerry went on to see about Filbert McKinnon and his toothache, but we've a wee bit of *cullen skink* if ye please."

He had not the vaguest idea of what "cullen skink"

could possibly be, but responded enthusiastically, "I would like it very much," and managed to refrain from snatching the steaming bowl clean from May's hands.

After he devoured—in an appallingly very few minutes—what turned out to be an excellent fish soup, he could scarcely keep his eyes open, but his pride demanded he accept the pipe Big Angus handed him. He drew the smoke into his lungs, very nearly turned green, and immediately presumed he had the distinct pleasure of inhaling peat. "Fine blend," he said, coughing.

Thomas and Angus exchanged a smile before continuing their conversation. Arthur quickly lost track; their speech was liberally sprinkled with Gaelic phrases and words that were foreign to him. As best he could tell, the two men were worried about the market value of the cattle they owned. He listened to Thomas's droning voice, his eyelids growing heavier with each new Gaelic phrase that filtered into his consciousness, wondering when Kerry might return. The last thing he knew, Big Angus was speaking of some poor chap who had been pushed from his land by sheepherders.

He was startled by the tapping of a finger on his shoulder. Bleary-eyed, Arthur jerked his head up. Of course it was Thomas, sporting what could only be termed a twisted grin. "Best to bed with ye then, laddie. We've more than our fair share of work on the morrow."

Arthur pushed himself into a sitting position, grimacing with the fire the movement caused through what seemed like all of his muscles. "I suppose we shall begin again at a suitably unreasonable hour."

Big Angus chuckled; Thomas leaned back with a grin. "Aye, we'll have an early start of it."

"*Splendid,*" Arthur drawled, and by some miracle, his legs actually supported his weight enough that he could move away from the table. With each step, his jaw clenched tighter—more, he knew, from the pain caused by the chuckling behind him than any ache in his limbs.

He shuffled into the narrow corridor, paused to rub

his back, at which point he noticed a thin shaft of light spilling into the hallway from the room he had been given.

Kerry.

She was still in his thoughts, playing at the corners of his mind. He moved stiffly toward the open door, where he eased his shoulder against the frame. His full weight sagged against it; with the last ounce of strength he had, he folded his arms and concentrated on the delectable sight of Kerry's bum.

That was because she was down on all fours, her round bum in the air, her head under the bed in which he had slept the night before. As he watched, she wiggled out from underneath it, a small tin box in her hands. Sitting back on her heels, she opened the box and extracted what looked to be a stack of letters. As she unfolded the first one, she glanced furtively at the door.

Her shriek was covered only by the sound of the tin box scudding across the floor. "God in heaven, you startled me," she gasped, thumping a fist against her breast.

"My sincerest apology. I did not realize you were . . ." he motioned lazily toward the bed, *"here."*

Her face colored instantly. "Oh. Aye," she muttered, and quickly moved to gather the letters she had scattered across the pine-plank floor.

"I can return later if you'd like."

"Oh no!" she practically shouted, and quickly stuffed the letters into the tin box before scrambling to her feet. She held the box closely to her side as she made an attempt to brush the dirty smudges from her knees. "I, um . . . forgot that I had some things in this room," she said sheepishly, now brushing her gown with a vengeance.

"Of course. It is your house after all."

"Aye." She glanced nervously about the room before switching the tin box to the crook of her other arm and smiling brightly at him. "Well then. Have you eaten? May made a batch of—"

"*Cullen skink.* Yes, I had some."

"Oh." Her gaze dipped to her feet for a moment. "Your clothes. We've laundered them," she said, nodding toward a corner.

Arthur shifted his gaze to see his clothes, laundered and pressed. Oddly enough, the sight of the waistcoat made him shudder. He actually preferred the freedom the borrowed linen shirt and trousers afforded him. "Thank you."

"Mmm," she said, peering up at him through thick lashes. "Well. I suppose you'd like to sleep."

Sleep. He had wanted to yes, but gazing at her now, the thick black braid draped over one shoulder, sleep was the farthest thing from his mind. It was amazing to him that a woman could be so appealing in a bland shade of gray, her hair unadorned, her lovely face without cosmetic enhancement. Oh, but Kerry McKinnon was appealing, terribly so, and in more ways than he cared to admit.

Regardless of the fact that she was a woman as far removed from his world as anyone could possibly be.

It was, unfortunately, almost laughable that he had somehow managed to end up in this remote little glen in Scotland, charmed by this woman . . . a woman who now cocked her head to one side and regarded him curiously.

Arthur managed to shove away from the door. "Yes, I should sleep while I can. McKinnon has a peculiar notion about what time a man should rise around here."

That brought a soft smile to Kerry's lips and a glimmer of amusement to her eye. "He willna harm you, not really."

Seeing as how he could scarcely move a limb, Arthur considered that open to debate.

"I'll leave you, then. Sweet dreams," she murmured, and started toward the door. As she moved to pass him, he caught a scent of lavender, and impetuously, instinctively, his arm shot out, catching her in the abdomen before she could pass and leaning into her before she could step away, breathing in her scent. "I would sleep better with the memory of your lips on mine."

Her fair cheeks flushed instantly; her smile deepened as she dropped her gaze to his arm around her midriff. "It is not wise."

"But I'd like it all the same, Kerry McKinnon, and I promise, so will you."

She laughed. "You are shameless."

Oh, he was shameless all right—she had no idea just how shameless. He pulled her into his side, his mouth on her hair. "Completely and irrevocably shameless," he muttered, and gently pushed her backward, out of the open doorway, so that she was standing directly in front of him.

Her arresting blue eyes were smiling up at him now, and Arthur lowered his head to hers, barely touching her lips with his, skimming the plump surface, purposefully tantalizing himself. With his hand, he gently touched her slender neck beside the thick rope of hair hanging over her shoulder, and moved his lips across hers. She sighed softly; he felt her breath in his mouth, her hand fall delicately to his waist.

He slipped one arm around her back, pulled her closer to him so that he could feel the length of her supple body against his, the swell of her breast in his chest, the slight curve of her stomach against his groin. Kerry sighed again, tilted her head backward, and Arthur deepened the kiss, devouring her like a French delicacy, tasting the valleys of her mouth. Her body arched into him, moved against him, pushed him once more past the point of a gentleman's reason.

He struggled to stay on the surface of that kiss, fighting the drag of desire that threatened to pull him under in a vortex and very gently, very reluctantly, broke away. Kerry remained pressed against him, her eyes closed, her lips, slightly pursed, wet and lush with the remnant of his kiss, until she, too, slowly opened her eyes.

They stood for a long moment, just looking at one another, his arm securely around her. He brushed a wisp of hair from her temple, touched the contour of her cheek with one finger. There was no need for words; the desire flowing between them was well understood. And Arthur believed they could have stood there all night like that, simply gazing at one another. But with nothing more than a softly seductive smile, Kerry silently slipped from his embrace and into the corridor, still clutching the tin box, one hand smoothing the side of her hair as she moved away from him, walking, Arthur noted, a little crooked.

Exhaling a long breath, he turned into the room and looked at the bed.

He wished for all the world that morning would go ahead and come, as there would be no sleep for him tonight.

Not after that kiss.

Chapter Ten

THE MEN WERE already gone by the time Kerry roused herself the next morning from a sleep made fitful by dreams—rather erotic dreams—of Arthur Christian.

Dreams that awakened a living, breathing beast within her that craved his touch, made her feel pleasingly faint when she recalled the feel of his hands and his lips on her skin, and made her imagine the many different ways and places those hands could touch her again.

Such thoughts were intensely distracting, and Kerry spent the morning weeding the floundering little kitchen garden so that she would not have to endure May's questioning looks, tackling a thick tangle of vines that could hang a grown man and plants of such strange appearance that she was almost afraid to touch them. *When had the garden become so overgrown?*

The work did little to soothe her fever.

As she yanked and pulled at the stubborn weeds, her mind wandered from her increasing anxiety about the glen, to torrid thoughts of Arthur, images of him holding himself above her in the throes of lovemaking that made her flush hot. What sort of woman had she become that she could dream of such blatantly carnal activities, and worse, *feel* them as she worked in her garden? She had not thought of lovemaking since long before her husband had died, and quite honestly, she could scarcely remember what it was like to be held by a man. *But Arthur* . . . Arthur evoked something in her she had never really known existed, something that yearned for the feel of a man deep inside her.

Kerry suddenly sat back on her heels, shocked by the indecency of her thoughts, and pressed her dirty hands against her face to douse the burn in her cheeks. Was this what she had become, a wanton, thinking such indecent, lewd . . . *delicious* thoughts?

Aye, they *were* delicious thoughts; thoughts that warmed her all over and made her belly tingle in that queer way she had not known in so many long years. Moving thoughts that banished all else from her mind, refusing entry even to a wee bit of common sense. Fluid thoughts that melted her, made her feel strangely pretty, made her want to look at him again and again, *touch* him.

Everywhere.

Embarrassed, Kerry impulsively shoved her hands into the black dirt, digging for the root ball of one large, purple-stalked plant. She should be concentrating on the problems at hand, not commending herself to hell.

And Lord, her problems needed all of her undivided attention now.

Reluctantly, and with more than a little difficulty, she forced herself to review her predicament again as she had a thousand times or more, searching for answers. Not that anything had changed, oh no—she had read the letters again last night, hoping in vain that perhaps she had misinterpreted something in Mr. Regis's letter. But she hadn't misinterpreted a bloody thing—Mr. Regis was nothing if not precise—they were to be evicted, and every day that passed was one more day she had lost in finding a solution.

Yet she felt an overwhelming and increasing determination to survive this catastrophe. Her journey to Dundee and back had awakened a staggering and surprising belief in herself. For the first time in her life, she thought herself capable of existing without a husband, or a mother, or a father. She had always thought of herself as her mother's unfortunate daughter, or her husband's wife and caregiver. Even when Fraser's ability to oversee their modest holdings had left him, and she oversaw the old McKinnon clan holdings, she still believed *he* was the one who provided for them all.

It had taken that extraordinary journey from Dundee to show her that she, Kerry McKinnon, was a survivor. She could survive without Fraser, without Lord Moncrieffe, without even Thomas. She was capable of shaping her destiny, capable of surviving the worst. And by God, she intended to survive this threat to her hearth, even though she hadn't the slightest notion how to stop what was happening. She only knew that she would not lose everything and be sent to the certain hell that awaited her in Glasgow. She would die first!

Kerry's shoulders sagged; her hands fell away from the purple plant.

Exactly who did she think she fooled with such bravado? What, did she think a pot of gold would suddenly appear and chase all her troubles away? This morning, after she had read the letters again, she had taken the old bonnet in which she kept the household funds, turned the lining inside out, and dumped the contents on the threadbare counterpane of her bed. And as she very carefully counted what she had, twice and three times to be very sure, she had realized that there wasn't enough there to even get them through the summer, much less into the autumn months.

Tears blinding her, she had stuffed the money into the bonnet lining and returned it to its hiding place.

She had pondered selling all of the McKinnon possessions that weren't nailed to a floor. Fraser had been fortunate enough to inherit many nice things from his father, but after carefully reviewing everything that she might sell—furniture, a bit of bone china, a few gold trinkets, an old plow—Kerry seriously doubted that all of it together was worth more than a few hundred pounds. Nowhere near the five thousand pounds she owed Baron Moncrieffe, not to mention the extraordinary sum owed the Bank of Scotland.

Perhaps, then, the McKinnon clan could move on as so many had done before them. Perhaps that was not such a bad solution after all—perhaps God did not intend for her to remain in Glenbaden as she had always believed.

But where would they go? Others had gone to the shore to earn a living harvesting the sea, but it was rumored that there was not enough in all of the sea to support so many dispossessed of their homes and livelihood.

America? She had heard tell of the abundant opportunities there for everyone, regardless of class or nationality. While she hadn't enough money for passage for all of them, the sale of the beeves might possibly bring enough. All right, then, but once in America, then what? They could hardly earn enough from the beeves to establish them all in a foreign land.

Kerry yanked hard at the purple-stalked plant again, flatly refusing to give in to its stubborn roots. She would not allow herself to think of what options were left to them all, but one thing was certain—she would *not* go to Glasgow.

She yanked again. And again, only harder.

There had to be another way. There *had* to be another way, and damn it, she would find it or die trying.

The plant finally came free of the earth, sending clumps of soil flying everywhere.

The next few days passed in a whirl of emotional distraction as Kerry frantically sought solutions to her dilemma.

The only bright spot in her miserable existence was the presence of Arthur.

He teased her mercilessly, stole intimate touches of her, would catch her alone and kiss her passionately before leaving her breathless and flushed and smiling like a lunatic. The stolen touches and the secret kisses helped to make her numb to the terrible dilemma she faced, if only for snatches of time. But even when she felt her looming disaster keenly, Arthur's tenacity and cheerful demeanor buoyed her.

He was even beginning to make a dent in Thomas's armor.

Not even Thomas could fault a man who could smile in the face of all he had put Arthur through. For reasons entirely unclear to Kerry, Thomas contrived every despicable, backbreaking chore he could throw at him, from maneuvering an ancient plow behind two old oxen, to duping him into climbing to the top of Din Fallon in search of a haggis nest. The nest, of course, was purely an invention of Thomas's imagination. Haggis was a Scottish dish made of the entrails of a sheep, which everyone knew.

Everyone except Arthur Christian.

Kerry had not seen this particular jest coming—she had been too worried about the hens, which were not laying. But when she discovered what Thomas had done, she had angrily threatened to strangle him herself, a threat to which Thomas had merely shrugged. "A man's got to know how to survive up here, lassie."

That scurrilous remark had only served to anger her further, and Thomas had rather sheepishly taken himself off to the barn when she had reminded him that Scots were known for their hospitality, and that she certainly hoped he met with the same hospitality he offered Arthur when he finally set off for his grand journey to America.

The afternoon passed at a turtle's pace; it seemed the arms on her father's clock would not move. When an hour stretched into several more, Kerry was frantically convinced that Arthur had met with some dire fate, if not his death. She could imagine his magnificent form sprawled, broken by a fall onto the rocky crags. So concerned was she that when dusk began to fall, she insisted Thomas form a search party, but it was interrupted by the sound of a horn from one of the other cottages in the glen.

Kerry rushed to the little yard of the white house, Thomas close on her heels.

Arthur had returned, whistling lightheartedly as he walked along—albeit with a limp he most decidedly had not left with—carrying a coarsely woven sack slung jauntily over one shoulder. Thomas and Kerry were quickly joined by Big Angus and May, and the four of them watched in awe as Arthur strolled crookedly but nonchalantly down the rutted path between the thatched cottages below, nodding and speaking to their neighbors.

As he approached the white house, Kerry noticed that his trousers were rent in at least two places, his beautiful boots scarred beyond repair, and the stain of his labor marked great circles on the back and the underarms of his shirt.

In spite of his down-at-the-heel appearance, he broke into a wide grin. "Thomas, my good friend," he called cheerfully. "What a clever chap you are, sir, very clever indeed! You were quite right in your estimation—the haggis nest is indeed atop the highest crag of Din Fallon, and in a most unreachable spot. I rather fancied myself a haggis bird, flopping about as I was. But being the limber fellow that I am, I managed to gain the top crag and am quite pleased that I did. You cannot imagine what a veritable treasure I beheld on that frosty peak!"

Thomas glanced uneasily at Big Angus and artfully ignored the murderous glare May bestowed on him before squinting closely at Arthur. "Aye?" he said cautiously.

"Oh *aye*," Arthur drawled. "I would that I had four bags, for I would easily have filled them all with the bountiful treasure of your haggis. I most eagerly anticipated what tasty pie our May might make of it all, and as I pondered that," he continued, carelessly swinging the bag from his shoulder, "I was inexplicably reminded of a particularly dull evening at the Kenilworth in Edinburgh, when I had occasion to speak with a chap who was dining on haggis stew."

With that, he tossed the bag at Thomas, who caught it, midair, in his fist.

"Yes sir, I did indeed recall that haggis stew, and now I pray that your haggis pie might be as . . . *tastefully* . . . prepared as that very delectable dish in Edinburgh. You will excuse me, won't you? I should very much like to wash the, ah, *haggis* from my hands." He nodded, walked on in his uneven gait toward the pump, whistling again.

Big Angus, May, and Kerry turned as one toward Thomas. He blinked at the sack; slowly, he lifted the thing and opened it, his nose immediately wrinkling at the foul odor that rushed up to greet him. Big Angus was instantly at Thomas's side, craning his neck to see inside before bursting into a gale of deep laughter. He snatched the sack from Thomas's hand and held it out for May to see. *"Sheep shit,"* he boomed gleefully, and roared at the unintelligible utterance Thomas made under his breath. May instantly burst into a string of Gaelic admonishing Thomas while Big Angus slapped him delightedly and repeatedly on the back.

Unnoticed by the others, Kerry turned to look at Arthur. Pumping water into a bucket, he seemed to sense her, and looked up, flashing a warm smile and a wink.

It was at that exact moment that Kerry realized she would never again know a man quite as wonderful as Arthur Christian. She loved him. With all her heart, she loved that beautiful stranger.

That sentiment was confirmed again the next day when Willie Keith brought the post and the news that one of Baron Moncrieffe's fine, dappled roans had been hurt in a riding mishap. The horse was loose just below the glen, but no one could get close enough to the frightened creature to tend its leg. The prevailing thought was that he'd have to be put down, presumably with a gun.

Arthur, working to repair the chicken coop, overheard this and immediately came striding forward. "Where is this horse?"

"You canna miss him, milord. He be just below the glen, at the end of Loch Eigg."

"How far?"

"A mile, no more," Kerry said. "We've a wagon—"

"No time for it. But if you've any oats you can spare, I'd be very obliged. Here, lad, show me where this horse is," he said, and put his arm around Willie Keith's shoulders, gently pushing him into the barley field so that he might lead him to where the injured horse was holding Baron Moncrieffe's shotgun at bay.

Following the rutted road from Glenbaden, Kerry and Thomas found the horse and a small gathering of people growing on the northern edge of Loch Eigg. Some were seated on wagons, others milled in small groups, all of them come for the blood sport of seeing someone shoot a young roan from a distance. In the middle of the crowd was the tall, imposing figure of Baron Moncrieffe, arms akimbo, his son Charles beside him, laughing as gaily as if this were a Sunday picnic.

Thomas had not even brought the wagon to a halt before Kerry was running toward them, a sack of oats clutched tightly in one hand. She came to a halt in their midst, her gaze sweeping ahead to where they looked and pointed.

Arthur stood alone in the heath, his hands stuffed in his pockets. The injured horse was pawing the ground a few yards away under the shelter of a lone oak tree. His terror was clearly evident from the whites of his eyes, which were visible even from where Kerry stood. Arthur removed one hand from his pocket and scratched the

back of his neck. He took one small, tentative step
forward, but the horse neighed and moved backward,
tripping on his bad leg. Arthur immediately went down
on his haunches, clasped his hands together, and appeared to be talking to the horse. The roan's ears pricked
forward; he lifted his head and swung it to one side to
better see Arthur, as if he was terribly interested in what
he had to say.

After a moment, Arthur rose very slowly and took
another unhurried step toward the horse, then another.
The horse whinnied at him, bared his teeth, but Arthur
kept moving, kept talking. Kerry could almost hear his
calm, soothing voice, and whatever he might have said
was having the desired effect. Slowly and evenly, he
moved closer, until he was an arm's length from the
horse.

The crowd around Kerry grew quiet as they watched,
gasping collectively when Arthur reached out and
touched the horse's nose. Everyone held their breath as
he moved forward, reached for the horse's neck. The
horse did not move, and in fact, he seemed to sag a little,
as if relief and a sense of comfort had touched him.

Arthur stroked the horse's neck for a long while before he went down again on his haunches to examine the
injured leg. After a moment, he stood again, stroked the
horse's neck and shoulders once more before turning and
striding purposefully across the heath. His gait was long
and sure, so sure, that Kerry could not help but smile
with pride as she watched him.

Unthinkingly, she glanced around her, starting inwardly at Baron Moncrieffe's piercing look. "Who is
he?" he asked curtly.

Her smile faded; Kerry couldn't think. "An Englishman, my lord. I, ah, he—"

"*Och,* he's naught but a wanderer."

Surprised, Kerry turned to look at Thomas, but he
was looking at Moncrieffe, his expression inscrutable.

"A wanderer?" Moncrieffe's voice was full of disbelief.

"Aye, an English wanderer he is, in search of poetry, naught more."

Moncrieffe eyed Thomas suspiciously before turning around to greet Arthur as he strode into their midst. "Well sir," he said, exaggerating a low bow, "it appears I owe you a debt of gratitude." He extended his hand and smiled thinly. "You must allow me to thank you properly at Moncrieffe House."

Arthur glanced at his proffered hand, hesitated briefly—enough for Moncrieffe to notice—before accepting it. "You owe me nothing, sir—I'm rather fond of horses all in all."

"You are an Englishman," Moncrieffe noted as Arthur let go his hand. "We've not many visitors to our little corner of the world . . . particularly Englishmen. You really must come for a wee *dram buidheach*. My man will take the horse now."

"Thank you, but I shouldn't want to impose on your hospitality."

"It's no imposition," Moncrieffe continued smoothly. "Especially for the late McKinnon's English acquaintance." He glanced over his shoulder at a weathered old man and nodded curtly.

"I beg your pardon, sir, but you are mistaken. I never met the late Mr. McKinnon," Arthur responded.

Moncrieffe shrugged indifferently. "No, then? I was quite certain McKinnon mentioned an English acquaintance. Ah, well then," Moncrieffe sighed, "if you willna accept my hospitality, then you will surely let me pay you, my lord . . . ?"

"As I said, you owe me nothing, but you do owe the roan—his leg was injured long before today. He's a gash on his fetlock that is festering and requires immediate attention," Arthur coolly informed him.

That pronouncement clearly surprised Moncrieffe;

his gaze instantly flew to Charles, who scruffed his toe in the dirt, smiling sheepishly at Kerry.

"Mrs. McKinnon, might I find oats in that sack?" Arthur asked impatiently, and took the sack from her hand. He did not wait for Moncrieffe to gain his composure; he was already striding across the heath before Moncrieffe could say more.

The baron was not amused; he turned to Kerry, his eyes blazing. "I willna be fooled, Mrs. McKinnon!" he snapped. "Fraser McKinnon looked to England and it served him naught!"

Fraser had looked to England? What did that mean? Kerry glanced at Thomas, but he looked just as baffled.

"Will the horse be all right?" Charles asked.

"Aye, Charles!" Moncrieffe responded hotly, and leveled another heated gaze on Kerry as he clamped a hand on his son's shoulder. "Doona be coy, Mrs. McKinnon. You may think your Englishman will help, but it changes nothing! Come then, Charles," he said, and pushed his son in the direction of a waiting carriage. He cast one last scathing glance across her as he followed Charles, and Kerry felt it rake her to the bone. Her stomach twisted; she looked away from the sight of Charles. *Never.* Never would she go to him, not for her clan, not for anyone. She needed to breathe, sucked in the air, but Thomas was in front of her, his expression dark.

"What did he mean, then, that it changes nothing?" Thomas demanded suspiciously.

She shrugged, shifted her gaze to Arthur, who was on his haunches again, inspecting the injured fetlock as the horse munched happily at his sack of oats. "I really canna say that I know," she lied. At Thomas's skeptical look, she threw up her hands. "He's got some maggot in his head, Thomas! I canna read his mind!" That only made Thomas's eyes narrow with more suspicion, so Kerry looked around him, to where Arthur tended the horse. "He's quite good with horses, is he not?"

"Aye," Thomas growled, reluctantly shifting his gaze

to watch Arthur soothe the horse and wrap his fetlock with a cloth one of the baron's men brought him.

Kerry watched him, too, careful not to show any emotion in spite of being greatly bothered by something Moncrieffe had said. She could not imagine that Fraser had an English acquaintance, for surely she would have known it. And even if he had known an Englishman, what could it possibly signify? It was obviously nothing more than Moncrieffe's intimidation of her, an attempt to confuse her.

Still, it puzzled her.

She fretted over it, turning it around and around in her mind, trying to make sense of it as she watched Arthur finish his work and give the roan over to Moncrieffe's man.

As the last of the group dissipated, Arthur, looking rather pleased with himself, strolled up the hill to where Kerry and Thomas stood waiting with the wagon. "I daresay the boy will feel much improved on the morrow. He's a fighter, that one. Won't let a nasty gash or a stubborn Scot get him down," he quipped.

"Aye, you've got a way with the horses," Thomas grudgingly admitted.

That caused Arthur's grin to broaden impossibly. "Good God, McKinnon, do my ears deceive me, or did I hear a kind word fall from your mouth?" he asked, then laughed roundly when Thomas rolled his eyes, muttered his opinion in Gaelic, and fairly vaulted onto the wagon.

Still chuckling, Arthur smiled down at Kerry. "I'll have that old goat you name cousin eating haggis from my hand before I'm gone, watch and see if I don't," he said, and casually put a hand on her back to help her up after Thomas.

Kerry's legs moved, but for once, there was no strange flash of heat that she seemed to experience every time he so casually touched her. She barely felt his hand on her back at all—his words had stunned her, rumbling like thunder through her, rattling her to the core.

"... before I'm gone ..."

It was the first time she had allowed herself to think of it, the first time she had seen the image of his back as he walked out her front door in her mind's eye.

Never to return again.

How? How could she stand there and watch him leave?

An odd sense of panic swept her; she felt a hard urge to fling herself into his arms and beg him not to go, to never leave her or Glenbaden ... but her head worked to overrule her foolish heart as Arthur climbed up beside her, settling comfortably against her, and reminding Thomas that he also had quite a way with milk cows, which immediately gained an argument from Thomas, who flatly refused to praise his skill *that* far. As the argument raged, Kerry's practical head calmly told her heart that he would walk out her front door in a matter of days—of course he would!—for what was there in Glenbaden for a man like Arthur Christian? Oh aye, he would walk out of her door, and when he did, she would have to face the inevitable fact that she would never see him again. His presence here was nothing more than an interesting quirk of fate, a moment in time that had brought her an unexpected measure of comfort in her darkest hour.

He had woken her up one morning, shown her the sun. How could she now watch him leave, knowing that with his departure she would slip into an eternal sleep again?

For as much as she loved him, *adored* him, Lord Arthur Christian of the English Sutherlands was as far removed from simple Kerry McKinnon and Glenbaden as any one human being could be. For as much as she *desired* him—*and oh God, she did*—he was never meant to be here. Not now. Not ever. Not with her.

This interlude would end.

He would walk out her door, leaving her broken heart in his wake.

And she convinced herself, as they bounced along the rutted road home, that it was perhaps quite all right that he should leave her heart in pieces—she certainly had no other use for it.

Not after him.

Chapter Eleven

Arthur rose before dawn the next morning, thanks to another hazy nocturnal visit from Phillip, who stood to one side as Arthur doctored the horse in the heath. Except that the horse had been shot and was dying, and Phillip stood, twirling his hat on one finger, yawning with boredom at Arthur's efforts to save the horse. "You won't save him—he prefers death to this life," he remarked nonchalantly, and Arthur had jerked around, intent on strangling Phillip for his indifference.

He had awakened before he could reach him.

He had also awakened before anyone else in the glen. So having had a breakfast of cold bread, he was sitting on a tree stump just in front of the white house, where he paused in the task of buffing his boots long enough to admire the sun rising above the horizon. He had discovered, having been in Glenbaden more than a week now, that much to his great surprise, the early morning hours were among the finest of the day. He loved the morning, a simple truth he had never known.

He had never risen with dawn's first light before now. But in Glenbaden, he did so each day and would wash and shave, dress in the simple clothes that allowed him enormous freedom of movement, then walk quietly down the hall, following the scent of ham May prepared for the men before they began their work.

But he would always pause before the door of Kerry's room, which she left slightly ajar, and push it open just enough so that he might gaze at her sleeping. She was angelic in those morning hours of sleep; she slept with her hair unbound, spilling all around her and framing her lovely face. Arthur longed to touch one of the delicate curls at her temple, touch two fingers to the place where the skin was tender and soft . . .

But he always continued on, taking care to keep his steps light so as not to wake her.

At the scarred wooden table, Arthur would devour the oats and ham May put before him, tending to eat twice as much food as he had ever had in London. He found this particularly interesting, because his trousers were looser than they had ever been in his life, despite his eating as much as the enormous sow they kept.

Once he had his fill of the hearty breakfast, he would join Thomas and Big Angus in the yard, where Thomas, having abandoned his considerable efforts to kill Arthur, would divide the chores among them. And then he would be off, walking briskly through the crisp, cool morning. It pleased him tremendously to watch the mist lift as the sun made its slow path across the morning sky, and he remained quietly astonished at how the light would begin to dance across the dew-soaked grass, its warmth spreading throughout the glen. It was a beauty he had not often seen in his six and thirty years on this earth, and only then as he approached it from a night of revelry. But in London, the air was often so thick with smoke and other unhealthy vapors that he wasn't entirely certain anything like dew existed.

Dew.

Good God, what was happening to him?

He was adrift in strange waters, that was what. He was floating and bobbing merrily around a question to which he had no answers. Astounding, but he *enjoyed* this existence in the Scottish glen. He relished the hard work, the sense of accomplishment . . . the sense of *purpose*. Yet this life was alien to him, and really, wholly unsuitable to a man of his stature in the *ton*. He was the proverbial fish out of water, the English gentleman playing at a bit of rustic farming. Yet he liked it, liked it very much indeed; there were so many things that touched him here, he thought, as he watched the sun chase away the morning mist. Touched him deeply.

A sound to his right caused him to turn, a smile slowly spread his lips. Kerry walked sleepily across the small yard toward the pump, her hand covering a yawn. She was barefoot; the hem of her gray skirts wet from dragging across the morning dew. She paused at the pump, stretched her arms high above her head for a moment, and then leaned forward, her back strong and lean as she filled a bucket with water.

That was, he thought idly, exactly what he found so beautiful about her. The more he watched Kerry in the midst of Glenbaden, the more he found her completely and utterly irresistible.

She had, in the course of these days, come to embody all the qualities of a woman he now realized he craved. Kerry McKinnon was real; there was no pretense about her, nothing false. She was not afraid of work, and in fact, he would wager that she worked as hard as any man he had ever known. It hadn't taken him long to realize that it was she who kept this little glen alive, kept them all moving, working, living. Even he, a jaded veteran of the highest reaches of cynicism, *believed* her cheerfulness when she greeted her neighbors and remarked on another fine day—even those that were miserably cold and wet. But that was what was so unique about Kerry—he truly respected her unwavering ability to endure hardship without the slightest complaint, and moreover, he truly admired her grit to survive when it was so painfully obvious that there was no money.

He had known men who could not and did not endure the hardships Kerry McKinnon seemed to balance on the tip of one finger.

She was the very soul of this glen, the single light shining on its meager existence, and the reason, he suspected, that many of these poor souls remained, inspired and rallied by her determination. Arthur had no doubt whatsoever that she was partly the reason Thomas McKinnon had never left the glen as he threatened to do at least twice daily.

And he could only thank God that Regis had defied his order and gone to Fort Williams instead of coming straightaway to Glenbaden as he had instructed him to do. He could no more evict Kerry McKinnon than he could cut off his right hand. Oh, he no longer doubted it was Kerry's eviction he had ordered; he had seen enough, heard enough to know.

It was astounding, if not oddly comical, that he had happened upon Phillip's land in such a bizarre fashion. It was so unbelievable that a man had to wonder if there hadn't been some sort of divine intervention. If Kerry hadn't shot him in the road that evening, he never would have known who he evicted, much less stopped it. He never would have known the simple pleasure and beauty of this glen.

He never would have known Kerry.

Ah, Kerry.

There he was again, drifting into uncharted waters. In a matter of days, he would leave Glenbaden, find Mr. Regis, and stop the eviction. He could not and would not remove Kerry from Glenbaden; no, he would find a way to somehow fix this little mess, a way that would enable her to remain in this idyllic portrait she had painted in his mind and in his heart.

As for him, well, he wasn't quite certain what he would do after that. He wasn't certain of a bloody thing any more, really. Nothing seemed familiar to him, not his emotions, not his thoughts, not his body or his desires.

And as he watched her turn toward the house—flashing a brilliant smile when she saw him sitting there, he noticed—he wondered what he would do to fix himself, for while he would see to it that Kerry remained in Glenbaden where she belonged, he could not. He was forced by birth and duty and circumstance to leave this place and this quality of life he was beginning to cherish.

As well as the beautiful woman walking toward him now.

"I suppose now that you mean to frighten Thomas from his wits by rising before the dawn," she said as she stepped into the yard.

"Actually, I was thinking that the sight of *you* up and about before the dawn should put him directly in his grave."

Kerry laughed, pausing at the gate to push a curl from her face with the back of her hand. "A body must rise early 'round here or starve—most mornings, you've not left even a wee bit of bread for the rest of us," she said, pushing through the gate.

"I beg your pardon, but I have merely followed the laws of nature—a man must eat what is placed in front of him or be devoured by Thomas in the course of some death-defying duty he has dictated."

Kerry's laughter spilled out into the morning mist as she gathered her skirts in one hand and moved forward. But her foot caught the sagging hem of her skirt and she stumbled; Arthur half stood, catching her by the elbow. She righted herself, but his hand closed tightly around her elbow, drew her to him. The sparkle in her pale blue eyes darkened; she flushed with a heat Arthur felt beneath his coarse linen shirt as the current of desire flowed between them.

His gaze locked with hers; slowly, he rose to his full height, unnoticing of the boot that slipped from his lap to the grass at his feet. He ignored the voice of warning in his brain and pulled her into his arms. A thought had been plaguing him for days now, teasing the far reaches of his mind, dueling with the sense of duty instilled in him from the cradle. *He could not leave her, not without caressing her, kissing her breast.* "Try as I might, I can't seem to stop wanting you," he admitted softly.

Her lashes fluttered; she dropped her gaze to his shoulder.

"I can't seem to stop wanting to taste your skin," he said, and brushed the curl at her temple with the back of his knuckle so that he could kiss the supple skin there. "You are my last thought as I sleep and my first thought as the sun rises."

Her body sighed; she whispered his name so softly that he barely heard her. He brushed his lips against her forehead. "You are beautiful," he said against her skin. "So beautiful. I want to possess you, possess you completely, every inch of you."

Her hands came up; she caught the open lapel of his shirt and closed her eyes. "You canna imagine how your words flutter like a bird inside me," she whispered. "But . . . but this is *so* very unwise."

Arthur sighed into her hair. "Yes," he responded truthfully, reluctantly. "It is unwise." He grasped her hands at his lapel, held them tightly in his own for a moment as he prepared to let her go.

"B-but I want to possess you, too," she whispered. "*Completely.*"

The utterance seized his heart; he felt an unusual tingling beneath his collar. He squeezed her hands tightly. "You don't know what you are saying."

A shy, lopsided smile spread her lips. "*Och,* have you forgotten I was married, lad?"

Arthur suddenly felt as wobbly as her smile. She knew exactly what she asked for, and he wanted her to possess him, wanted it badly. But he also realized in that extraordinary moment that he had brought her to this state of wanting, that in the time he had spent in

Glenbaden, he had seduced and cajoled and inveigled his way into her graces. Kerry had understated the obvious—this was not only unwise, it was insanity. Absolute insanity, and he had a moral obligation—albeit an extremely weak one at the moment—to stop this before it progressed any further and consumed them both.

He brought her hands to his mouth and kissed the backs of them before bestowing her with a roguish smile perfected through years of balls and routs and assemblies. "Madam, you could bring a man to a state of knee-bending devotion. It's small wonder that your cousin wields such a heavy hand," he said, and dropped her hands. "Speaking of that devil incarnate, I should best be about the odious tasks assigned to me today for God knows what he would do should he find me idle."

He shoved his hands, hands that strained to touch her, deep into his pockets and stepped back, still smiling, even though his heart had climbed up to his throat, choking him. Kerry looked confused, but sheepishly dropped her gaze to her feet, unconsciously smoothing the hair at her temple. "Aye. He'll not let you rest." And she turned awkwardly toward the house, her step quick but uneven as she moved away from him, dragging all the dew with her as she went.

Arthur bit his lip, battled the urge to call her back . . . and his deep regret.

The next day marked the beginning of the barley harvest. The inhabitants of Glenbaden were, in Arthur's opinion, overly excited about the prospect of such a small harvest, and he remarked as much to Thomas. That was because, Thomas stoically informed him, there was a crop to be harvested this year, unlike the previous two years, when the barley had not matured properly.

He showed Arthur the grass, explained how it would be used for bread and barley-bree, which Arthur understood to mean Scotch whiskey, and the stalks would make winter hay to feed the cattle. Thomas showed him how to hold and swing the long curved scythes they used to cut the grass, and they walked side by side, cutting together in a solid rhythm. They were followed by two more cutters, and behind them, May and Kerry stripped the grain from the stalks, which Big Angus and two older men bundled into big rounds.

The cutting was a relaxing endeavor, the sort of mindless activity Arthur had come to appreciate in the glen. But while his mind enjoyed the respite from weightier thoughts, his body was cramping in agony by late afternoon. The muscles of his back felt as if they would burn clear through to his chest; his right hand was covered with a bloody blister from the friction of the scythe handle he had gripped all day.

When the late afternoon sun began to weaken into evening, Thomas halted the work for the day. Stretching his back, Arthur glanced behind him to the path they had cut, certain they were near to finishing the harvest. To his great astonishment, however, it seemed that less than a quarter of the field had been cut. As he stood gaping in wonder at that phenomenon, Thomas slapped him hard on the back and laughed. "Doona fret, laddie. There'll be more for ye on the morrow," he said, and laughed again as he walked away.

Arthur smirked at Thomas's retreating back, taking some satisfaction in the knowledge that in two days' time, when he left for Dundee and Mr. Regis, Thomas McKinnon would miss him. Oh *aye,* he would miss him very much indeed.

He walked after Thomas, following him and the others who, he thought irritably, remained remarkably cheerful after a day of such excruciatingly hard labor. They moved away from the white house, where an old, unused barnlike structure stood. Arthur was mildly surprised when Thomas turned left, going with the others instead of toward the house, where he fully expected to enjoy one of May's delicious meals. Much to his great

chagrin on that score, Big Angus and May followed
Thomas. He paused, hands on hips, desiring of a suitable
explanation as to *why* his supper would not be ready at
the usual time.

"It is our custom to celebrate the start of a harvest
with a common meal."

Arthur turned toward the sound of Kerry's voice behind him, wincing at the sharp stiffness in the muscles of
his neck. "Indeed?"

Kerry nodded, walking easily to where he stood,
apparently unaffected by the hard work of stripping
the grain. "We've a Scotch broth, only we've not any
mutton."

He had no idea what that meant, but said lightly,
"Sounds delightful," and pressed his hands to the small
of his back. "And when does this veritable feast begin?"
he asked, glancing idly at his blistered hand.

She stopped, suddenly grabbed his hand. "Dear
God!" she exclaimed, and Arthur was shaken from the
cloud of her lavender scent as she peered closely at the
blistered hand, pulling his arm out so that she might better see his wound. She stared at it for a moment, then
glanced up, her eyes filled with empathy. "Arthur . . .
your *hand*."

He shrugged. "A bit of a blister, that's all."

"A *bit?*" she echoed incredulously, and probed it gently, looking up to him again when he flinched at the pain
that caused. "It must be tended," she said authoritatively. "Come." She released his hand and walked purposefully ahead. He did not dare think to do anything
else but follow her.

He followed her into the kitchen of the white house,
where Kerry pulled a small wooden stool before a shelf
lining the top border of the window. She stepped onto
the stool and, reaching up on the tips of her toes, extracted a jar filled with the strange green-colored sub-
stance he had seen her use on Red Donner.

She leapt from the stool, impatiently motioned him onto the bench at the table. "You'll not care for the scent, but it will draw the blood and water from beneath your skin." Then she opened the jar, and he instinctively recoiled against the pungent odor that filled the room.

"The odor willna last long," she pertly informed him, and stuck two fingers into the jar with a little more gusto than Arthur liked, digging out a thick dollop of the stuff.

"I do not fear it, madam, in small doses. Are you certain this requires so much of the stuff?"

Kerry ignored him. "Here now, give me your hand. This might sting a bit, but you'll be dancing with May when I'm through, you have my vow." When he did not move as quickly as she liked, she grabbed his hand and jerked his arm forward. Before he could even open his mouth, she had slapped the foul paste on his palm, and an immediate fire went racing up his arm and down his torso, causing him to yelp with surprise.

But Kerry was strong and held his hand firmly in hers as she rubbed the grainy paste across the blister. The fire was almost instantly followed by a tingling cool; Arthur could feel the blister begin to diminish as the pus was slowly drawn. After a moment, Kerry stopped rubbing the paste onto his hand and retrieved a strip of cloth from a basket near the stove. She sat next to him, his hand on her lap, and wrapped it tightly. "You must keep this wrapped for two days or it will not heal properly."

Arthur looked at his hand, then at Kerry. She smiled sweetly, wrinkling her nose a bit. "It didna hurt terribly, did it now?" she asked.

How could he know? He was too focused on the cute little wrinkle on the bridge of her nose. He leaned forward, intent on kissing that wrinkle, but Kerry abruptly turned her head, and his lips fell to her shoulder instead. They sat that way for what seemed an eternity—his lips on the gray gown that covered her shoulder, her head turned slightly away—until Kerry turned toward him. Arthur caught the corner of her mouth as she turned, seeking the full of her lips.

One slender hand came up to cup his jaw as her lips parted beneath his.

Unthinkingly, he clasped her to him in a fierce embrace and kissed her fully, aware of every place they touched, of the smell of lavender, of the feel of her thick braid between them, the silken feel of her fair skin. He kissed all of that without leaving the soft valleys of her mouth or her tongue or her ripe lips. He kissed it all, touched it all, until the knowledge of his imminent departure began to pound away at his conscience.

He lifted his head and pressed her head against his chest with his bandaged hand and tried to catch his breath. Kerry's hand fell limply from his cheek to his shoulder; he held her even more tightly to him then, feeling her disappointment and not wanting to ever let go. His heart felt jagged inside him—he was torn between his great desire and his sense of propriety, weak though it was. Somehow, propriety won, and he heard himself say the unthinkable: "You know I must go soon."

She did not move, did not speak.

"I must be to Dundee." *I must stop your eviction!* "You know this, don't you?"

He felt the tremble in her body before she lifted her head and pushed away from his embrace, looking across the room, away from him. "Aye, of course I do," she said, and rose to her feet, swiping up the jar of thick paste in one hand as she moved away from him, toward the shelf. "You will miss me when you are gone, you know," she said hoarsely, and tried to laugh.

"I . . . I shall miss you greatly, Kerry," he muttered helplessly.

She did not respond, but climbed up on the stool, put the jar away, then climbed down and picked up a potato, pretending to study it. "When?" she asked.

He sighed wearily, glanced at his bandaged hand and

tried desperately to ignore the tug at his heartstrings. "On the morrow." He looked up, saw her hand swipe at her cheek.

"Doona look at me so," she said, turning the potato anxiously in her hand. "It's naught but the onion."

Except that it was a potato. He did not know what to do, did not know how to comfort her, or himself for that matter. But when Kerry turned toward him a moment later, she was smiling.

Yet she avoided his gaze, looked everywhere around the kitchen but at him. "Well then, you are properly patched for your journey. Shall we join the celebration, then?" she asked, and moved toward the door as if she intended to go on, regardless of his answer.

His was a peculiar feeling at that moment, an odd mixture of true regret and a sense of relief, as if he had almost strayed too deep into the ocean, had almost lost his footing in it. He rose, smiled insouciantly. "Let's," he said simply, and followed Kerry out of the house and into the waning light of the sun as it cast gold shadows on the uneven path. He walked along that golden path into a circle of gay laughter as the little community Kerry nourished drank from a common jug of whiskey.

Chapter Twelve

Dusk HAD DESCENDED in Glenbaden, and Kerry could only hope that the shadows masked her devastation.

It was ridiculous, she thought as she took the whiskey jug May offered her, to be so *affected* by his announcement. She had known it would come, probably could have predicted the moment he would choose to go. Not for a single moment had she believed it would end any differently. So why then, did it feel as if her heart was being torn in two?

Because she had come to adore him, unlike any other man she had ever known.

She took a swig of bitter Scotch whiskey and passed the jug along.

He had proven himself a rock, a man with a strength of character and disposition that made him quite literally irresistible. He seemed so very capable, so able to take everything in stride that she had, on more than one occasion, longed to tell him of her troubles, to lay her head on his chest and let him solve them for her. She had even allowed herself the fantasy of what it would be like to grow old with him. She loved him. *She loved him.*

Therein lied the spring of the violent conflict of her emotions. She loved him, but she could never have him.

A man like Arthur Christian belonged in the fancy drawing rooms of England where such troubles as hers did not exist. She could not and would not entangle him in hers.

Of course he would go ... *but how would she ever bear to watch him walk away?*

Kerry shook her head, forced herself to focus on Red Donner playing a lively jig on his fiddle, his sliced finger obviously much improved. Molly McKinnon and Belinda Donner danced to his tune, their skirts hiked high over their legs, their arms linked as they spun round and round the small fire as if they had not a single care in the world.

The poor women had cares they were not even aware of, she thought morosely, at least not until the morrow. She had already decided to tell them the truth, that they had less than a fortnight to decide what to do with their lives, as she was incapable of devising a way to save Glenbaden.

She would tell them all, admit her failure.

Just as soon as she was certain Arthur was gone—she would not add humiliation to her hurt.

The jug was passed to her again, and Kerry took another healthy swig before passing it along to someone on her right. Just beyond the circle in which they danced, Arthur sat on the ground with his shoulder propped against an old oak keg, watching her. Watching her in just the way he had from almost the moment they met, with a piercing hazel gaze that made her skin heat beneath her woolen gown. She kept her gaze averted from his, trying desperately to overcome the overwhelming sentiments warring in her body, her heart, and soul. God help her, but her longing was greater than she could possibly fathom, and the fear of his leaving agonizingly real. She desperately craved that heat and the odd tingling in the pit of her belly when he looked at her. She craved her mind's image of him, holding himself above her, thrusting deeper still ...

The thought jarred her, and all at once, Kerry was on her feet, in the midst of the other dancers. Holding her skirts tight, she kicked her feet in time to the music, her heels lifting higher than anyone else. Snatches of Arthur's face rushed by her as she leapt and twirled, leapt and twirled, laughing almost hysterically when Big Angus caught her arm and linked it through his, spinning her faster. Red Donner quickened the tempo, pushing the dancers into a frenzy of movement; someone collided with her and she stumbled backward, but Thomas caught her and heaved her into the crowd again.

She danced on, ignoring the perspiration beading on her back, too intent on using the time-worn tune to purge her of this insane longing, or at least tamp it down to the black hole in which it belonged. But as hard as she danced, it did nothing to ease her anguish—if anything, it only seemed to increase it. Myriad thoughts tumbled through her head; her mind and heart warred with blatant physical desire, the impropriety of her thoughts, and the overwhelmingly prurient longing to have a night of lovemaking that she would never have again. The very idea drained her of reason; she was caught in a web of physical desire, entrapped by unfathomable passion that rose up like a beast within her, stirring the rabid hunger for his touch, for the solace only he could give her.

When Red Donner ended the jig, Kerry collapsed on the grass, catching her breath as others around her laughed. She could not stop herself from seeking Arthur's gaze; he was still leaning against the keg, still watching her. His gaze was more intent, harder than she had ever seen it—she could feel it piercing her consciousness, as if he knew exactly what she was thinking.

Her stomach leapt; she faltered then, breaking the gaze between them and looking around at the others. But it was no use—she could feel his gaze boring through her still.

When the last of the whiskey was drunk, the little group began to stagger off toward their cottages in twos and threes, their laughter drifting up in the silence of the cold night. Arthur noted that Thomas had left early on having imbibed more than his fair share of the whiskey, stumbling up the rutted path to his loft above the barn. Big Angus hoisted the community pot onto his shoulder and he and May made their way to the cottage they shared below the white house, talking softly with one another.

Arthur remained, watching the last of the McKinnon clan without really seeing them—his mind's eye was still full of the vision of Kerry dancing. She had sprung into their midst like a wood nymph, graceful and light on her feet but demonic in her intensity. It was a provocative image, one he could not scrape from the back of his eyes. One that inflamed him.

When there was no one left but Arthur and Kerry, he watched her again as she moved to douse the little fire, remembering her skirts held high, the turn of her ankle as she leapt into the air. She glanced up at him and smiled shyly as she fingered the tail of her long thick braid. "I'd wager you've naught seen a harvest celebration such as this."

He had never seen a harvest celebration. "Can't say that I have. Found it right entertaining."

Kerry's smile faded a bit; she clasped her hands behind her back. "You might miss our customs in London."

That was an understatement—she had no idea how much he'd miss everything about this little place—the work, the scenery, the camaraderie . . . *you, Kerry, I will miss you.*

"We've a fresh batch of biscuits. I'll see to it that you've enough for a few days."

"That would be very kind."

She glanced away for a moment, seemed to want to speak. But when she looked at him again, she shrugged her slender shoulders as if they carried some enormous weight. "Well then, I suppose there is naught left but a good night's sleep."

Oh Kerry, there is so much left, so much left behind, so much . . .

"I wonder if my hope of sleeping until the sun has at least touched the sky are improved given Thomas's inordinate admiration of Scotch whiskey," he drawled, falling in beside Kerry as she began to move toward the white house.

She laughed lightly at that, the sound of it dripped like honey over him. "I wouldna be too hopeful were I you. The man has an uncanny way of recovering from his excesses."

Arthur did not respond—he was too aware of her, every fiber in him shimmering with the nearness of her and the knowledge that he would soon be gone. *He would never see her again.*

They walked in silence.

When they stepped into the kitchen, the two of them paused—a bit awkwardly, Arthur thought, seeing as how he wasn't quite sure where to put his hands.

"You'll be gone early, I suppose—"

"Yes." He shoved his hands in his pockets.

Kerry brushed an imaginary piece of lint from the lap of her gray gown. "Might you send word? I mean . . . so we would know that you arrived safely."

"Of course." He withdrew his hands, clasped them behind his back.

She nodded, kept brushing the lap of her gown. "Well then—"

"Kerry, thank you," he blurted, shoving his hands in his pockets again. "This has been . . ." *What could he say?* There were no words to describe this experience, no way to convey to her how much this extraordinary journey into Scotland had meant to him.

"Yes, it has," she said quietly. "You've a long journey ahead—I'll wish you a good night," she added, and solved any dilemma of a response by walking out of the kitchen. Arthur stood alone next to the scarred table, staring after her, wishing he could say all the things he longed to say to her.

But it was better this way. Yes, definitely better this way.

And he silently repeated that in his mind, over and over again as he walked to the room he had slept in for two weeks now, moving past her door without hesitation. Once in his small room, he moved sluggishly; peeling the linen shirt from his back as if it was a bandage, grimacing to himself when he looked at his own clothes hanging neatly in the wardrobe. He washed idly, his mind wandering, then moved to one of two small windows adorning the room and gazed up at a Scottish moon that shone brightly on the land, unspoiled and pure.

He had no idea how long he stood there before a faint knock on the door startled him.

Arthur glanced over his shoulder as the door opened and his heart plummeted to his feet. Kerry stood in the doorway, her hair unbound, her bare feet peeking out from a white nightdress. He turned slowly toward her, uncertain how he should receive her in this circumstance, even more uncertain when she closed the door softly behind her.

He dropped the towel he was holding.

She folded her arms across her midriff and looked at the floor. Arthur stood rigidly, waiting for her to speak. But she pressed her lips firmly together, then opened her mouth as if she would speak, then closed it again.

Arthur swallowed. Hard.

She looked up, her gaze skimming quickly over the bed before landing on him. She looked so sad that Arthur felt a pull in his chest. "I doona ever want to forget the touch of your lips to mine," she whispered, unconsciously touching her fingers to her lips, "or the feel of your hand on my skin. You make me long to be held as I havna in years, Arthur. I . . . I canna bear for you to go without knowing you—"

Arthur's feet were moving before his brain, crossing the room in three strides so that he could gather her roughly in his arms. He understood completely, as if he had spoken those words himself, but his voice was lost. He wanted to tell her how he admired her. He wanted to say that he would that their lives were different, that he was anyone other than who he was—and he opened his mouth, drew his breath to speak, but she put a finger to his lips.

"Doona speak," she murmured, and moved her hand to untie her nightdress. Her gaze unwavering from his, she slowly pulled it open, pushed it so that it slid over her shoulders, then fell down her body, pooling at her feet.

Arthur could not breathe. He could not catch his breath as he gazed at her naked body. Her breasts were perfectly shaped to fill the palm of his hand; her slender waist flared gently into a woman's hips, from which two legs, as firm and strong as a stallion's stretched beneath. She was more beautiful than he imagined, more alluring—he suddenly fell to his knees, buried his face in the soft concave of her abdomen. He felt her hands on his head, her fingers in his hair, and then heard her soft sigh.

That sigh sent an eddy of voracious desire spiraling through him. He clutched her hips, kneading the flesh as he opened his mouth against the smooth skin of her belly, flicked his tongue into the crevice of her navel. Mindlessly, deliriously, he moved lower, to the springy curls that covered her mons, inhaling her womanly scent.

Kerry stroked his shoulders and arms as he held her tightly to him and vainly tried to drink her in, devour a piece of her that might live on permanently within him. The desire was overpowering, raging like a monster through him. He could not seem to have enough of her—

he was aware of only Kerry; every sense, every pore was filled with her, the sweet taste of her, the fragrant smell of her. The skin of his bare chest burned where her legs pressed against him, his shoulders singed by her fingers, the flames so deep inside him that they threatened to consume him altogether.

He struggled to his feet, his lips dragging across her belly, over a firm breast, and her neck, until he was upon her mouth, his tongue sweeping between her lips, savoring the recesses of her mouth and sweet breath. His hand slid to the side of her neck, spanning her cheek. Kerry's fingers curled around his wrist, and he felt her body mold effortlessly to the rigid contours of his.

Arthur's desire spread like molten lava through his veins, culminating in rigid attention against her belly. Kerry eagerly responded; her hips pressed against him, moving seductively in a primordial dance. He was fast losing his patience—he had to have more, had to have all of her, and he groped for the warmth of her breasts. She lifted her body to him, thrusting forward, into his palms, and then it was *his* sigh that melted between them.

It was more than a man could endure. With a soft groan, Arthur swept her into his arms and marched to the bed, falling with her onto the simple cotton spread. One arm swept into her loose flowing hair, grabbing handfuls of it as he hungrily devoured her lips. Kerry's urgency seemed equally intense—her hands were suddenly everywhere, sweeping over his arms, his chest, down his torso, over his hips.

He palmed her breast, carefully kneading the peak to stretch taut and firm, and dragged his mouth from her throat to lave it. The sensation of her smooth skin in his mouth was intoxicating; he suckled her while Kerry thrust her fingers through his hair, pushed his head against her breast, moaning low in her throat when he moved to lave the other breast. Reverberations of desire were rumbling hard through his body now, settling in his groin.

"Such beauty," he murmured, and reached for her thigh, brushing against the warm flesh between her legs. Kerry gasped; Arthur moved his hand upward, lightly skimming the damp curls between her legs. The heat was a full, raging inferno now, and Arthur found her mouth again, thrusting his tongue into her depths as his fingers slipped into her wet folds.

Kerry squirmed against him, arching her hips against him and digging her fingers deep into his skin as he skillfully stroked her, circling around and over the pinnacle of her pleasure.

"My darling," he murmured genuinely, "my beautiful Scottish darling." His lips fell to her neck, kissing the curve into her shoulder. Kerry's hands moved provocatively across his nipples, down his chest, but when she boldly stroked him through his trousers, the world seemed to tilt, the pressure in him building to intolerable, but oddly weightless proportions. She freed him from the confines of the buckskins with a white-hot wave of heat down his spine. But Arthur almost imploded when her hand folded around him, squeezing gently as she swept the velvet tip with her thumb, then slowly down his shaft.

The experience was staggering—each sensation more startling than the last. This woman, this young country widow who had captivated him, was driving him over the edge of a desire he had not felt in the arms of any other woman. He was dangerously close to the edge of an emotional and physical precipice from which he knew he might never recover should he fall.

It was too late.

He had fallen days ago, and Arthur suddenly grabbed her hand and pulled it away from his cock, forcing her pale blue eyes to open and gaze up at him. Tiny tufts of black curls swirled around her face. Long, silken tresses draped her skin and the linens of the bed. Her breasts, magnificently exposed to him, gave her a beguiling softness that made his heart pound. He had never desired a woman so intently. He had never yearned to show a woman what he was feeling, to give her all the pleasure he could, to fulfill her in ways she had never before experienced.

Then Kerry reached up to tenderly touch his temple, and he saw the light in her eyes, the glimmer from somewhere deep inside her. He felt himself falling into those eyes, drowning in them. Completely immersed, he could not tear his gaze away from hers as he moved between her thighs and slowly entered her. Her lips parted with her body; her eyes fluttered closed with her long sigh, and her back arched, pushing her breasts against his chest. As he slid deeper, her body tightened provocatively around him, luring him into her depths as he began to move, her body flowing instinctively with his.

To his great surprise, a flood of unfamiliar but intense emotion was all at once crashing through him, making him feel oddly tender. Kerry seemed to sense it; she suddenly opened her eyes and smiled brilliantly. *"Arthur,"* she whispered, stroking his cheek, and he was suddenly plunging deep into the tidal pool of her longing. His strokes took on greater urgency now; one of Kerry's arms flailed above her head, clutching at the linens, while the other raked his back. She tossed her head to one side, oblivious to the dark hair that covered her face as Arthur drove into her again and again.

It was an extraordinary journey, the press of his body into hers, extraordinary feelings, vague but earnest feelings he recalled having felt as a young man so desperately in love. But this was different somehow, so bloody *earthy.* As with everything in her life, there was no pretense with Kerry in this bed. She moaned without self-consciousness, moved just as fiercely as he each time her body rose up to meet him, and just when he thought he could bear no more, she shoved him, pushing him onto his back and rolled on top.

Her hair fell like a curtain around them; she smiled seductively as she braced herself with her hands against his chest. "You've unleashed a beast in me, Arthur Christian," she whispered, and began to move. *Ah God,* did she move. Arthur grasped her hips, pushed her down and tried to reach the heart of her. As his strokes began to quicken, she collapsed onto his chest, clinging to him, her breath hot and panting in his ear. "Reach for it, Kerry," he muttered as he reached for his own.

The pressure in his groin suddenly burst into a thousand shards that poured into the warm pool of her body. In the fog of that shattering climax he heard her cry from somewhere above and felt her body convulse tightly around him, drawing the life from him. With a final, powerful thrust, a guttural moan erupted from his throat as he released the last of the life into her.

Gasping for breath, Arthur slid his arms around her body, holding her close. Neither of them spoke; it seemed to him that they were both quite simply stunned by the sweet sensation, the flame ignited between them. He stroked her hair, the silken skin of her back. It was several moments before he realized that the dampness of his shoulder was not perspiration, but her tears.

He turned his head toward her, but Kerry slid off him, burying her face in the crook of his arm.

He silently gathered her into his arms and pulled her back into his chest, wrapped his legs around her.

She said nothing, but her hand covered his that anchored her to him. They lay there for what seemed like hours to Arthur, each lost in their own thoughts, staring at the moonbeam streaming in through the window. When at last she spoke, he had to strain to hear her. "You must know that I love you."

The admission hit him square in the gut. "No," he said. "It's just that it's been a terribly long time since you—"

She stopped him by chuckling softly. "Arthur, a blind man could see how much I love you." She paused; the chuckle died in her throat. "Doona say anything. Just promise me that you'll go before the sunrise, will you? And . . . and doona wake me. I canna bear to see you walk away."

No more than he could bear to walk away. He tenderly kissed the top of her head. "I promise."

"And once you've gone home again, you'll send word, promise that too."

"I promise that, too."

She sighed, a softly tortured sound that made his heart ache.

"Kerry . . . this has been an extraordinary fortnight. I shall never forget my experience here."

"Then perhaps you will think of me from time to time."

"Aye, lass, I'll think of you; every day I'll think of you," he murmured into her hair.

She turned in his arms then, seeking his mouth. They made love again, slowly and surely, taking their time to feel one another completely, prolong the experience. She whispered her love again just as they reached a glorious fulfillment together. Only then did they drift off to sleep, entwined in one another's arms.

Arthur woke well before the sun had risen, unable to sleep soundly. Thankful that she was such a heavy sleeper, he carefully extracted himself from her limbs and quietly donned his clothes—although he struggled with the restrictive waistcoat. When he was at last dressed, he picked up his boots and turned to gaze one more time at Kerry McKinnon. He stroked her long black hair, tried to brand the image of her in his mind's eye, the same lovely visage he had first seen on a bed of pine needles in the Scottish forest, and one that he would carry with him all his life.

He longed to kiss her one last time, to hold her, to

hear her whisper that she loved him once more, but true to his promise, he walked out of the room without waking her.

He tiptoed to the kitchen, only to have the wits startled from him by Thomas's presence—the ornery Scot looked half-dead. His head hung over a bowl of coffee he gripped tightly in his hands. He frowned when Arthur sat on the bench to don his boots. "Ye be leaving," he said flatly.

"That I be, old chap."

"Why, then? Ye seem to like it here well enough."

Arthur smiled at Thomas as he worked his second boot on his leg. "McKinnon, I suspected you to be a sentimental goat all along. I like it here quite well indeed, but it is time I was about my business. I've an appointment in Dundee that must be kept, and my family will be expecting me in London shortly."

Thomas snorted and slurped at his coffee. "Ye'll not find such heaven on this earth as Glenbaden, mark me."

"I know that," he agreed solemnly and stood, helped himself to several biscuits piled high on a plate in the middle of the table, which he stuffed into a woven sack May had given him. He turned and walked to the door and paused to glance over his shoulder one last time. "You should try your hand at a little wandering yourself, Thomas. There are many treasures to behold on this earth that you will not find in Glenbaden. Mark me," he said, and with a wave, walked out the door and into the cool early morning air.

And he kept walking, cutting through what was left of the barley field, his stride brisk and strong. He kept walking, kept forcing one foot in front of the other.

Not once did he look back, lest he crumble right there in the middle of this heaven on earth they called Glenbaden.

Chapter Thirteen

In hindsight, the journey to Dundee reminded Arthur of one of the bawdy burlesques that often played in Covent Garden, beginning with the stage right entrance of a little man possessing a manner highly reminiscent of the ubiquitous Richey Brothers. The troll had extracted a grand fortune from Arthur's pocket for the dubious pleasure of floating down Loch Eigg on little more than a piece of wood.

From the southern edge of Loch Eigg, Arthur walked to Perth, where he was once again subjected to an outrageous price for a less-than-desirable piece of horseflesh, which required the last few crowns Arthur had in his purse. He would have to survive on berries and tree bark, he supposed, until he could reach Dundee and the Bank of Scotland where he had, fortunately, put away a goodly sum. How the Scots normally procured their horses baffled Arthur—in the two instances he had been forced to buy, the seller had reacted as if he were quite mad to want to *purchase* a horse. Which really should not have surprised him, seeing as how he had yet to see a horse he would deem a suitable mount. This particular one had a bowed back, clopped along at an excruciating pace, dipping and heaving, and responded so testily when Arthur pushed her forward that he had named the old nag Thomas.

The journey to Dundee seemed to take weeks instead of days. For every hill Thomas managed to climb, there was another one just behind it, rising higher than the first. Worse, the mild summer weather suddenly turned foul. Thick gray clouds hung low and a cold, steady rain seemed to have no end. His disposition was hardly improved when he asked a farmer for directions to Blairgowrie. The man stroked his red beard very slowly, pondering the request for what Arthur swore was at least a quarter of an hour, then slowly extended a bony hand and an even bonier finger to the right.

And then he proceeded to explain his pointing with an accent so heavy and so quickly spoken that Arthur had no idea what he said. Instead of asking the farmer to repeat himself, he had simply followed the bony finger . . . in the wrong direction. A fact, naturally, he did not realize until he entered the same hamlet he had left just that morning—from the opposite end.

In the daylight hours—when he was in fact able to distinguish them from the night—he encountered a passel of odd people that convinced him he had ridden straight into the middle of a fairy tale. There was the young man he encountered digging a hole next to the road. He paused so that Thomas might have one of her seven daily meals and watched the young man. He in turn ignored Arthur completely, never broke his rhythm in digging and attended it so fervently that Arthur finally asked, "What, are you digging through to the Orient?" And he chuckled at his own jest.

The man hardly paused in his work. "No."

"A well, then?" he asked, more seriously.

The man flicked his gaze over Arthur, but kept digging. "No," he answered again.

The couple Arthur encountered near Lundie eclipsed that young man's odd behavior, however. He had stopped to water Thomas, naturally—the old hag could not walk more than forty feet without needing some sort of sustenance—and asked if he might let his horse drink of their stream. Upon hearing his accent, the woman clapped her hands and the man flashed a toothless grin at Arthur. They eagerly invited him to let his mount drink her fill, and just as eagerly urged him to come into their little cottage for a bit of stew while she did. At last, Arthur thought, a pair of Scots who actually *liked* the English. They had seemed perfectly normal, and he had gladly climbed down from Thomas, had walked into the cottage, expecting to find something as neat and cheery as May's cozy rooms, but stopped dead in his tracks. The main room of the cottage was filled with the presence of an enormous cow, steadily chewing from a pile of hay.

With the exception of that batty pair, who seemed to think nothing unusual about having a cow in their cottage, everyone he encountered greeted him with a thinly veiled disdain every time he opened his mouth. A Sassenach was not welcome in these parts, that was made sufficiently clear to him. The more miles he traveled, the more he came to understand that the universal contempt of the English had less to do with history and more to do with the perception that the English were behind the wholesale push of the Highlanders from their glens in favor of sheep. The Highlanders that could, eked out a living selling kelp from grossly overharvested seas. But when the coasts became too crowded to support them all, many were forced to sell everything for passage to America.

Arthur had no idea if it were truly only English investors behind the sweeping agrarian change, but by the time he reached Dundee, he was beginning to dislike the English, too.

However, in Dundee, any sympathetic feelings he might have had for the Scots rapidly evaporated.

First and foremost, Mr. Jamie Regis, Esquire, had not deigned to keep his appointment, which irritated Arthur to no end. If there was one thing he could not abide, it was for a man to give his word and renege. Jamie Regis had done exactly that in Arthur's opinion, and *twice* if he were to count his negligence in performing the eviction.

He did not, however, count the eviction.

Secondly, he could not find suitable lodging in the town. There was no grand hotel, no coaching inn where people of the *Quality* might reside for a time. The Wallace Arms, the best Dundee apparently had to offer, was a dilapidated old building in which he would not have housed even his mount. In the days he spent waiting for the stout little solicitor, he moved from public house to public house—Dundee seemed to have an ample supply of them—in search of a room where he might sleep without having to listen to boisterous laughter and song all through the night.

Fortunately, he was able to ascertain from the only solicitor offices in town that Mr. Regis was expected within a matter of days. He sorely wished he might have known that earlier, as he had not been able to shake the thoughts of Kerry that had plagued him from the moment he had walked into the mist of the half-shorn barley field and left her behind. It was worse now—there was nothing to occupy him; he seemed to dwell on the image of Kerry lying naked in bed the morning he had left. To know that he might have stayed on . . . watched her sleep . . .

Lord God, but she was often on his mind during the lonely, uncomfortable hours he spent on the swayed back of the contrary mare, and his memory fared no better in Dundee.

At first, he tried to ease his mind by writing to friends and family. He wrote what seemed to be dozens of letters, each one detailing his experience thus far in Scotland a little better than the last. When he had exhausted his mental roster of everyone he would even remotely consider sending a letter, he took to wandering the narrow streets of Dundee. But the pungent scent of jute and flax from the textile factories mixed with the heavy odor of fish drove him back to the public inn du jour, where he grew increasingly restless and increasingly obsessed with the fair memory of Kerry.

He dreamed of her. Night after night it seemed, her image slowly and steadily overtaking Phillip's in the nocturnal visage of his mind. Kerry laughing, Kerry walking, Kerry just *being* there—and always, *always* out of his reach.

Just like Phillip.

After a few days of that, Arthur determined he must absolutely have a diversion while he waited or else he might literally lose his feeble mind to those dreams.

So he took up golf.

He had seen the strange game played a time or two in England, but in Dundee, he noticed entire troops of people marching out to the country, the hardwood sticks they used to knock the ball about stuffed securely under their arm. One day, he saw three young boys, each carrying three such sticks. Having nothing better to do, Arthur followed them.

They led him to the top of a grassy hill, where he could see some sort of course, which he learned the Scots called *links,* had been laid out among the sand barriers and hills overlooking the Firth of Tay. One boy withdrew a small leather bag and placed it on the ground directly in front of him. Selecting one of three wooden clubs, he braced his skinny legs apart, put his head down, and swung the club at the ball. All three boys stood in silent, rapt attention as the leather bag arched high into the sun before landing in the middle of a water hole. That earned a cry of disgust from the boy who had swung the club and a round of laughter from the other two.

When a second boy took the place of the first, they noticed Arthur standing a few yards behind them.

By the time the sun had set that afternoon, Arthur had swung the club one hundred and fourteen times.

The next morning, he paced impatiently, waiting for the lads to appear, hoping that the black-headed one had remembered to bring along the stick with the hickory shaft and applewood head that Arthur had determined he preferred, along with the leather ball they called a *featherie*.

After another day of following the lads about, Arthur bought the sticks from one—at an extravagant price, naturally—but managed to talk him out of two of the *featheries,* and struck out on his own. He discovered a peaceful, pretty course a half-day's ride away, near Affleck Castle. And it was that course for which he struck out early every morning, then spent the better part of the day whacking away at the *featherie,* waiting for Mr. Regis to show himself and trying not to think.

Unfortunately, not even striking the *featherie* tens of hundreds of times could put his mind to rest.

His dreams never fully left him when he awoke each morning and chased him through the course of the day, making him question everything he had ever known. There was Phillip, his nocturnal visitor, and the anger Arthur could not, after three years, quite seem to release. Particularly not the anger over this impossible venture— why had Phillip invested so carelessly? It was ridiculous, just one more thing Arthur could add to Phillip's list of transgressions—a bad investment mangled by incompetence, the ultimate price being Kerry's livelihood.

If Phillip hadn't done what he did, he never would have met Kerry and would never have been so bloody tormented by her memory.

Yes, but how could he blame Phillip when he was guilty of having looked away when he might have helped? What sort of man was *he,* then, if he could turn away when Phillip needed him most? Phillip, the one person in his life who had ever wanted Arthur to lead him, the one person who *believed* he could lead him. Oh, he had lead him, hadn't he—right into his grave.

Arthur hated who he was, what he had become.

Would that he had become someone like Kerry.

Heaven help him, because he could not stop thinking about her or the exquisite sensation of her skin beneath his lips, her body beneath his, the warmth of her womb. He could not stop envisioning her walking across that barley field, her hand trailing along the top of the grass. Nor could he purge even simple memories of her talking gaily with May, her laughter running over them all like sunbeams, dancing to Red Donner's fiddle, smiling through her daily visit to the old crone Winifred, or stripping the grain from the barley stalk. He had never known a woman like her, never admired a woman so. Of all the women of the *ton* whom he had courted or had courted his favor, he had never seen one who possessed a fraction of the natural beauty Kerry possessed.

Ironic, wasn't it, that she was so unattainable? Kerry hailed from the wrong country, the wrong social strata, the wrong breeding. He might as well set his sights on the fictional moon queen—Kerry was just as elusive.

And he hated the world for it, hated more the legacy of his birth. He envied the modest and uncomplicated life of Thomas, a hard-working man who had nothing to clutter his mind but the desire to travel and see the world. But Arthur was neither a Scot nor a farmer of any sort. He was the son and brother of one of the most powerful dukes in the realm, hailed from the highest reaches of society, had entry to the most sought-after homes in all the British Isles. He could not, under any circumstance, real or imagined, picture himself in Glenbaden.

And that angered him.

Angered him so that he struck with fury at the *featherie,* knocking the little leather ball farther and farther each day, while his aim seemed to stray farther and farther from the hole. He hardly cared.

He was just returning from his latest attempts on the course near Affleck Castle when the innkeeper of the Hawk and Thistle came outside to meet him. Arthur immediately assumed he wanted more money for stabling

Thomas, which chafed him to no end—he could hardly
abide to waste good coin on such a worthless horse. But
the innkeeper surprised him with news that Mr. Jamie
Regis, Esquire, had left his card.

It was about goddamn time.

Arthur climbed down from Thomas and tossed the
reins to a freckle-faced lad and anxiously snatched the
card from the innkeeper. "I don't suppose he left word
where he may be reached?" he snapped.

"Aye, 'e did, milord," the innkeeper calmly responded, then turned and walked back inside without
bothering to tell Arthur exactly *where* he might reach
Regis. With a frown, Arthur flipped the card over.
There, in very neat script, was the name *Broughty Inn*.

Oh fine. He was to call on Mr. Regis at the Broughty
Inn, as if *he* were the solicitor and Regis the client. He
whipped around, gestured impatiently for the reins to his
mare, swung up on Thomas's swayed back and rode out
of the courtyard, happily reviewing exactly how he
would strangle the stout solicitor.

It so happened that the stout solicitor was in no mood to
suffer the dark mood of His High Almighty Self. Jamie
had had a very rough journey from Fort Williams—
he was tired, he was hungry, and so overworked that he
was beginning to feel as if he were sinking beneath the
weight of it all. When he saw Lord Christian striding
across the courtyard—his jaw tightly clenched—Jamie
groaned, rolled his eyes, and downed the last of his bitter
ale. As Lord Christian burst into the tiny common room
of the inn, Jamie pushed himself to his feet. But as the
insufferable Sassenach stalked toward him, Jamie had to
bite his tongue to keep a very derisive smile from his
lips—the flawless leather boots he had so admired not
three weeks past were scarred beyond redemption. Lord
Christian had, apparently, met with his own trials on
Scottish soil, and for that, Jamie could not be happier.

His spirits much improved, he extended his hand. "Milord, how do you do."

Christian barreled to a stop in front of him, looked at his hand, then frowned, unbelievably, even more darkly as he folded his arms tightly across his chest. He glared daggers at Jamie for a few moments, his jaw working frenetically before finally muttering tightly, *"Regis."*

Jamie grinned and gestured to a chair across from him. "Will you not sit?" The Sassenach looked suspiciously at the chair, then at Jamie. Almost reluctantly, it seemed, he slowly lowered himself onto the chair as Jamie settled comfortably in his own. "I apologize for the delay, milord. I was unavoidably detained in Fort Williams."

Christian shifted awkwardly in an apparent attempt to get his long legs under the table. "Not only are you delayed, Mr. Regis, but you did not follow my explicit instructions—"

"I beg your pardon, I did indeed!" Jamie quickly interrupted.

"I beg *your* pardon! Do you mean to imply that you carried out my instructions to evict Mr. Fraser?" Christian asked, his chest filling with superior air.

Pompous ass. "Perhaps not in the precise manner you dictated, but I certainly carried through with your instructions!"

Clearly baffled, Christian leaned slowly forward, peering intently at Jamie as if seeing some wee spot between his eyes. "Let us speak plainly, Regis. Did you or did you *not* call upon one Fraser McKinnon and inform him that—"

"I didna call personally, I sent proper correspondence," Jamie interjected. "I assure you, sir, it is an acceptable and effective form of communication in my occupation, and I think, in matters such as this, perhaps a better way of—"

The sudden and sharp sound of Christian's palm slapping the table made Jamie jump in mid-sentence.

"You did *what?*" he breathed, his voice quivering with what Jamie instinctively knew was fury ... white-hot fury.

He nervously cleared his throat. "I, ah, directed a letter to McKinnon informing him that I would be calling in a fortnight to discuss the particulars of his eviction and that—"

"Do you realize, Mr. Regis, that Fraser McKinnon is quite *dead?*" Christian fairly shouted.

Now there was a new piece of information. McKinnon dead? A pity, that. The man had himself a bonny lass, indeed he did.

"Had you bothered to look after Lord Rothembow's investment, you might have known as much," Christian snapped.

That only put Jamie's back up. "Now see here, milord, you've no right to insult me! I have seen my business triple in the last two years, and I canna possibly be expected to hike up into some remote Highland glen to see if everyone is quite alive!"

"You certainly might have done so when no payment was made, sir!"

Jamie did not appreciate the stab of guilt that brought him, and sat back, glowering. "That is neither here nor there. A letter has been delivered on your behalf to McKinnon's survivors, and I daresay they are quite capable of understanding the gravity of the situation ..." His voice trailed off; Jamie actually forgot what he was about to say because the transformation in Christian's countenance was nothing short of remarkable. The color seemed to bleed from his face; he gaped at Jamie, his gaze sharp enough to bore a hole clean through him, but Jamie had the distinct impression that Christian wasn't seeing him at all.

"Dear God," he muttered. *"DEAR GOD!"* he bellowed and suddenly surged to his feet, disappearing through the door before Jamie could stand.

Jamie thought to go after him and tell him that he

had prepared the necessary documents and had them delivered to the Bank of Scotland, but it was too late—Christian had already disappeared into the crowded street.

While Jamie Regis was trying to sort out the confusing behavior of the Englishman, Thomas McKinnon was seeing to it that the belongings of the last pair to leave Glenbaden were securely fastened onto the old wagon that would carry them to Loch Eigg.

Aye, but this was a colossal mess Fraser had left for them, the bloody fool.

As he tightened the rope around a piece of luggage, Thomas watched Kerry walking slowly through the shorn barley field. He would curse Fraser to his dying day for putting this on her, but he could not help marveling at how she had shouldered the burden of her husband's deception for so long. Admired her, aye, but he was also angry with her for having kept it to herself. What had made the lass believe she could generate five thousand pounds to save them all? The whole of what was standing in Glenbaden wasn't worth that much!

Evicted.

The word sounded harsh to his ears.

Harsh, but it had only been a matter of time before it was bound to have happened. Thomas turned his attention to the wagon again. It had happened in every glen and valley in these Highlands, and there was certainly naught about Glenbaden that would separate it from the rest of them. For a score of years, good, decent, hard-working Scots had been pushed out by landlords in favor of the Blackface and Cheviot sheep across the Highlands. The sheep needed a lot of room to graze, needed so much land that it was, by the very essence of it, a rich man's venture. Truthfully, the sheep seemed to suit the Highlands far better than the beeves, and sheep-farming was, for the barons, the most efficient means for making a profit. Which meant that the Scots who had lived and farmed in the same glens and valleys for centuries were in the way.

No matter how he tried to tell her that Moncrieffe was doing the same to them, Kerry would not accept it. The lass believed she was responsible for this mess, but God above, it was Fraser and his dealings with Moncrieffe who had brought them to this end. The land, the white house, all of its furnishings, the stables, and barn—all of it would go to pay the debt to Moncrieffe and the Bank of Scotland. The only thing Kerry and Thomas were determined to keep were the twelve beeves Fraser had bought before he died—they were the only thing of value left to them.

After a conference with Big Angus and May, they decided they would drive the cattle to market, get what they could for them, and hope to high heaven it was enough to buy passage to America for all who wanted to leave. Big Angus and May had decided to stay behind with his family who had migrated to the lowlands, where factory work was said to be abundant. "Doona ken how we'll manage, but I'll feed her," Big Angus had said to Thomas one night as they cleaned out the barn. "Ye will see America I think," he had predicted.

Thomas reckoned he would. After thirty-five years, the time had finally come for him to seek his way in the world. Since Kerry had told him of the eviction and shown him the letter, the thought of venturing into the unknown had both excited and frightened him. He had moved about in a sort of daze ever since, his thoughts miles from Glenbaden.

As for Kerry, well, she had not said what she would do. She had loved the Englishman, that he knew. But he had also known that Christian would never stay; he was too refined for this part of the world and the McKinnon clan. Ah, but her long face was enough to dishearten the sturdiest of souls, and he hoped, for her sake, that she would join him and the others in a journey to America.

Thomas had heard enough of a bountiful America to picture a sort of Eden, a land proving rich and prosperous for every man, regardless of his station. He had visions of stepping off a ship onto land green and fertile and brimming with flowers and sunshine.

Oh aye, he hoped she would join them and put the Sassenach out of her mind.

The last wagon, piled precariously high with luggage and belongings, bounced along the rutted road that snaked around the eastern shore of Loch Eigg toward Perth. Standing in the room Arthur had used, Kerry watched the wagon disappear over the crest with the last pair of Glenbaden residents clinging to the bench. There was no one left but Thomas and herself now, and even Thomas would leave before the sun rose the next morning, driving the cattle to Perth.

The plan was to give Thomas a good head start before she let Moncrieffe know Glenbaden was now his, in case Moncrieffe had the idea of going after the beeves. Kerry rather imagined he would not, as the beeves were rather sickly and would not bring him much profit. She would wait two days and collect the last post from Willie Keith before calling on Moncrieffe, then go immediately to Perth to meet Thomas. Together, they would travel on to Dundee, where the others would be waiting. And then she would . . . she would . . . *what?*

Of the fourteen residents of the glen, all but four had opted to go to America. What choice did they have? But Kerry doubted that the cattle would bring enough for half that number, and she could not, in good conscience, take someone's place on the ship to America.

Then what?

Not Glasgow. *Not Glasgow!*

What would become of her? She could hardly wander around the countryside hoping for the best. She had no marketable skill—she had heard of the textile factories that employed women like herself, but she hadn't a notion of how to spin wool. Worse, she had no concept of how one went about obtaining employment. It was rather ironic, she thought, that after all the years of superior education her father had given her, she had come away with little more than a forgotten appreciation of art and literature. Nothing very useful at all.

But she had, in the course of that education, met Regina Kilmore, a small, quiet girl from Edinburgh. Although Kerry had not spoken to or heard from Regina in twelve years, they had once shared a room and girls' secrets and a mad infatuation with the school's headmaster. Perhaps Regina could help her. She seemed to recall that her father was a prominent man—surely he could help her find employment in one of the factories. But how difficult would it be to find Regina in Edinburgh after all these years? And how would Regina receive her now, in her patched widow weeds?

What did it matter? Regina, bless her, was her last hope.

Arthur.

The thought of him never left her, pricked at her constantly. It felt as if she had misplaced a part of herself, as if she was sort of hobbling about. There seemed so many dreams of him, so many things left unsaid, so many things she longed to tell him. But it was as if he had died, for she would never have the opportunity to say what was in her heart. Or to see his smile, his eyes. Feel his lips on her skin . . .

The hot, burning tears of her grief filled her eyes, spilled onto her cheeks, and Kerry swiped at them, angered by them. How she longed for Arthur now, his quiet strength, the comfort of his arms.

The next morning, Kerry stood shivering in the mist, watching Thomas as he adjusted a bag onto his shoulder containing the last of the biscuits, some cheese and dried fish. Finally satisfied that he wore it securely, Thomas glanced up at Kerry and smiled thinly. "Well then. I'll be going now."

Kerry nodded.

"I'll be meeting ye on the far edge of Perthshire no later than Thursday, lass. If ye're not come by then, I'll come for ye."

"Doona worry, Thomas," she tried to assure him. "I will be quite all right. I went all the way to Dundee and back, remember?"

"Aye, I remember," he said, his eyes narrowing slightly. "You've got the gun?"

"Yes."

"And ye remember how to use it?"

"I do," she said, smiling.

Thomas frowned, looked across the barley field. Kerry's heart went out to him; for all his talk of wandering, she could not begin to imagine what he must be feeling now.

As if to answer her question, he said simply, "Canna put it off now, can I?" He shifted his gaze to her and smiled. "Ah, lassie, the world beckons me," he said, and leaned down to kiss her cheek. He turned and walked forward, into the mist. "Thursday!" he called sternly as the mist began to wrap around him.

"Thursday!" she called back, and watched until the mist swallowed him.

She stood there for what must have been an eternity before returning slowly to the house, each step dragging as if she had weights tied to her legs. She wondered what Arthur was doing now, as she did a thousand times a day since he had slipped out before the sun had come up, giving in to her wishes not to see him go. She imagined him in an ornate room, a dozen or more men gathered around and hanging on his every word as he regaled them with his journey through Scotland.

God, how she missed him!

Kerry made a breakfast but couldn't eat it; she was

too distracted by the silence. So she walked outside and looked around the glen, shivering with a strange chill that ran up her spine. No smoke rose from the chimneys of the empty cottages dotting the countryside, there were no sounds of laughter, no dogs barking, no chickens, no cows, no Big Angus bellowing. It was as if the life of Glenbaden had been stolen in the night, snuffed by some unseen force. It was eerie—she hoped Thomas was making good progress. She wanted to leave as soon as she could, escape this misery.

Escape his memory.

He had fallen into her life, left her breathless, and when she had at last gained her breath again, he was gone. But her dreams continued to surround him, and she could scarcely walk by the room where he had made such wonderful, passionate, glorious love to her without the tears welling. She had never known lovemaking could be so magical, had never known that a man could lift a woman to such surreal heights of pleasure. Oh, but he had lifted her, more than once he had lifted her and filled her with such tenderness that she still shivered when she recalled it.

It was little use to remember it now, she thought bitterly, and set about the business of cleaning the white house, putting the final chapter into place and leaving no sign of the McKinnons behind. The task took her all day; when night fell, she sat shivering on the old tree stump, gazing up at the stars, wondering if Arthur was gazing at these same stars, wherever he was.

The next day, she moved about like an imbecile, hardly thinking, packing the few belongings she would take from Glenbaden. In the afternoon, feeling very restless, she went outside and wandered around the kitchen garden. There were some beans left on the vine, but the rest of the garden—what little had actually grown in the summer—had been depleted in the last few weeks. It was a good thing they were going, she supposed, because they likely would have starved before autumn.

Kerry leaned down to pull the beans for wont of anything better to do, but something behind the white house caught her eye. There, on a rock protruding from the side of a hill, was a Black-faced sheep. As she slowly straightened, she noticed two more, higher than the first.

"Where have the people gone?"

Startled, Kerry whirled, dropping the beans. Charles Moncrieffe stood before her, his expression puzzled. She had not heard him approach.

"There were people here before," he said.

What was he doing here? "Charles! Have you come alone?" she asked, her chest now filling with the dread of encountering Moncrieffe. It was too soon! Thomas had not had enough time!

Charles nodded as he stepped inside the confines of the garden. "Just me. What happened to the people, then?"

"They, ah, they went on holiday."

That seemed to confuse him; he peered down the lane for a moment, his brow furrowed with his thoughts. But then a lewd smile slowly crept across his lips, and Kerry took a step backward as he shifted his gaze to her again. "My *da* sent me to fetch you."

Her stomach rose on a sudden surge of fear. She took another step backward, keenly aware that she was alone, unprotected—

Charles's tongue darted across his cracked lower lip. His eyes fastened on the bodice of her gray gown. "My *da* is impatient with you because you owe him money," he blithely informed her. "He says you are to come to Moncrieffe so arrangements can be made to repay him."

She swallowed. "What arrangements?"

"The wedding."

Fear seized her fully then; Kerry backed farther away from Charles and frantically looked around him for an exit. But Charles seemed to know what she was about; he walked deeper into the garden. "You canna run away because I'm to take you to Moncrieffe. My *da* says we will be married." He moved toward her again.

Frantic, Kerry threw up one hand. "Please, sir—"

He grasped her hand in a surprising show of agility before she could yank it back. "I will share a bed with you," he continued, and pulled her roughly to him, groping at her with his hand and mouth in an attempt to kiss her.

Revulsion filled her gullet; somehow, Kerry managed to squirm out of his grasp. "Please!" she said, stumbling away from him.

"You're to go with me!" The tenor of his voice had changed—it was menacing, and he suddenly lunged again.

Kerry scrambled out of the garden, cringing at the sound of Charles's laughter. *Think!* her mind screamed.

"Is it a game?" he called after her.

The gun. It was in the house in the bag she had packed. Frightened, she started to run. But Charles caught her from behind, knocking her to the ground. "I *like* this game," he laughed, and roughly nuzzled her neck as his hand groped for her breast.

Kerry bucked against him, surprising them both with her strength. It caught him off guard; she rolled onto her side, pushed him away with all her might before he could grasp her again. But Charles had a look in his eye that made Kerry's blood run cold—he was quick to catch her ankle and painfully jerk her onto her back. He came over her then, his mouth everywhere, his hands tearing at her clothing. Kerry fought back with sudden desperation, beating his shoulders, tearing at his hair, biting him. But she didn't succeed in getting his attention until she managed to wedge her leg in between his and bring her knee up hard.

Charles howled in agony and rolled off her, clutching his testicles. Kerry clambered to her feet, running as fast as her legs would carry her into the house and to her gun. She burst through the door, careered down the narrow corridor, colliding with the wall as she tried to navigate a sharp turn into her bedroom. The bag was on her bed; she ran to it, cursing herself for having packed it below her other belongings. Each *clip* of Charles's boots as he strode down the corridor behind her was like a hammer against her heart as she tore wildly through the carefully packed articles.

As her hand closed around the cold steel barrel, Charles reached her door. "You shouldna run from me!" he bellowed.

Kerry yanked the gun free of her things and sent the bag flying. She clumsily positioned the gun in her hand and twisted around, the long barrel pointed directly at Charles's chest, but she was shaking so badly that it quivered back and forth. He stepped across the threshold, his eyes blazing, and she saw that he gripped a large rock in one hand. She suddenly could not breathe. *Mother of God, help me!* she silently screamed.

Charles looked at her gun and laughed, belying the dark fury on his face. "Doona be a fool," he said, and stepped into the room. "That willna stop me."

Chapter Fourteen

How he managed to acquire a horse of acceptable caliber at all on Loch Eigg would remain a mystery to Arthur for the rest of his natural life, he supposed, but there had appeared an old man as bent and gnarled as an old oak tree, leading a very fine mount. Arthur stopped him, asked him if his horse might be for sale or let, and after some fierce haggling, handed over yet another royal fortune *and* Thomas in trade.

The steed was worth the investment; apparently grateful to be given his head, he flew from the banks of Loch Eigg, gobbling up yard after yard of Scottish heath in response to Arthur's anxiousness to reach Glenbaden and Kerry. But as the miles stretched long behind them, he was increasingly anxious that he had not exactly worked out the details of what he would do once he arrived in Glenbaden.

Assuming the McKinnons had actually received the letter from Regis, it hardly seemed appropriate to come barreling into their midst and announce that he was the one behind their eviction. Honestly, there didn't seem to be a very delicate way of telling them the truth, or making Kerry understand he hadn't known it was she. Or that he was determined to fix this mess, that he would never hurt her, never intentionally harm her . . . *never leave her.*

Bloody hell, it was *that* thought that kept coming back to him, again and again, intruding uninvited into his mind. The same thought that had dogged him about the links, trapped in the cage of his heart.

He didn't want to leave her.

He didn't want to spend another day without her.

It had taken four days of solitary golfing to reach that agonizing conclusion, four days of restless dreams, and worse, visions of her in broad daylight as he stared out over the course. He had at first assumed he was as infatuated as he had been when he was blinded and muted by Portia's beauty almost twenty years ago. And had assumed, therefore, that this, too, would pass.

But there was something that bothered him, something that didn't quite fit with the notion of a mere infatuation. It was something inextricably tangled with the memory of that fantastic night of lovemaking and the rather tender feelings that had very nearly bowled him over. Feelings so strong yet so strangely elusive that he wasn't at all certain what label to put on them, and hadn't known until the moment Regis said what he had done. In that moment, when he had understood that Kerry had received the letter evicting her, his heart seemed to explode within him. A burst of regret and anxiety had hit him square in the gut and he had no idea how he moved from there. He only knew that he had to get to Kerry and make her understand that *he hadn't known it was her,* that he could never do that to her because he . . . he . . .

Good God, he loved her.

The regret and anxiety had faded in the days that followed as he journeyed across the rough terrain of Scotland to reach her, replaced with the single and startling revelation that he *loved* her. It amazed him, frightened him, baffled him, but it was nonetheless as plain as the nose on his face—he loved Kerry McKinnon, had loved her from the moment she had connived their way onto the Richey Brothers' boat. He had loved her then and more as he watched her around Glenbaden, had loved her cheerful determination in the face of adversity, her natural beauty, her kindness, her gentle, giving spirit.

He loved her.

But goddamnit, what was he to do with that? Take her to London? The thought was so overwhelming that he shoved it aside, told himself he could not think of that now. At the moment, the only thing that mattered was to make her understand, and he spurred his newest mount—whom he had christened Sassenach in honor of spirited Englishmen everywhere—to run faster.

As Arthur crested the hill just beyond the barley field in Glenbaden, he noticed that something seemed not quite right. As Sassenach trotted easily across the cut field, a deep foreboding crept up his spine—something was terribly wrong. There was no one about, no smoke rising from the chimneys, no barking dogs, squawking chickens, or Thomas storming out to greet him. *No Kerry.*

The place was deserted.

As the horse cleared the barley field, Arthur guided him toward the white house, mentally running through the few plausible explanations he could imagine for the strange desertion. Perhaps there was some sort of gathering taking place; after all, they had all come out to watch him tend Moncrieffe's horse. But that did not explain the absence of the livestock. Perhaps they had moved the cattle to better grazing, but—

The sound of gunfire shattered the deadly quiet.

Arthur immediately spurred the horse forward. When he reached the white house, his feet were moving before he hit the ground. He drew his pistol as he reached the door, cautious of what he might find on the other side.

That was when he heard her bloodcurdling scream.

Kerry's scream was so shrill, so piercing, that it sent a raw shiver down his spine. Instantly, he kicked the door open with such force that it slammed against the wall and rushed inside, running toward the sound of her scream as his nostrils filled with the acrid smell of gunsmoke. His pulse pounding with terror, he raced for the first door on the right, caught himself on the doorframe, and trained his pistol on the room.

The scene stunned him; he slowly lowered his pistol.

A man who looked vaguely familiar lay on the floor, blood pooling thick and dark beneath him and oozing slowly across the pine-plank floor, puddling around a large, jagged rock. Arthur could not quite place him, but this much was certain: he was dead. His eyes stared up at Arthur, the astonishment with which he had met his death still in them. Kerry stood next to him, her old gun on the floor beside her, bloodstains on the knees of her disheveled gown where she had knelt beside the man. Her body trembled violently; tears streaked her cheeks, falling from terror-filled eyes as she stared at Arthur. Slowly, she lifted hands covered in blood out to him.

"Look at my hands," she whispered.

He couldn't look anywhere else.

"Get it off," she said, lifting them higher, but when Arthur did not move immediately, she began to shake them violently. *"Get it off!"* she screamed.

Her terror moved him at once; he grabbed her hands in his and attempted to cover the blood so she could not see it. At the same time, he dragged her across the room as she screamed at him to get the blood off and plunged her hands into the basin. The water turned scarlet red; Arthur shielded her as best he could while he washed the blood from her. Kerry babbled hysterically about what had happened, but he needed no explanation—it was clear what had occurred here. His only concern was getting her out of that room, away from the dead man, before they were discovered.

But who *was* he?

"Kerry!" he said sharply as he wiped her hands clean with a linen cloth. Kerry did not seem to hear him—her gaze was now riveted on the dead man. *"Kerry!"* he said again, shaking her roughly until she looked at him. "Who is he?"

"Charles Moncrieffe," she whispered, her eyes welling all over again. "Moncrieffe's son!"

Ah God.

He had not liked Moncrieffe from the moment he saw him, and his instincts had been confirmed when Thomas told him that Moncrieffe was a man of considerable power and influence who possessed the soul of a snake. A panic began to rumble in the pit of his belly as Arthur stared down at Moncrieffe's son, the same, gut-tightening, suffocating panic he had felt the moment Phillip had died.

He had no idea what to do. Were this England, he would feel quite secure in notifying the authorities. His word and his name alone would keep out any unnecessary inquiry into the matter and the whole unfortunate matter would be handled discreetly, with no harm to Kerry. But this was not England. Not only was he unfamiliar with the laws, he was a Sassenach, as detested as the lowest insect by some. If anything, his presence would create more scrutiny. And judging by what little he knew of Moncrieffe, there was no telling what the man could or would do once he learned of his son's death.

His only option—until he had time to think, at any rate—was to get her away from here before anyone discovered what had happened.

He grasped Kerry's arms, forced her to look at him. "Where is Thomas? May?"

She shook her head and looked again at Moncrieffe's son; Arthur shook her again. "Kerry, listen to me! Where is Thomas?" he fairly shouted.

"He's gone," she cried. When Arthur dug his fingers into her flesh, she winced. "Evicted, all of us," she said, closing her eyes as tears seeped from the corners. "Big Angus and May, they've taken everyone to Dundee to seek passage to America. Thomas and Red Donner drove the beeves to Perth. I am to meet him there. He'll not understand when I doona come."

Her explanation both shocked and confused him. Any hope he had of breaking the news to her gently was dashed with the understanding that not only had the McKinnons received the letter, but they had uprooted themselves and abandoned Glenbaden. Yet he did not understand why she had stayed behind. "Why in God's name are you here alone?"

"So Thomas would have time to reach Perth," she muttered helplessly, and looked at the dead man again. "The beeves, they're all we've got, and we feared Moncrieffe would take them—oh God, I will surely hang for this!" she cried.

Arthur rather feared that she would—he had to get her out of there, as far from Glenbaden as he could. Then he would think through it all, figure out what to do. He grabbed her hand and yanked her behind him, pausing only long enough to hurriedly stuff some of her scattered things into the old red satchel. He snatched it up with his free hand and quickly continued on, stepping over the body of Moncrieffe's son, then yanking a crying Kerry hard behind him when she whimpered at having to do the same.

Once they were outside, he tossed the satchel on the back of Sassenach, quickly fastened it down behind his. Kerry had not stopped crying, did not stop as he lifted her up onto Sassenach's back and swung up behind her. Anchoring her securely to him with one arm, he spurred

Sassenach on, hoping to high heaven the horse had the
mettle he suspected he did, because Arthur needed him
to ride just as hard for Loch Eigg as he had come.

And Sassenach did indeed give it his spirited best,
but he tired halfway to the loch, slowed to a steady trot,
and caused the panic in Arthur to expand to frightening
proportions. For the first time in his life, he had no idea
what he was doing or what he *ought* to be doing. He had
never, not once, walked into a situation that he did not
know how to walk away from. His fear for Kerry was
terrifying him, his only coherent thought was that he *had*
to get away from Glenbaden—*but to where?* To England? And what then? He could hardly take her to London, could he? How in God's name would she survive
that world?

There was her mother. He recalled that she had a
mother still living, somewhere near Glasgow. There was
something else about her mother, too, but it escaped him
at the moment. Would she be safe? Could he take her
there?

Kerry was no help in the matter. She had stopped
crying, and for that he was grateful. But she had fallen
into something of a silent shock, balling up against his
chest with her head down and her fingers gripping his
arm. He tried to speak to her and elicit some response,
any response, but Kerry could scarcely shake her head or
murmur anything more than she had killed a man.

When they neared the ferry crossing at Loch Eigg,
the sun was just beginning to sink into the horizon. A
handful of souls waited to cross over to the road to Perth
instead of walking the great distance around the loch.
Arthur decided against waiting for the ferry with
them—someone might later recall seeing him with
Kerry. But Sassenach was worn through; his head
bowed between his shoulders, his pace little more than
dragging. The horse had to be fed and watered if they
had any hope of making it around the loch.

Pulling his hat low over his eyes, Arthur shifted in

the saddle and tried to shield Kerry from the group gath-ered at the dock, nonchalantly raising a hand in greeting to two men who peered closely as they passed. One of them slowly raised his hand in return as they cleared the dock and headed away from the group. Arthur breathed a silent sigh of relief and anxiously spurred Sassenach forward, but the horse was barely moving at all.

They rode for another hour, Sassenach hardly man-aging to put one hoof in front of the other and Kerry seeming to fall deeper into her shock. His dismay was overwhelming—he panicked that they would be stranded out here, his horse dead, Kerry in some insensi-ble state. Once Moncrieffe discovered his son dead—if he hadn't already—there would be a full-scale hunt of the Highlands, and the two of them would hang from the nearest tree. This was a state of vulnerability he had never before in his life experienced, and it frightened him half unto death.

But as the path curved around the far end of the loch, he spotted a trail of smoke in the dusk sky, and he felt a faint glimmer of hope. He reined Sassenach toward the smoke, and after a quarter of an hour, had tethered the horse and helped Kerry down—or rather, caught her as she fell down—to rest against the trunk of a shaggy birch. "I'll be back," he murmured, and soothed a loose curl from her face. But Kerry turned away, lost in her shock, and the panic flared in him again. *Damnit,* he could not afford such panic now!

He forced himself to turn away from her and crept through the woods toward the trail of smoke, eventually espying the cluster of thatched-roof cottages nestled against the side of a hill. There were four of them, grouped to-gether at strange angles. A barn-like structure stood off to one side.

It was exactly what Arthur had hoped to find.

A quick search of the landscape told him no one was about, with the exception of a dog lying in front of one cottage, his head resting between his paws. Not an encouraging sight for someone who was about to steal a bucket of oats. Oh yes, he could scarcely believe it himself, but he, Arthur Christian, was about to cross the threshold into common thievery.

There was no time like the present.

The dog, however, gave him pause. Arthur pondered that dilemma for a moment, wondering exactly how a common thief would appraise the situation, until his gaze fell on some stones at his feet. A conniving little chuckle escaped him as he bent and picked up several of them. Selecting one of the larger ones, he stepped out from the cover of the trees and threw the rock as hard as he could in the opposite direction of the barn. It had the desired effect—the dog's head suddenly popped up, its ears pricked in the direction where the stone had landed. Arthur threw another stone and the dog scrambled up, trotting off in the direction of the noise, its snout to the ground. "One more for prosperity," he muttered, and threw another large stone to the right of the others.

The dog disappeared into the woods.

Arthur sprinted across the meadow for the barn, crouched low and running as fast as he ever had in his life.

Entering the barn was easy; he quickly slipped inside, scanned the four cottages to make sure no on had seen him, then slumped against the rotting door to catch his breath. As he dragged air into his lungs, a prickly feeling crept along his neck, and he suddenly realized he was not alone. Slowly, he turned his head . . . and instantly, instinctively, flashed a charming smile at the young girl seated beside the milk cow, as if he sneaked into barns all the time.

Caught in the act of milking, the girl's hands were still on the teats of the cow as she blinked up at him in evident surprise.

"Now aren't you a bonny lass," he tried, falling on habit as he shoved his hands into his pockets. "A bonny lass indeed."

The girl did not move.

"You'll forgive my manners, won't you? I'm afraid I've a bit of a problem," he whispered conspiratorially. "I've a rather sick mount, just below here on the road to Perth." Nor did that pronouncement elicit any response from the girl, with the sole exception of her hands, which she moved from the teats of the cow to her lap. Arthur cleared his throat. "I had rather hoped to borrow a few oats."

"Ye mean to steal," she said simply.

Well . . . not to put *too* fine a point on it. Arthur pulled his hands from his pockets and shrugged innocently, palms upward. "There you have it. I am quite appalled that it has come to this, I truly am, but you find me in rather a predicament, I'm afraid. My horse is in desperate need of a little sustenance, and the grazing in these parts is not particularly fit for horseflesh, is it?"

To his surprise and relief, she shook her head. He flashed his best roguish smile and very casually strolled into the middle of the barn. "You see? I was quite right about you. A very bonny lass with a heart of gold."

"My *da* will kill ye," she announced casually. "He doesna care for the English. Says they be thieves and robbers of all things Scottish."

Damn. Trumped before he had even laid his hand. The girl stood, carefully wiped her hands on her patched skirt, and Arthur frantically racked his brain for something to keep her there with him, short of physical force. He could not, *would* not, hit a young girl.

But he'd wrestle one if he absolutely had to.

"Your *da*," he drawled, "is an astute man. I should put the noose around my own neck, I swear I should, but you see, I cannot let my horse die. He's quite ill, and I have ridden all day. *All day*," he repeated vehemently as he frantically sought an explanation. "That's right, lass! Ridden all day to, ah . . . see a man here in the Highlands they say can cure any beast."

To his great and considerable surprise, the girl

paused in the straightening of her apron and looked up at him. "Roger Douglas?" she asked carefully.

"Why *yes*," he answered quickly, hoping to high heaven Roger Douglas was a good thing. "Do you know of him?"

The girl dropped her gaze, smiled softly, and if Arthur wasn't mistaken, even blushed a bit. *Aha.* "Aye, I know him," she said, her voice noticeably softer. "He's a bit of legend in the glens. For his cures, he is."

Thank you God. "A fine reputation that reaches into England, you know. I would not have come so far except that this mount has been with me since I was a lad . . . my grandfather made a gift of him when he was but a pony. I confess, I am quite attached to the old fellow," he said, marveling at how easily the lie flowed from his tongue.

"Has yer horse a name, then?" she asked.

Oh fine, a bloody name. "He does. I call him . . . Bruce," he said, pulling the name from some distant lesson on Scottish history.

The girl's countenance brightened considerably. "Bruce," she echoed softly, then suddenly moved toward him.

Arthur immediately braced his legs apart, prepared to battle the waifish girl if he must. "Now see here, lass—"

"The bucket be behind ye there," she said, pointing over his shoulder. "I'd ask that ye leave it on the road and I'll fetch it in the morning. Ye know where to find him, eh?" she said, gesturing for the bucket. Arthur hurriedly fetched the bucket and handed it to her. "Roger, I mean to say," she added sweetly.

"Mr. Douglas? Ah, I . . . actually, I'm rather glad you asked as I am not entirely certain. Might you point the way?" he asked as she walked to a wooden trough along one wall.

Lifting the lid, she bent over, her back to him. When she straightened and faced him again, she had filled the bucket with raw oats. " 'Round the dock of Loch Eigg ye'll see a path leading off to the right. He lives among the pines of Din Fallon. Aye, Roger Douglas will cure your horse," she said, blushing again when she said his name. "You'll tell him, will ye not, that Lucy McNair sends her warm regards?"

Arthur took the bucket from her hand and bowed deeply. "You may depend on it."

She blushed furiously now and awkwardly fingered the collar of her gown. "Be careful my *da* doesna see ye," she said.

Arthur smiled. "I shall be *quite* careful. Thank you, Miss McNair. You may very well have saved Bruce's life." With that, he left the blushing girl and walked quickly to the door, peeking outside to see about the dog before he slipped out. As it was nowhere in sight, he flashed one last roguish smile over his shoulder at Lucy and slipped outside, running quickly across the field and into the woods with his bucket of oats. Only when he was safely under the cover of the woods did Arthur stop, prop himself against a tree, and press a hand to a stitch in his side, amazed by his sudden sense of exhilaration.

Remarkable. He had just stolen a bucket of oats. Not only had he stolen it, but also he had lied to a pretty girl with no more remorse than a slug.

He pushed away from the tree, hurried down the path to where he had left Kerry.

Sassenach—or *Bruce,* for God's sake—didn't like that he couldn't have his oats immediately, but Arthur forced him to walk on a little farther, until he was well away from the McNair camp. He stopped by a small stream, helped Kerry down once again, then placed the bucket of oats in front of the horse. While he ate, Arthur unsaddled him and rubbed him down as best he could with the old blanket that had come with the deal.

Then he turned his attention to Kerry.

She was rocking back and forth at the foot of a tree, her forehead pressed to the tops of her knees, which she hugged tightly to her chest. She had barely said a word since they had left Glenbaden, had not inquired as to their destination. Nothing. Her shock was evident, her astonishment and grief palpable. Arthur had never shot a man in his life; the closest he could come to understanding her desolation was the manner of Phillip's death and the anguish he had seen in Adrian. In all of them.

His heart went out to her. The burdens Kerry had shouldered these last months were inconsequential to the burden of having taken a man's life if even to save her own.

And exactly how would he save her now? With a grunt of exasperation, he picked up the two bags he had unleashed from the saddle and carried them to where Kerry sat hugging herself. He then heard her faint moaning and squatted down beside her, put his hand on her shoulder. But she did not lift her head.

"Kerry," he said softly. "Kerry, look at me." She did not seem to hear him at all. Arthur shoved out of his riding coat, spread it on the ground next to her, then put his hands on her shoulders. "Sleep now," he said, and forced her onto her side. Kerry curled up in a ball on his coat; the weak evening light glimmered on her cheeks where her silent tears had charted a new path.

The girl was drowning in her grief.

Arthur sat at the base of the tree beside her and laid his hand on her shoulder. She startled him by suddenly curling up tightly next to him, putting her head on his lap. He laid his arm across her shoulders and with a sigh, leaned against the tree and debated what he should do.

The moon rose and slowly tracked across the sky as Arthur debated every conceivable option, watching Kerry drift from one bad dream to another. By the time the moon had begun its descent, he had decided: he would take Kerry to Glasgow, to her mother. It was the only plausible course of action. He could not take her to England—as much as he loved her, she was unsuited to his world. Nor could he take her to Perth. Moncrieffe would be looking for them, and he could not risk finding Thomas only to find Moncrieffe. At least in Glasgow, she might have a chance of hiding from Moncrieffe. It was not an ideal solution, but a reasonable one. He would offer her family money; urge them to migrate to America with the others given the circumstances.

It was the only practical solution.

He kept telling himself that, over and over, hoping he might actually believe it.

Kerry felt the jostling through a fog and forced her heavy eyes open. She blinked, focused on the moon and tried to remember where she was.

It all came rushing back to her, bearing down on her chest with great weight. *She had shot a man to death, had watched the shock in his eyes as he realized the life ebbed from his body.* She drew her breath, closed her eyes, prayed that it was a nightmare.

"Come now, sweetheart. We've got to go before the sun rises."

It was his voice, her Arthur, her knight-errant, who had appeared in the midst of that monstrous occurrence and taken her away. *She had shot a man to death.* The ache in her head, the pounding at her temples was fierce and relentless. She rolled away from the sound of his voice, unwilling to face reality.

"Kerry. We must be on our way before we are found."

She was a criminal. They would hang her if they found her.

"Come on then." She felt his hands beneath her arms, pulling her up. Her feet were numb; she stumbled as she tried to put them under her. Nothing seemed to move or work as it should. Arthur's arm came around her middle, mooring her to his body, moving her across the small clearing to the saddled horse nearby. "Be a good girl, up now," he muttered, lifting her onto the saddle and putting her hands on the pommel. "Hold tight now."

He disappeared from her view for a moment; she felt the tug of the saddle as he fastened the bags behind, then the pull of his weight as he swung up behind her. He put his arms around her as he gathered the reins and she felt his lips against the crown of her head as the horse started to move. "Ah, sweet lass," he murmured sorrowfully, spurring the horse into the night.

Ah, sweet lass, what have ye done?

Chapter Fifteen

SHE MUST HAVE slept again; when she awoke, the morning sun was rising and lifting the mist with it. Her every joint ached; Kerry shifted and immediately felt Arthur's arm tighten around her.

"Thank the Lord above—I was beginning to think your sleep was perhaps permanent," he said above her.

"Where are we?"

"Ah, and she speaks, too, thank God." He tenderly brushed the curls from her forehead. "We are to the west of Perth as best I can tell. I'm afraid I've not a suitable compass for this journey."

Kerry put a hand to her throbbing temple. West of Perth. *But Thomas was waiting.* He was, wasn't he? The terror began to fill in the edges around her clouded memory, creeping forward, bringing with it another, monstrous memory to her consciousness. "Thomas is waiting," she muttered, not wanting to relive the terror again.

"Yes, well, about that. I shall endeavor to find a way to get word to him, but you mustn't hold much hope of it."

That response confused her—she turned her head, wincing at the bright sunlight as she tried to peer up at him. "Get word to him?"

Arthur frowned, flicked the reins against the horse. "We cannot risk Perth. That is the first place Moncrieffe will look, particularly when he realizes the beeves are also missing. He will likely surmise they have been taken to market and will go to Perth to have a look about, so I'm afraid it's too great a risk at present."

Not to Perth? Then to where? And what of Thomas? The drum in her head pounded harder. She closed her eyes as the terror pushed forward into her consciousness, the memory growing sharper. "We must go to Perth," she mumbled. "There is no other place for me to go."

"There is Glasgow."

The soft tone of his voice did not dull the stab of his words—they sliced across her like a knife and she jerked away from Arthur's body, very nearly falling from the horse. "Careful! You'll break your neck!" Arthur sharply admonished her, tightening his hold on her and the reins.

"Not Glasgow!" she cried, ignoring his warning. "You canna mean it!"

"It is the only option—"

"*No!*" she shrieked, and struggled fiercely against his hold, suddenly desperate to be away from him. Her struggle forced him to rein to an abrupt halt, and Kerry immediately shoved away from him, leaping to the ground, landing on what felt like thousands of needles when her feet hit the earth. Arthur was right behind her, and she tried to run on her lifeless legs, to flee the very suggestion of Glasgow. The terror was now rifling through her, squeezing the breath from her lungs, choking her until she could scarcely draw her breath.

She felt the hard clamp of his hands on her shoulders just before he jerked her back into his chest, capturing her in a tight embrace. "Mind yourself, Kerry McKinnon," he breathed into her ear, "I am hardly of a mind to chase you into the brier. I know you don't want to go to Glasgow, but what choice do you have, given the circumstance?"

"Not Glasgow!" she cried, striking at his grip. "I

doona care what will come of me, but I willna go to Glasgow, I *will not!*"

"Stop it at once!" he bellowed, and with uncommon strength, grabbed her shoulders and whipped her around to face him. His expression was taut; dark circles stained the area beneath his eyes and a heavy beard shadowed his chin. He looked as exhausted as she felt. "Heed me, madam. I cannot let you go to Perth and risk Moncrieffe finding you there. I will not see you hanged, do you quite understand me? The only thing that seems to make even a bit of sense is to take you to Glasgow!"

He meant it, every word. The life quickly drained from her; her knees began to buckle. Kerry closed her eyes and felt herself falling.

"Come now," he said gruffly, shaking her, trying to make her stand. "It's hardly as bad as all that. I'll see to it that your mother has the means to see to your welfare—you won't be made to toil in some factory—"

"*No,*" she sobbed. "Please, no! I *canna* go to her, Arthur! You doona understand—"

"I understand that there is no one who can protect you, Kerry," he said, roughly forcing her chin up so that she would look at him. "You have no one, save your mum. Thomas cannot help you now. I've no choice but to take you—"

"Then leave me here to die!" she shrieked hysterically. "I'd rather die, I *deserve* to die for what I've done, so leave me to it then, out here among the wolves! But not Glasgow, Arthur! *Anything but Glasgow!*"

Clearly shocked by her hysteria, Arthur stared down at her, his hazel eyes searching her face in confusion. His grip on her arms began to hurt as a dozen waves of emotion scudded across his eyes, and for a moment, a single moment, Kerry hoped. But at last, he softly begged her to understand. "Kerry, sweetheart, what else can I *do?* Give me another choice, give me but one . . ."

There was one, all right. Death. Kerry preferred

death over life with her mother and the zealots she lived among. She preferred death to thinking about the loss of Glenbaden or killing Charles Moncrieffe. But when Arthur put his arm around her shoulders and began to coax her back to the horse, her legs moved of their own will to live. Mute, she stumbled along beside him, numb to his softly urgent reassurances, her mind filled with the incredible catastrophe that had suddenly become her life. It was as if some Greek tragedy was being played out here, on the stage she knew as Scotland, with everything she had ever known slowly disintegrating beneath her. Perhaps, she thought morosely as Arthur helped her up to the saddle, she had gotten her wish.

Perhaps this was death.

They rode until Sassenach could go no farther, plodding along for what seemed hours. Kerry did not speak—she seemed resigned to her fate, much like Arthur imagined a condemned man would face his certain death.

He was horribly, hopelessly confused.

It was clear that after all she had faced in the last year, the very thought of Glasgow was what would finally defeat her. God's blood, it defeated *him*. Who could look at her now, her despair filling the space around them, and deliver her to Glasgow? It was beyond his capacity as a man to commend her to a person or a place she would, obviously, rather die than inhabit. But it also was beyond his capacity as a member of the British aristocracy to take her to London, to a world she didn't yet know she would despise.

To a world that would despise her.

All that glittered in London was false—there was no natural light there, no sunlight to shine on her natural beauty, no Highland moon to illuminate her expressive face. Not only that, but the people of the *ton* could be so very false. They calculated every step, appraised every situation for what it could do for them. They possessed no true sense of camaraderie, no common bond—other than social status—that connected them with one another. Few had worked an honest day; even fewer knew the rewards of labor. They had no concept of what it would be to work together for the common good.

Oh yes, London was a very different world—Glenbaden was a dreamscape in comparison to the gritty reality he called home. How would a woman as vibrant and beautiful as Kerry McKinnon survive there?

They stopped midday to rest and water Sassenach. Arthur did not like the way the horse looked—he was beginning to show the signs of extreme fatigue. Kerry silently slumped into a heap of gray on the grassy knoll and watched with lifeless eyes as Arthur tried to make the horse as comfortable as he could. It was apparent that Sassenach would not last long at this rate. Five miles more? Maybe ten?

He troubled over it as he worked, but he was too exhausted to think clearly. When he had finished at last, he removed his coat, intending to rest for a time until they would travel again. He glanced at Kerry as he unbuttoned his waistcoat. Her expression had changed; she looked almost wistful as she gazed up at him, and it surprised him. "What?" he asked.

Her gaze fell to her lap. "I was thinking . . . remembering . . . how happy you made me."

Her utterance immediately unbalanced him, tossed him headlong into a pool of sharp regret. But he merely stared at her, his mind filled with all the things he could not say. *She* had been the only spot of brightness in his life, the only glimmer of pure joy he had known in so very long, in what seemed so many lifetimes. He loved her, adored her, yet he could hardly stand to look at her pale face now, uncertain as he was.

He said nothing, simply moved to lie on his side, his back to her, and closed his eyes, hoping her words would go away, leave him be. Fortunately, his body immediately gave way to exhaustion—the sleep came rapidly, carrying him into the depths of heavy slumber.

It seemed only moments before Phillip appeared, crouched down on his haunches, grinning at something on the ground in front of him that Arthur could not see. For once, Phillip was close enough that if he could have moved his arms, he might have finally seized the haunting figure. But he could merely gaze at Phillip's body, his ragged clothing stark against skin as pale as the Scottish mist. Something amused him, something in the grass. Arthur struggled to sit up, but he was weighed down by the heavy sleep, pressed against the earth so that he could not move.

Phillip leaned forward, his low chuckling turning to shrill laughter. Suddenly, he turned fully toward Arthur, paralyzing him with the horrific sight of a gaping hole where his chest should have been. As he watched, Phillip slowly rose to his feet, exceeding the six-foot height he had known in life, towering above the earth. He laughed again and bowed gallantly, sweeping his arm to one side.

"Glasgow," he said.

Arthur looked to where Phillip indicated and felt the horror rip like a scythe through his body—there in the heath lay Kerry, as pale as Phillip, a gaping hole in her breast as black and as wet as Phillip's. Arthur struggled in the terror of the moment, kicking with every ounce of strength he possessed to the surface of his sleep, shuddering awake with the force of ten men as he broke the surface of his dream.

He bolted upright and jerked around to where Phillip should have been standing.

Phillip was gone.

He quickly looked the other way and breathed a sigh of relief. Kerry had fallen asleep. There was no gaping hole in her chest. But her lips were moving in silent conversation, and her face bore an expression of perfect, sweet misery.

Glasgow.

Phillip's dreamy whisper continued to haunt Arthur well after he had bundled Kerry in front of him and pushed on with the early evening. *What had he meant?* Was it an omen? Did it mean anything at all, or was the stress of the last thirty hours making him sentimental? He was, after all, hardly accustomed to being a fugitive. He was hardly accustomed to anything anymore—the world was listing more sharply with each day.

The meaning of the dream escaped him, but it nonetheless propelled him to a full-fledged panic when the seldom-traveled path he had chosen suddenly ended on the banks of a small river south of Perth. Arthur's limited knowledge of the region's geography told him that the river emptied into the Firth of Tay, which meant heavy traffic and passage to the sea and England. If he crossed the river, continued on, they would reach Glasgow in two days, perhaps three. There, he would use his considerable resources to find Kerry's mother, leave her there, and obtain passage to England.

Glasgow.

The haunting memory came to him again as he restlessly paced the banks of the river. In these three long years since Phillip's death, Arthur had believed that the dreams of his fallen friend were Phillip's way of reaching out from the grave to crucify him for having let him fall. But as he paced along the banks of the tributary in the last hours of sunlight, he couldn't help wondering if perhaps Phillip was trying to relay another message altogether. *Glasgow.*

"What shall we do?"

Startled from his ruminations, Arthur turned toward

the sound of Kerry's voice. Standing with her hands clasped demurely in front of her, she gazed at him with wide blue eyes, devoid of the sparkle he cherished.

God, he was losing her, he was losing his very heart.

Her black hair was in wild disarray, her face colorless, all the life bled from it. And he realized in that moment he loved her far too much to deliver her to an uncertain fate in Glasgow. The instinctive need to protect her from that fate, to put the life back into her eyes suddenly surged through him.

Consequence be damned, he was taking her to England.

He suddenly and decisively moved forward, closing the ground between them in two long strides. Kerry's eyes widened as he reached for her and pulled her into his determined embrace. She opened her mouth to say something, but Arthur silenced her with a fierce kiss, his mouth moving hungrily over hers, devouring her lips, drawing her very breath into his lungs. That sweet breath sustained him, infused him with a will stronger than he had ever known to keep her in his arms for eternity and beyond, to endure whatever it might take.

Breathless, he lifted his head. "England," he managed. "Will you? Come with me to England, that is. I've no idea what awaits us there, but it is all I can offer you now—it's all I have at the moment."

Kerry blinked; the confusion scudded across her features like a summer cloud. Then suddenly she made a strange sound in her throat, closed her eyes as tears sprang from the corners.

"What then, I've upset you? I am sorry, Kerry, but there is nothing more I can do—"

A cry of laughter escaped her, and she threw her arms around his neck. "Oh God. Oh God, thank you!"

His arms quickly tightened around her, crushing her safely to him as he buried his face in the curve of her neck. They stood that way, holding one another tightly, until the need to be practical made Arthur let her go and pull her arms from his neck. "There is the small matter of transportation," he said, and walked to where the horse stood grazing. He relieved the poor beast of their baggage, then the saddle, which he placed behind a small stand of shrubbery.

Standing there, looking at the exhausted beast, he felt a peculiar burning in the back of his eyes. "Godspeed," he mumbled, and hit the horse on the rump, sent him trotting off toward greener blades of grass. He then picked up the two bags and, gripping them in one hand, motioned to a path leading east. "Mrs. McKinnon, if you will allow me to escort you to God knows where, I shall endeavor to find a boat to ease your travel."

Kerry smiled. The sight of it sent a rush of warmth all through him, invigorated him.

"Escort me to the ends of the earth, on foot, on horseback, by boat. I doona care as long as you are with me," she said, and just as she had so many weeks ago, walked bravely on before him on the narrow, overgrown path.

They walked for an hour or more, following the path of the tributary as it curved around and widened, indicating that they were nearing the Firth of Tay. As they climbed up a small hill, Arthur spied a flatboat anchored alongside a dock on the opposite bank; a handful of men worked to load small crates onto one end of the boat. At last, a hope of transportation out of the Highlands.

Kerry had seen the flatboat, too; she was squinting into the dusk trying to make it out.

"I shall speak with them," he said, setting the bags aside and strode briskly to a point that put him directly across from the flatboat.

"Ho there, lad!" he called, bracing his hands against his hips. One man straightened, said something to the other. There was something familiar about him, something—

"Aye?" the man asked, folding his beefy arms across his barrel chest, and Arthur groaned at the sight of the familiar, uncompromising stance of the Richey brothers.

As if this little journey could not *possibly* get any worse.

Fortunately, as Arthur had become quite the expert in dealing with the Richey brothers, he succeeded in gaining passage to Newbergh and a promise to at least *attempt* to deliver a message to Thomas, all for the bargain price of roughly half his personal fortune. In exchange, the Richey brothers agreed that the fact the Sassenach and Mrs. McKinnon had sought passage on their boat a *third* time would remain their little secret. Arthur was rather confident they would keep that promise—Mr. Richey One relayed to him, in a mere four words, that he could gain passage to Dundee at Newbergh, and from there, passage to England. Assuming, of course, there was anything left in the coffers of the Duchy of Sutherland at that point.

So loaded once more on the flatboat, they drifted silently into the night. Kerry's exhaustion gave way to a fitful sleep. Arthur's nerves were too raw; he dozed off once or twice, no more—the slightest noise or movement jarred him awake. He was beset with a vicious cycle of doubt as to the wisdom of what he was doing, to the absurd hope that he might have Kerry with him forever, only to doubt again. The confusion made him feel as if he was treading water as his strength slowly bled from him. More than once, a silent and deep fear welled in him that he might actually be pulled under by the enormity of what was happening to him. His life was sedate in comparison to this, the quality of his life safe and uneventful. Nothing the Rogues had ever done compared with the extraordinary experiences he had had in the last weeks, or the extraordinary, foolish, dangerous escape he found himself in the middle of now. His life was suddenly frightening.

But then he would look down at Kerry's dark head in his lap, touch the curl at her temple, feel his blood come alive and believe. When the morning finally dawned,

Arthur had come to the single conclusion that he had plunged headfirst into deep water when he stumbled across that red satchel weeks ago, and now, he must fight to the death to keep from sinking and taking Kerry with him.

Chapter Sixteen

Although they reached Dundee without further incident, they were forced to wait two full days until Arthur could secure passage to England aboard a shipping vessel. The price of passage however, left Arthur precious little; the seemingly substantial amount he had brought to Scotland had dwindled to almost nothing. Afraid that Moncrieffe would search for her even as far as Dundee, Arthur found a cheap, nondescript inn near the docks where they waited.

It was an interminable, intolerable wait; the small room smelled of fish and bodies. Arthur left her each day to seek passage on any ship he could find and, at Kerry's insistence, to look for Big Angus and May. He came back each evening to find Kerry sitting cross-legged on the sagging bed, fighting her imagination.

And when Arthur told her he could not find Big Angus or May, or anyone from Glenbaden, her imagination went wild, filling her mind with ominous theories of what had happened to her clan, and visions of men coming to drag her off to the gallows. Every sound, every creak of wood beneath a boot beyond the door sent her heart racing. When she closed her eyes, she saw the hangman's noose swinging in front of her. When sheer fatigue finally forced her to sleep, she would inevitably

dream of standing on the gallows, watching a hooded ex-
ecutioner put the noose over her head and pull it tight
around her neck. If by some miracle she could sleep
without seeing herself hanged for her crime, she
dreamed of Charles Moncrieffe lying lifeless before her,
the blood pooling black beneath him.

But in those bleak moments when she was jolted
awake by the horror of her dreams, Arthur was always
there, cocooning her in the comfort of his arms and whispering soothing little nothings into her ear until the
tremors had ceased. It was as if he had actually seen her
dreams, had actually felt the terror himself.

On the morning they at last set sail for England,
Kerry stood on the deck of the schooner and watched the
land slowly fade to a dark strip on the horizon. Myriad
emotions assailed her at once—relief, profound sadness,
and fear. She gripped the railing hard, felt a pull in her
chest, as if Scotland actually called to her, tried to keep
her home.

But she had no home. What Fraser had not destroyed, she had. She had no one, nothing to hold her to
Scotland now; all that she had was the charity of an extraordinary man, a beautiful stranger who had felt the
anguish in her heart and had come back for her. Kerry
believed that with all her heart.

It was that belief that enabled her to turn her back
for God knew how long on the last glimpse of her home-
land. Carefully, she made her way to the small cabin
where Arthur waited.

The ship he had found was carrying a hull full of jute
and tobacco. Arthur had explained to her that they
would first cross to Hoek-van-Holland to unload then
take on new cargo before sailing to England, where they
would dock at Kingston-upon-Hull. From there, they
would travel to a place called Longbridge. It was the
home of a friend, he said, and a place they might stay for
a time until he determined what they should do.

What he should do with her, he surely meant, but

was far too kind to say so. Nonetheless, Kerry knew exactly what sort of burden she presented—she had little more than the gray gown on her back that signified her status as widow. The contents of her satchel amounted to two pairs of drawers, a chemise, and the blouse and black bombazine skirt she wore to work in the garden. She had no real skills to speak of—she supposed she could hire on as a governess somewhere, but without credentials, the likelihood of securing a suitable situation were slim. It was more likely that she should end up in the kitchen service of some English household—assuming, of course, Arthur could help her find such employment.

As the ship sailed farther into calm seas, Kerry remained in the cabin, heartsick and confused. She thought often of Thomas—what must he be thinking now? It broke her heart to imagine his confusion, but it made her positively ill to think that he must have gone back to Glenbaden to find her, only to find what she had done. And the others, Big Angus and May. What had become of them?

And of course there was the guilt. All-consuming guilt, a persistently nagging thought that she should turn back, throw herself on Moncrieffe's mercy, and face what she had done.

Had it not been for Arthur, she might very well have thrown herself over the rail of the ship and let her misery sink her. As the first day turned into the second, he became her lifeline, keeping her carefully tethered to him and reality.

But he was obviously restless, too; he bustled in and out of the little cabin, putting things here and there then rearranging them again, and talking to fill the silence that seemed to engulf them. He told her about his closest friends, starting with the earl of Albright, whose home they would visit first, and how he had turned a small estate in severe disrepair into one of the most powerful agricultural centers in all of England. He laughed about the earl of Kettering, who had raised four younger sisters from the time he was a lad of sixteen. He was proud of his own family, clearly admired and loved his brother Alex. And he smiled fondly when he told her about his mother and even his Aunt Paddy and her friend, Mrs. Clark, who, Arthur said with a roll of his eyes, spent the better part of their lives looking for marriageable young women for him. He was obviously a man who held his family dear, and it was just one more of the many qualities that endeared him eternally to Kerry.

When night fell on the second day, the seas turned rough. Arthur returned from the deck to tell her that they were sailing into a late summer storm and that he would lend a hand to the crew. Kerry assured him she was quite all right, and he left her lying on the narrow little bed, unaware that she swallowed down nausea that rose with each swell of the sea.

As the ship rocked into the night, Kerry kept the nausea at bay by concentrating on Arthur, forcing herself to recount in detail everything about him from the moment she had shot him on the road to Perth.

It was an easy task. Everything Arthur had ever done in her presence lived on in her heart. She recalled waking next to him the morning they had set off for Glenbaden, inadvertently sprawled across his body, and the dangerous look on his face that made her heart flutter like a bird. And the moment he had removed the boots from her feet and had wrapped his neckcloth around her battered heels. And, oh God, she recalled the searing kiss he had given her when he had pulled her from the waters of the river.

Kerry pressed a palm to her damp forehead as she recalled his last night at Glenbaden and the hours she had spent in his arms and beneath him. The memory turned molten; her face flushed hot with the memory. It was that night she had understood how she truly loved him, completely and irrevocably, for the rest of her life. She had never felt for her husband what she felt for her beautiful stranger, and the intense longing filled her again, swelling inside her heart until it felt as if it would burst from her chest. She suddenly rolled onto her side, curling into a ball.

She should not long for him. She should not wish that he would kiss her like that again. She should not look at his hand and remember how tenderly he had caressed her naked breast. God help her, but she should not notice how magnificent he was, or let his smile melt her, or let his cheery laughter wash over her like rain. But every time Arthur touched her—a hand to her shoulder, a finger to her temple—she wished he would take her into his arms, kiss her, make love to her again like he had that night, and banish every ugly thing from her life. *She loved him.*

Oh God, what sort of cruel life was this that she should know such love and tenderness but never truly possess it?

In the blackness of the cabin, she lay there listening to the wind batter the ship like her sorrow battered her soul. She mourned her losses, but above all, she mourned the inevitable loss of Arthur. Nothing had changed. They came from two different worlds and in spite of his heroic act of rescuing her—not once, but twice now—he would, eventually, continue on with his life, as would she.

The dreaded vision of her life was the last thing she knew before she drifted off to sleep.

Sometime later, a noise awoke her, and as she opened her eyes, she noticed that the ship was no longer listing. A single lamp burned low. She blinked against the dim light, her eyes slowly adjusting to the sight of Arthur trying to fit his long body across two chairs.

With his legs stretched onto a chair, he held his arms folded across his stomach, and rested his chin on his chest with his eyes closed. After a moment, his head jerked up; he groaned softly before stabbing his elbow onto the table and his chin atop his fist.

A surge of tenderness swept through her; Kerry pushed herself up onto her elbows. *"Arthur."*

His head instantly jerked up and around to the sound of her voice, his feet landing hard on the floor.

Kerry held out her hand to him.

It seemed to take him aback. He pivoted in his chair, facing her, his hands braced on his knees as he stared at her outstretched hand. He swallowed. "Don't," he said roughly. "Don't offer me your hand because I can't be satisfied with only that. If I have any part of you, I must have all of you. And if you take me, Kerry, you must take all of me."

"Then come to me," she murmured.

He lifted a gaze from her hand that was both smoldering and bewildered. A scorching heat instantly filled her; she spread her hand over the coarse linen cover. *"Come."*

Arthur stood, quickly removed his waistcoat as he crossed the cabin to her, pulling his lawn shirt from the waist of his trousers as he reached the edge of the bed. "Kerry," he said, falling onto one knee on the bed beside her, lifting his hands to cup her face. *"Kerry,"* he whispered earnestly, "have you any idea what you've done to me? Have you any idea how I have longed for you, how I have dreamed of you? Do you know that you entered my daydreams, rode alongside me, slept in my arms at night? My regard for you has not changed nor abated with time, it has only grown stronger."

His earnest admission shocked her—she had heard his declarations of adoration the night they had made love, but she had believed they were voiced for the moment. How many times had she replayed the words in her head, wishing—no, *praying*—that they were true? And how many more times had she berated herself for her foolish dreaming, her childish hopes? Yet here he knelt before her, uttering words she had ached to hear.

"Arthur," she said, pressing her palm to his rough cheek, "how I love you . . ."

A warmth filled his eyes, and he pulled her face to his, drinking the words from her lips as he gently pushed her onto her back and came over her. He kissed her tenderly, straying from her mouth to her eyes and her cheeks. His moist lips slowly touched every part of her face and neck, deliberately teasing her while his hands caressed her, his palms skimming lightly over her arms and bosom, his fingers flittering across her neck.

His gentle, near reverent exploration of her was stoking a blaze that begged to be doused. Her hands swept the hard lines of his body. She slipped her hands inside his shirt, fingered his hardened nipples. Arthur's low moan reverberated against the skin of her neck, and he reached for the buttons of her gown, deftly freeing each one as his hands moved quickly down her spine.

"I have often thought of our night together," he murmured as he slipped the gray wool from her shoulders to her waist and gazed down to where her breasts spilled from the top of her corset. "More times than I might count," he added softly, and sat back on his feet, pulling her to a sitting position. He kissed her forehead and the tip of her nose as he unfastened her corset. With a smile, he threw it aside. But the smile slowly faded as he carefully cupped her breasts, rubbing the peaks with the pad of his thumb through the thin cotton chemise she wore. "I thought of you constantly."

"And I of you," she said, carefully brushing a thick curl of hair from his forehead. "I dared not dream that you would come back."

His gaze dropped to her lips. "Many was the time I would look at you in Glenbaden and wonder at such natural beauty, wish that such beauty could be mine, that I could hold it in my arms." He nipped her bottom lip before drawing it fully between his. He pushed her back onto the narrow bed, breaking the kiss only to remove her skirt and his shirt. But then he came over her again with an urgency and heat that Kerry felt burning inside her.

With his hands, he began a more anxious exploration of her body, pushing the chemise aside so that he could feel her skin. Kerry's body was jolted alive by his touch; his fingers seemed to scorch every place he touched her, detonating something inside her—she was suddenly raking her hands through his hair, kissing him fiercely, her body straining to meet his.

Arthur seemed to share her desperate abandon; his hands worked with a fever of their own, stroking her everywhere, inflaming her flesh, striving to caress every inch of her and know every contour, every flaw. Her hands trailed down his chest, to the soft down that disappeared into his trousers.

He caught a drag of air in his throat when she flicked her tongue across his nipple. The sound of his ardor turned her into a churning, molten mass, and she realized it was her hands that fumbled with his trousers, her hands that sought to free his rigid arousal straining against the fabric. When the last button sprang free, she reached for him, felt him swell hot in the palm of her hand.

Arthur anxiously freed her breast from the confines of her chemise, smothered it with warm kisses. When he took it in his mouth, Kerry felt the draw of desire from the bottom of her belly, the ethereal weight of it rising rapidly to the surface, boiling there as he laved her with deliberate laziness, sucking her into his mouth and tongue.

The ache for him was more than she could bear; her hand surrounded his rigid erection, squeezing gently, stroking him with the same deliberate laziness that he showed her, until Arthur could endure no more. His head suddenly came up; planting his hands on either side of her head, he moved over her.

"You seduce me as no other woman has," he said brusquely. "You compel me to an insane desire, Kerry McKinnon." With that, he lowered himself to her, kissing her passionately as one hand moved lithely between her thighs. Kerry gasped against his mouth; the molten heat she had been feeling was spilling from her, she could feel it. Arthur's fingers moved expertly against her, swirling over and around, in and out, driving her to the brink of a well of desire, battering her senses for release. And just when she thought she would surely drown in it, he moved his hand, positioned himself between her legs, and slid inside her as smoothly as the tide washes ashore. She felt her body as she had never felt it before—every sense was inflamed, every fiber ablaze, the air around her filled with the scent and flesh of Arthur.

With every stroke of his staff, every kiss of his lips, he was pushing her closer and closer to him. It was so fluid, so without beginning or end that she could scarcely tell where his body ended and hers began. He flowed into her like water, then rushed out again like the tide, only to come again, deeper still. Kerry's body rose to meet every stroke, but she felt herself fast losing control, spiraling headlong into a physical release so pure that the anticipation of it had already taken her breath away.

Above her, Arthur pressed his cheek against hers and buried his hand in the wild tangle of her hair. With his other hand, he continued to stroke her in rhythm with his body's thrusting until Kerry could endure the immaculate torture no more. It happened suddenly—a sensation of sinking fast then floating on the swell as the tide rushed out again. The wondrous sensation caused her to cry out with the joy of it; her arms fell away, landing limply to either side of her.

Arthur's strokes suddenly intensified; he shoved his hands beneath her hips, lifting her to him, thrusting fiercely and quickly until he shuddered against her with a strangled sob of his own. Kerry felt the powerful surge of his seed deep inside her and was immediately overcome with a sense of completion.

They lay with their arms around one another, both of them panting lightly. After a few moments, Arthur somberly gathered Kerry to him and rolled to his side so that they lay facing each other. She felt him slip out of her and the warmth of his lifeblood spilling onto her thighs. Sighing, he brushed a damp strand of hair from her face. "You have captured my poor heart, madam."

Oh, but he had captured her heart weeks ago, plucked it like a ripe fruit. Suddenly overwhelmed, she buried her face in his neck—it seemed to her that in this moment, out here on the open sea as they were, they were just man and woman, sharing the most extraordinary intimacy two people could share, and she loved him for sharing it so completely.

They lay entwined in each other's arms for what seemed hours, hardly speaking, simply enjoying the feel and scent and look of one another in the flickering light of the lantern. When they drifted to sleep Kerry would never know, but she would carry with her for the rest of her days the memory of their lovemaking that night, when they had become one upon the sea.

The next morning, she was coaxed awake from the first deep sleep she had known in days by Arthur's hands and mouth. He made slow, deliberate love to her, taking his time to bring her to climax, taking even more to reach his own with a joyous smile on his face. He did not leave the cabin again until they docked in Hoek-van-Holland, except occasionally to find food and to give Kerry some privacy. Except for those rare occasions, they lay together on the tiny shelf of a bed, carefully but thoroughly exploring one another's bodies, laughing softly at private little jests, and speaking low of their lives, their hopes, their dreams.

Whispering tenderly of the love growing between them.

It was as if the world did not exist for that space of time. By the time the ship sailed for England, the intimate surroundings and prolonged togetherness had brought them impossibly close. On the sea, there were no differences between them, no ugly realities to disturb them. It seemed to Kerry that she had known Arthur much longer than a handful of weeks—they had so much more in common than she would ever have thought possible. She actually *felt* him—as inexplicable as it was, at times she had the intimate sensation that she was looking at herself.

Even her debilitating guilt was beginning to melt away in the comfort and safety of Arthur's arms. What had happened seemed a lifetime ago, and in some moments, she dreamed that perhaps it hadn't happened at all. There was no Scotland, no Moncrieffe, nothing of Fraser's legacy in that cabin. Nothing but her and Arthur and the love between them.

But on the afternoon the ship docked at Kingston-upon-Hull, the first rays of ugly reality filtered into the little cabin. The sights and sounds of the busy little harbor brought the cold truth crashing into the world they had created and the stark reality of who she was and what she had done.

Arthur left the cabin for a time, and Kerry moved woodenly about, donning the plain skirt and blouse from her satchel, fastening her hair into an austere knot at her neck. When the tears began to slip from her eyes, they were quick and silent, taking the magic of the last few days with them. What they had shared in this cabin was over, forever gone, and Kerry was certain she would never know such peace again.

When Arthur returned, she managed to keep her back to him so that he would not see the redness in her eyes. But in that uncanny way he had, Arthur seemed to sense her distress. He walked up behind her as she packed her few things and slipped a strong arm around her waist, drawing her into his chest.

He brushed his lips against her bare neck, pressed his cheek against hers as he tightened his hold. "It will be quite all right," he said softly. "I will not allow any harm to come to you, on my life I won't."

His solemn pledge warmed her, but she twisted in his embrace and kissed him hungrily, silencing any more vows he might make, because she couldn't bear to hear them.

She couldn't bear to face the truth—it wasn't her crime she feared, it was *him.*

Oh, there was no doubt in her mind that he meant every word he said. He had shown her glorious love, completely and unselfishly, and readily vowed with his life to keep her safe. But it was his very life she feared. It was his name, his position in the British aristocracy, and everything else that separated him from her.

A different world, she thought later as Arthur took her hand in his to walk among the fishmongers and sailors and various tradesman in the crowded streets of Kingston, not the realm of make-believe they had created in the last few days. And as she watched him haggle over a carriage—a covered carriage, he insisted loudly to the man, as he would not expose the lady to the elements—she pretended she was watching a man who would love her forever, would cherish her for all of eternity.

And then swallowed down the bitter taste of reality that crept into her throat.

Chapter Seventeen

If HE HADN'T known better, Arthur would have sworn they were still in Scotland, for hiring a suitable traveling chaise in Kingston was just barely more tolerable than purchasing a horse in the Highlands. He sincerely hoped his brother Alex hadn't made some major investment of funds in the last several weeks, for he had certainly spent a bloody fortune since he had wandered off to see after Phillip's holdings.

And as if he hadn't had enough bloody vexations for one day, the driver was not terribly keen on the idea of driving to Longbridge. "Roads are rather thick with mud, milord," he said, clutching his cap anxiously in his hands. "We've had an awful lot of rain of late. Would you not rather go south?"

Had the whole of England gone mad in his absence? Since when did a journeyman argue with him? "I am *quite* certain," he said through clenched teeth. "In fact, I am rather *unyieldingly* certain. Now, sir, if you will do me the great favor of getting *on* with it, I should be eternally grateful!"

The man frowned, shoved his hat on his head. "Mud, I say," he muttered under his breath as he swung up onto the driver's seat, and followed that up with something Arthur did not quite catch, but which sounded terribly snide. "I can hear you very clearly, sir!" he snapped, and shoved through the opening of the chaise, slammed the little door behind him, and landed irritably on the bench across from Kerry.

But with only one look at her, Arthur quickly forgot his annoyance. He smiled. "It would seem our driver has a particular aversion to mud. Rather causes one to wonder why he should aspire to be a driver a'tall."

Kerry merely smiled and looked out the dingy, gray window.

Arthur frowned, straightening himself against the squabs. Two days ago, Kerry would have laughed. This quiet, contemplative demeanor of hers had come about the moment he told her they were sailing into the harbor at Kingston. Not that he was any sort of expert in the ever-changing dispositions of women—nor did he have any aspiration to be—but he had noticed it then and had guessed that the change had to do with memories of Scotland—and Thomas. In the course of the last several days she had worried aloud more than once about her cousin. Privately, Arthur thought her worries a tragic waste of good humor; Thomas, that horse's ass, would make his way in this world. Bloody hell, Arthur wouldn't be surprised to see the obstinate goat rise to great fame and fortune on some lark. That was always the way with men like McKinnon—

"Your friend, the earl? He willna think we are imposing, truly?"

Kerry's small voice roused Arthur from his ruminations; he saw the worry on her face, and immediately leaned across the coach and put a comforting hand on her knee. "Trust me, Albright shall be delighted to receive us."

Kerry glanced down at her worn black skirt; a faint grimace creased her brow.

Arthur suddenly understood. For perhaps the first time in his life, he wished for an entire kingdom at his disposal and the instant means to give Kerry her choice of gowns and jewels and shoes, right there in the bleak country of the north. He would do anything to please her, anything to raise her joyous smile once again.

He had, of course, given trinkets to lovers or little gifts to appease ruffled feathers for one perceived slight or another. But he had never so much *desired* to give a woman something until now, never felt such burning need to make her happy. And never had he felt so hopelessly inept at doing so. In spite of his considerable influence and resources, in the rural north as they were, without any ready funds left to speak of, there was nothing he could do—they would be accepted at the door of Longbridge as they were. Or not . . . Arthur was not quite certain what he would do if Lilliana objected to their unannounced and untoward arrival. Worse, he realized that uncertainty about every bloody thing was a feeling that was becoming quite familiar to him of late.

Such was life with Kerry McKinnon about.

By the time they reached the mile-long drive leading to the house and grounds of Longbridge, Arthur could not have possibly cared less how they might appear to Albright, or the whole bloody *ton* for that matter. They had been stuck twice, which naturally meant he had to push. A cold rain had started up again, chilling him through to his very marrow. He had never in his life been as tired or cold or ravenous as he was at that moment, and by God, Adrian Spence would receive him.

The driver, naturally, flatly refused to attempt the drive to the house when the deluge of rain began anew. Arthur and Kerry had, therefore, stood under a very slim space of shelter built into the massive brick gate until the rain had abated. *Somewhat* abated. As it appeared to Arthur that the sun would never shine again, he had taken up their bags, forced a smile for Kerry's benefit, and had started down the muddied road to the house, pulling one foot after the other from the muck. It was a miserable trek—but not once did Kerry complain or suggest that she could not go on. Hers was a valiant soul, he would certainly give her that, more valiant than he, for he was on the verge of sitting on his arse next to the road and wailing like a baby.

They walked until they were standing side by side on the huge round porch that surrounded the massive oak entry to Longbridge, staring at the gruesome face fashioned on the brass knocker. Neither of them spoke for a long moment. When Arthur finally glanced at Kerry from the corner of his eye, she turned and gazed at him with a look of such dismay that he could not, no matter how hard he tried, summon words of encouragement. He shifted his gaze to the ugly brass knocker, and might have studied the workmanship of the thing all bloody evening had the door not swung open so suddenly that he and Kerry were blinded by the bright light behind it. Arthur blinked until he could clearly focus on the marble tile and gilded fixtures that adorned the foyer.

"Oh my. Oh *my!*"

That voice Arthur instantly recognized as belonging to Max, Adrian's fastidious butler. "Max," he drawled, focusing his bleary gaze, "I don't suppose Albright is about?"

A good six inches shorter than Arthur, Max gaped up at him, his round eyes clearly relaying his shock. "My Lord *Arthur!*" he squealed. "What tragedy has befallen you?"

What tragedy? What *tragedy?* An adventure so bizarre as not to be believed had befallen him, but a tragedy? This was no tragedy; this was a blasted comedy! Arthur could not help himself; the situation suddenly struck him as full of hilarity, and he laughed hard. "A thousand stars have befallen me if you must know," he said through his laughter, knowing full well he looked quite mad. "A thousand stars, right on top of my noggin,

Max. Now if you would be so kind, let the old boy know
that I've come to call, will you?"

Max flicked his gaze down the length of Arthur's
body, then looked at Kerry. "He is indeed in residence,
my lord. Please forgive me," he said, and stepped aside,
gesturing weakly into the foyer. Still chuckling, Arthur
put his hand on the small of Kerry's back to usher her inside. But she surprised him by pushing back against him
and refusing to move forward. "It's quite all right. Just
step inside," he murmured.

"No," she muttered, and shoved back against him so
hard in her attempt to back away from the door that she
unbalanced him.

Max looked mortified; Arthur plastered a smile to his
face for the butler's benefit, and slowly leaned to one
side so that his mouth was just above Kerry's ear. "What
would you do, stand out here all night?" he whispered
through his smile. "Come on then, just step inside."

"No!" she hissed, and elbowed him in the ribs. "I will
not go in *there* looking like *this!*"

Oh fine. Just bloody *fine.* He had dragged her all the
way from Scotland and she would choose *now* for a
tantrum? All right, all right, he could see why she might
be a bit reluctant—Albright never did anything halfway,
and the elaborate foyer with its painted ceiling moldings,
gilded door and window fixtures, marble tile, and great
sweeping staircase was merely a sample of what one
would find in the rest of the mansion. Nevertheless, it
was the only shelter within miles of where they stood,
and wet to the bone as they were, Arthur was in no
mood to argue the point. "Step inside," he said, the tone
of his voice brooking no debate. "We can argue in
warmth just as effectively as we can in the rain."

"No!"

With a sharp sigh, Arthur turned and grabbed Kerry
by the shoulders, not caring what Max heard or saw
now. "You have no choice, Kerry! It is either *this* house

or the stable, and trust me, you will not want to share a stall with the likes of Thunder!"

Kerry defiantly tipped her head back. "I prefer the stables!"

"That can definitely be arranged!" he shot back querulously.

"Good! Then please point me in the proper direction as I should very much like to be gone before another living soul lays eyes on me!"

"Arthur?"

Startled by the female voice, Arthur and Kerry simultaneously jerked their gazes toward it. Lilliana Spence stood in the foyer, looking very elegant and very bewildered. Her green eyes flicked the full length of his personal disarray, then to Kerry's. One sculpted blonde brow lifted above the other in silent question.

Bloody hell. Arthur cleared his throat. "Lilliana. I must apologize for arriving so . . . ah, so . . . no doubt you are wondering—"

"Please come in, won't you? You must be very cold," she said to Kerry, and extended her hand as she suddenly moved toward them.

"N-no thank you," Kerry muttered, stepping backward and putting her heel down on Arthur's toes. "I wouldna think of spoiling your house—I mean, the mud—"

"Nonsense. It's merely a floor and you could not spoil it if you tried, Miss . . . ?"

"Lady Albright, may I introduce you to Mrs. McKinnon of Glenbaden, Scotland," Arthur quickly interjected.

"*Scotland!*" Lilliana's face lit with her smile. "I thought I detected a bit of an accent! Ooh, how very lovely, Mrs. McKinnon! I have been desperate to travel to Scotland, and I have read all the beautiful poetry of Wordsworth. My husband promises to take me there once our children are a bit older." Lilliana paused to peer at the gray sky through the open doorway, then at the grimy red satchel before bestowing a warm smile on Kerry. "We must get you into some dry clothing," she said, motioning for Max to close the door.

"No," Kerry said instantly, "I wouldna impose—"

"It is no imposition, Mrs. McKinnon. It is a wonderful treat for me to have a true Scot in my very own house. And Arthur," Lilliana said firmly, "you are in need of a bath, if you will pardon my saying so. Max, do have two baths drawn at once, please," she said as she extended her hand and wrapped it around Kerry's, seemingly oblivious to the mud caked to her wrist. "Please come in, Mrs. McKinnon. You will catch your death."

With a scowl for Arthur, Kerry allowed Lilliana to pull her deeper into the foyer. "Arthur, Max will attend you momentarily," Lilliana called over her shoulder, and began a march up the spiraling staircase, dragging Kerry behind her.

Arthur could see why Adrian loved the woman so— she never once looked back to see how Kerry's soiled skirts dragged the blue carpet of the stairs, nor did she look at her hair or stained clothing. She spoke to Kerry as if she were an equal, and for that alone, Arthur would adore Lilliana Spence for the rest of his days.

"What in God's name has happened to your boots?"

Arthur closed his eyes and prayed that the rest of his days would not include many like this. He opened them slowly, turned reluctantly to see Adrian leaning negligently against a wall, one ankle crossed over the other, his hands shoved deep in his pockets, observing Arthur with a very pointed look of amusement on his face. "If you don't mind me saying, you look like hell."

"Why thank you, Albright, for the kind compliment."

Adrian ignored that, and inclined his head to the floors above where Lilliana and Kerry had just disappeared. "I suppose you know that I am all aflutter with anticipation of the tale of how you have come to be here—looking like *that,* naturally—and with a new charge."

Yes, Arthur rather imagined he was all aflutter, and

with an impatient sigh, he raked a dirty hand through his tangled hair. "I'd be right happy to oblige you in exchange for a hot bath and a bottle of your best whiskey."

Adrian's brows lifted. "A bottle, is it? Very well then, I shall have Max fetch our best—I shouldn't want to hear what I am quite certain is a delightful tale with anything less than that."

And he apparently meant to hear it at once, seeing as he followed Arthur into the bathing room when Max had announced his bath ready. Arthur ignored Adrian; he was too busy luxuriating in the steaming waters. With his eyes closed and his head propped lazily against the edge of the porcelain tub, he let the water seep beneath his skin and scald the grime of the last ten days from his body. Every now and again he would open one eye to see Adrian sprawled along a long, silk-covered window bench, one leg bent at the knee and heel propped against it without regard for the fine fabric. In one hand, he held his head; with the other he held a crystal glass from which he languidly sipped aged Scotch whiskey when he wasn't peering intently at Arthur.

Arthur was just beginning to feel human again when Adrian at last asked, "Well then, let's have it."

Arthur merely snorted, kept his eyes closed.

"Ah, Christian, you don't mean to taunt me, do you? Really, you must consider this from my point of view. You appear from nowhere after a strange foray into Scotland and a lengthy absence, inexplicably covered head to foot with mud and a Scottish woman on your arm to boot. And now you would play coy? *Tsk, tsk.*"

Arthur chuckled. "You act as if you never appeared at Mount Street under suspect circumstances, Albright. You can't deny that you have and you must acknowledge that I did not insist on interrogating you on those occasions," he responded, and sank lower into the water.

"Yes, well, perhaps. But you are *Arthur.* And besides, I never appeared with a strange woman on my arm— you surely have me confused with Kettering."

That earned another chuckle—Julian had, indeed, appeared at his door on several occasions with unknown women on his arm . . . and some quite well known. "Nor did I interrogate Kettering, though God knows I should have."

"Come on, then. Your brother has sent two letters asking if I have had occasion to see you. We were all beginning to fret a bit—so who is this woman, where in the hell have you been, and what have you done to those fine boots?"

Funny, but Arthur had not, until this very moment, imagined what words he might use to explain Kerry. Or his whereabouts the last few weeks. Or why he had risked his bloody neck to bring her here. He slowly opened his eyes and glanced at one of his oldest friends.

Adrian had righted himself, was leaning forward with his arms propped against his thighs, the glass dangling carelessly from one hand, watching Arthur closely. "Who is she, Arthur?"

God, if only he knew! He sank lower until his chin skimmed the surface of the hot water, contemplating that. What was he doing? What madness had overcome him, what demon had possessed him and allowed him to believe that he could bring Kerry here, no questions asked, no explanations?

"I can't imagine what happened in Scotland, but I think she must be someone rather dear for you to have gone to such trouble," Adrian said.

If only he knew. "Dearer than my own life," Arthur muttered. The admission surprised him far more than it seemed to surprise Adrian. He had not meant to say any such thing, but it had sprung involuntarily from his lips, had escaped him before he could pull them back.

"She is Scottish. And the widow of a poor, landless one at that. She is . . . no one."

"I beg your pardon," Adrian drawled, "she is clearly someone to you."

Arthur looked at his friend then, searching his face

for any sign of condemnation, any hint that he would not accept her.

He saw none.

But he saw the lines of aristocracy in Adrian, the placid expression and years of practiced indifference in his voice. Undoubtedly, he was trying to be accepting of this strange situation, trying to understand, but how could he possibly make him see? How could he explain to Adrian that Kerry had taught him how to *live?*

"Do you recall," he asked slowly, "the evening the four of us accompanied Alex to the opera? It was the night he unveiled his newly appointed box."

Adrian stared at the whiskey in his glass for a moment. "I recall clearly," he said, looking up from his glass. "Quite clearly. Phillip had drunk far too much brandy as usual."

"You will surely recall, then, how he angered Alex beyond compare by bringing Miss Daphne into the box."

Adrian nodded.

Arthur looked toward the fire. He could almost see Phillip there, his blond head bent over Daphne, explaining the opera to her. Alex—a duke, a man of propriety—had been livid. Daphne was one of Madame Farantino's charges, a woman who pleasured men of the aristocracy in a discreet brothel behind the Tam O'Shanter. She was Phillip's favorite, and indeed, he had developed quite an attachment to her in those days, one that almost rivaled his attachment to brandy.

Alex had invited the four Rogues of Regent Street to his box on the opening night of the opera. That was their era, the days when the *Times* hardly went to press without some mention of their exploits. Phillip had disappeared during the opening act, reappearing with Daphne on his arm at the most inopportune time of all—at intermission, when everyone was crowding the box to pay a call or request introductions. Alex was furious with Phillip and quite embarrassed, but there was nothing he could do without causing a scene.

"I was quite angry on Alex's behalf," Arthur continued. "When I later confronted Phillip about his reprehensible behavior, he looked at me as though I had disappointed him somehow. I remember thinking that it was a rather odd reaction to my anger. 'You consort with women just like Daphne,' he said to me. 'Do you think the women you ride like a dog are so insignificant beyond your bed that you would deny them the very simple pleasure of music?' "

Arthur paused, remembering how the question had mortified him on many levels, not the least of which was the grain of truth in it. Adrian said nothing, remained very still, waiting for him to continue. "Of course I held more regard for the woman than that," he said, silently questioning whether or not that was entirely true. "But Alex's opera box? It was unimaginable, incomprehensible. I had to think of his reputation—a young duke, so much he was trying to accomplish, so many who would have delighted in seeing him fail. I said as much to Phillip, and reminded him that Daphne was not of suitable situation, that her very presence tainted the important work my brother was trying to accomplish in gaining the social reforms that would help women like her."

"I've no doubt he responded with something terribly mocking," Adrian muttered.

"He said, 'Then your brother touts false reform, Arthur, if it is people like Daphne he professes to save, for Daphne is a living, breathing human being, as much God's child as you or I. She is as deserving of his esteem as anyone, but if she is not good enough to sit in his box, then there is no hope that she can be saved from men like your brother.' "

Arthur looked at Adrian. "Kerry *is* someone to me—she is someone I never dreamed could touch me, someone not of my class, someone whose *situation* could taint my family's good name. Yet she *did* touch me—she touched me in a way I can scarcely understand, much less describe to you. She is someone to me, all right. She is everything to me—she is a living, breathing human being, as much God's child as you or I, and as deserving of my esteem as anyone."

Adrian blinked, held Arthur's gaze for a long moment before suddenly tossing the last of his whiskey down his throat. "Well then, that makes her someone to me. Now I suggest you remove yourself from that pond before you drown and *I* am forced to think what to do with her."

He flashed a droll smile at Arthur and stood, strolled to the door. "I've no doubt Max has fetched you the best of my clothing," he said with a roll of his eyes. "We'll gather in the gold salon before supper." With that, he walked out of the room, and Arthur heard him tell Max to bring another bottle up from the cellar, as "Christian was going to be in desperate need of it."

He chuckled to himself before submerging completely into the warm waters of his bath.

Chapter Eighteen

STANDING IN FRONT of a full-length mirror, Kerry turned again, unable to believe her eyes. The transformation in her was . . . *remarkable*.

The gown she wore was finer than any she had ever seen or imagined. It was a pale blue silk trimmed in white satin—not black, not gray, or some other morosely drab widow color. Never had she looked so bloody elegant. Even her hair—Mrs. Dismuke, Lady Albright's personal maid, had dressed her wet hair with her big hands, artfully rolling it into a thick chignon and fastening it with jewel-tipped pins to the back of her head.

Lady Albright had given her a pair of large pearl earrings to wear to supper and a matching necklace. It was odd, Kerry thought, that the pearls she had cherished as her most valued possession all these years would have looked so terribly small and ordinary compared to these. No wonder Mr. Abernathy had chuckled so when she had shown them to him and then carelessly tossed them into the safe box.

The memory of that interview had her suddenly feeling like a fraud, and she quickly glanced away from the mirror, unable to look at herself. What was she doing—pretending she was some sort of lady? She no more belonged in clothes this fine than she belonged in this house! House? Lord God, it was a *palace,* with gold and marble and crystal everywhere she looked. For the past two hours she had felt she was living inside some dream, moving from one fantasy to another, afraid to move too fast or too suddenly lest it all evaporate.

"Oh, Mrs. McKinnon, how beautiful you look!"

Kerry forced a smile and glanced self-consciously at Lady Albright as she glided into the dressing room wearing a lavender gown even lovelier than the one Kerry wore. "I . . . I doona know how to thank you for the bath and . . . *this,*" she said, motioning awkwardly to the gown.

Lady Albright gave the gown a dismissive flick of her wrist. "I haven't worn that gown in ages. Actually, I haven't worn *any* of my old gowns since my son was born. Unfortunately, I cannot fasten the silly things around my middle. It suits you so well! You must keep it."

Kerry gasped at the suggestion. "Oh *no!* I canna keep anything as fine as this!"

"Posh!" muttered Mrs. Dismuke.

"I insist. No, no," Lady Albright said cheerfully, throwing up a hand, "we'll have no more discussion of it. If you don't accept the gown as my gift, Polly will hang it in some wardrobe and feed a colony of moths."

Kerry shifted her gaze to the mirror again, smoothing the embroidered fabric of the bodice. A dozen seamstresses must have labored over the intricate stitching.

"Ah, won't our Arthur be quite surprised?" Lady Albright said from behind her.

Oh, he'd be surprised, all right. Would possibly fall over in a fit of apoplexy. But frankly, Kerry was quite anxious to know what Arthur would think of her now. She turned and smiled at her hostess. "I am indebted to you for your kindness."

The woman laughed brightly and motioned her to follow. "You are too easily pleased, Mrs. McKinnon. Now then, if you are quite ready, the gentlemen await us in the gold salon."

They descended the curving flight of stairs and moved down what seemed like an endless stretch of thick blue carpet in a corridor larger than Moncrieffe's ballroom. Kerry gaped at the many portraits and porcelain vases and bouquets of fresh hothouse flowers as she hurried after Lady Albright. She was taken aback by the footman who flung open a pair of doors as they approached, and almost collided with Lady Albright when she stepped across the threshold and saw the enormous salon, dominated by a full-length portrait of her hostess wearing a gown encrusted with jewels and a coronet on her fair head.

Before she could fully absorb the magnificence of the room, a movement to her right caught her eye. Kerry turned and immediately felt the blood drain from her face as Arthur rose slowly from his seat, literally snatching the air from her lungs as he did so.

Lord God. Dressed in a coat of dark blue superfine and a silk waistcoat of silver and blue, he looked absolutely regal. His neckcloth, silver silk that exactly matched the waistcoat, was tied to perfection and shone against the pure white frills of his shirt. The trousers he wore, a dark gray, hugged every masculine inch of him, tapering into black patent shoes polished to a sheen.

He was beautiful. Stunningly so. But . . . he had cut his hair. His long, golden brown hair had been shorn to just above his collar and was perfectly arranged.

"Kerry . . ." he muttered, and she realized he was staring at her as if in shock. His gaze moved slowly across her, taking her in. He was, as she had guessed, very surprised by her elegant appearance.

"Are we to stand here all night whilst you openly admire Mrs. McKinnon, or did you intend to make proper introductions?" a deep male voice drawled.

Kerry looked to her right and immediately blushed at the sight of the powerful build of Lord Albright. The darkly handsome man was standing so close that he might have touched her, yet she had not noticed him until this very moment.

"I should rue the day I do not pause to admire the brilliance of true beauty, Albright," Arthur responded. *He thought her beautiful.* "Please allow me to introduce to you Adrian Spence, Lord Albright," he said softly, then to Lord Albright, "Mrs. McKinnon of Glenbaden, Scotland."

Kerry dropped into an awkward curtsey, but Lord Albright immediately shook his head and grasped her hand, pulling her up. "We do not stand on ceremony at Longbridge, Mrs. McKinnon. It is my great pleasure to make your acquaintance, I must say. I have heard quite a lot of you already," he said, and bowed gallantly over her hand. "Welcome to our home."

"Thank you," she said, inwardly grimacing at how weak her voice sounded. "You are very kind to receive me."

"Ooh, your accent is positively lyrical!" Lady Albright said from somewhere beyond her husband. "Max, please fetch a wine for Mrs. McKinnon. I rather imagine she is parched after such a very long day. Arthur, will you join her?"

"Thank you, Lilliana, but the earl had the good sense to bring up his best whiskey."

"I shall apparently have to bring up the entire stock," Lord Albright drawled, and put Kerry's hand on the crook of his arm as he motioned toward a cluster of sofas and chairs near the massive hearth at the far end of the room. "It is our habit to indulge in a bit of brandy prior to supper, Mrs. McKinnon. I hope you aren't too terribly famished."

Her nerves were so frayed she would not be able to choke down a single bite, and shook her head.

"Splendid," said Lord Albright, and seated her in a chair covered in red brocade. "I would guess my Lillie has already squeezed you dry with questions of Scotland—

she's of a mind to visit there soon, I am sure she told you," he said, casting a warm smile at his wife, who had seated herself daintily on the edge of a sofa. "Nonetheless, I must insist you repeat it all for me. I traveled there once as a young man many years ago, and I confess, I don't recall much of it"—he paused at Arthur's disdainful snort to toss a frown over his shoulder—"as I was quite caught up with some pressing business."

He joined his wife on the sofa. Arthur took the chair next to Kerry and winked covertly before draining what was left in his glass and handing it to Max.

"Mrs. McKinnon, please tell Adrian of Glenbaden. It sounds simply divine from your description," Lady Albright asked.

Describe Glenbaden. It wasn't enough that she felt awkward and out of place here, in this house . . . in this *room*. How could she describe Glenbaden? She hardly knew where to begin, how one could possibly describe the purple hue of the heather, or the blue morning mists, or the dark green hills that seemed to touch the sky. How did she convey the familiarity of that glen, the deep connection to the land or the sense of clan she had shared with all who lived there?

"It's too beautiful to describe, really," Arthur said.

He had read her mind. Surprised, Kerry looked at him; Arthur smiled. "Would you mind terribly if I attempted to describe it?" he asked, and not waiting for an answer, turned his attention to the Albrights. "The first thing one learns about Scotland is that she has her own special stars. If you were to lie in the heather under a full moon, the stars are so close that you might swear they lay upon your very face. And the moon—ah God, the moon! I have never seen one so bright or so large as in that glen. It's amazing, really, remarkably tranquil, and the colors of the morning are rich, purer than you can possibly imagine . . ."

Overwhelmed with surprise and emotion, Kerry sat

mutely, watching Arthur's expressive face as he spoke of Glenbaden. It was inconceivable to her that he could describe the Scotland that lived in her heart, how he might have, in the short time he was there, grasped and absorbed the very essence of it. The improbable, impossible sensation struck her that she had known Arthur all her life, the feeling that something more connected them than the few weeks they had spent in Glenbaden.

The sensation grew stronger over supper, as Arthur recounted the story of their first meeting and the incredible journey through the Highlands she had inadvertently taken them on. It touched her to learn that he had been so uncertain of what he was doing—she had thought him so capable, had been duly impressed that he never seemed to take a false step. She laughed with the Albrights when he described his first meeting with the Richey brothers, then sobered quietly when he spoke of how the first sight of Glenbaden had taken his breath away. Even Thomas—he spoke fondly of Thomas, capturing his character so very well that an invisible band tightened around Kerry's heart.

His conversation kept everyone's rapt attention, so that the Albrights did not notice that she didn't know which utensil to use, or which wine to take with her meal. Confounded by the array of dishes and glasses, it wasn't until hours later that Kerry realized he had managed to omit the reason they were in Longbridge altogether.

By the time they had adjourned to the salon again, Kerry's love for him had expanded ten fathoms deeper into her soul.

Arthur thought they would never escape Adrian's watchful eye or Lilliana's cheerful banter. Not that he wasn't terribly pleased to see them both, but he had been wholly unprepared for the sight of Kerry and his body's corporeal reaction to her. From the moment she had floated across the threshold on a cloud of blue silk, he had been deliriously enchanted.

She was stunningly beautiful in that gown; it seemed especially tailored for her, fitting perfectly to every lovely curve. And he had been astonished at how easily she moved in such finery, how she seemed almost born of the *haute ton*. He wanted to hold the image in his arms, devour the bare skin of her shoulders with his lips, feel her body beneath the rich fabric then and there.

He had only endured the interminable supper by monopolizing the conversation. Afterward, when they had gathered in the gold salon once again for port, he had managed to pass the hour by simply gazing at Kerry as she spoke with that soft, intoxicating voice of hers about her family and school days in Edinburgh.

When Arthur was certain the Albrights had wrung every bit of useful information from her, he thought he would go quite mad, and was thinking how exactly the two of them might take their leave of their hosts when Max appeared announcing a messenger from London in the study. Arthur had never heard more welcome news in his life.

"At this hour?" Lilliana exclaimed, and stood with Adrian.

"I can attest to the impassable roads, poor chap," Arthur remarked.

"Best see what it is about. If you will excuse me, Mrs. McKinnon," Adrian said to Kerry, and began striding across the salon, Lilliana on his heels. The moment the door closed, Arthur leapt to his feet and grabbed Kerry's hand. She fairly bounced to her feet when he tugged on her arm, and he quickly put his hand to the small of her back and steered her toward the door at the opposite end of the salon.

"What are you doing?" she asked. Arthur threw a finger to his lips, carefully opened the door, and glanced furtively up and down the corridor.

They were quite alone.

He caught Kerry's arm, turned her into his body as he pushed her against the mahogany door.

"Arthur!" she exclaimed through a luscious smile. He captured that smile with his lips, one hand snaking around her hips and pressing her against him. Her lips were like nectar, teasing him with the promise of her mouth and body—

His head snapped back with the surprise of a sharp pain in his shin; he caught a groan in his throat.

"Are you insane?" Kerry whispered frantically, and shoved hard against his chest.

"One cannot help out wonder," he muttered, still grimacing at the pain in his shin. But she did have a point—it would not do to tumble her in the salon with the door wide open. So he grabbed her hand and yanked her into the corridor, pulling her along in his wake as he marched in the opposite direction of the study, forcing her to keep up with him as he rounded the corner for the terrace sitting room.

He went a little too quickly through the French doors leading into the sitting room and crashed his shoulder into the doorframe. Kerry laughed a breathless, anxious laugh fraught with anticipation. In a whisper, Arthur urged her to be quiet and to hurry.

"Hurry to *where?*" she insisted in an equally urgent whisper.

"To the gardens, love," he said, as if that was understood, when in fact he had no idea where he was going. He only knew that he had to have her in his arms and for what he intended to do to her once there, he needed privacy.

They stumbled into the gardens, running down the gravel path with their arms entwined with one another, trying to keep their laughter from spilling into the cold night air. They ran until Arthur spied the gazebo. He had forgotten that Adrian had built one to rival the grandest gazebos in all of England, and in particular, his

father's. At the time, he had thought it a foolish expense.
At the moment, he thought it a very wise investment. He
pulled Kerry into his side and hastened his step; the two
of them clambered up the steps of the gazebo and fairly
burst inside.

They came to an abrupt and breathless halt. The
gazebo obviously was used quite often; it still bore the
remnants of a recent picnic, visible in the light of
the moon that shone through one open window. A bench
circled around the entire room, cushioned with green-
and-white-striped pillows. A blanket and two books
were stacked neatly on the bench directly under the
south awnings; a small brazier, recently used, nearby. A
wicker chair had also been pulled inside, and in it was a
china plate, obviously missed by the servants who had
picked up after the picnic.

Kerry slipped from Arthur's embrace and walked
into the middle of the gazebo. "It's beautiful." She turned
slightly, glancing over her shoulder at Arthur. "I've not
seen such luxury, Arthur. I wouldna have believed a
gazebo could be so beautiful."

"I shall tell you about beautiful, darling," he said
softly. "You are the most beautiful sight I think I've ever
seen. You astound me with it."

Kerry smiled and glanced down at her gown. "Lady
Albright gave this to me. She said it was too small—"

"There will be more, many more just like it, in every
conceivable color," he said, walking slowly toward her.
"Whatever your heart desires."

She glanced up. "Pardon?"

"You deserve the very best. I shall endeavor to give
you just that."

"Arthur," she said, laughing a little. "I think you must
have drunk more of that whiskey than I know. You
speak nonsense now."

"Do I?" he asked, reaching for her. "Why shouldn't
you have the very best, Kerry? I can afford to give it
to you."

"Oh aye, that is very fine, eh? And what do you think I should do with such fine gowns in Scotland?"

"Scotland?" he echoed, momentarily confused by the scent of lavender on her skin. He bent his head, brushed his nose against her bare neck.

"Aye, Scotland. Where I live, or have you forgotten your pretty speech of it?"

Arthur lifted his head. "You can't go back to Scotland, have you forgotten that?"

Kerry instantly reared back, but Arthur caught her before she could pull away. "It's not safe for you there."

"No, not now, that I know," she stammered, her luminous blue eyes wildly roaming his chest. "But eventually I shall return."

"Why?"

"Why?" she fairly shouted. "I am a *Scot,* Arthur, or have you not noticed the burr in my voice? I canna live in England forever! What would I do?"

The conversation was starting to annoy him. All he had wanted to do was make love to her, not discuss the future, blurry as it was. "It can wait," he murmured soothingly. "There is nothing we can resolve tonight. Would you waste this moon?" She looked toward the railing, where the moonlight was spilling onto the bench. "I would gather it up and carry it in my pocket if I could," he said, bending to nuzzle her neck again. "And I should take it out every time I wanted to recall how beautiful you looked this night."

Kerry sighed then, kissed his cheek, and Arthur felt himself spiraling down into the clutches of earnest desire once again.

They made love on the cushioned bench, the blue silk gown bunched carelessly around her waist. They moved languidly with one another, neither wanting to rush the moment or the moonlight. When Kerry at last closed her eyes and moaned, Arthur felt her body tighten around him . . . felt his love for her score his heart, mark it with everything that was Kerry.

Long afterward, when the chill of the night air began to overtake the warmth they had shared, they stole into the house, giggling like children as they hurried down the long corridor, shoes in one hand, clasping one another with the other. At the top of the grand staircase, Arthur kissed her fully and deeply, unwilling to let go, now or ever. But Kerry at last forced him awake by playfully biting his lip.

"Ouch!" he exclaimed, and watched through something of a haze as Kerry scampered down the corridor to her suite. When her door had shut quietly behind her, he turned slowly and reluctantly headed in the opposite direction.

He dreamed of their lovemaking that night, of her above him on the bench of the gazebo, her eyes a watery shade of blue, glistening with her pleasure as she reached her climax. And then Phillip appeared, strolling in a circle around the gazebo. The moon sent a shaft of eerie light through the hole in his chest when he passed the western façade. With his hands clasped behind his back, Phillip shook his blond head again and again. "Arthur, lad," he whispered sadly. "What is it you do?"

Arthur came up out of the dream with a bad start; perspiration pasted the linen nightshirt to his back. He sat up, stared at the glass-paned window. "When, Phillip?" he muttered, and thrust his hands through his hair. "When will you at last sleep in peace?"

Chapter Nineteen

IN THE EARLY afternoon the next day, Lilliana—she had adamantly insisted that Kerry address her so—dragged Kerry to the orangery to show her where she painted. As Lilliana proudly showed each of her paintings, Kerry began to see a glimpse of a past that could have been Arthur's—idyllic paintings of languid picnics, hunting, and May Day games. There were portraits of the Albright ancestors, dressed formally in sashes and coronets and heavy rings.

There was one in particular, however, that caught her attention. Kerry gaped at the painting of four men. She recognized Arthur and Adrian right away; Arthur standing with one foot propped on a large stone, Adrian with his hat in his hand. She assumed the taller, black-headed man standing behind them was Julian Dane. And the handsome blond man kneeling in front, his arm lazily propped on one knee, had to be Phillip.

"The Rogues of Regent Street," Lilliana said proudly.

"Who?" Kerry asked.

Lilliana blinked. *"Who?"* she echoed, and when Kerry confessed she had never heard that name, Lilliana eagerly sat her in a cushioned wicker chair near a bank of floor-to-ceiling windows overlooking the northern meadows and launched into a tale of four young men who had met at Eton and had grown to men together. Kerry was not surprised to hear this—Arthur had told her the same thing. But what she was surprised to hear was exactly *how* they had come to be known as Rogues, and more significantly, apparently, the four infamous Rogues of Regent Street.

Spellbound by the tale, Kerry sat on the edge of the chair, hanging on every word that fell from Lilliana's lips. She blushed when Lilliana whispered the roots of their reputation—complete with names, and in some cases, actual dates. She held her breath when Lilliana spoke conspiratorially of the half-dozen fracases the four of them had started, engaged in, or ended at what sounded like bawdy gatherings in London.

But she sagged into the chair with emotion when Lilliana told her of the death of Phillip. Naturally, Arthur had referred to Phillip, just as he had referred to all of them at one time or another. But she had noticed something was different when he spoke of Phillip, she had sensed a deep sorrow in him. Now she understood; now she felt that sorrow a little herself.

When she had finished, Lilliana glanced at the painting. "This is to be a surprise for Adrian, but I confess, I've no idea when to give it to him. He still carries such guilt over Phillip's death, yet he misses him terribly. I pray one day he will be at peace with what Phillip did."

She looked at Kerry again. "What do you think? Do you like it? I took each likeness from other paintings and arranged them as if they had posed together. I had a deuce of a time finding a portrait of Phillip, however— but Adrian's brother, Benedict, found this one at Kealing Park and had it delivered to me. I think he is rather young, don't you?"

Oh, he was young, all right. Far too young to have frozen in time forever this face, this smile. Kerry gazed at the portrait, at the smiling eyes beneath the blond curls, and wondered what had gone so terribly wrong that he would seek to end his life. She looked at the other three men, all looking terribly relaxed and jovial, with the exception of the stern Lord Albright. They were four men whose lives had grown and stretched around one another like vines of ivy until one could not tell where one ended and the other began, all inextricably tied to one another and to Phillip.

No wonder Arthur had set out to Scotland as he had—in a moment of clarion vision, Kerry suddenly realized that the journey to Scotland had as much to do with Arthur's life as it had Phillip's.

And she couldn't help but wonder, standing there in the orangery of Longbridge, if he had found what he was looking for.

Arthur was in grand spirits as he dressed for supper in another set of Albright's finest coats and trousers. Having politely refused the services of Adrian's valet—he thought taking his clothes *and* his valet a bit much—he hummed as he wrapped the neckcloth around his collar. The return to Longbridge had been so easy, *much* easier than he had anticipated. He smiled at his reflection in the mirror above the basin, recalling their inglorious arrival. He should have known his old friend would accept him and Kerry without qualification.

And it was precisely that acceptance that held Arthur in such good spirits. If Adrian Spence of *all* people could accept Kerry into his home so readily, then so too could his friends and family in London. *Of course they would!* They would hardly refuse *him* entry, and if accepting him meant including Kerry, they would not dare object. It was so simple, really, he wondered why he hadn't realized it before now. Now he was rather anxious to return to London. Lately, he had begun to worry about his business interests; there was much to be done, not the least of which was finding good counsel in the matter of Moncrieffe's death, should the need arise.

Even *that* ugly incident had seemed to fade with

their arrival at Longbridge. Kerry was as genteel as he had ever seen her; had he not known from where she hailed, he would have thought her a lady of the country, quite accustomed to quiet days and leisurely evenings. Even more encouraging to him was that she and Lilliana seemed to have formed a fast friendship. It gave him great hope that similar friendships could be forged among the *ton* in spite of her less than acceptable background.

But his smile faded as he slowly finished tying his neckcloth. Thoughts had been whirling around his head the last few days, thoughts that were disturbing him, stirring the deep waters of his soul. His pleasure at seeing how easily she adapted to her surroundings continued to translate into thoughts of the future, of Kerry by his side, of home and children and growing old together.

Arthur groaned, exasperated with himself. That simply wasn't possible. *Was it?* No! He could never justify such a marriage, and Lord knew his family would not sanction it. Yes, well then, what exactly *did* he intend? The shadowy thought of a mistress flitted briefly into his consciousness, but he dismissed the notion immediately. He loved Kerry; he could not bear to ask such a thing of her.

Then what?

With his palm, Arthur smoothed his newly trimmed hair. *Then what?*

He turned and strode across the room, ignoring his conscience, pushing down the inevitable question to its proper place. He would think of an answer sometime soon, but not now. Now, he would tell Kerry that they were to London in two days' time. Really, there were more immediate dilemmas. As he strode down the corridor to the gold salon, he crushed the small, niggling thought that perhaps there was no answer to the question of *then what?*

At least none that he would ever accept.

Kerry somehow managed to make her way through supper, thankful once again that the Albrights and Arthur were engaged in a lively discussion of places and people that were foreign to her, something to do with a debut. She felt terribly out of place, longed for May's simple stews instead of the plates of artfully arranged foods she could not name.

But that was all forgotten with Arthur's blithe announcement over custard pudding that he and Kerry would be continuing on to London by the week's end. It not only stunned her, it *appalled* her. What did he think, that they would simply traipse into London dressed in someone else's clothes and on a borrowed horse?

She lowered her spoon and looked around her as Arthur fit a spoonful of pudding into his mouth, apparently oblivious to the silence that had suddenly fallen around them. Lord Albright, she noticed, looked just as horrified as she felt.

He, too, lowered his spoon and glared at Arthur. "To London?" he asked, stealing a glimpse of Kerry. "Are you quite certain?"

Arthur shrugged nonchalantly. "Of course. I've been gone far too long—there are several matters that need my attention."

"I should think you could easily dispose of those matters from Sutherland Hall."

Arthur frowned at Adrian as if that were a perfectly absurd suggestion. "Sutherland Hall? It's as remote as Longbridge. My interests are in London."

Adrian looked at Kerry again with a pained expression, as if there was something he could not quite bring himself to say. Well Good God, *she* could say it, and would, the moment they were private. Had he lost his bloody mind? How did he think he would explain *her?* She could not go to London!

Then where, Kerry?

She could not stay here, she knew that. As much as she liked Longbridge, as much as she admired Lilliana, she was wearing another woman's clothing, sitting in another woman's orangery, admiring another woman's children and furnishings—another woman's *life*. She was only a visitor, and an uninvited one at that. There was no choice but to follow Arthur for the time being, unless she wanted to return to Scotland to face what she had done.

The conflict made her suddenly queasy, and Kerry slowly shifted her gaze to Arthur. Sitting across from her, framed artfully between two candelabras, he smiled reassuringly. "You've never seen London, Kerry. I think you will like it very much."

His ability to divine what she was thinking was nothing short of unnatural. Kerry's gaze dipped to her pudding. There was no place for her to go. She didn't belong anywhere. *Except Glenbaden.*

"Julian is in London, is he not? He was rather determined to stay through the autumn," Arthur easily continued.

"He is," Adrian muttered, shoving his pudding away. "Lilliana, darling, perhaps you and Kerry would allow a couple of old Rogues a port and cigar?"

"Certainly." She smiled at Kerry and came to her feet. "Max, the blue drawing room?" Her heart in her throat, Kerry came slowly to her feet and followed Lilliana. When she reached the door, she glanced over her shoulder at Arthur, her beautiful stranger, sitting there so regally. *Oh God,* what was to become of her?

She walked through the door, to where Lilliana was waiting. She looped her arm through Kerry's as they moved down the corridor. "You mustn't fret," she said kindly. "We'll see to it that you have a proper wardrobe. I've some slippers, too, that I think—"

Slippers and gowns! "Lilliana!" Kerry cried, pulling

her to a halt in the corridor. "Do you know who I am? No—do you know who I am *not?*"

Lilliana's smile faded. "Let's go to the drawing room. This corridor is rather drafty—"

"Please stop," Kerry begged her. "Please doona pretend I am someone I am not. This corridor is not drafty, it is far warmer than I could ever seem to heat my little house in Glenbaden!"

"Well, then," Lilliana responded coolly, her arm falling away from Kerry's, "the blue drawing room is very small and should suit your sensibilities nicely."

That brought Kerry up short. She stared at the woman who had shown her nothing but kindness from the moment she had landed on her doorstep.

"Yes, I know who you are not, Kerry. I know that your circumstance must be quite different from mine. But I also know that Arthur Christian loves you, and if I were you, I would not seek reason to reject it."

Kerry blinked.

Lilliana sighed and grasped her hand. "Oh honestly. Come on, then," she muttered, and began a solemn march to the blue drawing room. Once there, she asked that they be left alone and waited until the door shut behind the footman. Then Lilliana began pacing, her gold skirts rustling loudly with each sharp turn.

"I will apologize—" Kerry started.

"There is hardly any need for that," Lilliana interjected. "You've every right to be upset with your situation. I've no idea, and shouldn't want to know, thank you, how you and Arthur came to be here . . . together . . . but it was plainly not a, ah, *suitable* situation."

Kerry cringed with shame and sank into an overstuffed armchair.

"I really don't care how," Lilliana hastily assured her. "All I know is that you have endured more hardship than a woman has a right to know, I think, and survived it. It is so terribly plain to see how Arthur adores you. I know how the desire to help someone you love can burn in your soul, especially when that someone feels pain. I know how desperately Arthur must want to take your burdens for his own."

"But I canna allow that," Kerry muttered miserably.

"Do you remember what I told you in the orangery about the Rogues?" Lilliana asked, sinking onto an ottoman directly in front of Kerry. "Arthur has always been the one among them that could adapt to any circumstance. He stood by Phillip during the worst of times, he helped Julian through a horrid scandal, he has been a rock of support to Adrian through the years. If there is anyone who can help you now, it is Arthur. He loves you, Kerry. He wants to help you, and you may trust me, with the Sutherland name to help you, you could not possibly ask for more. And frankly, I don't see what choice you have."

Kerry sank back into the cushions of the chair, trying to conjure up even one reason that Lilliana could be wrong. Nothing came to mind. Lilliana was right, of course—she truly had no other choice. Her choices had been taken from her the day Fraser died. There was nowhere for her to turn, nowhere she could go.

Except Scotland.

Arthur did not fare as well as Kerry in the course of his interview. Adrian was up immediately once the ladies left the room, pacing like a wild animal as he apparently tried to gather his thoughts. Arthur waited patiently for the barrage he knew would come, quietly finishing a most excellent custard pudding.

Just as he pushed the dish away, Adrian turned from a rigid stance at the windows overlooking the lake and pointed a long finger at him. "You've lost your bloody mind, you know that," he said flatly.

Arthur shrugged, signaled the footman for port.

"You cannot be serious, Christian! Have you any idea a'tall as to the sort of scandalous rumors that will circulate about London? Did Kettering's troubles teach you nothing? Arriving in London with this woman from Scotland? The *ton* will label her a whore! She will be ruined, you *must* know that!"

Arthur was well aware, probably more so than Adrian, that Julian's forced marriage and sister's elopement had been the greatest scandal the *ton* had seen in some time. But this was different. He accepted the port from the footman and sipped before turning to look at Adrian. "Would you sit? You are disturbing my digestion with all that bellowing."

"I should like to do more than bellow, my friend," Adrian growled.

"Yes, yes, I know you would. Come, sit, and at least consider the dilemma from my point of view, will you? Here I have had the bloody misfortune to grow quite attached to the woman and she cannot go back to Scotland, not now, at least. I am therefore left with the option of hiding her away at Sutherland Hall, or taking her to London and letting the world know that I, for one, cherish her. If I leave her at Sutherland Hall, I am quite certain it will extinguish the light in her."

"That *light*," Adrian spat, "will quickly be snuffed in London! Arthur, think! What in God's name do you intend to do with her?" When Arthur did not answer and sipped again at his port, Adrian stalked angrily to his seat and fell into it, ignoring the port the footman placed in front of him. "You are a sentimental fool! Look here, I know you are overly fond of her, but you must admit the facts! You *cannot* keep her at Mount Street without ruining her! You *cannot* marry her, for God's sake. You've no choice but to find a suitable situation for her, something that puts her out of harm's way and the sooner the better. But I would kindly suggest that whatever situation you may choose, it is *not* in London and *not* associated with your good name! Think of your family, man!"

"What, do you think my brother will not accept her? Do you think my mother afraid of a bit of scandal? Good God, Adrian, Hannah *urged* Alex to break his engagement to Marlaine Reese in favor of Lauren Hill, and she was hardly solvent! Alex has spent the last ten years building on reforms designed to help people just like Kerry! How could he possibly find fault with me for loving a poor woman?"

"It is not Kerry's poverty that offends, Arthur. It is her *birth*—she is of common Scottish stock."

Adrian said it with such disdain that Arthur inwardly shuddered. Is that what he was? Did he, too, judge people on the basis of their birth? "Are you offended?" he asked quietly.

"No! Of course not! But I have known my share of hardship and the *ton* . . . God, Arthur, they would sooner cut you as accept her into their circle."

Arthur supposed that was true for Adrian. But Adrian was not a Sutherland, and Adrian didn't know Kerry. He didn't understand how a man might move mountains to see her smile, or plow a field to hear her laughter, or sit in one place for hours hoping that she might dance. He had hoped Adrian would understand, but perhaps it was asking too much.

As it had been since the day he had first encountered Kerry, everything was uncertain, unreal, unbelievable. What he thought he knew, he no longer understood. In the last weeks of his life, he had not been able to do more than greet each day and hope for the best. But he was *certain* his family and friends would learn to accept her, class be damned.

He smiled at Adrian.

Adrian groaned, rolled his eyes.

"You really don't understand, Albright. Please allow me to explain again . . ."

———

They argued well into the night, long after Lilliana and Kerry had retired, consuming more whiskey than they ought to have done. Somewhere in the early hours of the morning the debate changed from what was best for Kerry to a hodgepodge of faulty memories and events that had made up their lives. It amused Arthur greatly to learn that Adrian had somehow gotten it into his brain that Phillip had once thought to join the ranks of naval officers.

He howled, clumsily wiping tears of laughter from his eyes. "You cannot be serious, Albright! Rothembow abhorred the sea! Do you not recall when we escaped to France in '20 that we feared he might be permanently affixed over the railing? The lad puked himself into a fevered delirium!"

"No!" Adrian loudly disagreed. "That was most certainly Julian! Kettering couldn't stomach a boat across the Thames!"

"What, have you lost what was is left of your feeble mind? Julian was a frequent visitor to Southwark—across the Thames. Think hard, old chap, and you will recall the bit of trouble he got us into there."

Adrian frowned with concentration, and slowly, the light of his memory dawned on his face. "Ah yes . . . Kettering," he said as a slow smile spread his lips. "The imbecile almost had us killed that night."

"Yes," Arthur laughed. "*That* was Kettering. And you will recall that Rothembow was a bit green around the gills for the entire event."

Adrian sobered a bit, looked into his empty whiskey glass. "It seems another lifetime, does it not? I scarcely remember what Phillip looked like."

"I remember. I still see him so often in my dreams."

That brought Adrian's head up. "Do you?" he asked quietly. "I can say that, thankfully, I have not dreamed of him since my son was born. I know it sounds rather strange, but I have often thought that Richard's birth somehow freed him . . . or me."

Arthur said nothing, drained his whiskey. He would give anything to have his dreams free of Phillip, but he had a macabre suspicion that he would never be entirely free of him.

"So there is nothing I can say that might change your mind?"

"I beg your pardon?"

"This foolish notion you have of going to London. You'll not change your mind?"

With a heavy sigh, Arthur put his glass down. "Tell me truly, Adrian, what choice do I have? My home . . . my *life* is in London. I made my choice the moment I took her from Scotland. I will now face the consequence of having done so. I just need time to think what to do, that's all."

"God grant you the time then," Adrian said on a sigh. "But it may already be too late."

Chapter Twenty

ARTHUR'S AUNT PADDY gave Kerry a thorough once-over as they stood in the cheerful morning room of his house on Mount Street. The bundle of tight ringlets over Paddy's ears bounced like a child's toy as she nodded her approval of the last gown the modiste was fitting to Kerry.

"Absolutely *perfect*," she chirped.

"Absolutely," agreed Lady Paddington's constant companion, Mrs. Clark.

Lady Paddington clasped her pudgy hands together and cocked her head to one side, squinting at Kerry. After a moment, she shook her head. "The hair, my dear. I'm afraid it simply won't do."

That her hair was unsatisfactory hardly surprised Kerry—it was, after all, the only thing remaining that was truly her. Everything else had been hastily created in the last several days. A half-dozen new gowns from the finest dressmakers in London, drawers and chemises made of silk, slippers so delicate that she was afraid to walk in them—these new things replaced her sensible woolens, her sturdy shoes, her cotton undergarments.

These things had replaced Kerry McKinnon—she hardly knew who she was anymore.

"Please turn, madam," the modiste said.

"Yes, do turn! Let's have a look from behind!" Mrs. Clark said.

Her arms held perpendicular from her body, Kerry dutifully turned and let the women examine her for any defects as the modiste marked the hem.

"Perhaps a lovely plum for a walking gown, do you think, Paddy? A lovely plum would so compliment her pale complexion, I should think."

"It's true there isn't as much sunshine in Scotland," Lady Paddington quickly agreed, and Kerry looked heavenward for strength. She was beginning to despise her circumstance. It wasn't that she wasn't extremely grateful and humbled by Arthur's generosity; the magnitude of his largesse shocked her, as did his wealth. The moment they had arrived in London—only a few days past, she reminded herself—he had immediately sent his butler, Barnaby, on a mission to bring modistes and milliners and purveyors of all things feminine to his magnificent home. And at first, she had been pleased; wearing Lilliana's clothes made her feel like a poor relation. The finery was enticing—what fool *wouldn't* have enjoyed the opportunity to wear such wonderful things?

But as the number of gowns and shoes and hats and gloves began to mount, the more disturbed she became. The fine clothing, the furnishings, the people to do her slightest bidding were terribly alluring on a base level, but she was acutely aware that she had begun to resemble a woman she did not know. This, she thought miserably as she glanced down at the green-and-blue gown, was not Kerry McKinnon.

This was a woman Arthur Christian could love, a woman who should be used to the best the world had to offer, worthy of such splendid attire. *Oh, Arthur.*

It was so plainly obvious how very proud he was to give her such beautiful things. He beamed with joy each time he saw her in a new gown, all of them commissioned at a premium so that he might have them in days instead of weeks. And truthfully, it made her feel beautiful—every time he looked at her, she felt desirable, sensual, worthy of his affection—all the things she had never felt with Fraser.

Yet no matter how much she enjoyed his attentions and the clothing and a world that glittered with crystal and gold and beeswax candles, she could not ignore the little voice inside her with the Scottish accent. The voice that reminded her she was a fraud, a woman more comfortable in coarse wool than silk.

Even Arthur was different now. A perfect coif had replaced his thick, wavy long hair. Gone were the linen shirts and buckskins, replaced by silk waistcoats and neckcloths and fine woolen coats. His ruggedness was fast fading into the softness of the aristocracy.

"If you would turn again, madam," the modiste said.

"Ooh, how very—"

"Fetching!" Mrs. Clark interrupted.

"Fetching!" Lady Paddington agreed.

"There you are, madam. Does it meet with your approval?"

Kerry dropped her arms and looked down. Of course it met with her approval. Aware that the women were waiting for her response, Kerry tried to find her voice, but to her horror, the bitter taste of tears welled in the back of her throat, and she could not speak for fear of suddenly weeping.

Lady Paddington and Mrs. Clark exchanged a look; Lady Paddington looked at her again, her cheerful countenance soured. "I should *hope* you do indeed approve of the gown, Mrs. McKinnon, as I assure you, my Arthur paid quite handsomely for it!"

"That is China silk!" Mrs. Clark added, folding her arms across her chest.

The modiste peered up at her as if she might be ill. "Madam? Is there something not to your liking?"

"No. I mean *aye*. I mean, I *adore* it, I do!" Kerry quickly assured them. "I didna mean to seem ungrateful, I suppose I'm a wee bit overwhelmed."

Lady Paddington's expression softened. "Well of *course* you are, dear! And having come such a long way in a short amount of time, too! Mrs. Clark and I journeyed to Alnwick one summer—which, although in England, is really just the same as travelling to Scotland—"

"Well not *really* the same," Mrs. Clark interrupted Lady Paddington. "But very close by—"

"Extremely close by!" Lady Paddington echoed, "and it took us one fortnight and four days plus!"

"Aye," Kerry said wearily, accepting the modiste's hand to step down from the fitting stool. She allowed the modiste to undress her as Lady Paddington and Mrs. Clark prattled on at length about what sounded like an afternoon outing gone awry. As she let the modiste settle a blue-and-white-striped day gown over her head, Kerry wondered what it must be like to have so little to occupy one's time that an afternoon trip could turn into a fortnight. How did these women move through their lives with nothing more than chatter?

In London only a few days now, Kerry already felt as if she might claw her way out of her own skin. She was accustomed to working from sunup to sundown, tending to a house, and animals, and crops, and *people*. She was *not* accustomed to sitting and contemplating which gown should be worn to supper that evening. And as she was not allowed to leave Arthur's home except for a daily walk in Hyde Park—*"It's the propriety of the thing, darling. A woman wandering about alone like that, well, really, it's just not done"*—there was nothing to keep her occupied, nothing but her thoughts of Scotland, Charles Moncrieffe, Thomas, May, and Big Angus.

Lord God, what was she doing here?

It was time, she thought numbly as the modiste tied a blue satin ribbon around her waist, to speak with Arthur. She could not continue this farce much longer.

The moment Arthur arrived home that evening, Lady Paddington eagerly sailed out, informing her nephew as she did that she would be off to South Hampton on the morrow, and he therefore needed to be about the business of finding another chaperone. "This evening's supper and opera are my last engagements until the Christmas season, you know."

"I know."

"I should hope so," Lady Paddington said absently, as she tried to fit her hands into gloves that were far too small. "There is a bit of talk going around town. We really can't have that."

"No, of course not."

"I daresay Alex will not be pleased when he returns from Sutherland Hall," she added, and paused to check her ringlets in a large oval mirror.

Arthur took her red velvet cloak from a footman. "Now, Paddy," he said, holding the cloak out, "You know as well as I, Alex shall be delighted to make Mrs. McKinnon's acquaintance."

"Oh! Of course!" the woman said, and shot a quick, sheepish glance at Kerry as she slid into her cloak. "Yes, of course he shall! I am merely making comment."

Arthur pulled the cloak around her throat and nodded at the footman. "You best be going now or you'll be late for your supper with Mrs. Clark." He pressed a kiss to her fleshy cheek.

Lady Paddington blushed with pleasure. "Such a dear boy." Her gaze flicked to Kerry. "Good evening, Mrs. McKinnon."

"Good evening, Lady Paddington," Kerry responded, and presented an awkward curtsey, uncertain whether it was a proper moment for doing so or not.

"Well then!" said Lady Paddington, and nodded to the footman to open the door. As she marched out, Arthur behind her, Kerry could hear her calling to the coachman to be quick and open the carriage door before she caught her death of cold.

Arthur returned a few moments later, smiling sheepishly. "Forgive her. She is an old woman with some rather definite ideas." He paused; his smile broadening. "Ah, my darling, how beautiful you are tonight." He caught her hand and lifted it to his mouth.

That warm, sweet flush she always felt when Arthur complimented her seeped through her skin so quickly that Kerry had to remind herself there were things that had to be resolved. But before she could say anything, Arthur caught her around the waist, began to lead her away from the foyer. "I've a surprise for you," he said. "I know you have been missing Scotland."

With every breath, she missed it. "That is true," she murmured.

"Well then, we simply must do something about it, mustn't we?" he asked as they walked into the salon.

An uninvited, insane little hope suddenly invaded Kerry's mind. Her heart began to beat a little faster; she quickly looked up, examining his expression, the hope becoming more absurd and larger as her imagination raced—

He meant to take her home.

He meant to take her home! Somehow, he had devised a plan that would allow her to return to Scotland! She abruptly pulled away from his embrace, twirling to face him. "I'm going home!"

The puzzlement that washed over his expression instantly dashed her hope. "Oh, my love, I would not think of taking you back, not now, not under the circumstance! I think it will be a long while before we sort through your troubles, and until then, I wouldn't allow you within a hundred miles of Scotland."

Her heart sank. Of course he wasn't going to take her back. Her fear was quickly turning into a stark reality— she would never see Scotland again.

Clearly confused by her reaction, Arthur watched her closely. She turned abruptly away from his watchful gaze, fell limply onto a chair and tried to catch her fool breath.

"I am sorry, darling. I did not mean to imply that we . . . You understand that we cannot go to Scotland, do you not?"

Oh, she understood all right. Understood so clearly that her heart felt leaden in her throat. "I . . . I doona know why I thought so."

"Kerry." Arthur squatted down on his haunches beside her, and with a sad sigh, touched her cheekbone. "I know you miss Scotland. So do I." He flashed a quick, wry smile and withdrew a small velvet box from his coat pocket and looked down at it in his hand. "When I saw this, it instantly reminded me of the blue morning mist in Glenbaden. And when I moved it, it fractured the light, and I could not help but see the heath, the green hills, the dark blue of the loch. But when I picked it up, it reminded me of a star. It reminded me of you—you are like a Scottish star I caught hold of in my hand."

Kerry gasped softly.

"My hope is that you will think of Scotland every time you look at it." He reached for her hand, turned it palm upward, and placed the box in it. "And when I look at it, I shall think of your eyes, the stars of Scotland."

What was in the box left her speechless—never in her life had she seen such a precious jewel. It looked to be a diamond, pale blue and about the size and shape of a robin's egg. She had never seen anything like it; it hung from a simple braid of gold and was beveled all the way around so that light was refracted into every color on God's earth. The gem was magnificent, worthy of a queen . . . *not a poor widow.*

Kerry's vision suddenly blurred; raw emotion filled her heart as quickly as the tears filled her eyes. His generosity was overwhelming. She did not deserve anything so fine, and it was inconceivable to her that a man of Arthur's stature could believe that she did. She felt him take the box from her hand, felt his fingers brushing the bare skin of her neck as he fastened the necklace on her. The gem hung like a stone against her chest.

"I canna take it. It's too much, Arthur."

His hand moved over hers, squeezing tightly. "I've only begun, Kerry. Look here, feel it," he said, lifting her hand to it around her neck. "This was made for you—it *is* Scotland, clear and beautiful and shining, just like you. No other woman could wear this stone, only you."

"I doona deserve this—"

He suddenly clasped her face between his hands, forcing her to look up. "*Never* say that. You deserve the finest the world has to offer! You deserve this and much more! Oh God, Kerry, can't you see what you have done to me? Can't you see how much happiness your smile brings me? And if this brings even a *hint* of that smile, it is worth every farthing I have! I want you to have it!"

How easily he banished every doubt, every worry from her head. Kerry suddenly threw her arms around his neck, burying her face in his collar and squeezing her eyes tightly shut so that she would not cry. Arthur laughed, the sound of it reverberating in his chest. With a quick tug, he toppled backward, pulling Kerry along with him, so that they were prone on the expensive Aubusson carpet, Kerry on top of him.

Arthur groaned. "Now this, madam, will very quickly bring a smile to *my* face," he teased her, and laughed into her mouth when Kerry kissed him with all that she had.

They made fast, hard love on the carpet in the salon—neither showing any fear of discovery—then afterward arranged their clothes and hair as best they could and rang for tea.

After the tea was drunk and the teacakes devoured—by Arthur, that was, as Kerry was too awed by the stone around her neck to eat—Arthur said, "I've spoken to

Kettering and all is arranged, but I shall greatly miss these interludes."

"What?" she asked.

Arthur smiled, casually told her what he had planned to ensure that she was properly chaperoned. She was to reside with the earl of Kettering.

Kerry was immediately on her feet, pacing wildly, Arthur calmly watching her. "I willna go, Arthur. You canna ask me to—"

"But you must. Sweetheart, you can't know how it pains me to let you go, if even so close by, but I cannot allow you to remain under my roof without a proper chaperone. There is nothing else to be done for it—until Alex and my mother return from Sutherland Hall, there is really no one to see after your virtue."

"My virtue!" she fairly shrieked, and gave a shout of hysterical laughter. "My virtue is of no consequence! I willna go!"

"Yes, you will," he said as if discussing the weather. "I'm very sorry for it, but staying at Mount Street is impossible. Paddy was right—talk is already beginning to circulate among the *ton*. When I encountered Lord Enderby at the Tam O'Shanter earlier today, he inquired after my houseguest—don't you see? For the sake of propriety—*your* propriety, you must go."

"Why should you care about propriety now, may I ask? We came all the way from Scotland with no regard for it!"

That earned her a dark frown. "It is your reputation I would protect, madam. This is not something I will debate—you will go to Kettering House first thing on the morrow."

"You didna care so much for propriety in Glenbaden!"

And that brought Arthur to his feet. "Glenbaden," he said evenly, "is a far cry from London, where I've my family name to protect, my brother's position in the House of Lords to consider. I will avoid scandal to the extent that I can, Kerry. There is no point in arguing."

There was to Kerry, but Arthur was clearly determined. He refused to listen to her pleas, and at one point, threatened to leave for his club if she didn't stop debating him. But Kerry was born of stubborn Scottish stock; the debate raged on over supper until, in a moment of sheer frustration, Arthur slapped his palm to the table and roared, *"Enough!"*

Silence quickly descended. After a moment, Arthur picked up his fork.

"How long do you mean to leave me there, then?" she asked.

He slowly lifted his gaze to a painting of a fox hunt above her head, his jaw working, his fork frozen in midair. "I don't rightly know."

The truth . . . the regret . . . in his voice was plain. Neither of them could deny any longer the quandary in which they found themselves. Kerry put both hands flat on the table and spread her fingers, staring blindly at them as her mind whirled. "We canna continue on like this," she said softly. "This . . . this dilemma must have a solution."

"It is not a dilemma!" he said sharply.

Kerry looked at him, saw the doubt swimming with the determination in his hazel eyes. She loved him, and God, she could see that he loved her. But it was impossible. "Arthur . . . we canna pretend forever."

A strange look came over him; he dropped his fork, his hand curling into an unconscious fist. "What is it you think we pretend? Do you think I pretend to love you? Do you pretend to love me?"

"No, of course not. But this," she said, flicking her wrist at the space around them, "this finery, this grandeur isna real, Arthur. Pretending that you and I . . . well, it can never be real—"

His whole body seemed to jerk as if she had struck him. His goblet toppled over, the fine crystal breaking into several large pieces when it hit the cherrywood table, wine spilling onto his lap.

Arthur surged to his feet, tossed a linen napkin on to the spill and stared down at the dark stain on his thigh. Kerry stood, too, but Arthur quickly gestured for her to sit. "Please, finish your meal. Jesus, where is Barnaby?" he fairly spat, and stalked from the table in search of his butler before Kerry could even open her mouth.

Chapter Twenty-One

CLAUDIA WHITNEY-DANE, the countess of Kettering, could not have been happier if Arthur had announced he was the long lost brother of little Queen Victoria. She actually had to physically restrain herself from covering him with kisses for having the courage to follow his heart instead of social convention.

And she had to restrain herself from punching Julian for laughing so hard.

In the spacious study of Kettering House on St. James Square, Julian was almost doubled over with laughter as Arthur dryly related the shooting that had introduced him to Mrs. McKinnon.

Claudia didn't think it so amusing. She might have done the same thing in Mrs. McKinnon's shoes. She glanced at the woman, sitting stiffly on the edge of a chair, her hands gripped tightly in her lap. Her white knuckles were the only outward sign of discomfort. She watched Arthur, smiled pleasantly when Julian laughed, politely declined Claudia's offer of more tea. To look at her, one would not know she was an impoverished widow from Scotland. One would not guess that Arthur Christian had fallen in love with a woman so scandalously without pedigree.

She did not have to be told that Arthur loved

Mrs. McKinnon—she had deduced it the moment she saw Arthur look at her, for it was the same expression of hunger and longing she had seen on Julian at one time. Arthur could not keep his eyes from her. Claudia could see why he was so entranced. Mrs. McKinnon, while not a beauty in the classic sense of the word, was lovely. With stark black hair, pale blue eyes, and skin that looked like porcelain, she had an air of pretty simplicity about her, an openness that was not often seen in London. Her expressions, unlike those of the ladies of the *ton*, were natural and unaffected. When she smiled, she smiled fully, the skin around her eyes crinkling. When surprised, her body radiated with it. There did not seem an ounce of pretension in Mrs. McKinnon.

Which was precisely the problem. One look at the two of them and it was obvious they were in love. Not that Claudia wasn't all for a happy union between them, oh no. As a champion of women's rights, she was thrilled that someone like Mrs. McKinnon could catch Arthur's eye. But having suffered from the scandal surrounding her marriage to Julian, Claudia had no desire to see how scandal might unfold with Mrs. McKinnon. And it would. There would be no hiding who she was—no connections, no blood ties, no sophistication borne of spending years in drawing rooms of the uppermost echelons of society. The *ton* could be merciless when it came to women like Mrs. McKinnon.

No, this had to be handled very delicately. *Very* delicately.

A supper party with a few of their most trusted friends was the first step, Claudia had already determined as much. Mrs. McKinnon would be slowly introduced, her entry into Arthur's world carefully constructed as their good friend come to visit for a time. The launching would begin just as soon as Julian stopped laughing at Arthur's tale of what sounded like a rather adventurous summer in Scotland.

There were moments, albeit brief ones, over the next two days that Kerry felt as if she could somehow learn to live in this world. She secretly liked the fact that she was allowed to sleep past sunup, and that a very cheerful woman brought her hot chocolate and toast every morning before she had even put a foot to the floor. But for every moment she believed she could live like this, there were two more that left her feeling restless, out of sorts, and woefully inadequate for the salons of London.

It seemed as if she was forever doing the wrong thing. Brenda, the personal maid to the countess, seemed quite upset when Kerry washed her undergarments and hung them in the dressing room to dry. She had turned and looked at Kerry with such a look of shock that for a moment, Kerry thought she might be apoplectic. "If you've clothing to be laundered, mu'um, you need only say so," she had said tightly, then had proceeded to snatch the clothing down. Where she took them, Kerry was afraid to ask.

And there was Brian, the footman. The first time Claudia had taken her out for a turn about the town, the young man had met them in the foyer with wraps. He held one out to Kerry. "If you please, miss," he had murmured, and Kerry had started at the familiar sound of his accent.

"A Scot," she had all but whispered.

The footman glanced at Claudia from the corner of his eye. "Aye, mu'um."

Claudia put her hand on Kerry's arm. "Kerry? Is the wrap not to your liking?"

It was odd—it was almost as if Claudia did not even see the man standing there. In a moment of confusion, of not knowing the right thing to do, Kerry said, "No, it's quite nice," and awkwardly turned away from the footman. But not before she saw the change in his expression, and when she had walked out of the house behind

Claudia without looking back, she had felt his eyes boring a hole in her back, as he had seen her for the fraud that she was.

Moments like those left her feeling adrift and at odds with her conscience. There was so much of this life that was foreign to her.

The supper party Claudia was determined to host was not only foreign, it was a nightmare. Claudia had explained her thinking, but it made little sense to Kerry. Actually, it seemed rather contrived—a series of introductions, a hope that one or two of the most influential guests would like her well enough to tell one or two of their most influential friends—all of the intricate maneuvering made Kerry's head spin.

And for what? What she could not seem to convey to Claudia was that she did not *need* to be introduced to society. In fact, she abhorred the idea, particularly since she wasn't to be in London long. Soon, Arthur would determine where she would go next, and soon she would leave here.

Claudia was very good at waving a dismissive hand at her when Kerry insisted the supper party was an unnecessary expense, and immediately resumed the planning of an affair that was sounding less and less like supper and more and more like one of the grand events they used to read of in school. The cold fist of dread was already gripping her heart.

Her clothing for the evening was the first major issue. Claudia produced a gown of violet satin trimmed delicately in green. It looked like something Kerry was certain the Queen should wear, and she said as much, along with her hesitation to don it. What followed was a bit of an argument, with Claudia insisting that the gown was perfect for her coming out, and Kerry insisting just as adamantly that she was not *coming out,* that she was merely dining, and reluctantly at that.

Claudia won.

Even the choice of her clothing was not her own.

When Arthur called that afternoon, Claudia had kindly left them alone under the pretense of searching down old Tinley, the senile butler Julian kept in his employ. Once they were alone, Kerry rushed into Arthur's arms, seeking comfort from the only thing familiar about her life anymore.

"Kerry, sweetheart, you must allow me to at least breathe," he said with a chuckle.

"Arthur, please tell me now, when will you take me from here?"

He kissed her forehead. "As soon as Alex returns from the country—"

"When?" she interrupted.

"A fortnight, not more," he said, stroking her cheek with his knuckle. "Have you any idea how much I miss you? I think about you constantly." His gaze dropped to the blue diamond around her neck. Lifting it in his hand, he smiled. "The moon last night was so bright, I could have sworn I was in Glenbaden again. But it couldn't be—you weren't with me. There is no Glenbaden without you."

There was no earth, no heaven, no world without him. How could she make him understand how out of place she was here? With a weary sigh, she laid her forehead against his shoulder. "Arthur, please, will you listen to me now—I doona belong here."

"It's just a while longer."

"I canna make you understand that I am not like Claudia. I am not like anyone in London. I doona belong in these clothes or this house. I should be home, in Glenbaden."

"I miss Glenbaden, too," he said, missing her point. "But I can't let you go back to Scotland—"

"I doona ask to go back," she said wearily.

"Then what are you asking, Kerry? Can you not endure it another fortnight? Is it truly so unbearable? You have every comfort—what would you have me do instead?"

The question silenced her—she had no idea what she asked. To be taken back to Mount Street? It was really no different than Kettering House, the sole exception being that Arthur was there. She loved him desperately, but even he couldn't shield her from this life every moment of every day—he was as much a part of London as she was an outsider. So what, then, did she ask?

"Don't look so despairing, will you? It won't be long now." He folded her in his arms and kissed her fully. Kerry could not help herself; she clung to him, wishing she could somehow crawl inside him and hide there. For a few blissful moments, she felt as if she had almost succeeded, felt the security and comfort in his arms. But when Claudia rejoined them, and Arthur moved away, he fell into an easy conversation about the supper party the following evening, the invited guests, the menu, and the seating arrangements, paying particular attention to protocol. He seemed to understand the many nuances, the intricate network of introductions. They were speaking another language altogether that Arthur understood and she didn't.

Kerry's anxiety grew to such monstrous proportions the night of the gathering that she feared she would be ill. The credentials and social standing of the dozen invited guests had been thoroughly explained to her, so that, presumably, she might understand how important they were to her. It did not help her understand, it made her feel faint. The list sounded like royalty, and as Brenda helped her dress in the elaborate costume, Kerry felt more than inadequate to the task. Although she had been taught some high-society etiquette in school, most of it was lost to her memory.

"What will I do?" she frantically asked the maid.

Brenda blinked. "I don't know, mu'um. I suppose you should do as Lady Kettering does."

As if she could ever be so beautiful and cultured.

When Brenda finished with her, Kerry looked in the mirror. The gown of violet and green was very nice, but she moved woodenly, unaccustomed to the weight of the skirts and petticoats and slippers with heels. Brenda had done very well with her hair, too, she noticed, sweeping it up and fastening it to the back of her head. Soft wisps of curls trailed down her neck, one wrapping around one of the earrings Claudia had loaned her. The blue diamond sparkled like a star above the low-cut bodice of the gown. Perhaps if she didn't open her mouth all evening, no one would know that she was a fraud.

Oh God, what a catastrophe!

A moment later, Claudia came sailing in, but pulled up short when she saw Kerry. "Oh my. Oh *my*. You are beautiful, Kerry! How stunning! Oh Lord, Arthur shall strut about like a little peacock, won't he, especially since he is bringing that cousin of his, Lord Westfall. They are quite the pair, you know."

No, she didn't know. She didn't know he even *had* a cousin.

"Julian's sister Ann is absolutely beside herself in anticipation of meeting you," she continued as she walked around Kerry, assessing her from all sides. "She is quite desperate to meet a true Scot."

"Why?" Kerry asked.

Claudia laughed. "I suppose she thinks it rather exotic."

Exotic. Hardly certain what that meant, the vise of fear tightened a little more. "W-what will I say?" she asked, her voice growing fainter.

"Say? Oh, something shall come to you. You mustn't worry about that—chances are you won't have much opportunity to speak at all," Claudia said blithely, and flashed a charming grin at Kerry. "There are many of our guests who rather delight in hearing themselves talk. You shall merely have to nod and smile at the appropriate moment."

Kerry forced a smile.

"Oh, I am so *pleased!*" Claudia chirped, clapping her

hands. "This shall be the perfect evening, mark my words!"

Aye, a perfectly disastrous one.

Many of the guests were already gathered in the gold salon when Kerry entered behind Claudia. The sight of so many people, so much finery, glistening jewels, crystal—much to Kerry's horror, she realized that her hands were shaking as the earl of Kettering introduced each guest to her. It was hopeless—her tongue tangled so badly that she might as well have been speaking Gaelic. She was curtseying wrong, too, at first dipping to everyone, then fearing it was all wrong and dipping to no one, then again when Claudia whispered sharply in her ear, *curtsey!*

Arthur was, as usual, a rock of strength for her. He was the first to greet her and introduce her to his cousin, then was never again very far from her side. Honestly, he did not seem to notice how terribly awkward she was, and it was a blessed relief when he answered questions posed to her—such as when Lord Farlaine asked how long she intended to visit London.

"Aha, you must be asking in the event she might like to see your theatrical debut?" Arthur quickly interceded.

Lord Farlaine blushed. "I suppose the thought did indeed cross my mind." And he proceeded to explain to her in detail how he had stumbled into a role in a play that would be playing on Drury Lane for a period of two weeks. He went on explaining, in spite of Arthur's increasing scowl, right down to reciting some of the lines he found particularly moving.

At supper, she was, thankfully, seated directly across from Arthur, but across from the watchful eye of Lady Pritchett. Arthur was, of course, very engaging. She admired the easy way he regaled the guests around them with meaningless chatter—he was a master at turning the conversation around so that whomever he had engaged was suddenly talking about themselves and not asking pointed questions of her. Throughout the meal, he laughed at the droll wit of his supper companions, complimented the host and hostess profusely, and charmed all of the ladies with his easy banter. Frequently, he caught her eye and smiled reassuringly. It was plain he was very much at home at such affairs as this.

And it was outlandishly clear that she was not. Kerry began the first course with the wrong spoon, fumbled with the serving utensil when the Scottish footman tried to serve her. He whispered harshly to her in Gaelic to put it down—much to the considerable interest of Lady Pritchett—and only then did Kerry realize she was to be served by him. And she was the only one who did not seem to understand the apparently very funny joke Lord Reynolds made that had the entire table laughing politely. Feeling clumsy and oafish, she found herself sinking farther into her seat as the supper wore on, praying no one would speak to her or God forbid, try and *serve* her anything, and catching the watchful eye of the Scottish footman more than once.

She foolishly believed the worst had passed when the dishes were cleared after the last course. Breathing a sigh of relief, she smiled at Arthur, answered Lady Billingsly's questions about the weather in Scotland— "Aye, it *is* rather cold in the winter"—and even chuckled when Claudia made a face that only Kerry saw.

But then the footmen advanced like an army, laying small crystal goblets in front of the men. Before anything was poured, however, the men stood and the women came to their feet, filing out of the dining room in twos and threes. Kerry thought this practice was another indication of the great divide between her and them. In Glenbaden, the men went directly to bed after their evening meal so that they might begin anew with the sunrise.

Claudia caught up with Kerry as they filed out. "It's wonderful, isn't it?" she whispered excitedly, and slipped her arm through Kerry's. "You are very much complimented."

That brought the first real laughter from Kerry and a roll of her eyes. "That's absurd! I've not spoken but a word all night!"

Claudia shrugged. "What matters is that they *think* you did."

In the salon, they joined the other women in a cozy gathering of furniture in the center of the room. One of the women asked Claudia about her school for girls. Surprised, Kerry listened with rapt attention as Claudia described the school she had built for young girls of the factories. Fascinated with a side of the countess she had not seen, Kerry was humbled by the knowledge that Claudia was apparently the force behind many charitable endeavors.

"And what of you, Mrs. McKinnon? Is there a particular charity you enjoy?"

The question, from Lady Darlington, startled Kerry. She sat up, looked around at the faces turned toward her. "Ah . . . charity," she said. Lady Darlington nodded. Ladies Filmore and Barstone leaned forward as if they were afraid they might miss her answer. "Umm . . . there are no charities in Glenbaden."

"Why, Mrs. McKinnon! You must give yourself credit where credit is due. You told me how you helped the people of the McKinnon clan."

Confused, Kerry looked at Claudia. Claudia eyed her hopefully, trying very hard to help her, but she could not, for the life of her, take credit for her clan. "The McKinnon clan," she said uncertainly. Claudia nodded eagerly. "I, ah . . . well. I really canna take credit there, for we all helped one another. We shared responsibility for the land and worked it together."

The room was so silent one could hear Lady Barstone's stomach disagree with her supper.

"You worked?" asked one woman.

Kerry realized her great mistake. She tried to laugh it off. "Oh, I doona suppose I'd be so bold as to call it *work,* really, what but a bit of cooking now and then—"

"Mrs. McKinnon enjoys cooking as a hobby," Claudia quickly interjected.

"Aye, that I do." At least she had the presence of mind to agree with Claudia, in spite of it being an enormous lie. She detested cooking.

Lady Phillipot wiggled her enormous body forward and eagerly thrust her hands onto her knees to steady herself. "This is quite *fascinating,* Mrs. McKinnon! What other hobbies do you enjoy?"

"Milking cows?" asked someone, and all the women tittered.

Kerry felt her blood begin to race through her, heating her skin, uncertain if she was mortified or angry. Did these women think milk magically appeared on their table? "Actually, I have milked a cow," she said softly.

"*Oooh,* how wonderful!" Lady Phillipot crowed. "Do tell us more, Mrs. McKinnon!"

She was about to tell Lady Phillipot that they did not have an army of splendidly attired footmen to feed them, but Claudia said sharply, "Honestly, Olympia, one would think you had never seen a cow milked before! Come then, would you be so kind as to share your lovely voice with us in song? I am sure Lady Boxworth can be persuaded to accompany you on the pianoforte."

"I should be delighted," Lady Boxworth said and was at once on her feet.

"Very well, if you insist," Lady Phillipot said, and somehow managed to hoist herself from her seat. As the two women made their way to the far end of the room, Kerry smiled thinly at Claudia. "I should like a wee bit of air," she said, and stood, walking away from the group before anyone could call her back and expose her further.

She slipped out one door at the opposite end of the room and found herself in yet another, darkened room.

Using her fingers to feel along the wall, she slowly moved along the perimeter of the large room until she found another door, and opened it, thankful to see a thin ray of light at the end of what looked like a corridor. God in heaven, would she now be *lost?* It was rather fitting, she supposed, as she made her way toward the light. She had been wandering around without direction or purpose since the morning Charles Moncrieffe had laid his dirty hands on her.

As her sight adjusted to the darkness, she realized that the light was coming from a door ajar at the end of the corridor. When she reached the door, she pushed it open wider, and walked inside.

She heard the click of boots on the plain wood floor before she saw anyone and whirled about, her palm pressed to her thundering heart. It was the Scottish footman; he stood before her holding two bottles of wine. They stared at one another for a long moment before he finally spoke. "Are ye lost, then, lassie?"

She heard Thomas McKinnon's voice in that burr and closed her eyes. The tears stung the back of her throat, and for a moment, a brief fleeting moment, she was transported home.

"Mrs. McKinnon."

Her eyes fluttered open; she looked at the young footman. "I, ah, seem to have lost my way to the salon."

He did not move at first, just kept looking at her as if he wanted to speak. Kerry lifted a hand to her flushed neck; the movement seemed to spur him; he suddenly moved past her. "Follow me."

She followed him into the darkened corridor and immediately through a door that led into the main corridor awash with light. When they reached the main door of the salon, he reached for it, but his hand paused on the brass handle. With a furtive glance about, he whispered quickly, "If yer in need of help, lass, ye ask for Brian. Do ye understand me now? Brian."

He did not wait for her answer. He swung the door

open, bowed lightly as he stepped aside so that she might pass. The men had rejoined the ladies; the din from the room was high and voices and music seemed to rush at her. Grasping her skirt tightly in her hand, Kerry lifted her chin. "Aye, I do," she said, and walked into the room, looking for Arthur.

It was the early hours of the morning when Arthur finally arrived at his empty house on Mount Street. He climbed the stairs slowly, unraveling his black neckcloth as he went, a smile playing on the corners of his lips as he recalled the evening. Claudia had been right, of course. A supper party had been just the thing to introduce Kerry to influential members of their circle. And oh Lord, she had been magnificent this evening. An ethereal vision in that violet gown, the soft lilt in her voice intoxicating every male in the room. Granted, she had been rather subdued this evening—he had felt her nerves. But her mien had seemed one of quiet sophistication, of observation and polite refrain. She had easily been the most alluring, the most intriguing woman present.

She had fit so perfectly in that all-important setting that Arthur had finally found the answer for which he had been searching since they had arrived in London.

He would marry her.

It was the answer that had been playing on the fringes of his mind for days now, the only course of action.

That, and the only answer his heart would accept.

Why, then, had he not come to the conclusion sooner?

Because, he told himself as he entered his suite of rooms, of who Kerry was. Having seen her tonight, he was now loath to admit to himself that his reluctance had stemmed from the simple fact that she was a poor Scot's widow. It was unthinkable for a man of his stature to marry a woman like her. But it was also unthinkable—at least to him—to allow something like the circumstance of her birth guide what could very well be the most important decision of his life.

Tonight, however, he had seen their situation through a different lens. He had seen that she *could* fit into a world to which she had not been born, could move among those who *had* been born to it. He had seen that she not only fit, but that she could, with some training, become one of the most sought-after women among the *ton*.

Still smiling, Arthur sent his sleepy valet away and stripped down to nothing. He sprawled nude onto the massive four-poster bed and slung an arm over his eyes. His last conscious thought was of Kerry, gliding toward him in that lovely violet gown, smiling at him as if he was the only man in the world.

He dreamed of a ball that night; dazzling women dressed in shimmering golds and greens twirled in the arms of men dressed in formal black tails. In the center of the crowded ballroom stood Kerry, dressed in a white velvet gown, her hair curled and piled atop her head with slim gold chains. A Greek goddess. As he walked toward her, the dancers parted, and she held out her hands to him. He took her in his arms, swept her into a waltz beneath a thousand candles, and asked her, "Are you happy, my love?"

Kerry laughed, her dark red lips sliding over perfect white teeth.

"Are you happy?" he asked her again, but Kerry did not answer, was distracted by something to her left. Arthur's gaze followed hers, and the dancers seemed to melt away as an impeccably dressed Phillip, save the hole in his chest, strolled onto the dance floor.

"Are you happy?" he asked again, but when he turned to look at Kerry, she was gone.

And Phillip was laughing.

Chapter Twenty-Two

KERRY DREAMED THAT night, too—unpleasant dreams of a supper where she was the object of ridicule. She awoke before dawn and lay on her back, staring up at the embroidered canopy above her as she silently begged God for help.

After luncheon, she left Claudia with some excuse of napping, pulled on a new pair of gloves—delivered just that morning along with a half-dozen pairs of slippers—and walked into the foyer. She asked the footman there for a carriage, fully expecting to be denied on the grounds of improper protocol or something equally obscure. But he merely nodded and went off to fetch her a carriage.

In the drive, a coachman helped her into the carriage, then stuck his head in and inquired as to her direction.

"To the Christian House on Mount Street," she said, and again waited to be told no. But once again, the coachman merely nodded, and the next thing she knew, the carriage was rocking forward.

Kerry leaned back against the plush velvet squabs and smiled to herself as the carriage rolled onto St. James Square. Perhaps God had heard her pleas after all.

At Mount Street, Barnaby greeted her at the door. He

did not seem surprised to see her, nor did he so much as flinch when she asked if she might speak with Arthur. He gave a quick glance over her head to the street, then stepped aside, bowing low and sweeping his hand to indicate she should enter. Kerry stepped into the two-story foyer, let a footman divest her of her wrap, and then followed Barnaby to the study.

"My lord is with his solicitor at present, madam. If you would be so kind as to wait here, I shall inform him you have called." He bowed again and pulled the door shut, leaving her alone.

Kerry instantly removed her gloves and nervously flexed her fingers. Her mind raced with what exactly she would say to Arthur. She absently wandered about the study as she tried to settle on a proper speech—how did she tell the man she loved with all her heart that she could not exist in his world? How did she tell him that she could not wear so many pairs of slippers, or that the number of gowns now hanging in a wardrobe at Kettering House was enough to clothe the entire population of Glenbaden several times over? How exactly did she express to him how much she loved him, but that she had to return to Scotland?

That she had to return to Scotland had settled on her just this morning. It had been weeks since she shot Charles Moncrieffe dead and had entered her own private hell, alternating between guilt and remorse at having taken a human life, and anger for having the situation forced upon her. Weeks in which she had jumped at every shadow, her nerves frayed to the very ends, convinced that Baron Moncrieffe had finally found her. Certainly it had occurred to her that the one thing that might end her nightmarish existence was to return and face the consequences of what she had done. Just as certainly she had rejected that idea, more interested in living than swinging at the end of a rope.

Aye, that she should return and face the consequences of her actions had come to her in vivid clarity this morning as she was brushing her hair. Come what may, she owed it to herself and to Charles Moncrieffe to return to Glenbaden and explain what had happened. And she was not entirely without hope. Cameron Moncrieffe surely knew his son—he could not help but understand what had transpired that awful morning. Perhaps he would show her mercy . . .

Perhaps he would not. But she would never rest again as long as she ran from what she had done. It would eat at her soul like a disease, slowly killing her.

Kerry moved from the vase to the desk where she had often seen Arthur working. An old quill pen was perched on one corner of the desk; an ink blotter and small porcelain bowl of sand rested near a stack of papers, opened to be read. Kerry paused and looked down, not really seeing the words on the page as her fingers traced the fine grain of the wood, her mind on Moncrieffe and what he might do.

With a quick draw of breath, she closed her eyes. She couldn't think of such things now or she would lose her fragile resolve to do what was right. Slowly, she opened her eyes, concentrated on the paper in front of her to banish the brutal images of her fate from her mind's eye . . . and saw the name Thomas McKinnon.

The name jolted her; she gasped, recoiling slightly before immediately leaning forward again to look at the paper. It was his name, all right, but why would Arthur have a paper with Thomas's name on it? Confusion and curiosity overwhelmed her, with only a twinge of conscience, she snatched up the paper and read it.

The letter was addressed to Lord Arthur Christian. Kerry glanced at the bottom of the page and instantly recognized the neat little signature before she actually read Mr. Jamie Regis, Esquire. *Why should Mr. Regis be writing Arthur?* She lifted her gaze and began to read, slowly sinking into the tall leather chair at the desk as she read, finally covering the silent scream in her throat with a hand over her mouth.

Jamie Regis very perfunctorily reported that the eviction of the tenants Lord Arthur Christian had ordered from Lord Rothembow's land had been completed, and that a written offer of settlement of the land and assets had been made to the Bank of Scotland.

It was inconceivable. *Impossible!* This could not be, it simply could not be, that Arthur was the one who had ordered her eviction! Or that he was the one who had deigned to settle her property! But he had, apparently, done it in the name of Lord Rothembow . . . Phillip. *Fraser's English investor.*

Oh God.

The realization that it was no accident Arthur had come to be on that rural road a lifetime ago made her nauseous. He had come looking for *her,* looking for her land, looking to throw her off like so much rubbish so that he might sell all that she had in the world to a bank and then replace her life with *sheep.*

Kerry dropped the paper, covered her face with her hands as she tried to absorb it. He had lived with her, eaten from the dwindling bounty of Glenbaden, accepted the kindness and hospitality of her family and kin. He had worked alongside them, knowing that he would cast them all to the wind when it was said and done.

Thomas. Kerry looked up. *What of Thomas?* She grabbed the letter again, searching frantically for the name she had seen only moments ago, finding it in a last thought from Regis.

> *I regret to inform you of an unfortunate turn of events. It would appear that Mr. Thomas McKinnon has been taken into the custody of Baron Moncrieffe by the authority of the sheriff in Perth for the murder of his son, Charles Moncrieffe. It is also suspected that Mr. McKinnon may have very well murdered the widow McKinnon, as her whereabouts are unknown to this day . . .*

Kerry cried out and sprang to her feet. She had to get out of there, arrange to be taken back to Scotland at once. *Thomas!* What if she was too late? What if they hanged him before she could reach Glenbaden? Her heart cried out to God, and a sudden, blinding pain behind her eyes very nearly brought her to her knees. *God, no. No, no, no.*

Kerry stumbled forward—her gloves. Where in the bloody hell were her gloves?

Arthur was surprised but terribly pleased when Barnaby leaned over and whispered in his ear that Mrs. McKinnon had come to call and was waiting in the study. He quickly dismissed his solicitor with a promise to meet again on the morrow, saw the man out, then worked to pace his stride so that it did not appear that he rushed off like a young lad to see his love.

It was actually rather hard to do, for he was eager to tell Kerry of his decision, even more eager to see her glorious face when he did. She would be surprised, grateful, touched beyond words. She would love him always.

He quickened his step.

When he walked into the study, he could not keep what he was quite certain was an idiot grin from his face. Kerry had her back to him; she was bent over the map table.

"Kerry?"

She whirled, and Arthur felt the grin slip from his mouth.

Her face was pale, too pale—the gloves she gripped in her right hand were shaking, and her left hand gripped the diamond at her throat. For one insane instant Arthur thought she might tear it from the slender chain that held it.

"My God, what has happened?" he exclaimed, hurrying toward her. Kerry jerked awkwardly to one side, away from him, and opened her mouth, but there was no sound. His heart began to beat hard, flooding his body with alarm. "Kerry, speak to me. Tell me what is wrong!" he demanded frantically.

"Thomas," she managed to get out, and pointed to the desk.

Thomas. Thomas? Arthur crossed the room to where she pointed, grabbed all the papers there. "What? What would you have me see?"

"A letter . . ."

His heart dropped to the bottom of his stomach. He frantically searched through the papers he held and found the one that bore Regis's signature at the bottom. As he quickly scanned the missive, he felt his heart turn to lead, sink to his belly. He had not seen the letter before now. He certainly had not anticipated that she would discover his role in the demise of Glenbaden in this way. He supposed he had thought she would never know of it—why should she? She was never going back there.

He looked up; she stared at him as if he was a monster—no love shining in her blue eyes, just horror. "Kerry, please allow me to explain—"

"What could you possibly say? The letter explains it very clearly, does it not? You evicted me, Arthur. You scattered the McKinnons to all corners of the earth so that Moncrieffe could put his sheep there."

"No, Kerry, Phillip Rothembow and your late husband did that. I might have directed the final outcome, but it was done well before I arrived in Scotland."

She stared at him with such disbelief and hurt in her eyes that Arthur could feel it slice into his skin. "Why didna you tell me this, Arthur?" she asked hoarsely. "Why didna you tell me you would evict me? How could you eat from my table, drink our whiskey . . . *sleep in my bed?*"

"Kerry," he moaned, reaching for her, but she backed away. His hands fell to his side. "I didn't know it was you when I gave the orders, you must believe me."

She blinked back tears, looked down at the gloves she gripped so tightly.

"When I came to Scotland and met with Mr. Regis, not only did he not know that your husband was dead, but he made me believe that the man with whom Phillip had partnered had a *surname* of Fraser. It wasn't until my arrival in Glenbaden that I realized it was *you* I had ordered evicted."

She recoiled from the word, bumping into the map table. Arthur made another move toward her, but she quickly shook her head and held up her hand. "No," she muttered.

Panic. Sheer panic invaded him and suddenly frantic, Arthur quickly continued. "Look here, once I realized it was you, I did not say anything because I thought I could repair the thing. I had instructed Mr. Regis to pay a personal call, so I reasoned he had not yet come. When I left Glenbaden, I went directly to Dundee to stop the eviction and see what might be done about the debt."

That earned him a skeptical look.

"Kerry, listen!" he said, hearing the desperation in his voice. "When I met with Regis in Dundee I realized I was too late. That is why I came back, do you see? I came back to tell you what had happened and to help you somehow."

Her eyes rounded and filled with tears. "That is why you came back?"

"I came back because I loved you, Kerry. I love you *now,* only more, and so much that I was going to tell you today that we will marry—"

Her shout of hysterical laughter cut him like a knife, flaying open an old, ancient wound. A cold rush swept down his skin, and he unconsciously dropped the papers he held.

"You were going to tell me we would marry, is that it, then? Was I to have a say in it at all?"

"I thought you would want the same," he heard himself say, and the words burned him—he sounded just like he had all those years ago when Portia had so sweetly denied him. *I thought you would want the same.*

"Just like you thought I would want all these clothes, and these slippers, and these bloody gloves?" she asked, throwing the kid leather pair onto the map table. "I think you've not any idea who I truly am, Arthur! I am not these things! I canna live this life of leisure and unimaginable wealth! I doona know which spoon is appropriate, I feel myself rot with disuse, and I canna seem to shake the guilt or the fear of being discovered! I *belonged* in Glenbaden! It was my life, my very soul, and you took it away from me!"

His hands fisted tightly at his side in an effort to maintain his control. "I did not take it from you! Your husband robbed you of Glenbaden *long* before I came along! I merely tried to dispose of a bad investment, and in the course of it, I made the unforgivable error of falling in love with you!"

Kerry made a pitiful sound; a tear raced down her face. "Oh aye, I know, for I made the very same unforgivable error, I did. I love you like I have never loved another in my life, Arthur Christian, but I canna be what you want me to be and I willna stay here and pretend that I can! And dear God in heaven, I will *not* let Thomas hang for what I have done!"

"Thomas will not hang!" Arthur shouted at the ceiling. "For God's sake, I will send my man to Perth at once with a very generous offer to allow Thomas to come to London!"

"You canna simply *buy* his freedom!" Kerry exclaimed angrily. "You canna buy his freedom any more than you can buy my love!"

That stung him badly. *"Damn you,"* he said low. "I gave you those things because I love you and I wanted you to have the finest the world has to offer."

"No. No, Arthur, you wanted me to be like Lady Albright and Lady Kettering. You wanted me to learn to live like them, *behave* like them. You wanted me to live in a world where it is acceptable to evict people from their homes without even so much as seeing their faces.

You should never have to worry where you might live, or
how you might put food on your table! You have no idea
what you did to us!"

The truth in that made him furious, and he stalked
away from the desk, glared out the window as he fought
for control. After all he had done for her, she would throw
it back in his face? "Is it so awful, Kerry? Is what I offer
you so detestable?"

"No," she said, her voice softer. "It is highly desirable.
But I find it not as desirable as Glenbaden ... or my
peace of mind."

Somehow he found a glimmer of hope in that statement and pivoted around. Guilt was keeping her from
him; guilt was giving all that she had seen in London a
bitter taste. "Then I will find a way to free Thomas and
bring him here, and you may rest easy, Kerry. And when
you do, you will surely agree to marry me." *God, how
desperate he sounded.* How desperate he felt. The chaos
of it all was slowly churning, slowly spinning them out of
control. Arthur held his breath, waited for her response,
waited for her to throw herself in his arms and beg his
forgiveness for having been so cruel.

But Kerry slowly shook her head. "You truly doona
understand how different we are, do you?"

Her simple rejection stunned him. He had to tell himself to breathe, to move. He never would have believed
it, not in a thousand years would he have believed Kerry
could hurt him so. "Then what do you want?" he asked
coolly, finding that small part of himself that had not
been cut dead by her rejection.

Tears welled in her pale blue eyes. "I want to go
home."

He closed his eyes, willed the pain from his chest.

"Please doona make me stay here, Arthur," she softly
pleaded.

The final blow, the one that effectively slew him. He
could scarcely believe what he was hearing. He had
saved this woman from hanging, had brought her to his

home, clothed her in the finest gowns, draped her in jewels, imposed on his friends for her welfare ... and she wanted to go home? God in heaven, what sort of woman rejected the highest circle of British aristocracy out of hand? What sort of woman would take the love he had offered her under moonlit skies and silk tapestries and dismiss it so completely? *What sort of woman was she?* Perhaps Kerry was right. Perhaps they were very different indeed.

The old defenses came up after so many years, defenses he had erected and fortified in two dealings with Portia. Defenses he was certain he would never know again, because Kerry had seemed so different. *So real.* Everything he had thought she was seemed false to him now.

"I will think on it," he said simply, and turned his back to her, unwilling to let her see how she had wounded him so deeply. "I rather imagine if you found your way in you might find your way out again?"

Silence. And then, a very soft *"Aye."*

He listened to the rustle of her new petticoats as she moved across the room and passed through the door. He stood there, staring down at the desk for what seemed an eternity before finally turning to face the room again.

She had left her gloves behind.

Silently, woodenly, Arthur moved to the map table and picked up one of the small kid leather gloves. He turned it over in his palm, unable to stop the memory of the feel of her hand in his from instantly flooding his heart. He abruptly dropped the glove on the table and walked out of the study.

It was over. His extraordinary little journey was over, and the quality of his life had, once again, been altered permanently by a woman's perfidy.

Julian expressed some surprise before supper that Arthur had not been to call. Kerry shrugged it off as she pretended to closely examine a painting, and mumbled something about another engagement. But she was aware of the look Claudia and Julian exchanged, and felt the heat crawl up the back of her neck.

After supper, she complained of a headache and retired early. When she was certain the Danes were ensconced in the small sitting room, she stole from her room and down to the kitchens through the servant's stairway.

She startled Cook badly. "Miss? Is there something I can do for you?"

Kerry flushed furiously, fingered a curl touching her shoulder. "I would speak to Brian, the footman, if you please. Would you be so kind then to tell me where he might be?"

Cook's mouth gaped open. "Oh no. No indeed, miss, I won't be party to any such—

"He is from Scotland," Kerry quickly interrupted. "Like me. I . . . I've a message for him, that's all."

Cook stopped shaking her head. "From his brother?"

Kerry nodded.

Cook smiled. "Ah, he's been waiting to hear from him, the poor lad."

"Where might he be, then?"

"I will take it for you, mu'um—"

"Ah, no—" *Dear God, she had to think fast.* "It's . . . it's written in Gaelic, you see, and ah, the lad, he canna read it. I shall have to read it to him."

Cook frowned, obviously thinking. After a moment, she shrugged. "He's done for the day. I reckon you can find him in his room on the top floor. Third door on the left."

Kerry thanked her and left quickly before Cook could say anything else. She used the servant's stairwell again, silently rejoicing each time a floor was gained and she had not met anyone who would question her. When she reached the fourth floor, she hurried to the third door on the left and rapped. She waited, her pulse quickening.

She was about to rap again when she heard the sound of shuffling feet. The door cracked open a hair.

"Brian!"

The door shut. She heard the sound of feet again—more than a pair, she was certain—and then muffled voices. A minute passed, maybe two, before the door opened again. "Aye?"

"Brian?"

The door opened wider, and Brian appeared before her, wearing nothing but a pair of trousers. His red hair was mussed, his lips swollen. A long, very thin and red line ran from his shoulder to his breast, the mark of a fingernail. A furious blush raced to her face as the footman peered down at her. "Aye, lass, what would ye be needing, then?"

She reached in the pocket of her skirt and fished out the blue diamond and held it up. Brian's green eyes rounded; he flicked her an inquisitive look, then shifted his gaze to the diamond dangling before him. "I need to reach Scotland as quickly as possible."

Chapter Twenty-Three

IF THERE WAS one thing Julian Dane abhorred, it was meddling in another man's affairs. He usually left that sort of thing up to Arthur—he was so damn good at it. But when it was time for someone to meddle in Arthur's affairs, he supposed it would have to be him, and he cursed Albright for staying at Longbridge through the autumn!

Julian handed the reins of his horse to a freckle-faced lad at Arthur's Mount Street house and jogged up the steps to the entry, wondering how exactly he would inquire as to the delicate relationship between Arthur and Mrs. McKinnon. What words did he use to ask if the houseguest delivered to him was ever leaving? Not that he minded having Kerry about—she was actually very pleasant and Claudia seemed to adore her. And naturally, he couldn't be happier that it had been *his* idea for Christian to trot off to Scotland in the first place. But the woman hadn't come out of her room since yesterday afternoon, and Arthur hadn't been to call in three full days now. When Claudia began to fret, Julian had finally reached the inevitable conclusion that he would, unfortunately, have to inquire as to exactly what had transpired between the two lovers to cause this sudden rift.

Barnaby showed him to the study where Arthur was hard at work poring over a stack of papers.

"Kettering," he said, barely glancing up. "I expected you well before now."

Julian smiled and strolled deeper into the room. "I am unaccustomed to meddling, as you know. You must instruct me as to the proper procedure for it."

"It's rather simple, really." Arthur shoved the stack of papers away and leaned back. "First, you ascertain that there is some sort of trouble," he said blandly, "then you pay a call and inquire as to exactly the root of the trouble. If you are fortunate, the object of your meddling will tell all without much prompting from you. If you aren't so very fortunate, you may be forced to ask uncomfortable questions. Nevertheless, once you are satisfied that you understand the facts, you offer a truthful perspective and your very profound advice on the matter at hand. Quite simple, really."

"Aha. Then in this instance, I might ask if there has been a row between you and the woman you dragged here all the way from Scotland?"

"I see no reason to cover old ground. I would suggest you go straight to the heart of the matter and ask why someone like Kerry McKinnon would refuse an offer of marriage from someone like me."

The announcement shocked Julian—he hoped he managed to hide his great surprise from Arthur, but it was inconceivable that he would seriously entertain marriage with someone of Kerry's background. "Oh, is that all there is?" he drawled. "Then my work here should be concluded quickly. Well then, why *would* Kerry McKinnon refuse you?"

Arthur shrugged. "She says we are quite different."

"You are."

Arthur frowned. "I know her like I know myself, Julian. We are not so very different."

"All right," Julian conceded. "You share thoughts in

common, perhaps even some profound experiences in common. You enjoy the same pastimes and pursuits. But you are the son of a duke, Arthur. She is a widow of a Scottish farmer. In that regard, you are very different."

"Are you saying such differences cannot be overcome?" Arthur snapped.

"You heard no such claim from me," Julian quickly responded, raising his hand in supplication. "But you cannot deny that the differences in your background and pedigree are substantial."

Arthur looked down at his hands with a frown. "I . . . I love her, Julian. I don't care about such superficial differences. They *can* be overcome."

Julian sighed, reached in his breast pocket for his spectacles, and put them on. He peered at Arthur for a long moment, wondering if he should tell his friend how long it would be before such differences were overcome, if ever. Perhaps not even in their lifetime. Even if Kerry learned the proper table manners and how to speak and move like a woman of *Quality* the *ton* would never accept her. They were merciless in that way, repudiating anyone without the proper credentials to have gained entry into their circles. They would sooner forgive indiscretion or infidelity than they would the lack of connections. God help his dear old friend Arthur. It was just like the sentimental fool to believe he could change centuries of thinking among the whole bloody *ton* for the sake of love.

"Differences can be overcome, but only to a certain extent."

Arthur raked a look of disappointment over Julian.

"You said I should speak the truth. I am giving you the truth. Kerry is . . . lovely. Charming. Refreshingly original. Certainly she can be taught the proper etiquette for any occasion. But the odds are against her of ever being completely accepted here. There will be those who accept her for who she is and because you love her. But there will be more who shun her because of her background. Do you think your love alone can sustain her?"

Arthur suddenly shoved to his feet and stalked to the drink cart. He poured two whiskeys, handed one to Julian. "Don't think I haven't thought of it. Don't think I haven't lain awake every night wondering how we might overcome such bloody obstacles. Even Paddy treated her with not a little disdain. But I keep coming round to the same conclusion—I love her. I am quite certain I will never love another woman as I love her. And you would have me deny that because some goddamn blue blood would cut her?"

Julian looked at the amber liquid in the glass Arthur had handed him and asked quietly, "Have you considered setting her up in a house nearby?"

Arthur downed the whiskey and fairly tossed the glass aside. "Oh, I've thought of it. Believe me, I have thought of it. But I cannot—I care for her far too much for that."

That prompted Julian to down his whiskey, too. There was obviously nothing he could say that would convince the old boy to forget the ludicrous idea of marriage; oh no, Julian knew the set of that jaw—Arthur Christian would defy every known social custom in this country, offend his family honor in the process, all for the sake of his heart.

One had to love a man like that.

"Well then, if you are to be so very pigheaded about the whole thing, you may as well go and speak with her. Having endured the raising of four girls, all of whom moped over a lost love at one time or another, I would thank you not to force me to do it again."

"Will she see me?"

Julian's heart wrenched at the sound of hopeful uncertainty in Arthur's voice. It reminded him of his own troubles with Claudia when they were first married and he knew very well how much it hurt, knew very well indeed the pain of loving so deeply and believing that love unrequited. And how it was to wish hopelessly for it every waking hour.

He stood, walked to Arthur and clapped a hand on his shoulder. "I don't rightly know, old chap. She hasn't come out of her rooms since yesterday afternoon."

Arthur hesitated for a moment before he muttered, "Then we had best be about it." And he was already striding to the door.

They walked into the gold salon at Kettering House after Julian sent a maid to rap on Mrs. McKinnon's door and tell her that Arthur had come. Arthur was too restless to sit; he stood at the bow windows overlooking St. James Square and stared blindly into the street.

The sting of her rejection had lessened somewhat in the last few days. He could count himself among all unfeeling cads if he didn't realize what a great shock the discovery of the letter from Regis must have been for her. He should have told her his role in it, and truthfully, he had fully intended to do so—but the shock of finding her over Moncrieffe's body, the flight from Glenbaden, all of it . . . the more days that passed, the less important it seemed.

Nonetheless, her rejection of his offer of marriage stuck like a lump in his throat, a constant but dull source of pain. He wondered for the thousandth time if perhaps he had imagined her love for him, if he had somehow manufactured it to match his own increasing ardor. Had she truly lain beneath him, expressing her love for him in the most primitive terms, or had it been a dream? What of the things she had said? Had he misconstrued them somehow, misunderstood her intent? For the last three days he had tortured himself with every distinct memory of her.

He had thought he knew her as well as he knew himself. Now he wondered if he ever really knew her at all.

"Milord."

Arthur turned around as the maid Julian had sent up to Kerry entered the salon and curtseyed low.

"Well, Peg? What did Mrs. McKinnon have to say?"

"She wouldn't answer, milord."

"Nor when I called to her this morning," Claudia said, sweeping into the room behind the maid. "Julian, I think something is wrong."

It was not like Kerry. Arthur was already moving, his mind resisting the jagged edges of fear that tried to stab his consciousness. "Where?" he asked simply, and followed Julian out.

He rapped hard on the door Julian showed him to, and listened closely. There was no sound behind the door. He frowned at Julian and Claudia and knocked again. "Kerry, open this door!"

Silence.

Arthur twisted the knob; it was locked.

"Through the dressing room," Julian said, leading the way. Arthur strode through the adjoining bedroom, thrust the door to the dressing room open and walked through it, oblivious to its contents, to Kerry's room.

It was empty.

A window stood open, the long chiffon drapes floating on a cool autumn breeze. The bed was neatly made; there was no sign of anyone having lived in the room at all.

"Oh no," Claudia murmured behind him.

Oh God. She was gone. Kerry was gone. Arthur spun around, looking for anything, *any* sign that she had been here, *was* here, somewhere they weren't looking.

"Are you certain this is the right room?" Julian asked, obviously thinking the same thing, and receiving a withering look from Claudia for it.

"Where could she have gone?" Claudia asked.

Arthur pivoted on his heel, stalked to the dressing room and looked around him. Boxes of slippers and hats were lined neatly on one shelf, some of them with ribbons still tied—never opened. He flung open a wardrobe; her gowns, the expensive gowns he had commissioned for her, were stuffed tightly within. His mind could not absorb it, he whipped around again, strode into her room, glared at the objects on the vanity. Jars of creams—where had those come from?—a handful of ribbons, a comb. A jewelry box sat on one corner of the vanity, and Arthur felt himself moving there through some force that was not truly his own.

"She could not have gone far. She's no knowledge of London a'tall," Julian said as Arthur opened the jewelry box. Everything was there, all the pieces of jewelry he had given her.

Except the blue diamond.

He picked up a strand of pearls and let them fall through his fingers. "When was the last time you saw her?"

"After luncheon yesterday. She complained of a headache and came up to rest."

"What of supper?"

"She didn't come down," Claudia said, pressing a finger to her bottom lip as she thought. "I had a tray sent up, and the footman returned with it. I believe he said she refused it."

"He said she didn't answer," Julian clarified, and met Arthur's gaze from across the room.

His heart stopped working, laid dead. "She is gone," he said flatly. *Gone*. Gone, disappeared without a trace. *How could this have happened?* Not three days ago, he was happily contemplating marriage. How could it all have unraveled? *He had to find her*. All right then, *think!* Where would she have gone? It was inconceivable that she had started for Scotland. With what? She had no money, no means of transportation—

The diamond.

The understanding kicked him in the gut. The one thing she had not left behind was the one thing she could easily trade for cash, and quite a lot of it at that. Arthur started for the door, but his eye caught a glimmer of pale yellow on the stand next to the bed, and he paused.

It was a folded piece of vellum. He changed course, practically lunging for it, tearing it open. It was a note, all right, one written in a shaky hand, the words marred by several inkblots. As the words sank into his consciousness, his vision blurred with his despair, all else settled into a distant noise. She apologized for leaving in such a contemptible manner, of course, but wrote that she had come to realize their lives were vastly different, and that she was too simple to pretend she was someone she was not, too honest to allow Thomas to hang for her crime. As Kerry McKinnon apparently saw things, she no more belonged in his world than he in hers, for she urged Arthur not to follow her.

There was no hope of that, he thought, crumpling the note in his hand. As stunned as he was, he knew there was no hope of that. How could he? Her abandonment had broken him in two.

He turned and looked at the stricken Danes. "She has left. Gone to Scotland."

"But *how?*" Claudia exclaimed as Julian put an arm around her. "She can't simply walk there!"

"I suspect she found a way to sell the diamond necklace I gave her." It sounded so ruthless when he said it; he looked blindly around the room, thrust a hand through his hair, feeling suddenly numb.

"Oh, Arthur," Claudia murmured.

Unconsciously, he dropped the note. "I will send someone for her things," he said, moving for the door.

"Arthur . . ."

But he kept walking, deaf to Julian's call. Deaf to everything, but the pain of his loss and anger.

She had left him without so much as a fare-thee-well.

The first hours following the discovery of that monumental fact passed in a white blur of soul-consuming devastation.

She might as well have died.

The end was the same. He had no opportunity to hear her reasoning for leaving him like she did, no opportunity to present his side of things, to try and change her mind. She hadn't even extended him the common courtesy of saying good-bye. Oh no, she had cut herself from his life without a word, suddenly and completely, without giving him even a single chance to say the things that were in his heart. *How could he live without her? How could he pass the days without her smile, the nights without her breath on his neck?*

She might as well have died.

Arthur slept badly that night, tossing and turning through dreams of Phillip, of Kerry. He was again in the ballroom among glittering objects and people, searching for Kerry, struggling through a sea of dancers, finally finding her in the arms of a laughing Phillip. He grabbed her, pulled her into his arms, but she melted. Just melted into nothing.

The two days following were the blackest. Her betrayal of his trust and his love was the cruelest thing he had ever known, and it ate away at him like a cancer. He tried to numb it at the Tam O'Shanter with copious amounts of wine, but it had no effect on the pain. Even his mind played tricks on him—she hadn't really left, she was still in London, and he found himself looking for her in every woman he encountered on the street.

The worst of it was his body's traitorous ache for her. He remembered every touch, every kiss, every whisper. He remembered how her eyes would sparkle with desire when he kissed her, how her smile would warm him to the very pit of his soul, often leaving him to grin at her like a lovesick pup. The memories came to him unwanted, uninvited, filling him with perfect misery. In his thirty-six years on this earth, he had never known such personal annihilation. The woman had succeeded in shattering his fool heart.

A trip to Madame Farantino's brothel was even less successful than the wine. He sought to erase the memory of her body with that of another, but it was a wholly and humiliatingly futile endeavor. Nothing could take Kerry from his mind. Nothing.

A week later, Alex returned from Sutherland Hall with his sister-in-law Lauren and their three young sons. It took Arthur another two days to rouse himself from his doldrums to pay a call on his brother. When he arrived at twenty-two Audley Street, it was apparent Alex had already heard the news of his unfortunate bout of love. A copy of the latest *Times* sat folded on the edge of Alex's desk. Arthur had seen the *on-dit* in the society pages that speculated what a certain brother of an influential duke might have done with his Scottish bumpkin after amusing half the *ton* with her.

He waited for Alex to chastise him, remind him he was the son of the eighth duke of Sutherland and the brother of the tenth. He fell into a chair, lazily accepted a cup of tea from a maid, and stared at a picture of his father and mother.

"I ran into Kettering at White's last evening."

Arthur said nothing, waited for the lecture. Much to his great surprise, however, Alex merely studied his French cuffs and remarked, "I gather it has been a very trying time for you."

A gross understatement. It had been hell.

"I was reminded of the weeks before Lauren and I married."

Arthur glanced at his brother. "This is hardly the same thing." That was true—Lauren was a countess in her own right; her family had connections to the *ton*. And when she had fled home, it had been only miles from Sutherland Hall, a place Alex could easily reach her. Furthermore, Alex was engaged to be married to another woman at the time. He had not given everything he had to Lauren only to have her disappear into thin air.

Alex shrugged, lifted his gaze from his French cuff. "Isn't it? I recall sitting in this very room with our mother. Lauren had left; I was engaged to marry Marlaine Reese. They were terribly black days. And do you know what Hannah said to me?"

Arthur shook his head.

"She said, 'the French have a saying: *True love is like ghosts, which everyone talks about and few have ever seen.*'"

Arthur shrugged indifferently. "And?"

"And," said Alex calmly, "she urged me to break my engagement and go after Lauren for the sake of true love."

Now he was only confusing Arthur, who irritably shook his head. "I know all that, but this is not the same thing, Alex. You would hardly suggest that I toddle off to Scotland—"

"What is keeping you here?"

That brought him up short. He stared at his older brother as if he had lost his mind. Alex lifted a dark brow and God in heaven, Arthur wasn't sure that he hadn't. "Do you know who she is, Alex? She is the widow of a poor Scottish farmer who tried to dig himself out of bad investments by taking Phillip's money. Only he squandered that, too, and lost everything. Kerry McKinnon hasn't so much as a farthing to her name."

Alex laughed. "There are worse histories in our family background," he said with a smile. "If poverty is her only crime, I should think you could easily alleviate that."

"What of her lack of connections? Even Paddy was cool to her."

"I wouldn't know what her lack of connections means in Edinburgh drawing rooms, but here? Paddy will accept her once Mother is through with her. Kettering, Albright, our cousin Westfall—Darfield, certainly. They will most assuredly ignore anything as superficial as connections. Who else concerns you?"

Arthur gaped at his brother. "And what invitations do you think we shall receive at the height of the Season?" he asked disgustedly. "When you and the others are off to some ball, who exactly do you think will want us at their supper table?"

With a frown, Alex resumed the study of his French cuff. "What does it matter if you are in Scotland?" He looked up, gauging Arthur's reaction, and quickly continued before Arthur could speak. "Look here, Arthur, you have lived your life in the shadow of others. Don't deny it—you are the third son of a duke and could not help being thrust into mine or Anthony's shadow. You were one of the Rogues of Regent Street, true, but you stood aside and watched *them* live. And you have complained to me on more than one occasion that the Christian Brothers' Enterprise does not need you. Very well, then. It is time you lived for yourself, high time you sought your own meaning in life and perhaps improved the quality of it. Kettering said you had a fine time of it in Scotland, that you actually *liked* working the land. What do you have here that could possibly compare?"

Arthur was speechless.

He was speechless long after he left his brother's study. He had offered no answer to Alex's challenge, and Alex had let it lie. But as Arthur walked home along Audley Street, he was struck with the thought that perhaps Alex was right. He had never really lived, not like the others. He had often thought his life lacking somehow, as if there wasn't enough to it to justify his existence.

But to Scotland?

Ah God, he missed her. In spite of his anger, he missed her. And as much as he was loath to feel so, he was deathly worried about her. The foolish lass intended to hand herself over in some noble gesture to free Thomas. If he had known when she left, or *how* she left, he might have tried to stop her, but her head start was devastating to any hope of stopping her.

It was that which he was contemplating when he almost collided with a party of ladies out for an afternoon walkabout. The group of women startled him; he clumsily tipped his hat before he saw Portia among them, smiling up at him beneath her parasol.

"Lord Christian," she purred. "What a delight."

"Lady Roth," he responded coolly, bowing, and greeted the three women who accompanied her.

"I am surprised to see you about. I had heard you were quite indisposed once your little friend had run back to Scotland." The women giggled as Portia looked at him with a devilish glint in her eye.

How he despised her. The woman was devious, calculating. He glanced at her three friends, all of whom he knew very well by reputation. They were no better than Portia, all of them sporting identical, knowing smiles. "You should take better care of whom you select as confidantes, Lady Roth. As you can see, I am quite well."

"And we are very glad to see it, sir. I should hate to think of you pining away for some poor Scottish lassie." The women tittered again, and Portia smiled so broadly that it creased the heavy cosmetics she had applied to her face.

Arthur smirked, tipped his hat again. "You are as considerate as always, Lady Roth. Good day, ladies." He stepped around them and continued walking, aware of Portia's low laughter behind him.

And as he strolled on, he silently agreed with Kerry. She could never fit in this world; she could never possess the gall it required. His world did an injustice to her and for the first time, Arthur wondered seriously why he couldn't fit into hers. The days he had spent in Glenbaden had been some of the happiest of his life. He had felt like a man there, invincible, strong.

The idea teased him for the rest of the day. Over a solitary supper, Arthur reached an epiphany of sorts. As much as he was hurting, he truly did understand why Kerry did what she did—her integrity was one of the things he so very much admired about her. And while he might quibble with the how of it, he had not exactly listened to her wishes. He had imposed what he thought was best, assuming she had no knowledge of what was best for herself. How bloody arrogant of him. And he knew of the familial bond that existed between her and Thomas, and damn well *should* have known that she would move heaven and earth to clear his name.

The truth was, he thought as he picked at the lamb on his plate, that he would do anything at this moment to have her back, including leaving behind everything that he was and all that he had for Scotland.

And why not? He had nothing to lose but himself.

Chapter Twenty-Four

THE SEASON WAS already beginning to turn in the Central Highlands of Scotland. From the small window of her cell, Kerry could see bright red, yellow, and orange leaves falling and skating across the small courtyard. With each leaf that fell, she wondered if she would live to see the trees in Glenbaden again.

Their trial would occur, Moncrieffe said, when the justice of the peace came through the Perthshire region to hear criminal matters. Maybe a fortnight. Maybe longer. She and Thomas would be tried together.

Thomas. She had seen him for only a quarter of an hour before they had taken her away. Drawn and terribly thin, he had been shocked to see her, having believed her dead. He had been too overwhelmed with relief to tell her much, other than everything would be all right. At the time, she had believed him, because she had believed that once she explained what had happened, they would free Thomas.

But no.

Cameron Moncrieffe had leveled an accusation that she and Thomas were lovers, and had killed Charles so that Kerry would not have to honor her late husband's agreement to marry the poor, simple lad.

It was an absurd accusation—there were several

people who knew the true relationship between Kerry and Thomas, and furthermore, had seen him leave with the cattle. Unfortunately, most of those people had left Glenbaden for good, and Kerry had no idea where Big Angus and May may have gone. Nonetheless, she naively believed that the truth would prevail, and she had tried to convince the sheriff who had brought her here that she had killed Charles in self-defense. But the more she insisted on the truth, the deafer he and Moncrieffe seemed to be. No one believed her—no one would *listen* to her.

So she and Thomas were to be tried for murder and the penalty for their crime was, as Moncrieffe had maliciously delighted in telling her, death by hanging. To emphasize that point, he had put her in the cell of an ancient tower on the Moncrieffe estate that overlooked the site on which they were building the gallows.

Alone in that cell, with nothing to amuse her but the changing season and the progress on the gallows, Kerry inevitably spent her days thinking of Arthur. She missed him terribly. Oh, she had forgotten all about the eviction—it had not taken her long to see that he was right, that Fraser had lost her land, not him. She believed what he told her about his role in it all.

The hardest thing she had ever done in her life was to leave without seeing him. But she could hardly blame him for not wanting to see her, not after she had refused to marry him in the manner that she had. She had been angry, confused . . . and even in the best of circumstances, it was impossible to explain to him how terribly ill suited she was for London. Arthur had moved in those circles all his life; he could not possibly fathom how foreign it was to someone like her, how out of place she seemed. How everyone, including his own lady aunt, had felt it, too.

Only Arthur had believed she would be accepted.

She missed him, cried herself to sleep almost every night thinking of him, and woke every morning longing for his smile and soft caress. But then the matron would come with a bowl of what passed for oats, the cold seeping in through the thick walls of the tower would penetrate her bones, and she would begin her prayers all over again, until her thoughts bled into memories of Arthur.

How she had loved him. And she would, apparently, go to her grave loving him.

On a particularly cold morning, her gaoler—Mrs. Muir, Kerry was finally able to coax out of her—brought a basin of cold water and a rag. "Yer to clean yerself up, lassie. The baron would speak with ye."

Kerry moaned. Mrs. Muir lifted her thick brows and thrust a dirty rag forward. With inhuman strength, Kerry willed herself from the lumpy mattress that passed for a bed and walked to the basin.

She washed, managed to knot her hair at her nape by the time Moncrieffe sailed into her cell, seeming to fill what little space there was. He looked remarkably fresh; his gray hair was perfectly arranged; a diamond pin winked from his throat where it held his neckcloth in place. With his hands clasped behind his back, he slowly circled Kerry, thoroughly examining her.

He came to a halt in front of her. "A fortnight within these walls hasna done you any favors, Mrs. McKinnon. Yet I think you are salvageable."

Kerry shrugged indifferently. "How kind of you to remark so. But why should you bother? You intend, do you not, to see me hang before winter comes?"

Moncrieffe smiled. "Rather an acerbic tongue for one in as much trouble as we find you, Mrs. McKinnon."

Her patience had long since drained from her and Kerry was in no mood to play games with the baron. She folded her arms across her middle, drummed her fingers on one arm. "I am well aware of the sort of trouble *we* find ourselves in, my lord. If there is something you would say, I'd ask that you get on with it and spare me the childish games."

The man actually laughed. He strolled casually to the

window and gazed out at the gallows construction. "Not a terribly good view, is it?" he asked idly, and turned around. "I suppose I could change this view for you, if I were of a mind."

"Aye, and how would you do that?"

"Simply move you to a more suitable location, my dear."

A silent warning flagged in her chest; her eyes narrowed. "And where might this 'more suitable' location be, then?"

Moncrieffe moved to where she stood, standing so close that she could smell the cloying scent of his cologne. He lifted his hand; with one finger, he stroked her cheekbone. "Moncrieffe House," he murmured. "The view from the master suite is superb."

Kerry instinctively recoiled in horror. Moncrieffe, however, was not abashed by her revulsion. He chuckled, caught her by the mess of her hair.

"Think, Mrs. McKinnon—your life for my bed. I shouldna think it such a horrid suggestion then," he said, and leaned closer, his mouth brushing her hair. "You would delight in my skill as a lover."

Her stomach roiled; Kerry stumbled away from him and covered her mouth with her hand. "Never," she managed to choke out. "I would rather die—"

"Are you insane? I offer you freedom—"

"That is not *freedom!*"

"It is as close to freedom as you will ever be, madam! Do you think yourself such a prize as to hold yourself away from me?"

The image nauseated her; Kerry swallowed it down, shook her head.

"Then why in God's name do you refuse me? I would give you your life for it!" he snapped angrily.

"Why should you make this offer now?" she choked. "What of your son? What of avenging his death as you so publicly proclaimed you would do?"

Moncrieffe shrugged. "It was destined that one of us

would have you. As Charles couldna seem to manage it
without getting himself killed, it seems appropriate that
I should. I've admired you for long, Kerry McKinnon,
and I doona intend to force my affections on you like a
beast. But it seems that you have solved a dilemma for
us both."

Her stomach roiled again, only stronger, and she
pressed her hands flat against her abdomen. "Do you
mean to say you *knew* what Charles intended to do?"

Moncrieffe laughed, a sharp, mocking laugh. "Of
course I knew! I sent him there, did I not? How else was
I to make sure you would honor your husband's commit-
ment?"

She would be sick. Looking at the man standing before her as if it were perfectly natural to send his son off
to rape a woman, she felt the oats she had eaten move in
her belly. She whirled away, rushed toward the chamber
pot in the corner of the room, and fell to her knees, unable to contain the purge of her revulsion.

Behind her, Moncrieffe chuckled nastily. "There now,
lassie. Charles wasna a genius, but he wasna a cruel boy.
In time, with my help, he would have learned to be gentle with you."

She closed her eyes, tried to block the sound of his
voice, but he was suddenly crouching behind her, his
hand on her neck. "Now *I*, on the other hand, will be as
gentle or as wild as you want me to be. You will not regret it," he murmured, and licked her ear.

"I would die before I would submit to you," she whispered.

Moncrieffe suddenly shoved her aside; she fell hard,
hitting her head against the stone wall. "Think long and
hard before you speak to me thus again," he said low.
His boots rang sharply on the stone floor as he stalked
away from her. "I will return, Kerry McKinnon." The
boots stopped. "Perhaps I will give you a sample of what
you might expect in my bed, hmmm?" He laughed again;
his boots clicked across the floor. She heard the door

open and close, the grind of the lock in the ancient key-
hole. Only then did she push herself up. With trembling
fingers, she felt her forehead. Blood trickled from where
her head had struck the wall. She slowly pushed herself
to her knees, and then to her feet, and stumbled to the
small window for some air.

Arthur.

Where was her beautiful stranger?

She passed two days in a nervous state of anticipation
waiting for Moncrieffe to come again. Mrs. Muir finally
brought food more than a day after Moncrieffe had
come. Another full day passed before the woman appeared again, this time with a bowl of what Kerry could
only call gruel. Moncrieffe was, apparently, trying to
starve her into submission.

Mrs. Muir left the bowl on a small table and walked
to the door. She paused, turned halfway around and
said, "Yer barrister's come."

Her heart skipped a beat. "My barrister?"

But that was all she was going to offer, and left her
cell, locking the door behind her. Kerry was at once on
her feet. *Her barrister?* What did that mean? Had the
justice of the peace come? She ran to the door, pressed
her hands against it. Was her trial to begin, then? *Was
her life to end?* The thought frightened her, and Kerry
banged on the door, yelled for Mrs. Muir at the top of her
lungs until she was hoarse. When she could yell no more,
she turned and pressed her back to the thick, oak-
planked door and slid down, like a rag doll, to her
haunches.

This was the end of her life.

Sobs suddenly racked her body; she buried her face
on her knees. She was only eight and twenty! *She did
not want to die*—there were so many things she wanted
to do yet, so many things she had not finished! *She had
never had a child. . . .*

The weight of her regrets threatened to bury her. With supreme effort, she forced herself to stop crying and lifted her head. "There is naught to be done for it, Kerry McKinnon," she muttered and sniffed loudly. "Pray that justice will prevail, but you took the man's very life! And if they determine your life will be had for his, then you will meet your maker with dignity, you will."

She pushed herself to her feet, felt the swim in her head, knew that the lack of food was beginning to affect her. She wandered to the little table to look at the foul stuff in the bowl, pondering why she should eat anything if she were to die so soon.

When the door swung open behind her, she turned indifferently, expecting to see the old woman again, but her heart dropped and swelled all at once with great passion.

Arthur.

No, it was an illusion! *An apparition!* She glanced at the gruel again—she would force herself to eat it, for she was beginning to hallucinate, and she'd need all her wits about her in the next few hours or days . . .

"Kerry . . ."

The sound of his voice, so unexpected, so dear, drove her to her knees. She landed awkwardly, breaking her fall by catching the table with both hands. It was no apparition; it was *him*, her beautiful stranger. *"Arthur,"* she sobbed, and felt herself being pulled up, wrapped securely in his strong embrace. She buried her face in his shoulder, inhaled his scent.

"Kerry—Lord God how I have missed you!"

A fresh torrent of tears erupted within her, and Kerry sobbed with relief and longing, soaking his coat.

"Don't cry, darling, don't cry now. We'll get you out of this . . . place."

"How did you find me?" she choked.

"It was not easy. I found Thomas—he told me you were somewhere nearby—"

"Thomas, is he all right?"

"He's fine, considering the circumstance," he said soothingly.

"Arthur . . . oh, Arthur, I canna believe you have come!"

He pressed his cheek to the side of her head. "Of course I came! I don't seem to be capable of existing without you, Kerry."

The words curled around her heart, buoyed it. She lifted her head, gazed into his hazel eyes, saw the glistening of tears and the ravages of fatigue, and her heart went out to him. "Please forgive me. *Forgive* me! I am so sorry for what I did. I thought—"

"It doesn't matter," he interrupted, and kissed her cheek.

"I would that I could go back and change it all—"

"No, don't wish for that, my love, I wouldn't have you change a thing. I intend to stay here, with you."

That confused her; she blinked up at him. He couldn't mean . . . "You mean until the trial?"

"I mean forever, Kerry. I intend to stay here, with you, in Glenbaden."

Glenbaden. She had once dreamed of them there, living with one another, children . . . "But . . . but Glenbaden is gone!"

"For the moment, perhaps, but you leave that to me. When I get you out of here, I am taking you to Glenbaden. And then I shall find a parson to marry us."

"Marry?" Her hands slowly slipped from his neck; roughly, he caught them.

"Oh no, Kerry, you will not deny me again."

"No," she muttered, shaking her head. "You doona understand—"

"I understand that whatever our differences they seem only to exist in London, not here. I *love* you, Kerry McKinnon. I love you so much that London means nothing to me without you—I am nothing without you. I would have your answer now, Kerry, do you love me?"

"More than my heart. More than my life! But . . ." she

lowered her gaze, fixated on the perfect knot of his neck-cloth. "Arthur, I will hang for what I did."

"Ha!" he scoffed, and tightened his embrace. "Over my dead body will you hang! And if I—"

"Or I will warm Moncrieffe's bed," she muttered.

That stopped him. Arthur put a finger under her chin and roughly forced her gaze to his. "What did you say?"

She quietly told him everything with ragged breath, of how she had come to free Thomas, had confessed to what had happened, and how Moncrieffe had accused them of Charles's death. She told him of Moncrieffe's visit, how food had disappeared since then. And she told him, based on what she knew of Moncrieffe's influence in the shire, that she would undoubtedly hang . . . or be his whore. By the time she had finished, Arthur had turned a deadly shade of white; she could see the hatred burning in his hazel eyes.

"You will not hang, nor will you step foot in Moncrieffe's house," he said through clenched teeth. "I will get you out. You must trust me on this, Kerry—I did not come here to lose you! Keep faith with me." When she did not immediately respond, he grabbed her by the arms and shook her once. "Give me your word you will keep faith with me!"

"You have my word!" she cried, but she could not put down the fear that the force of Moncrieffe was more than Arthur could combat.

Before she could tell him so, the door opened behind them; Arthur quickly let her go and stepped back. He mouthed the words, *I love you,* and turned around.

"Ye been long enough," Mrs. Muir said.

"You will get Mrs. McKinnon some decent food, madam, or the justice will hear of it!" he snapped, and strode from the room. The door swung shut behind him, the key turned in the lock. Kerry sank, unconsciously, to her knees, straining to hear his voice. When she could no longer hear him, she fell in a heap onto the mattress and sobbed herself to sleep.

Arthur walked into the courtyard of the ancient keep and looked up at the small window of the tower, his jaw working frenetically. He swung up onto the stallion he had brought from York—he had no desire to attempt to find a horse again in this country—and snapped the reins, sending the horse on a trot out of the old castle grounds, pointedly refusing to look at the half-constructed gallows.

It was a foreboding place; he had learned from a sheepherder that what was left of the old castle was still used for a variety of purposes, including a gaol in the rare circumstance one was required. But it was well fortified and virtually impenetrable. He had promised Kerry he would see her freed, and he meant it with every ounce of his being. There was only one small problem—he had absolutely no idea how.

One thing was certain—he could not steal her away and escape to England again. No, this battle would have to be waged on Scottish ground. The first thing he had to do was find a barrister, and he spurred the stallion he had so prophetically named Freedom.

Freedom thundered through the countryside, chewing up the earth. They passed the old Celtic cross erected in the middle of nowhere for God knew what reason, past the crumbling remains of crofter cottages now overtaken by sheep, through the pines that towered so high as to almost block the sun. These landmarks now seemed vaguely familiar to him, as if they were somehow a part of him. They *were* a part of him—everything he had become in the last few months had started here, in this ruggedly beautiful countryside.

When he had made the extraordinary decision to give up all that he had in England to come here, to be with Kerry, his friends and family had been shocked. Only Alex had smiled and shrugged his shoulders. Julian had tried to talk him out of it, but in the end, he had clapped him on the shoulder, reminded him that it was *his* brilliant idea that he should go to Scotland in the first place, then pointed out to everyone gathered in his Mount Street home that the world had never known a greater sentimental fool than Arthur Christian. He had, at last, wished him Godspeed.

The decision had been the right one, his conviction strengthening every day as he moved north. It occurred to him, when the ship had set sail from Kingston, that he had spent his entire life treading water, working hard to stay in one place, never allowing himself the luxury of simply living. He thought of Phillip, how he had seemed to delight in skirting the edge of danger, pushing the limits of propriety, and ultimately living life to its fullest. In her own way, so did Kerry. She let nothing stand in the way of her beliefs; she risked all for the sake of those she loved.

Arthur had never pursued a conviction that he could recall, had never believed so firmly in anything that he would risk all for it.

Until now.

Kerry had pushed him into the deep of life, had made him swim for the first time. *This* was the quality of life the vicar was speaking of at Phillip's funeral; these last few months, complete with the unpredictable highs and lows, had enriched him beyond measure.

Kerry had enriched his soul.

And he would do anything it took—he would part the heavens, rearrange the stars, turn mountains upside down if that was what it required. But he *would* have Kerry to love and cherish the rest of his natural life, and he *would* figure a way out of his mess.

As he and Freedom hurtled into the dusk, he prayed for a bit of divine guidance.

And then he prayed that the divine guidance might come in the next half-hour, if at all possible.

Chapter Twenty-Five

Arthur wandered the narrow streets of Pitlochry like a vagabond, poking his head in various establishments and inquiring as to where he might find a barrister, not caring that he appeared half-crazed. But the Scots were nothing if not unflappable—he received nothing but blank looks for his efforts, an occasional sneer from those who were not exactly accepting of the English, and one or two suggestions as to where he might look.

He refused to allow himself to think it was hopeless, but the anxiety was mushrooming in him. There was no time to go to Edinburgh where the best of the legal profession in Scotland was to be had. Every hour that passed was adding to his blossoming panic—he was running out of time.

He was debating whether or not he should ride on to Dunkeld and search there when he happened upon an inn he had not previously seen. From the street, he could hear the loud commotion in the common room. It appeared to be a popular gathering place, and Arthur thought that he might try one last time.

At the very least, he could use a dram of good Scottish whiskey.

He walked into the common room, ignored the looks

he inevitably received—the Scots, he had discovered, could sniff out an Englishman at one hundred paces— and walked to where the innkeeper was standing.

"Whiskey," he said simply, and tossed two coins on a scarred barrel that served as a counter of sorts. As he waited for the innkeeper to pour his whiskey, he glanced around, his eyes scanning the crowded tables. Laborers, mostly, one or two gentlemen in the lot.

"Yer whiskey, sir," the innkeeper said, and Arthur swung around, reached for the heavy glass, was lifting it to his lips when he saw him.

Jamie Regis.

Arthur glanced heavenward, said a silent thank you to God for giving him this gift, and sauntered forward, a smile on his face.

There were times that Jamie Regis wished he could turn his cousin into a fish, or some other object that could not talk. Propping his head against his fist, he fought to keep his eyes open as his cousin droned on about something to do with the shoring of an old barn he had recently engaged in. Blair had begun the fascinating discourse on the exact size of the truss he had lathed himself, when Jamie was jostled awake by someone seating themselves at their table. Not that Blair would notice, he thought, marveling at how his cousin continued to talk, and lazily lifted his head to have a look.

He jerked upright when he saw the smiling Englishman. "Good *God!* Here now, milord, I believe my work is done—"

"And a good day to you, too, Mr. Regis," the insufferable Sassenach said, his smile broadening.

At the very least, his clipped English accent shut Blair up. "All right then, how do you do," Jamie said testily. "As I was saying, my work is done."

"Naturally. And settled quite nicely, thank you. But

I've another matter about which I should very much like to speak with you."

Blair looked at Jamie. "Aye then, who is 'e?"

"No one," Jamie muttered. "A former client."

"Ah, Mr. Regis, you wound me. A *former* client? And here I a sit, prepared to offer you a princely sum."

Jamie grabbed his ale and took a long swig, eyeing Christian over the rim of his mug. The one redeeming quality the man had was that he did indeed pay quite well. Jamie carefully set his ale down again, cocked his head to one side. "And how exactly did you find me?"

"Now you see, there's the beauty of it. If you believe in divine guidance—"

"I doona put much stock in it—"

"Well then, let's just say we have a situation of uncommon coincidence. I just happened to see you sitting here and could not believe my grand fortune—"

"Grand fortune," Jamie repeated suspiciously.

"—nor *your* grand fortune."

"Go on then with ye, Jamie. If 'e's got the coin to spend, ye should at least listen to the man," urged Blair.

As he was in no need of the addlepated Blair's help, Jamie glared at his cousin. He shifted his gaze to Christian again. This was a bad idea, a very bad idea, he thought. "All right then, let's have it."

And then he proceeded to question his own sanity as the imperious Christian explained what he needed. While Christian did not give him all the details, Jamie surmised from his brief description of the legal services he required that a friend had inadvertently murdered a Scot in what Christian claimed was an act of self-defense. Right. The friends of Arthur Christian did not seem to make very intelligent choices.

"I am not a barrister, sir," he said at once.

"Really, I've always wondered after the difference between a solicitor and a barrister, haven't you? Nonetheless, you are as close as I am likely to get to a barrister in the next few days. Time is of the essence, Mr. Regis."

"That may be, milord, but there is not enough time in all of Scotland to turn me into a barrister, or an advocate as we know it here. I would think you could find a suitable one in Edinburgh."

"There is no *time!*" Christian said sharply, then caught himself and took a deep breath. "The truth is, Mr. Regis, this matter is one that is very, ah . . . dear to me. It is imperative that I get help before it is too late."

Jamie shook his head. "I canna help you. I am not an advocate and I am not familiar with criminal law. For what you need, you must understand that my counsel would be insufficient. I urge you to go quickly to Edinburgh." He stood up, preparing to take his leave, but Christian surprised him by lunging across the table and grabbing him by the lapels. Jamie grabbed his wrists and yanked at his hands. "Unhand me, sir!"

"Listen to me, Regis!" Christian said roughly. "I *need* you! You are my best and last hope, do you understand me? I will pay you a bloody fortune for your assistance if that is what you want, but I will not allow Kerry McKinnon to *hang!*" he exclaimed desperately.

Jamie froze. He blinked, struggling to absorb the image of the fair Kerry McKinnon hanging from the end of a noose. His hands fell away from Christian's wrists; Christian let go of his lapels with a slight shove and quietly straightened his clothing as Jamie stared at him. "Kerry McKinnon? Fraser McKinnon's widow?" he asked, incredulous.

"Along with her cousin Thomas."

Jamie sank into the chair he had just vacated and drained the last of his ale. Christian resumed his seat, watching him closely. "They say he murdered her."

"Now they say the two of them conspired to murder Charles Moncrieffe," Christian said.

Jamie sucked in his breath. "You canna be serious!"

"I am deadly serious."

Jamie could hardly believe it. His memory of Mrs. McKinnon was a fond one—a lovely woman, dedicated to her ill husband and the little enclave of clan she lived among. His memory of Moncrieffe was less favorable. Through the years, he had had occasion to run across the man on various matters. He despised Cameron Moncrieffe, because he, more so than any other baron Jamie had known, pushed plain folk from their land with no regard for their welfare, all so that he could put more sheep on the land and make himself an even richer man. He hardly needed to do so—Moncrieffe was a wealthy, powerful baron, possessing of a tremendous amount of influence among the elite of Scottish society and lawmakers.

Jamie glanced up at Christian. "How did it happen?"

He sat very still, listening to Christian explain, his mind spinning with the fantastic story. He did not flinch when Christian told him of his part in her escape, nor did he move when Christian explained that Moncrieffe likely knew what his son was about. He did not even speak when he learned that Mrs. McKinnon had returned to Scotland to free Thomas McKinnon, giving up her own liberty to save her cousin.

When Christian had finished, Jamie knew the request was difficult to refuse. A man could not leave a woman like Mrs. McKinnon in such straits. He sighed, raked both hands through his hair. "I am not an advocate," he repeated. "I doona know that the justice will even entertain my advocacy."

"He cannot refuse it, can he? The woman has no one to speak on her behalf."

Jamie supposed that was true. The legal system guaranteed some sort of advocacy in situations such as this. "There's an awful lot of work to be done. I've got to study the law, and we must find someone who knows what happened to the McKinnon clan."

Christian eagerly leaned forward, nodding. "I shall look from sunrise to sunset if I must."

Still, Jamie shook his head; this was lunacy. What he knew of criminal law could be put on the head of a daisy. "I can offer you no guarantee. It may do more harm than good—"

"Nonsense, man! She cannot possibly do worse than she does now in that tower prison where he holds her!" He leaned forward farther still, the piercing hazel eyes for once beseeching. "I've nowhere to turn, Mr. Regis! I will bring all my power to bear in helping you, I will pay a highwayman's rate, but I *cannot* do this alone!"

That much was obviously true, and Jamie frowned. Alone, this vainglorious English aristocrat would certainly hang her. Bloody hell, he *was* all Kerry McKinnon had! He groaned. "All right, then, I will help you, but on one condition. You *must* do as I say, do I have your word?"

Christian beamed at him, his relief and joy apparent. "Naturally! Whatever you say, Mr. Regis," he exclaimed, and offered his hand to shake on their agreement.

"We'll need a place to work. I reside in Stirling—"

"I have just the place," Christian said, still grinning. He gripped Jamie's hand tightly. "We'll be quite the pair, you and I."

Oh yes, Jamie imagined they would be *quite* the pair.

The place Arthur had in mind was the scene of the alleged crime. Regis thought he had lost his mind, and had no qualms about saying so. Arthur could hardly argue. But his instincts were right; the place was deserted, save a few hundred grazing sheep. Regis complained that they were trespassing and were sure to be caught, but Arthur wrapped a friendly yet firm arm around the man's shoulders and forced him to walk into the white house while trying to convince him that it wasn't *technically* trespassing. After all, the papers settling Phillip's debts had not yet been signed.

Regis remained unconvinced.

They spent the evening chasing two sheep from the interior of the house and shaking the two mattresses that had been left behind to ensure no other creatures had taken up residence. After a frosty night—no thanks to Regis, who adamantly refused to allow a fire to be built, lest they alert the glen and signal Moncrieffe—the two men rose with the sun, washed in the cold stream, and dined on cheese and bread hard as stone.

They began work in the room Kerry had once occupied. It was practically empty now, except for the ugly, dark stain of blood. The bed was gone, as was the vanity—to what fate, Arthur did not know. Nothing but a wooden chair remained, a small rug, and a wardrobe with one door missing. There was also a tin box and a scattering of papers in one corner. With the toe of his boot, Arthur nudged them so that he could read what was written. One was a letter from Alva Tavish, another from Mr. Abernathy of Dundee. He stooped down, picked up the letters, and put them in his pocket while Regis measured the room with his stride, then made some notations on a paper.

They milled around the small room far too long to suit Arthur. Much to his great irritation, Regis insisted that he repeat the sequence of events as he knew them over and over again. After the fourth telling of it, Arthur had reached the limits of his patience. The longer they stood there, the longer Kerry languished in that godforsaken medieval tower. It seemed to him that there was something they ought to be doing—such as reviewing the bloody law—instead of discussing where Charles's body had lain when Arthur found them. When Regis asked for the hundredth time where exactly Kerry had been standing, Arthur lost what was left of his patience.

"I have told you, Regis! She was standing just there!" he snapped, waving his hand in the general direction he had indicated earlier. Regis paused in his examination of the floor and bestowed a look of pure tedium on him. Arthur bristled; he was unaccustomed to being treated in such a . . . *common* . . . manner. He was about to make issue of it, but Regis spoke first.

"I thought you wanted my help."

"Bloody hell!" he groused, rolling his eyes. "Of *course* I want your help! But I hardly see the point of repeating over and over again who was standing where!"

"I am attempting to ascertain exactly *how* this happened so that I might effectively argue self-defense on Mrs. McKinnon's behalf! If he were lying inside the room facedown, and she at the door, then it would not be quite so easy to argue, would it? Every detail, no matter how small, can only help us, sir! And while you may not have realized it, you have added some new detail to each telling of it!"

Regis had a point there.

Arthur sighed, glanced around the filthy room again, made a supreme effort to get hold of his emotions. "You are right, of course. What was your question?"

It was the afternoon before Regis was finally satisfied with his copious notes. His forehead furrowed in a frown, he walked slowly into the kitchen, Arthur on his heels, and sat down at the scarred table that had been left behind. With his arm, he brushed off a place where he could lay his paper, then ran his palms over his notes to flatten it before bending over to study it further.

Arthur fell onto the bench across from him and pulled out the letters he had found. Using his thumb to break the wax seal, he opened the first. In handwriting sharply angled, the missive began with a curt salutation and moved directly into a demand for Kerry to come to Glasgow, where she could apparently repent her evil ways and seek mercy from God by teaching the heathens of His Word. The letter continued in that vein, and when he reached the signature, a cold little shiver ran up his spine.

Kerry had, of course, alluded to discord with her mother. And he remembered vividly her hysterical reaction to his suggestion that she go to Glasgow. At the time, he had attributed it to the trauma of what had happened to her, but had he known her mother was this . . . *rabid,* he never would have suggested such a thing. He glanced at the letter again and noticed that it was dated 18 July 1837. He had found Kerry standing over Charles Moncrieffe's body on 29 July. Eleven days later.

"How long do you suppose it should take a letter to arrive here from Glasgow?" he asked.

Regis did not glance up from his work and answered distractedly, "Ten days, perhaps a fortnight."

Kerry must have just received the letter around the time of the unfortunate incident with Moncrieffe.

He forced the ugly image from his mind and picked up the other letter. This one was from a Mr. Abernathy of Dundee. When he broke the seal, he discovered that Mr. Abernathy was an agent of the Bank of Scotland. He had written to inform Kerry that her time had come to an end, and as much as it pained Mr. Abernathy to do so, he would be forced to foreclose on her property to settle her husband's debts. This meant, naturally, that the bank would take possession of her assets, and unfortunately, the pearls she had given him to secure a portion—albeit a very *small* portion—of the debt.

A peculiar wave of disgust and regret rolled over Arthur. Had he known, had he understood, he would have settled the debts at the bank for Phillip and Kerry. He looked again at the letter; it was dated 21 July.

What a burden Glenbaden must have been for her, he thought sadly, and unconsciously ran his thumb over a deep groove in the table. He despised her dead husband—it was unfathomable to him that a man might leave his wife with such monumental matters such as loans and accruing interest and collateral.

"Well then," Regis abruptly said, yanking Arthur back to the present. "I believe our course is clear. First, there is the matter of Thomas McKinnon. I should think there is someone in Perth who could swear to his being there on the day of Moncrieffe's death. We need a credible witness to that effect. I suggest you go to Perth and find one."

"*Me?*" Arthur blustered. "And what of you? Am I not paying you a bloody king's ransom to gather evidence of their innocence?"

"*I* will be gathering evidence of Mrs. McKinnon's innocence, sir."

"I will help you—"

"You can help me by finding a credible witness in Perth who will vouch for Mr. McKinnon's whereabouts. Look here, Christian, we've not much time. We must divide the work, and I think I am better qualified to develop the critical evidence we need to convince the justice of Mrs. McKinnon's innocence. If you prefer to waste time arguing—"

"All right, all *right*," Arthur snapped. "I will go to Perth and find the fellow who was fortunate enough to speak with the congenial Thomas McKinnon!"

"Excellent," drawled Regis, and for the first time Arthur could recall, the man smiled.

In Perth, it seemed that no one, from the markets to the public inns, had noticed a wiry Scot with a dozen head of sickly cattle. It was as if Thomas had never existed. But he *had* come to Perth, he had told Arthur so, had sold the cattle and waited for Kerry as they had previously arranged. When the appointed meeting time came and went, and two days more, he had gone looking for her. That was when Moncrieffe apprehended him.

After a full day and a half of wandering about, a dejected and exhausted Arthur stepped into the Dog and Duck Public Inn, an establishment he had been in more than once to inquire after Thomas. He fell into a rickety wooden chair and asked a barmaid to bring him a dram of Scottish whiskey. Defeat was not a familiar sensation to him, nor was the feeling of the lack of power to do anything. He stared morosely at the small glass the barmaid set in front of him, not really seeing it, his gut churning with his inability to affect a bloody thing.

"Bless me, sir, ye look so sad. Can I naught put a smile on that handsome face?"

Arthur gave the girl a weary smile. "I would that you could, lass, but unless you can bring me someone who saw my friend—"

"Who be yer friend then?"

He thought about waving the girl away. Too exhausted to speak, it seemed hopeless to engage her. But she smiled at him so prettily and twirled a thick strand of red hair around one finger that he could not help himself. Pure male instinct kicked in, and he smiled back. "Thomas McKinnon—"

"Tommy?" she interjected, and brightened considerably.

Arthur's heart skipped several beats. "You knew him? Thomas McKinnon of Glenbaden?"

The girl flushed. "Aye, I knew the lad," she said, and giggled shyly.

That old dog . . . Arthur smiled broadly and moved his chair around, pulling another one up beside him. "Please, sit . . . what did you say your name was?" he asked, and patted the chair next to him.

"Penny," she said, falling into the chair, and began to talk of "her Tommy."

And Arthur began to feel as if he had found his way again.

Chapter Twenty-Six

Regis wanted a credible witness? Well Arthur had brought him one, and it was no small feat.

It seemed that the barmaid Penny was the daughter of the rather blustery innkeeper, Mr. Newbigging, who remembered Thomas quite clearly, having tossed him out of Penny's room on more than one occasion. But in the mornings, when Mr. Newbigging was of a clearer mind, he had occasion to speak with Thomas man-to-man.

Newbigging had not wanted to come, of course, and had been rather loudly adamant about it—he had a thriving business to manage, after all. Why, the common room alone of the Dog and Duck Public Inn brought him twelve hundred pounds per annum.

Twelve hundred pounds later, Arthur had his credible witness, and was all smiles when the two of them rode across the barley field at Glenbaden.

Regis met them in front of the white house, his expression grim. "You are late," he said.

"Well good *God*, Regis, it's not as if witnesses to Thomas McKinnon were springing into the streets of Perth to greet me! Look here," Arthur tried to reassure him, "Mr. Newbigging has come to testify on Thomas's behalf!"

Regis nodded curtly to the man, swung his gaze to Arthur. "Justice Longcrier has come," he said simply.

His jovial spirit drained rapidly; a cold vise seized his heart. He turned to Freedom, stroked his nose. "How many days have we got, then?"

"None. He would hear the accusations on the morrow."

The earth seemed to shift under Arthur's feet. It simply could not be—they had no time to prepare! One look at Regis did nothing to reassure him, and Arthur lifted his gaze to the pinkening evening sky, squinting at the first strand of blue mist stretching across the horizon. He thought of Kerry in that cell, imagined her standing on the gallows, her long unruly hair flying wildly behind her, and the cold vise reached further, gripped his entrails. "This justice, do you know him?"

Regis nodded, looked at Newbigging. "Longcrier has a reputation for punishing the guilty accordingly, but he's also of a reputation for being fair."

"There's nothing fair about this ordeal," Arthur muttered. "Come on then, we've not much time." He turned abruptly toward the innkeeper. "Mr. Newbigging, meet Mr. Regis, our advocate. I am sure the two of you have a lot to discuss. I'll tend to the horses," he said calmly, and took the reins of Newbigging's horse as the man heaved himself off and vigorously rubbed his broad bum with the palms of his hands.

Regis grabbed Newbigging's beefy arm. "A pleasure, Mr. Newbigging."

As Regis hustled Mr. Newbigging into the white house, Arthur was unable to see the bridle he had lifted from Freedom's head, unable to focus on anything except the image of Kerry swinging from the end of a rope.

And somewhere in the distance, out near the loch, he could have sworn he heard Phillip calling her.

They worked long into the night. Arthur must have fallen asleep at some point; Regis was shaking him out of a deep slumber. He pushed himself up from the kitchen table, ground the heels of his hands into his eyes. "What time is it?"

"Four o'clock."

Arthur focused, looked around him. Newbigging was sitting by the fire, fussing with a boot.

"We've enough to set Thomas McKinnon free, I think," Regis announced.

Mr. Newbigging nodded. "Aye, my dau wasna the only one to have seen his sorry hide. He played his hand at cards, spent the better part of that day under me roof, taking two hundred guineas for 'is trouble."

"What of Kerry?" Arthur asked.

Regis looked down at a leather-bound volume of Scots law he had managed to obtain. "I'm struggling a bit with that."

Arthur did not ask more—he could not bear to know more. He helped Regis gather his things, cleaned himself up as best he could, then tried to choke down some of the biscuits he had attempted to make last evening while Newbigging barked the instructions at him. But he could not make himself eat—he felt strangely ill, nauseated by his own roiling emotions.

The three of them were en route for Moncrieffe's estate before the sun was up. When they started the descent down Din Fallon, they could see the wagons and horses and groups of people gathered around the old tower where the justice would hear the charges against Kerry and Thomas.

They could scarcely squeeze into the crowded bailey. They passed by the newly erected gallows, at which Arthur refused to look.

The crowd in the bailey was nothing compared to the number of souls gathered in what was once the great hall. People stood shoulder to shoulder, moving like a sea as dogs and children dove between their legs. A dais had been raised against one wall; two crude boxes stood on either end of a long table between them, marked by two ornate leather chairs.

With Newbigging at his back, Arthur pushed Regis forward through the throng and toward the dais where a group of official-looking men milled about. Regis reached the first one, removed his hat. Arthur strained to hear what was said, but the din was too high. The man removed a piece of paper from a sheaf he was carrying and scratched something onto it while Regis looked on. When he at last turned around, Arthur was quickly on him. "What have you learned?"

"There are a number of common matters to be heard this morning by the sheriff. The High Court of the Justiciary will be convened upon conclusion of the common matters to hear the cause of Kerry and Thomas McKinnon in the matter of the murder of Charles William Edgar Moncrieffe."

"Do you mean to say that we must *wait?*" Arthur demanded.

"This is hardly the House of Lords, sir!" Regis snapped irritably.

Obviously not. Bloody fabulous—they would be forced to stand idly by while a variety of inconsequential matters were heard. It was not to be borne. He could not possibly endure it.

He could endure it.

The interminable morning began with a protracted wait for the justice and the sheriff. The incessant shuffling and movement of the crowd forced Arthur, Regis, and Newbigging to one side of the hall. From his vantage point, Arthur could watch the bailey as more adults and children and various genre of livestock squeezed inside, and eventually, into the great hall, all wanting their petitions to be heard. Somehow, he managed to pace restlessly in the throng while Regis reviewed his book on Scots law. Mr. Newbigging disappeared for a time to take in the sights, he said, as if this were some sort of festival.

The crowd, the stench of animal and man, and the increasing delay only made Arthur's anxiety increase, and it nearly exploded into a fit of murderous rage when he saw Cameron Moncrieffe enter the gates of the bailey on a steed fourteen hands tall, two men riding at his flanks. He nodded imperiously to the people around him as the steed trotted into the midst of the crowd. He reined to a halt, swung down, and handed his reins to a young man without even looking at him. Arthur nudged Regis as Moncrieffe strolled into the great hall and disappeared through a dark door leading into the tower, his entourage behind him.

Regis shrugged as Moncrieffe disappeared into the tower and turned back to his study. But raw rage boiled in Arthur's veins. He pivoted sharply on his heel, resumed his pacing, knocking against people as they tried to move past him. The weight of his hopelessness, his *uselessness,* hammered away at him, destroying him piece by piece. There was nothing he could do, no influence he could exercise, no task he could perform to change a goddamn thing. *Nothing.*

The justice and the sheriff at last sauntered into the hall. Justice Longcrier was round and squat and wearing a purple robe and powdered wig; the sheriff only slightly taller, just as squat, wearing a black robe and powdered wig that sat rather crookedly on his head. Towering over both of them was Moncrieffe, who walked casually behind them, as if he owned the bloody tower.

The crowd began moving forward, all of them wanting to be heard first as the two situated themselves at the makeshift dais—there seemed to be an initial disagreement over chairs—then thumbed through a sheaf of papers that looked inches thick. Moncrieffe positioned himself directly behind the two men. Once they seemed fully satisfied that they had the right seats and the right stack of petitions, the sheriff called the first of what was to seem like dozens of injured parties.

What followed was a parade of disputes over such

matters as pigs, a leather harness, a bushel of hay owed for blacksmith services. As the petitions continued on— there seemed no lack of disputes in Perthshire, to be sure—Arthur's anxiety gave way to despair. The more he was forced to contemplate their chances, the more he became convinced there was no way out of this mess. Regis was hardly reassuring him—he seemed so intent on his law book that Arthur began to fear he had made a terrible mistake. The man had no more knowledge of criminal law than Newbigging.

But when the last of the common petitions were heard and the High Court of the Justiciary was convened, Regis suddenly jerked upright. He anxiously fished his glasses out of his breast pocket, stuffed them onto the bridge of his nose. "Newbigging?" he asked.

"Here," Arthur said, glancing at the rotund innkeeper, who was propped against the stone wall, napping.

Regis nodded, looked at Arthur again. "Best start your prayers now, Christian," he said low, and started pushing his way through the crowd toward the dais.

It was too late for that. Arthur swallowed the rising lump of trepidation in his throat as he urged Newbigging to pick up his pace a bit in following Regis, and fell in behind the mountain of man.

When they reached the dais, Regis conferred with a frumpy little man with the neck of a goose, then paced anxiously, his head down, his hands behind his back as the little man read aloud the names of the fifteen men selected to hear the charge against Thomas McKinnon and Kerry McKinnon of Glenbaden. When he had finished, the man asked, "Who advocates on behalf of Thomas McKinnon and Kerry MacGregor McKinnon?"

Regis lifted his head, called out, "I do, if you please, my lord commissioner."

"Who speaks?" Justice Longcrier asked, not bothering to look up from his papers.

"Mr. Jamie Regis, Esquire."

"Continue on," the justice said to the clerk.

"Who advocates on behalf of Charles William Edgar Moncrieffe?"

"If it pleases the court, I do," Moncrieffe said. "Baron Cameron Moncrieffe."

"Very well then. Let us hear the evidence of this murder *in toto*. Bring forth the accused," the justice decreed.

The first to be brought forth was Thomas, emerging from the dark door behind the dais as the crowd shouted at him. He looked disoriented, almost surprised by the size of the crowd. As he was led to one of the boxes on the dais, the gaoler shoved him into the witness box; Thomas stumbled, caught himself on the rail, then drew to his full height of six feet and faced the justice.

A cry from somewhere, and the body of people swelled, straining to see as Kerry was led out of the tower by a man Arthur recognized as having been with Moncrieffe the day of the roan's injury. He paraded her across the dais, obviously delighting in the shouts of *whore* and *murderess* that were hurled from the crowd. A slow, red-hot burn began to crawl up Arthur's spine; he wished for the strength of ten thousand men so that he might take every one of them in hand and strangle the vile words from their throats. Regis glanced at him, his expression grim.

As Kerry stepped into the witness box, her eyes swept the crowd; Arthur tried to step forward, but was instantly jostled backward. He realized in a panic that Kerry could not see him. *She could not see him!* She looked up from the crowd and across the dais to Thomas. The two of them stood gazing at one another as the justice shouted for order, and God bless Kerry, she smiled. In the bleakest moment of her life, she sought to comfort Thomas.

Arthur was moving before he knew it, shoving hard against those who called her names, forcing them apart, struggling to see her, to be *seen* by her. *"I am here, Kerry!"* he shouted, lifting his hand and waving it, but she could not see him, not in that mass of hostile humanity.

Above him, someone bellowed for quiet. Justice Longcrier leaned forward; his heavy jowls now propped up by two fists. "Your name?" he asked Thomas.

"Thomas McKinnon."

"Thomas McKinnon you have been charged with the crime of murder in the death of Charles William Edgar Moncrieffe of Glenbhainn. How do you plead?"

A sardonic smile drifted across Thomas's face. "Not guilty."

The justice paused to study Thomas for a moment, then turned his attention to Kerry. "Your name?"

"Kerry MacGregor McKinnon," she answered, her voice surprisingly clear.

"Kerry MacGregor McKinnon you have been charged with the crime of murder in the death of Charles William Edgar Moncrieffe of Glenbhainn. How do you plead?"

"I . . . I did kill him, my lord, in self-defense."

Her admission sparked a jeering outcry from the crowd. Arthur's heart sank like a weight and he abruptly shoved Regis. "*Do* something, man," he demanded angrily.

But Regis shoved right back. "Do *not* interfere! I know what I am doing!"

Above them, the justice looked at the sheriff, who did nothing to stop the clamor for Kerry's blood, and with a scowl, he lifted his hands. "All right, all *right!*" he bellowed, slapping his broad hand on the table until the crowd quieted. With a great sigh of exasperation, he nodded toward Moncrieffe. "The burden of proof rests with you, sir, as the accuser. You may proceed."

Moncrieffe exchanged a quick look with the sheriff, clasped his hands behind his back, bowed his head. "My son has been murdered, my lord," he said softly. "Thomas McKinnon conspired with Kerry MacGregor McKinnon in his death."

He waited, letting that accusation wash over his audience as he strolled to where Kerry was standing. She kept her eyes on the justice, her chin held high, refusing to look at the cretin. The foolish ass smirked at her courage; Arthur's hands itched to be around his throat.

"My lord commissioner, the late Fraser McKinnon, a dear friend of mine, suffered from a debilitating illness that eventually took his life. In the course of his last years, he was quite unable to oversee his own affairs and his livelihood was considerably diminished. He did everything a man in his condition might do—he sought help from investment partners, but had the singular misfortune of purchasing a sick herd of cattle. The plague took all of the beeves he had hoped to turn to profit.

"Fraser McKinnon turned to me for help then, and again the next year, when the bull he had purchased refused to sire. He found himself unable to pay the bank, and unfortunately, as he neared the end of his life, he ceased trying to appease any of his debts. As he lay on his deathbed, he owed me five thousand pounds, and I shudder to think of the sum he most likely owed the Bank of Scotland."

A collective gasp went through the crowd at the extraordinary sum Moncrieffe had tossed them.

"My lord commissioner!" Regis called.

"Mr. Regis."

"What Fraser McKinnon owed the Bank of Scotland *or* Lord Moncrieffe isna the issue here. The issue is—"

"It is *precisely* the issue, my lord, as Fraser McKinnon sought to settle his debts from his deathbed, which led to the murder of my son!" Moncrieffe loudly interjected.

"I beg your—"

"Mr. Regis," the justice interrupted, lazily lifting his hand, "I shall allow Lord Moncrieffe to state his case."

Arthur felt the roots of helplessness sink farther into the pit of his stomach. He groaned, closed his eyes.

"Thank you, my lord commissioner," Moncrieffe said, and casually adjusted the sleeve of his coat before continuing. "As Fraser McKinnon lay dying, he summoned me to his bedside, which I naturally attended. It was there that I first heard the rumors of Mrs. McKinnon's amoral relations with her cousin."

The crowd released a collective *hiss;* Kerry visibly stiffened, lifted her chin a notch, but it was the only outward sign she gave that Moncrieffe's lies affected her. *Good girl. Give him nothing.*

Thomas, however, snorted loudly at the charge, muttered under his breath.

"Poor Fraser McKinnon explained to me his plan for eliminating his debts and providing for his wife on the occasion of his imminent death. His plan was simple: allow the bank to repossess the land against that which he had borrowed, and deed to me the remaining McKinnon lands and holdings, whose value came very close to covering his debt. And for the portion of his debt that went unpaid, he offered his widow to marry my son."

The crowd could hardly contain their titillation at that scandalous arrangement. The justice frowned at Moncrieffe. "A rather unusual arrangement," he remarked.

"Unusual perhaps, my lord, but not unsound. As McKinnon had lost all the property he owned to debt, it seemed to him the most expedient way to provide for his young widow. I thought it an especially suitable arrangement, as my son was not afforded the usual opportunities for such a match."

The justice looked puzzled by that; Regis seized the opportunity. "My lord commissioner, I fail to see how the machinations of a man on his deathbed might contribute to the outrageous charge of murder. Charles Moncrieffe was not afforded the usual opportunities for a satisfactory marriage because of his unfortunate condition, which ultimately led—"

"*Unfortunate* condition?" the justice demanded.

"My son," Moncrieffe interjected, "was perhaps not as . . . developed . . . as other men of the age of thirty."

"Do you mean to say his growth was stunted?"

"I mean to say he was a bit slow. His was a difficult birth."

The women in the crowd responded to that with a faint murmur of understanding, and Moncrieffe turned, smiled sadly at them over his shoulder. "I thought it a fair settlement of the debt," he added, his voice full of feigned emotion.

"A settlement to which Mrs. McKinnon had no say or knowledge!" Regis insisted loudly.

Longcrier nodded absently at Regis, gestured with his hand for Moncrieffe to continue. "When Fraser McKinnon passed, God rest his soul, I did not immediately approach Mrs. McKinnon. I respected an appropriate mourning period. Unfortunately, Mrs. McKinnon used that time to further degrade her husband's honor in a flagrant affair with Thomas McKinnon!"

"That is a lie!" Regis angrily countered.

"Mr. Regis, you will have your opportunity," said the justice irritably, and looked at Moncrieffe again. "You can prove this abominable accusation, I trust?"

Moncrieffe nodded. "Unfortunately, there are witnesses to her debauchery, my lord, which I will happily bring forth to you."

"Very well then," Longcrier said, and looked at Regis. "Mr. Regis?"

Regis jerked at his waistcoat and stepped forward. "My lord commissioner, Baron Moncrieffe would have you believe that Mrs. McKinnon conspired with her late husband's cousin Thomas McKinnon to renege on her husband's agreement to settle his debt. He would have you believe that they conspired to steal the beeves he avows belonged to him and kill his son so that she would not be forced to marry him. If Baron Moncrieffe is successful in having you believe this, milord, then the McKinnon property would revert to the Bank of

Scotland, and undoubtedly, the Bank of Scotland would dispose of the land as soon as possible to retire the debt owed them. I would imagine that the Baron could have the whole of Glenbaden for a mere pittance."

"My lord commissioner, really—"

"Moncrieffe," the justice wearily interrupted. "You had your say. Mr. Regis will have a go of it." He nodded at Regis.

"Baron Moncrieffe has several thousand heads of sheep, my lord. He has expanded his grazing rights to the north and the south, all at the expense of poor Scots he has willfully displaced from their homes. It is not inconceivable, therefore, that Baron Moncrieffe—knowing Fraser McKinnon's illness would soon lead to his death—planned on obtaining the whole of Glenbaden, a prime grazing land for sheep. It is likewise not inconceivable that Baron Moncrieffe seized the opportunity to push his friend further and further into debt in hopes of securing that land and perhaps even forced a dying man to an agreement that he was without proper faculty to consider."

"I beg your pardon!" Moncrieffe blustered.

"And I beg yours!" Regis shouted back.

"*Gentlemen!*" the justice roared. "Let's get on with it, shall we? Lord Moncrieffe, have you witnesses?"

"I do, my lord commissioner. If the court pleases, I present Mrs. Alva MacGregor Tavish of Glasgow, the mother of Kerry MacGregor McKinnon," he said, sweeping his arm dramatically toward the door behind the justice.

Kerry jerked around to Moncrieffe then, gaping at him with incredulity, her eyes stark blue against her morbidly pale face, then dragged her gaze to the door where her mother was emerging, escorted by two men. In her hand, she carried a crude, wooden cross. Her hair was gray, although Arthur could see that it might have once had the black sheen of Kerry's. She was small; her plain gray gown hung loosely on her. As she was led to stand in front of Justice Longcrier, she looked heaven-ward, clasping her hands together around the cross she carried.

And Arthur felt the world begin to crumble beneath his feet.

Chapter Twenty-Seven

SHE WAS LIVING, breathing, in a nightmare; nothing seemed real in the drama unfolding before her—it was as if someone had summoned actors together, given them words that would falsely condemn her as a whore, an adulteress, and a thief.

She stood rigid in her box as the witnesses were paraded before her, her eyes fixed on the justice who occasionally looked at her, his brown eyes rimmed with what she could only term as sadness. The shock of seeing her mother after all these years—*Lord God, how the bitterness had aged her!*—had numbed her, sunk her into a pool of indifference. The vile lies and accusations Alva screeched as proof of her affair with Thomas were nothing new to her—she received those same condemnations at least monthly in a letter. But to hear them spoken out loud . . . it sickened her. There was nothing they could do to her now that could hurt any more than her own mother.

Where was Arthur? Had he given in to the impossibility of it all? Found her situation as hopeless as she? How she longed to see the reassuring smile of her beautiful stranger one last time.

One by one, the witnesses against her stood in front of Justice Longerier: Moncrieffe's butler, who testified

that she and Thomas had plotted against the baron; a
peddler, who had once come to Glenbaden to sell his pots
and pans, swearing that Thomas presented himself as
her husband while Fraser lay dying in the last room; a
doctor, who said he saw Thomas driving the beeves they
had stolen to the market in Perth.

Mr. Regis was scarcely able to argue on their behalf
at all, so hostile was the crowd toward them. To every
question the justice asked, she answered truthfully, but
the crowd responded angrily. They wanted to see a
hanging. They wanted someone to pay for the death of
Charles Moncrieffe.

Kerry looked across the dais to Thomas. He was
propped against the railing, his arms folded across his
chest. He caught her eye, smiled wryly. Her heart
swelled with remorse for having done this to him.
Thomas had been her rock through those years with
Fraser, and for that she would hand him his death war-
rant. She dropped her head, unable to look at him any
longer; tears filled her eyes. *Please, God, let them hang
me, then. But let Thomas go free!*

"Kerry! Kerry, listen to me!"

Ah God . . . Arthur's voice touched her like a caress
against her cheek, a kiss to her neck in the middle of the
maelstrom. She opened her eyes, searched for him, saw
him standing below her box, off to one side, straining to
be heard through the din. His hazel eyes glittered
strangely, but he smiled at her, that same, cheerful smile
she had come to love. "Hold your head *up,* Kerry! Do not
let them believe they have defeated you!"

But they *had* defeated her. It was too late, far too late.
She opened her mouth to tell him she loved him, but faltered. Arthur's face clouded; he clenched his jaw, raised
his hand and pointed at her. "Keep faith with me, Kerry
McKinnon!" he shouted. *"You promised you would keep
faith with me!"*

Tears slipped from her eyes, raced down her cheeks.

Aye, she had promised him once, but only to keep him from swimming in the same despair that threatened to drown her now. *How had it all come to this?* She didn't want Arthur to see her hang. It was her last and final wish—he could *not* see her hang! He was trying to move forward, to be closer, and she suddenly panicked, certain if he got any nearer she would lose the last fragments of her composure. "Go!" she shouted at him, drawing the attention of several around her. A few men looked over their shoulders to see whom she addressed. It caught him off guard, drew him up short, his face colored slightly. He clenched his jaw even tighter, glared at her. *"Go!"* she shrieked at him.

"Mrs. McKinnon!" the justice called to her, craning his neck to see who she addressed.

Kerry turned away from Arthur, her last sight of him his pained bewilderment.

Her heart felt as if it was shattering into a thousand different pieces.

There was nothing left of her, nothing left to hang but an empty shell. A strange calm descended over her, and impassive, she looked at the justice as he demanded some semblance of order in the hall.

When the crowd finally settled, the justice frowned at Moncrieffe. "You were saying, sir?"

"My lord commissioner, upon receipt of the letter from the Bank of Scotland, Thomas and Kerry McKinnon scattered their clan, stole the beeves, and murdered my Charles when he happened upon them! They killed the poor boy because the only way Kerry McKinnon could honor the debts owed the Bank of Scotland was applying the terms of her husband's agreement, which meant marriage to my son!"

The justice looked at Kerry. "You received word the debts were due?" he asked gently.

The question confused Kerry. She had received a letter from the Bank of Scotland, weeks before Charles's death. She slowly nodded. "Several weeks before," she said wearily. "I received word of the debts several weeks before . . . before this happened."

Moncrieffe snorted. "My lord, if the court pleases, Mr. Durwood Abernathy of the Bank of Scotland!" Moncrieffe called dramatically.

Mr. Abernathy, too?

As Mr. Abernathy walked to stand in front of the justice, he looked at Kerry with such regret that she cringed with shame. In a trembling voice, he informed the justice that he had indeed sent a letter to Mrs. McKinnon informing her that the McKinnon debt was to be collected on 21 July. Although she had never received that letter, when Mr. Abernathy stepped down, Kerry believed her fate was sealed.

But not Arthur. He knew Kerry had not seen that letter—*he* had broken the seal himself! A thought suddenly occurred to him, and he pushed through the crowd, to Mr. Regis, who was busily searching through a sheaf of papers.

"Regis!"

"Not now, Christian!"

"Listen to me—"

"Can you not see I am presently engaged? Good *God,* man. If you want her to live, you willna bother me now!"

The anxiety and the fear in Arthur had reached a desperate pitch. They had one small chance as he saw it, one very slim hope. He lunged at Regis, knocked him against a small table where his things were stacked. "Listen to me, Regis," he breathed. "I need time. I know how to free her, but—"

Regis shoved hard against his chest. "Do not *tell* me what to do!" he spat. "I told you I couldna save her bloody neck! Surely even *you* can see how grim the situation is now!" He sliced a murderous look across Arthur, turned back to his papers.

The terror suddenly exploded in Arthur's chest, ripping through his heart and his mind. He grabbed

Regis, whirled him around and caught his throat in one hand. *"I need time!"* he bellowed. "She never saw the letter, Regis! *I* broke the seal! *She never saw the goddamn letter!"*

Regis grabbed Arthur's wrist with both hands, his eyes now reflecting his fear as he gasped for breath. "All right, then, she never saw the letter! How can that help us now?"

He didn't understand! The sudden feel of dampness on his cheeks astounded and mortified Arthur. He lifted his free hand, touched his cheek. Tears. *Tears.* He looked heavenward, blinking, silently pleading—pleading that he might lead *this* loved one out of the morass, might know the richness of life only she could show him. *Please God, let me have this chance.* He lowered his gaze, dropped his hand. "Willie Keith," he said hoarsely. "The lad who delivers the post . . ."

Regis's mouth dropped open. No other explanation was apparently necessary; his eyes rounded with surprise and he whirled quickly around, riffled through his papers. "Go then. But be quick! I've a shepherd here, but I . . ."

Arthur did not hear the rest of what Regis said. He was already pushing through the crowd to the bailey.

How in God's name did one *find* Willie Keith? He had no notion of where the boy lived! Arthur rode Freedom hard, reining to a wild stop in the first hamlet he came to. No one was about; they were all apparently at the tower. Frustration and fear groped at him, tried to sweep him under with their current. He swung down from Freedom, left the horse to drink from a trough as he stalked from one cottage to the next, pounding at each door. At the last one, he did not bother to knock, but in a fit of frustration, lifted his leg and kicked it open. "Is there *no one* in this godforsaken place?" he roared.

The cry of an infant startled him; he lurched forward, through the door. A woman stood against one wall, her suckling infant at her breast. She cried out, brought her hand up to the baby's head. A strange heat instantly swept through Arthur, he quickly held up his hands to show her he meant no harm. "Forgive me, madam, but it is with some urgency that I find the lad Willie Keith. He delivers the post."

Too stunned to speak, she could only nod. Arthur dug his nails into his palms in a mad effort to maintain his composure and forced himself to ask, *"Where . . . might . . . I . . . find . . . Willie Keith?"*

"Killiecrankie," she whispered, and Arthur's heart surged on a new wave of hope. He pivoted away, raced for Freedom. He did not allow himself to think how far Killiecrankie was, just spurred Freedom to the west, lowered his head, and forced all thoughts from his head except that of Willie Keith.

Freedom covered the distance in a quarter of an hour, but the hamlet was just as deserted as the last. Only a blacksmith remained behind, hard at work. Arthur strode to him, his hand resting on the butt of his gun holstered at his side. "I beg your pardon, sir, but it is imperative that I find Willie Keith at once!"

The blacksmith looked up, eyed him casually before turning back to his work of forging a horseshoe. "He's delivering the post, just as he does every week."

"Yes, but *where?* It is a matter of great importance!"

"Aye, but I canna help you, milord. Willie travels many different roads, he does. I've no notion where he might be."

Calmly. "Have you any idea then when he might return?"

"Oh aye," said the blacksmith, thrusting the shoe into cold water. "Not 'ere dusk, you can be sure."

That was too late. *That was too goddamned late!*

The world at last crumbled under his feet, and Arthur turned away, walking unevenly. He felt himself sinking, rapidly descending down into the brink of hopelessness. He felt his failure keenly, felt it as sharply and as fresh as a knife to his heart, and his mind's eye was suddenly filled with the deadly pallor of Kerry's skin as she stood in the box, swaying with the fatigue and weight of the testimony—the *lies*—against her.

He walked, blindly, paralyzed by his inability to save her, the crushing knowledge that it was done, that he could not stop the tide of this ordeal from taking her, from taking the one person he loved above all others.

That thought overwhelmed him; his legs buckled and he suddenly found himself on his knees in the middle of the rutted lane that marked the center of the hamlet. Tears filled his eyes, tears of gross frustration, of loss—*he had lost her.* He had lost the one person who could make him believe heaven existed on earth. The loss was so devastating, so suffocating that he was insanely reminded of Phillip. How often he had tried to imagine the despair that might bring a man to end his own life.

How he hoped to God Phillip had not felt anything as keenly as this.

A sound, a faint whistle brought his head up and he looked to the right, gasping. Phillip stood leaning against a cottage, his arms folded beneath the hole in his chest, his legs crossed negligently, his blond hair wildly mussed. Arthur sucked in his breath, and slowly sank back on his heels. He had lost his bloody mind. *Was he mad?* How could he see Phillip now if he hadn't gone completely mad—

Phillip nodded his head in the direction of a cluster of cottages. A movement between them, the flash of red, and the faint whistle again. Arthur struggled to his feet, followed the sound of the whistle, moving backward, until he saw the flash of red again, coming toward him now.

Willie Keith.

Arthur hastily wiped his sleeve across one eye. "Willie," he said, holding out his hand. "Willie, listen to me now, lad. You must help me."

Willie eyed him apprehensively. "Aye," he said uncertainly.

"You care for our Mrs. McKinnon, do you not?"

The boy's face instantly flamed. He looked down at his satchel and bit his lip.

"She needs you now, Willie," Arthur said slowly, and took a tentative step forward. "You know that she needs you now, don't you?" he asked softly.

Willie nodded very slowly, took one small step backward without looking up.

Arthur knew then. How he knew it, he did not know, but he knew the poor child had seen Charles Moncrieffe die. He moved slowly, very carefully placed his arm around the boy's shoulders, gave him a comforting squeeze. "There are times, Willie, when a man must help his friends, even if he's very afraid. What do you think, we'll have us a bit of a chat, shall we? Man-to-man," he said calmly.

Willie Keith sniffed, dug his fingers into his eyes. Arthur patted his arm and quietly led him toward Freedom, holding him tightly against his side, comforting him.

Only when he had the boy securely on Freedom's back did he look back to where Phillip had stood and shown him Willie Keith.

He was gone.

Kerry did not believe her legs would hold her much longer. She gazed up at the rafters of the old tower, swaying slightly, wondering if she would hear the angels singing when she died.

She had long since lost track of what Mr. Regis was doing. He was questioning an old shepherd about the best grasses on which to graze sheep, and then cattle. She actually agreed with Moncrieffe—she had no idea what the relevance of it was. It had gone on for what seemed hours; Justice Longcrier seemed to be losing patience, too. With his head propped against his fist, the fingers of his left hand drummed incessantly against the table as he frowned at Regis.

At the very least, Arthur had heeded her and gone. At least she hoped so. Her vision was blurred now, but she looked around her, looked for his face, the familiar aristocratic stance. He had gone. Squinting, she dragged her gaze to Thomas, who seemed quite intent on the old shepherd. She wished she could tear her thoughts away from the inevitable. Part of her wanted to throw herself on the mercy of the justice and beg him to spare her the agony of waiting. Another part of her wanted to live as long as she could, every second of every moment she had left.

If only she could sit for a moment.

"Mr. Regis!" Longcrier suddenly blurted. "I've learned quite enough about sheep herding. Whatever do you mean by all of this?"

"My lord commissioner, I had intended to demonstrate that the best grazing land for sheep were on the lands that Mrs. McKinnon owned."

"Yes, yes, so you have! What of it?" the justice pressed.

Regis frowned, splayed his hands across the table and seemed to silently debate the question. "I would put forth a theory, my lord."

Justice Longcrier sighed loudly. "Very well then. But this shall be your last theory, Mr. Regis."

"I believe Baron Moncrieffe coveted Glenbaden—"

"I beg your pardon once again, sir!" Moncrieffe bristled.

"You advised Mrs. McKinnon not to raise sheep, did you not?" Mr. Regis shot back. "By her own, undisputed testimony, you advised her to raise beeves, even though it was obvious the land couldna support the herd! Did you not tell her thus so that she might fall further into debt and then *you* could have her land to graze sheep? Was that not keeping with your previous expansions of the sheep farming, sir?"

The hall grew quiet. Kerry blinked, tried to focus on Regis.

"My lord commissioner, we have heard from a

peddler who claims Thomas McKinnon presented himself as Mrs. McKinnon's husband while Fraser McKinnon lay dying in a back room. I would suggest that her cousin sought to give the illusion of a husband in case the peddler thought to prey on an innocent woman. As for Mrs. McKinnon's mother, the woman is a religious zealot with a history of condemning every thing and everyone, regardless of the truth! We have also heard from a doctor who saw Thomas McKinnon driving the beeves to market. We know that at this point, Mrs. McKinnon had dispatched her kin to Dundee, where she hoped they might gain passage to America. Why would she send her kin away if not for their own welfare? They had lived in that glen for several generations, alongside her, alongside Thomas McKinnon. It doesna seem particularly prudent if she conspired murder—who better to witness on her behalf than her own kin?"

Justice Longcrier was sitting up now, watching Mr. Regis with some interest. "That may very well be, sir," he said. "But you have not accounted for two facts: first, that Mr. Abernathy sent word that her debts were due just before she sent her clan wandering, and second, how did Charles Moncrieffe come to be killed?"

The hall grew quiet as the crowd waited for his answer. Mr. Regis looked across to Kerry; his desperation was plain. "Mrs. McKinnon told you that she hadna seen the letter, my lord," he said quietly. "I believe that to be true. I believe that letter, and another from her mother, were delivered about the time Charles Moncrieffe came to call."

Kerry blinked.

"Kerry McKinnon did everything she knew to do to save her home, but when she couldna raise the money, she did what she had to do—she sent them away, tried to sell the beeves to provide passage to America. But Baron Moncrieffe wanted her land. Kerry McKinnon never saw that letter—she saw only Charles Moncrieffe as he attempted to force himself on her at the direction of his father!"

Moncrieffe looked absolutely livid as he moved wildly in front of Longcrier. "My lord commissioner, I willna stand for these lies!"

"The only lies in this hall are the ones *you* have told, Moncrieffe!" Arthur's voice rang clear and loud above the din; Kerry stopped breathing. He came striding through the crowd toward the dais, Willie Keith firmly in hand. His expression was one of mad determination; his jaw was bulging with it.

"Who are *you?*" Justice Longcrier exclaimed.

"Lord Arthur Christian, my lord. But more importantly, *this* is Willie Keith of Killiecrankie. Willie delivers the post to the hamlets in the glens, and on the day in question, he delivered the last post to Glenbaden."

Moncrieffe roared his complaint, but the justice ignored him. Kerry still could not breathe, could not catch her breath. The justice leaned forward, peered closely at Willie. "What is your name, lad?"

"Willie Keith," he mumbled.

"Willie Keith, two people have been accused of murdering Charles William Edgar Moncrieffe. Do you have information to the contrary?"

Clearly frightened, the boy looked up at Arthur, and Arthur smiled warmly, the same, comforting smile he had bestowed on Kerry so many times. She could feel the strength of it now seep into her bones. Willie must have, too, because he nodded, turned his attention to the justice, and in a clear voice, told him that he had witnessed Charles Moncrieffe's attempt to have his way with Mrs. McKinnon, that he was afraid and had hidden himself, had peeked in the window when Moncrieffe followed her into her house. He matched her story with every detail, and Kerry's stomach lurched with the telling of it, sickened by the knowledge that he had seen such animal behavior.

"What did you do when she shot him?" the justice asked.

Willie colored, looked at his scruffed boots. "I . . . I hid for a time, milord. And then . . . I went inside, I did, to look at 'im." The poor child flushed as red as an apple. "I've naught seen a dead man, not up close, milord. I dropped the post by accident."

The justice pondered that for a moment, then asked, "Do you recall what was in the post?"

Willie nodded. "A letter from her ma and one from the Bank of Scotland. I remember because Mrs. McKinnon, she always looks a wee bit ill when those letters come."

The justice slowly shifted his gaze to Moncrieffe, his eyes narrowed. "Thank you, Willie Keith. You've been a good help to us, lad. It would seem, my Lord Moncrieffe, that Mr. Regis's theory is perhaps correct—"

"This is ludicrous!" Moncrieffe raged.

Justice Longcrier pushed to his full height of a little more than five feet and folded his arms across his large belly. "You may think this court *ludicrous,* my lord, but I think that you found a way to cast out a dozen Scots so that you might farm your sheep *and* marry off your simple son! Unless someone here can prove otherwise, these people are to be released at once!" He whipped around to one of his men. "Release them! Bring Mr. Abernathy to me forthwith! Mr. Regis, you are with me!" he roared, and marched off the dais.

The crowd went wild; they were suddenly pushing toward Moncrieffe, their convictions having changed with the justice's verdict. The blood drained from Moncrieffe's face; he pivoted around in search of an exit, and with his entourage, quickly followed the justice into the tower. Across the dais, Newbigging helped Thomas down, jovially slapping him on the back. Mr. Regis stood at the foot of the dais, looking a bit dazed as he stared at the door leading to the tower, finally moving.

Kerry was numb, could not seem to make her limbs move. The witness stand was jostled about as people clamored toward her, past her, wanting to reach Moncrieffe. The sudden clamp of a hand on her shoulder did not wake her from her stupor; she stood gaping at the scene, unable to believe she had been pulled back from the brink of death.

"My God, my love . . ."

She crumbled then, hard against him, her legs incapable of holding her under the enormous weight of her emotions. He caught her, turned her around, covered her grimy face in kisses. "Dear God, I thought I had lost you," he murmured against her skin. "I was so certain that I had!"

The noise in the hall seemed to recede to a distance; she could hear nothing but his voice, his heartbeat, feel nothing but his body, his warmth. She would do anything, she realized, to remain in his arms forever. "You willna lose me, Arthur," she said, her voice quivering with emotion. "I will go where you go, I doona care where it is, but you willna lose me again."

"Then come home with me now," he said, and helped her down from the dais.

Chapter Twenty-Eight

GLENBADEN,
THE CENTRAL HIGHLANDS,
SCOTLAND, 1838

THE SUMMER SUN broke the morning mist that drifted over the tops of barley stalks standing as high as a man's head. On the hill behind the white house, four Black-faced sheep huddled together and eyed one of ten new lambs that had been birthed that spring. The white house had a new roof, new shutters, and a team of men who worked diligently to add a new wing that some said would be bigger than even Moncrieffe House.

The cottages scattered across the glen were newly thatched; lazy curls of smoke drifted up to the morning sky from three of them, signaling the day had begun for the families who had found their way back from the coastal plains, most of them arriving on the Richey brothers' flatboat.

Willie Keith made his way through the barley field, marching along nicely in his new leather boots, his new leather satchel slung over his shoulder, both gifts from Lord Christian that he was especially proud of. As he neared the white house, he paused to look at Lady Christian—that was Mrs. McKinnon's name now, had been since she promised herself to Lord Christian under the old oak on the southern edge of Loch Eigg. She was squatting down, playing with the pups that had been birthed by Mr. Gilgarry's sheep dog a few weeks past.

A sigh full of longing escaped Willie; he supposed that he would always love her.

He reached into his bag and took out the packet of letters that had come. There were several for Lord Christian—one from an earl and one even from a duke, for he had seen the seals—he and Mary Shane liked to look at the seals and guess where they had come from before Willie made the long trek to Glenbaden every week.

There was one addressed to Lady Christian from Mr. Regis, Esquire, now of Pitlochry. Willie knew all about Mr. Regis. He'd done such fine work that Justice Longcrier had made him his special advocate for Perthshire. His was a thriving business, for there was not a want of disputes in Perthshire, especially now that every one was making claims against Baron Moncrieffe.

There was a special letter, too, and Willie smiled. Every week, she asked if he had word from Thomas McKinnon or Big Angus Grant. He hated to tell her no. Well, today he carried a letter thick as his arm, all the way from America. From Thomas McKinnon.

As Willie cleared the barley field, he saw Lord Christian come around the corner of the house and grab Lady Christian by the waist, twirl her around, and kiss her deep, just like Willie dreamed of doing.

As he walked into the yard, startling them, she blushed prettily, smoothed her hair at the temple. "Willie Keith! Is it time for the post already, then?"

"Aye," he said simply, and unable to bite back his smile, handed her the bundle. She glanced through them, her gaze settling on the one from Thomas McKinnon. It took a moment to sink in, but with a shriek of joy, she thrust the others at her husband and hurried to the oak below the white house to read it. Two pups waddled after her.

Clutching the letters, Lord Christian looked quizzically at him.

"Thomas McKinnon, it is."

A smile broke his face. "Aha. So the old dog has finally written home, has he? Probably rich as Croesus by now." He patted Willie on the shoulder, smiling. "There's a biscuit or two for you, lad, in the kitchen." With that, he turned and walked toward the oak where Lady Christian had sunk to her knees. Willie watched as Lord Christian went down on his haunches beside her, put his arm around her shoulder and his head next to hers to read the letter with her.

It gave him a warm feeling to watch the two of them like that, and as he made his way into the kitchen for his biscuits, he wondered if Mary Shane would ever let him follow her home like Mrs. McKinnon had let the Sassenach do.

Epilogue

DUNWOODY, SOUTHERN ENGLAND, 1848

THE THREE GRAYING men walked through the field of yellow grass that was now thigh high, slightly apart from one another, each lost in his own thoughts. One of them paused near a small stand of trees, peering into them as he rubbed his neck. "Here," he called to the other two. "This is it." His two companions turned and looked to where he pointed.

"Aye, that would be it then," said Arthur, his voice betraying the years spent in Scotland.

"Are you certain? I thought it was farther down."

Arthur turned and looked at Adrian. "I am certain," he said solemnly, and walked toward Julian, who was already moving toward the stand of trees. Adrian followed, a bit more slowly than the other two, his knee giving him a bit of grief on this cool fall day.

When they reached him, Julian adjusted his spectacles and pointed to a tree stump. "Do you recall? You were here, Adrian, when Arthur called out to you."

"I recall very clearly," Adrian said, and as if hearing the gunshot fired at his back, he pivoted sharply on his heel and looked behind him. "It still seems a dream."

"I've never understood it," Julian said. "I suppose I shall go to my grave wondering why he did it." They stood in silence a moment, looking about them, each reliving that dreadful morning almost fifteen years past.

"Do you recall the words of the vicar the morning of his funeral?" Julian asked.

" 'Know ye in his death the quality of mercy,' " Adrian readily offered. "Yes, I recall. I have thought of it quite often, for it is exactly that I found in his death. Had it not been for Phillip, I should never have married Lilliana. The woman has taught me the true meaning of mercy."

Julian chuckled. "You've gotten a bit daft in your old age, Albright. The vicar said, 'Know ye in his death the quality of *love*.' I recall because at the time I thought it such an absurd thing to say. But strangely, in a roundabout way, I might never have known the true quality of love had I not married Claudia. And we all know I would not have married Claudia had it not been for Phillip's death."

"*Och,* you are both mistaken," Arthur said with a dismissive flick of his hand. "The vicar said quite precisely, 'Know ye in his death the quality of life.' Believe me now, for I have heard it in my head over and over again through the years, just as he said it, and it was exactly that which sent me to Scotland . . . and Kerry. I would never have done so if Phillip hadn't so badly mangled his investments. That little journey showed me a quality of life I had not known existed. I would not have Kerry had Phillip not pointed me to her."

Julian and Adrian looked at him strangely; Arthur rolled his eyes. "I meant through my *dreams*. I dreamed of him so often, *too* often, until I finally made the decision to leave England behind and follow Kerry home."

"Still suffering from an overabundance of sentiment, are you?" Julian asked on a laugh.

Arthur cuffed him on the shoulder.

"*Ouch!* Must you hit so hard!"

"Look there, the two of you," Adrian said, pointing. The three men turned, looked toward the stream that babbled behind Dunwoody. There, on its grassy banks, strolled three women—one blonde, one auburn, and one dark-haired. They walked easily together; talking and laughing like young girls, pausing to admire a troop of butterflies. Nearby were their children—Adrian's daughter and two sons, Julian's four young girls, and Arthur's two boys, playing on the banks of the stream, the older ones screeching with delight at some tale Adrian's son was embellishing, the younger ones squatting in a circle, their heads bent together as they studied something in the grass.

Adrian smiled, looked around at the yellow field where Phillip had met his death. "We will never know why, will we? So many unanswered questions. But we can be certain of this: had it not been for that bitterly cold morning in this very field, we would never have known or seen such beauty as is before us now. My friends, in his death, Phillip gave us our lives."

No one spoke for a long moment. Adrian at last turned and looked at Julian and Arthur; they were standing like two old Rogues, Julian's arm propped on Arthur's shoulder; Arthur's arms folded across his chest, a quiet smile on his face.

Arthur chuckled, shook his head.

"What, more gushing sentiment?" Julian quipped, nudging him playfully as he stepped away.

"Actually, I was just wondering . . ."

"Yes?" Adrian prompted.

"What in heaven's name is Julian trying to do to us? *Four* girls? Honestly, Kettering, did you not learn life's little lesson the first time around? Could you not have spaced them a bit apart, perhaps? At least Adrian had the decency to keep his children home until they were old enough to call. Last month, when you sent those four to Glenbaden, I was quite convinced you had done it just to torture me—"

"*Me?* What of you?" Julian cried indignantly as he turned and strolled farther afield. "Those little demons you call sons are enough to make a man want to flee for the Continent. What, are you beginning your own little Scots army, then? For God's sake man, the war is over . . ."

Adrian laughed, and smiling, glanced once more at their beautiful, perfect families before turning and following his old friends—still arguing, naturally—deeper into the field, to the spot where Julian was convinced Adrian had once left a perfectly good walking stick so that he might fill both hands with a young tavern wench.

About the Author

JULIA LONDON is the *New York Times* and *USA Today* bestselling author of more than a dozen historical romance novels, including the acclaimed Desperate Debutantes series, the Lockhart Family Highland trilogy (for which she was twice a finalist for the prestigious RITA award for excellence in romantic ficiton), and the Rogues of Regent Street series, including *The Dangerous Gentleman, The Ruthless Charmer, The Beautiful Stranger,* and *The Secret Lover.* You may write Julia at P.O. Box 228, Georgetown, Texas, 78627, or at julia@julialondon.com. For news and updates, please visit her website, www.julialondon.com.

Stories of passion and romance, adventure and intrigue,
from bestselling author

Julia London

The Devil's Love
____22631-4 $6.99/$8.99 in Canada

Wicked Angel
____22632-1 $6.99/$8.99

The Secret Lover
____23694-8 $6.99/$8.99

The Rogues of Regent Street:
The Dangerous Gentleman
____23561-3 $6.99/$9.99

The Ruthless Charmer
____23562-0 $6.99/$9.99

The Beautiful Stranger
____23690-0 $6.99/$8.99